AFTER EARTH

Peter David

Based on the Screenplay by
Gary Whitta and M. Night Shyamalan

Story by Will Smith

DEL REY

1 3 5 7 9 10 8 6 4 2

First published in the US in 2013 by Del Rey,
an imprint of The Random House Publishing Group,
a division of Random House, Inc.,
New York.
Published in the UK in 2013 by Del Rey,
an imprint of Ebury Publishing
A Random House Group Company

The Random House Group Limited Reg. No. 954009

Addresses for companies within the Random House Group can be found at:
www.randomhouse.co.uk

A CIP catalogue record for this book is available from the British Library

The Random House Group Limited supports The Forest Stewardship
Council® (FSC®), the leading international forest-certification organisation.
Our books carrying the FSC label are printed on FSC® -certified paper. FSC is
the only forest-certification scheme supported by the leading environmental
organisations, including Greenpeace. Our paper procurement policy can be
found at: www.randomhouse.co.uk/environment

Printed and bound by CPI Group (UK) Ltd, Croydon, CR0 4YY

ISBN 9780091952907

To buy books by your favourite authors and register for offers visit:
www.randomhouse.co.uk
www.delreyuk.com

AFTER
EARTH

By Peter David

After Earth: A Perfect Beast (with Michael Jan Friedman and
Robert Greenberger)

Fable
Fable: The Balverine Order
Fable: Blood Ties
Fable: Reaver
Fable: Theresa
Fable: Jack of Blades

Movie Adaptations
Battleship
Transformers: Dark of the Moon
Spider-Man 3
Spider-Man 2
Spider-Man
The Incredible Hulk
Fantastic Four
Iron Man

The Camelot Papers
Tigerheart: A Tale of the Anyplace

Knight Life
One Knight Only
Fall of Knight

The Hidden Earth Chronicles
Book 1: Darkness of the Light
Book 2: Heights of the Depths

Sir Apropos of Nothing
Book 1: Sir Apropos of Nothing
Book 2: The Woad to Wuin
Book 3: Tong Lashing
Book 4: Pyramid Schemes (forthcoming)

Blind Man's Bluff (Star Trek: The New Frontier)
Year of the Black Rainbow (with Claudio Sanchez)

To Bob and Mike, two of my best friends ever

Acknowledgments

This book exists because of Will Smith and Caleeb Pinkett. I would also like to thank Gaetano Mastropasqua, Clarence Hammond, and Kristy Creighton for their input. At Random House, editor Frank Parisi and publisher Scott Shannon showed grace under impossible pressure.

AFTER
EARTH

PRELUDE

Kitai is sleeping soundly, dreaming of his future.

It is not an unusual dream. He has it all the time. His dream is simple and remarkably consistent. He is running in the dream, always running, across the plateaus that served as training grounds for the Rangers. He does not see himself as any older than he is right now: eight years old. Eight going on eighteen is what his mother often says. He's not entirely sure what she means by that, but every time she says it, she does so with such a wide smile on her face that it's clearly not intended to be insulting. As a result, he doesn't take offense.

In his dream, Kitai is running alongside other members of the United Ranger Corps. They are not children such as he is but instead tall and powerful and confident in their abilities. And they are all carrying cutlasses, the formidable weapon that each of them depends on to do the job that they have long been trained to perform. Also, they are all adults.

And he is bypassing every single one of them.

Kitai's speed is quite simply unparalleled. He is moving so quickly, so fluidly, that it is impossible for any of the others to keep up with him. "Slow it down, Kitai!" "You're killing us, kid!" Comments such as these often rain down on him as he runs, but he makes a point of ignoring them. The others' lack of speed is not his problem. All he cares about is being the fastest, being the best. Being the greatest Ranger in the history of . . . well, of great Rangers, really.

If there is one thing he knows about, it's great Rangers. His family is composed of nothing but great Rangers, and he is determined to surpass all of them, up to and including the general.

Kitai runs, he dashes, he vaults, he jumps. At one point he leaps off a cliff and actually soars through the air, free as a bird, while the other Rangers point and shout and collectively agree that he is, without a doubt, the best of all.

Somewhere in the distance, he hears a whining. It means nothing to him: just another loud sound to serve as a minor distraction, that's all. But he doesn't ever get distracted. He's too great and glorious a Ranger to succumb to such things.

Suddenly Kitai is jolted awake. He sits there in his bed, listening to his breathing, surprised by the realization that he had been asleep. The last thing he recalled was lying in bed, reading a book. He prided himself on always being awake and ready for anything. The fact that he had dozed off was bad; having to be awakened by a whining sound was even worse. Embarrassing, in fact. Or it would be if he were awake enough to appreciate the danger to which he was being exposed.

It takes him a few more moments to realize what the whining is: an air raid alert. The colony's alien enemies, the Skrel, have attacked. He's not hearing any explosions, though. If they're not bombing us, then what . . . ?

Ursa.

The creatures have persisted on Nova Prime for some years now. The Rangers, led by Kitai's father, managed to annihilate most of them, but the Ursa remain a genuine threat to the Novans. An unknown number of them remained, and they attacked the city without warning or pattern.

But what if it was the Ursa the alert was whining about? The thought paralyzed Kitai. If Ursa were being dropped off in the midst of humanity, all bets were off. For all he knew, Ursa could have made it to the interior of the compound. There could be one of them or a hundred. Since even one could kill hundreds of human beings, it didn't seem to matter all that much. Every single Ursa was a one-creature massacre machine. And considering the Raiges' apartment is only two floors from the ground, their home is right along the Ursa's projected path of destruction.

Kitai is in immediate danger. He confronts the fact. It makes him nervous.

He's eight years old. They're currently making plans to celebrate Landing Day: the day centuries ago when they first landed on Nova Prime, the world that became their new home. Landing Day is the one celebration to be found in the Nova Prime calendar. It's filled with dancing and feasting and gifts for small children.

Lately, Landing Day has occupied all of Kitai's attention. Despite the dangers that face the Novans on a daily basis, the notion that he might not live to see Landing Day had never occurred to him until just now. "I want Landing Day," he whispers. "I don't want to die. I want Landing Day."

He can hear running feet in the distance. His family's apartment is one of many in a cramped living area, and he hears voices in the distance directing people to a survival shelter. The apartments are fine for day-to-day living, but when the Skrel or one of their agents is threatening the Novans, it is standard procedure for them to take up residence in a shelter. A shelter is a heavily reinforced structure with thicker walls and only one way in and out that can be protected by a squad of armed Rangers.

At that moment, Kitai hears Rangers going through the hallways, making sure that everyone is heading down to the place where he or she is supposed to be.

One female voice in particular leaps out from the cacophony of shouts flooding over him. "Senshi?" he shouts, but he doesn't think anyone can hear him. His voice is too small, and the noise of others too big.

The apartment building itself is integrated into the

face of towering cliffs. It took years for the apartments to be carved out of the rock; during that time, humanity resided in thrown-together shelters on the sandy red ground. But it was not an issue then, for the alien race known as the Skrel had not yet noticed the presence of humanity on Nova Prime. The assaults had not yet begun. By the time they did—by the time the ships had come swooping in, firing away at the Novans, trying to kill them from on high—the cliffside apartments provided a good chunk of the protection humanity required.

A few hundred or so years later, that all changed.

When the Ursa landed.

That, of course, was centuries before Kitai was born. He doesn't know much about that. Years don't have the same meaning to him that they would to an older person. All he knows for sure is that people all around him are trying not to panic. Instead, they're trying to behave in the manner in which they have been trained. Kitai has been trained as well. Why is he not doing what he is supposed to do?

Because he is eight years old, that's why. This would be an acceptable excuse in another time and place. Here and now, it is not, and Kitai is aware of the fact.

Nevertheless he remains frozen in his bed, as if hoping in some small corner of his mind that he will pull slumber around him once more. That perhaps the dream world of happiness and superiority is the real one and all of this—a world of constant fear and barely restrained panic—is the fiction.

"Senshi!" he calls again, and this time his voice is louder and stronger.

For a moment there is no response, and then he hears her from a distance. "Kit?" her voice comes to him.

He sags in relief against his pillows even as he calls her name once more.

There is the noise of feet pounding in his direction. The smart cloth veils that serve as a door to his room *are pushed aside moments later, and he sees the concerned expression on his sister's face.*

Senshi is nineteen years old. Relatively young for a Ranger; she's working her way through the ranks. Most of her responsibilities keep her in the immediate vicinity of the city. She doesn't have much experience in genuine fieldwork. That's fine with her mother, less so with her father. Fantastic as far as Kitai is concerned.

"Kitai!" she says with frustration. "Why aren't you out in the hallway? Why didn't you come when you were supposed to?"

He is not entirely certain. What is he supposed to say? I was scared?

"Never mind," she says. "Kit, we have to go. Right now."

Despite the potential dangers awaiting them, he is filled with nothing but confidence in his sister. She looks brave in her Ranger outfit. For a flash he recalls when he first saw her in it, so tall and proud. The huge smile on her face was reflected in the face of their father, who didn't smile a whole lot otherwise. Senshi is holding her cutlass, ready to lash out at anything threatening her.

"Right now!" she says, her voice louder, more insistent.

His bed is nothing more than a hammock suspended across his room, which is filled with clothes and toys. As he attempts to get out, his foot snags on the ropes. Instead of clambering out of the bed, he falls forward and lands hard on the floor, twisting the hammock around on himself.

"Oh, for God's sake," she mutters as she starts to move toward him so that she can disengage him.

That is when a loud, terrifying screech cuts through the air.

Kitai freezes. He does not do so consciously. The shriek is an inhuman noise that thoroughly immobilizes him.

Senshi's head snaps in the direction of the screeching.

The blades on the cutlass—a large, ornately carved metal staff—snap out from either side.

"Is that . . . ?" Kitai manages to get out in a strangled whisper.

Senshi nods. Something has changed in the way she looks, in the way she holds herself. She's all business, 100 percent professional. It's as if she were merely pretending to be a Ranger until that moment.

"They surprised us," she tells Kitai. "They keep invading the city at random times . . ." She steps forward quickly and swings the cutlass right at him.

Kitai lets out a startled cry, and then the cutlass slices through the ropes in his bed. It severs the bindings instantly, and he tumbles to the ground. Quickly Kitai starts pulling the remains of the bindings off himself. As he does so, Senshi asks him briskly, "You're not afraid, are you?"

"No," Kitai says. Then there is another high-pitched howl of animal fury, and he jumps several feet in the air. "Yes," he admits, feeling ashamed but compelled by his lifelong tendency to be truthful.

This second source of howling is far louder, which means far closer, than the previous one. Senshi whirls and looks behind her, and Kitai cannot see the expression on her face. For some reason he is grateful for that. He suspects he wouldn't like the way she looks.

"Kit," she says softly, "get under the bed."

There isn't that much of a bed to get under, but it's sufficient. Kitai scrambles under the torn and twisted hammock, useless now for supporting him but still good for hiding under. Having pulled it completely over his head, Kitai then backs up toward the corner. Squeezing himself into a small ball, he is certain that he cannot be seen by anyone or anything under the coverings.

"Senshi, come on," he calls to her. The answer is simple as far as he is concerned. They hide together and wait for someone else to deal with the Ursa. To him, that's the most reasonable way of handling the current situation.

He watches in confusion as Senshi continues to look around the room. Her eyes dart around and fix on a round glass container with plants in it. It is his garden, or at least the closest thing that he could have to a garden.

Quickly Senshi brings her fist down on a button at the end. The lid obediently slides open. Senshi sweeps her cutlass around and expertly attaches it to her back with its magnetic clasp. Then she quickly starts unloading the plants from the box. She dumps them all over the floor, sending dirt flying everywhere.

Kitai watches in confusion. He has no idea what she is doing. He finds out moments later, though, when Senshi drops the plant box onto its side and slides it across the floor to him. "Climb in here, okay?"

"But . . . why?" He does what he's told even as he questions it.

"So it won't be able to smell you. Hurry up!"

He climbs and pulls his legs in after him, shrugging off the remains of the hammock. The moment he is completely enclosed, his sister drops the remote control into his hands. "Hold on to this."

"But what do I use it for?" he asks.

"You use this when I tell you to. Or when a Ranger tells you to. Other than that, don't come out. No matter what. That's an order," she adds sternly, because she knows that those are words that Kitai will respect.

Then she takes his face in her hands. Her beautiful eyes are emotional and deadly serious. "Did you hear what I said, little brother?"

"Yes, Sen—"

He is unable to complete the sentence because there is another thunderous roar, this time from much, much too close.

Kitai starts to say her name again, but she doesn't wait around to hear it. She hits the remote that is in Kitai's hands and then yanks her own hands clear as the glass box closes. He is now completely closed in as Senshi backs up, pulling the cutlass off her back.

It is a C-30 weapon. He knows that because she boasted about it when she brought it home the first time. He recalls clearly the first time she demonstrated it around the house. It moved so quickly in her grasp that he could not even see the blades. Her mother had been impressed. Her father had pointed out things she was doing wrong and had spent an hour or two with her going over all of her mistakes. She took the corrections without comment or any evidence of frustration. That was just the way she was.

Once the cutlass is in Senshi's hand, she taps a pattern on the weapon's handle. Instantly it responds as thousands of steel-like fibers extend on either side. They form razor-sharp points that she can use to cut deep through the Ursa's hide and squarely into its heart.

The cutlass is now two meters long and ready to be employed. Kitai watches and takes comfort from seeing it. He knows that once his sister is wielding her weapon, nothing is going to be able to get past her. She is a Ranger. She has been trained for exactly this sort of situation.

Then he sees a shadow in the adjoining room. It is the room his mother uses for various handcraft projects. Her "relaxation room," as she calls it. It used to be Senshi's room, but that is no longer the case since she has become a Ranger and resides in the Ranger barracks. So the room was made over.

Now, though, as the shadow moves across it, the room has become a place of danger.

Senshi spots the shadow. She doesn't make a big deal about it. She doesn't scream or point it out. She simply whips the cutlass around in her hand so that it is in attack mode.

Then she takes one final look toward Kitai. She nods confidently and makes a down-handed gesture to indicate that he should stay low, that everything is going to turn out just fine.

Senshi moves into the next room, spinning the cutlass in her hand, whipping it around in a figure eight pattern. Even as she does this, she is speaking in low, sharp tones to what Kitai realizes are other Rangers. She is bringing them up to speed, telling them that she is about to engage an enemy and that the sooner they arrive there, the better it's going to be for everyone involved.

That is when Kitai sees the creature enter the adjoining room.

He cannot make out very much of it. What he is able to discern is that it's huge, moving forward slowly on its six legs. At least that's how many he is able to count in the shadow. It is growling low in its throat, seeing its enemy, ready to strike.

Senshi is still moving her cutlass as it darts up and down, back and forth. She spins it so quickly that Kitai can scarcely follow it, and so he is sure that the Ursa is having the same problem.

That is when Senshi suddenly lunges at it. She is endeavoring to make a quick strike, to drive it out of the room, out of the apartment.

The Ursa, at least as far as Kitai can determine, doesn't fall for the maneuver. Instead of striking at her, it drops back several feet. A quick thrust from one of its legs sends furniture crashing about.

Senshi sidesteps, allowing the furniture to tumble past her. At the same time the Ursa tries to move in on her. Senshi pivots, jabs. The creature knocks the point of her weapon aside but fails to knock it out of her hands.

For long, awful seconds it goes on, the give-and-take, the thrusting and the jabbing. Then the Ursa bunches its powerful hind legs and lunges for her—and Senshi goes low, bringing up her cutlass in a move that is certain to impale the creature.

But it doesn't.

Instead, the Ursa lands clear of the cutlass. It is a moment that Senshi wasn't expecting, and she tries to bring the cutlass back around so that she can slice into the beast's body.

Whether she is too slow or the creature too fast is something that Kitai would never know for sure. All he is certain of is that the Ursa lashes out with its clawed foot, striking out at his sister. Its claws catch her right shoulder, and she cries out in pain, stumbling backward beyond the creature's reach.

Or at least that is her intention. Her backpedaling is too slow, her movements clearly impaired by pain.

Kitai still cannot see the monster clearly, hidden as it is behind the cloth between the rooms. But he can hear. Oh, God, can he hear. He can hear as Senshi tries to thrust forward with the cutlass, and he can hear as the cutlass is struck from her hand, landing noisily on the ground. He can get a brief glimpse of her shadow as she tries to move toward it and can hear the triumphant howl of the Ursa as it intercepts her.

Another claw lashes out, and the sound of flesh, his sister's flesh, being torn from her body is so deep and so loud that Kitai wants to do nothing but scream in terror. And he hears Senshi's high-pitched shriek of agony. Kitai can briefly see an image of her clutching at some point of her upper body, wherever it is exactly that the Ursa has struck her. Then, suddenly, just like that, she goes down, and that is when Kitai realizes that the Ursa has knocked her feet out from under her.

It lunges forward then, the Ursa does, and it lets out a deafening roar that mingles with Senshi's terrified shriek.

In the distance Kitai can hear rushing feet, the shouts of Rangers. He tells himself that they're going to be in time, that they're going to rescue Senshi. Everything is going to be just fine, and years from now they will laugh at this time when Senshi almost died squaring off against an Ursa to protect her kid brother.

It is at that moment that Kitai wants to leap out from his enclosure and go up against the Ursa. He heard Senshi's cutlass fall away, and he can see that it is lying not all that far away. All he has to do is emerge from his enclosure and grab it, and he can attack the Ursa him-

self. He is completely positive that he can take the creature out. He can attack, thrust forward with the cutlass, and strike the monster where it's not expecting any sort of attack.

He can do it. He can take the creature on. He can defeat it. All this he knows with absolute certainty.

Instead he does nothing. He lies paralyzed within the enclosure, and hot tears roll down his face. Kitai cannot move. He is terrified.

Then there is a final crunching noise, and he can actually hear Senshi. She doesn't sound like a Ranger at all. Instead she sounds like nothing but a terrified young girl, and a single word passes through her lips.

"Dad," she says softly.

And it's not because he's just entered to save her.

Kitai knows that his father is nowhere nearby, that he's on a "mission," wherever that meant. Maybe Senshi is saying "Dad" because she is seeing him in her own mind, or maybe she's apologizing because she has somehow let him down. Or maybe she's just scared.

Then there is more crunching and a final gasp from Senshi, and just like that, she is gone and Kitai is alone in the world.

The Ursa grabs Senshi's unmoving body with its teeth and lifts it up to within range of the nearest window. Senshi's shredded form is thrust into view, and Kitai can hear Novans screaming in the distance.

The Novans are as fearful as Kitai, perhaps even more so. Kitai can hear their footfalls as they run, can hear the growling and derisive snort from the triumphant Ursa. Then it drops Senshi's corpse right before Kitai's eyes.

Senshi's body lies on the floor, her face turned in Kitai's general direction. He sees her stare at him in what appears to be accusation, and he wants to turn away from her. Instead, all he can do is continue to look at her, his eyes wide and horrified, for what seems like a long, long time. Finally, he manages to look away, but even then he feels as if he's abandoning her somehow.

The Ursa leaps out of the room then to go search for other prey. Kitai lies there within the cabinet, no longer staring at Senshi but instead deeply into the narrow wall that constitutes the makeshift shelter Senshi has shoved him into.

It takes nearly an hour for the Rangers to find him. It's nobody's fault in particular, except perhaps Senshi's, for she had told him to stay there until a Ranger showed up. And that didn't happen until the Rangers who arrived had done everything they could to try to bring Senshi back. Only then did they entertain the off chance that someone else in the apartment might have managed to survive.

Until then, Kitai had had to remain there silent and immobile, his tears drying on his face.

It is not until Kitai's mother's arms are wrapped securely around him that he finally starts crying again. He keeps saying the same thing over and over: "I'm sorry. I'm so sorry." He blames himself for what has happened, but no matter how much he says it, his mother refuses to accept his apology—because she is certain that she might well have had two children die this night.

Oddly, knowing that doesn't make Kitai feel any better.

United Ranger Corps Training Camp

i

The alarm jolted Kitai awake.

He sat up, gasping for breath. He had been dreaming, but he didn't remember the dream. He had a vague notion that it had something to do with his sister, but he couldn't be sure.

It probably had to do with her. Most of his nightmares did.

Kitai flopped back down onto his bed and lay there despite the howling of his alarm. Long moments passed as it continued to shout at him. Finally he reached over and slapped it, hard. The alarm's cry finally ceased, allowing him a few more moments in bed. Another person might have been tempted to roll over and return to sleep, but that wasn't Kitai Raige. All he had needed was the jolt to wakefulness; after that, he was good to go.

Kitai finally sat up, rubbing at his face. He managed to bring himself to glance outside and begin to get a feel for what the day was going to be like. This was *his* day, after all, and he needed to have some idea of what the weather was going to be like. Of course, bright skies or pouring rain, it made no difference. Today was the day, and if he was going to have to do his stuff in soggy ground, well, that was the way it was going to be.

It didn't mean he was looking forward to it, though, and when he looked outside and saw that the day promised to be decent, he gave a silent "thank you" to the powers that be. He couldn't be absolutely sure since it was still dark outside, but from what he could see, it looked promising enough.

For just a moment he allowed himself to drift back to his dream. His recollections were vague at best, but he was reasonably sure that he'd been dreaming that awful day from five years ago when he had hidden from danger while his beloved sister was torn to shreds.

The notion that he had done so—that he had relived the deep guilt that still festered within him—was one of the hardest things for him to handle. Yet he dreamed of it with a frequency that was almost sickening. He did his best to brush away all recollection of it, yet that never seemed to work for very long.

Part of him occasionally toyed with the notion of going to see a psychiatrist, but every time he thought seriously about it, he ultimately rejected the idea. It would not go over well with his father. Members of the Raige family simply had no truck with people whose job it was to muck around with the human mind.

"You are who you are," his father had said when Kitai had very subtly (he thought) brought up the topic of psychiatrists in the first place, "and you live with the hand that you were dealt." That had been pretty much that.

The thirteen-year-old Kitai rolled out of bed and stretched. Waking was not something he did the way other people did. There was a procedure. First came a series of isometric stretching exercises. Then he dropped to the ground and did a hundred push-ups, which were followed by a hundred jumping jacks counted off in brisk fashion. He then crossed his room to the chinning bar he had installed back when he was eleven and did as many pull-ups as he could manage: twenty this morning.

Not bad. Not great, but not bad. Perhaps he was simply saving himself for his time out on the field this morning.

Yes, that made a vast amount of sense. He knew what

he was facing this morning and how important it was going to be. His father was going to be home this evening, eagerly expecting the news they all wanted to hear. It was Kitai's job to make sure the news would be good news.

"Kitai!" It was the voice of his mother, Faia, calling to him from downstairs. "You up yet?"

"Yeah. Why are you?"

"Made you breakfast. Thought you could use some this morning."

He was surprised that she was taking the time. Her hours at the turbine factory were long, and mornings were the only time she ever had to catch up on her sleep. She usually wasn't even awake before Kitai was out the door; that she had rousted herself this morning was sweet of her.

"Okay, be down in a few minutes." It was only after that that he realized he might want to say something along the lines of "Thank you." But he decided that it would come out as weak and indecisive, and so he simply nodded to remind himself to offer thanks after he went downstairs.

He took an actual shower this morning. Water had been in short supply recently, and although they weren't at drought levels yet, people were being conscientious about water usage these days. If nothing else, there was a bit more of a general aroma from people. It wasn't that big a deal. Once you decided to ignore the smells of other people's bodies, you more or less made yourself used to it. However, with all the running around he was going to be doing, getting off to a fresh start wouldn't be such a bad idea.

As he showered, he took the opportunity to check out his body. Tall and slender he was, catching up to his father in height. His skin was dark, his head was triangular, and his hair was cut down to standard Ranger length, which was one step above a buzz cut. He flexed his biceps as the shower water poured over him. The muscles were solid, compact. He did a few aerobic movements in the shower, then ran through a self-defense sequence before he was satisfied.

Minutes later he had toweled himself off and dressed in his two-tone gray and white Ranger cadet uniform. It lacked the decorations that were common to the full Ranger uniform, which of course made sense. How could one work toward being a full Ranger if one already had the accoutrements?

He trotted downstairs to find that Faia had made him two eggs, scrambled, plus a scattering of local fruits. His mother smiled when she saw him come downstairs. She was still wearing her nightgown with a robe draped over it. For all Kitai knew, she was going to go back to bed after he was off and grab another hour's sleep.

"Thought you might like this for a change," she said with a smile. "It's a step up from protein bars, I figure." That was true enough. Typically he grabbed a single bar for breakfast and launched himself into his day's activities. This was unusual.

"Thanks," he said. "For getting up and making it, I mean. Uh . . . thanks."

"You can stop thanking me, Kitai. It's all fine."

He nodded and started plowing into the eggs. They were pretty damned good. He could taste the flavor of cheese intermixed with the eggs; she'd obviously put some in. "Good," he said as he chowed down. "Really good."

"Excellent." His mother sat across from him, her fingers interlaced. She was smiling at him, but there was something about that smile that seemed to be . . . missing. That was it. It was missing . . . something.

"What's wrong?" he said.

"Hmmm?"

"Wrong. Something's wrong." He hadn't slowed his eating. Bits of egg were falling out the edges of his mouth.

"Nothing. Nothing at all."

"Something is," he insisted. He lay down the utensil and looked at her with concern. "What's going on?"

She hesitated and then shrugged. "I just want you to

do your best today. I know it's important and all that. So just . . . you know . . . your best. That's all you should be worried about."

"I'm not worried," Kitai said.

"Honey, I'm your mom." She reached out and placed a hand atop his. "You can admit—"

"There's nothing to admit. I'm going to do this. I'm going to go out there today on the course and finish on top on every subject, and by the time I see you this evening, I'm going to be a Ranger. That's all." He hesitated and looked at her warily. "You don't have a problem with that, do you?"

"What? No! No, of course not." She laughed slightly. "Why would you think that?"

Because you're afraid I'll become just like Dad.

"No reason," he said. "No reason at all."

"Well, that's good. I wouldn't want you to do anything other than your best."

"That's no problem," Kitai said confidently. "And I'll make you proud."

Her hand was still on his. She squeezed it tightly and said with a smile, "You already make me proud."

They were meant to be comforting words. Instead, for no reason that he could come up with, they made him nervous.

ii

The suns beat down on the thirty-two Ranger cadets— twenty males, twelve females—as they pounded across the course that would determine their futures. The terrain was red and rocky, with peaks that seemed to stretch so high that they scraped the sky.

Kitai was somewhere in the middle of the crowd, and his positioning was helping to drive home some of the disadvantages he had to face simply because of his physical condition. For starters, despite the solidity of his body, he was still at least a head shorter than most of the other candidates.

Consequently, as the group moved across the rugged terrain, he had to take two steps to keep up with every single step of the others. He worked on maintaining a steady inhaling and exhaling rhythm, but it was definitely not easy. He was supposed to keep a consistent pace, but instead he was practically sprinting to keep up.

A huge river cut through the stunning red mountain range. Both suns were high in the sky, beating down on the planet's surface. Kitai remembered reading some old science texts from Earth—back when there *was* an Earth—that swore that life-providing planets could not possibly exist in a two-star system, that any planets would be crushed between the gravity wells of the competing suns. He wondered what those scientists, dead for a thousand years, would have said about Nova Prime.

Don't let your mind drift. Pay attention to what's going on around you.

Kitai splashed through the river, sending water spraying, as did the others. However, the river also aided him in his positioning in the crowd. Others slowed down for whatever reason, and Kitai was able to take that opportunity to speed if not into the lead, then at least considerably closer than he had been before. When he hit the land on the other side, he was actually able to advance so that only a couple of the others were now ahead of him.

But he knew that a couple was not enough. When they reached the end of the trail, he had to be first. It was the tradition of the Raige family. Not second, not third—nothing but first would do.

The course of the race took them past a growing station. It was a huge open-fabric structure that shielded the crops from the weather. It allowed moisture to reach the plants but protected them from some of the more threatening weather. The station seemed to spread forever, although he knew that it was actually only a few hundred hectares.

Kitai felt his second wind kicking in and worked to shove his progress into high gear. He saw that Bo was leading the pack and started working to move his legs even faster despite the fact that Bo was built like a large tree. Bo was sixteen years old, farther along than Kitai in every regard: bigger, smarter, faster. But he was also breathing a bit more raggedly than Kitai was. Obviously, the stress of the run was starting to wear him down, and that was spectacular as far as Kitai was concerned.

There was a sudden drop in the terrain directly in front of them. Bo cut to the left to avoid it, and that gave Kitai the opportunity he needed. Rather than cut around the drop, he picked up speed and leaped directly over it. The trick was going to be sticking the landing, and that Kitai was able to do with style. He hit the downsloping ground ahead of him, stumbled only slightly, and then kept going. One leap and just like that, he was finally in the lead.

Bo, now behind him, called out to him, "This isn't a race, cadet!"

Kitai didn't care what Bo had to say on the subject. It hadn't been a race until Bo was behind him. And now that Kitai had grabbed the lead, he had absolutely no intention of allowing it to slip from his grasp.

Instead of heeding Bo's advice, Kitai stepped it up. His arms pumped, and his legs scissored with greater speed than he had displayed before. Slowly but steadily, he left the rest of the pack behind, separating himself from the leader and those in close proximity to the leader by a good ten or twenty meters.

The finish line was a kilometer ahead, but it might as well have been directly in front of him. He never slowed down for a moment, his feet flying across the terrain. One moment it was in front of him, and then it was behind. Kitai clapped his hands joyously in self-congratulation and then turned and faced the rest of the Ranger cadets, prepared to receive their congratulations as well.

Instead, one by one and then a few at a time, they jogged past him. The triumph he felt in crossing the finish line first was somewhat defeated by the fact that no one seemed the least bit willing to acknowledge it. Sure, granted, no one had actually been timing how long it took the Ranger cadets to cover the distance, but still, would it kill them to acknowledge his personal triumph?

Apparently so. Bo barely afforded him a glance, and then it was just a rolling of his eyes and a slow shake of his head, as if Kitai's accomplishment meant nothing.

Fine. Be that way. Kitai tried not to let his irritation get the better of him. Sure, the other cadets might not have been at all interested in offering him kudos for his achievement. But certainly the Ranger officers who were watching from a remote distance would have made note of it. They, at least, would understand: It wasn't enough that Kitai simply passed the course and was designated a Ranger. He had to be the best, and they undoubtedly knew why.

So what if the other cadets were unwilling to care about that? *He* cared. The Rangers who were judging him would care, too. In the end, that was all he really needed to worry about.

Once the Ranger cadets had a few minutes to gather themselves and recuperate from the run, the Ranger Instructors—RIs, as they were called—gathered them and marched them to a canyon about a mile away. Kitai noticed that a number of the Ranger cadets were chatting with one another intermittently. No one, however, seemed the least bit interested in chatting with *him*.

Okay, fine. That's how they want to play it? That's how we'll play it.

As they approached the canyon, Kitai could spot RIs at the top. They had small, multiple layered devices in front of them that were giving individual readouts on each of the Rangers. Kitai knew exactly what they were for. They tracked fear levels, because the Rangers were about to be attacked there, down in the twists and turns of the canyon below. The readouts would provide exact details of their reactions, an overall score that would be called the fear prospectus.

Fear was the thing over which Rangers were supposed to triumph. Fear was the weakness that could wind up getting a Ranger killed. And they all knew why.

It was because the Ursa were sensitive to fear in their prey. They could smell it.

Over the last few hundred years the Skrel had put a half dozen or so different generations of Ursa up against humanity, and the most recent incarnations of the creatures had been the most formidable that humans had ever faced. Six-legged monsters they were, with huge maws full of teeth, not to mention the ability to blend in so perfectly with their backgrounds that they were practically invisible.

But it was their ability to smell the pheromones that denote fear, to lock on with unswerving concentration, that made them the deadliest of creatures.

So there was no ability more valuable to a Ranger than the mastery of one's fear. More important than skill with the cutlass, more important than just about anything. That was why Kitai was determined to nail this part of the testing. This, more than anything, was going to determine his relative viability as a Ranger, and there was no way in hell he was going to screw it up.

The Rangers gathered at the entrance to the valley. Some were glancing up toward the RIs who were going to be monitoring them. Kitai was not. He'd already seen them and had buried that knowledge deep in the back of his mind. The presence of the RIs was no longer of any consequence to him. Only the challenges they would be facing in the valley mattered.

"All right, cadets," called an RI who was down in the valley with them. "Take your equipment."

The equipment dispensary had been set up. The dispensary had only two things in it, with enough for every one of the cadets: a protective helmet and a practice cutlass. These cutlasses would not change shape. There were no blades on the cutlass; it was to be used strictly for practice combat. It didn't necessarily mean that someone couldn't be hurt by it, but it was a lot more difficult.

Kitai slid the helmet over his head. He held up his hand briefly, looking at it front and back to make sure that his vision wasn't impaired. *Looks okay.*

As soon as all the cadets were properly outfitted, the RI who had spoken before addressed them again. "Cadets . . . enter the field of combat!" He pointed straight toward the entrance to the narrow field that ran between the cliff's sides.

"Sir, yes, sir!" called out the cadets, and marched straight into the unknown.

If there had been any means by which the Rangers could have dropped one or more Ursa into the canyons without worrying about dead cadets, they would have done so. But even Rangers had their limits, and no one in any command capacity was going to put three dozen or so cadets into one-on-one combat situations with the most vicious killing machines on Nova Prime. There would be challenges awaiting Kitai and the others, but of a more human kind.

Kitai once again found himself in the middle of the pack as they made their way slowly through the valley. This, however, was more by his choice than anything else. His positioning meant that other cadets would be the first to be attacked, giving him more time to react. He looked around as if his head were on a swivel, trying to see potential hot spots all around him, certain that the testers had come up with something special for the cadets this time.

There!

He reacted before he even saw it clearly. From the corner of his eye, he had spotted a quick flash of light.

Could be nothing, but much more likely, it was everything.

"Left, left!" he shouted, and charged straight toward where he had seen the flash of light. *"I got it!"*

"Cadet!" Bo shouted, clearly getting tired of what he considered to be Kitai's attitude. "Fall back into formation!"

Kitai paid him no mind whatever. Instead he charged, and other cadets got the hell out of his way.

As it turned out, he was right in doing so.

An RI hiding behind an invisibility field shifted it so that he could be perceived. He had his staff out as Kitai leaped through the air, bringing his own cutlass whipping around.

The two practice staves cracked together in midair. The RI staggered from the impact as Kitai charged forward and slammed a foot into his gut. The instructor let out a startled gasp and bent over, which Kitai took as an opportunity to slam the side of his staff down into the back of his neck. The RI went down to one knee, which was something of an accomplishment. Another man might well have been sent sprawling.

Kitai leaped past him, spun around, and was ready to bring his practice cutlass slamming down as hard as he could.

Then he lost the visual.

For no reason that he could discern, Kitai suddenly couldn't see a damned thing. A screen slid horizontally across his field of vision, blocking his ability to perceive the area around him.

"I'm dark, I'm dark!" Kitai shouted, and started to reach up to the helmet restraints so that he could pull the helmet clear of his head.

Before he could do so, the screen across his face retracted. Just like that, he could see, and what he saw in specific was the extremely irritated RI whipping his body toward him. Before Kitai could move or react, the RI flipped him over his back, Kitai landing hard on the ground.

Yet he was up just as quickly as he'd gone down. His vision restored, Kitai came in as fast as he ever had. He delivered a series of quick blows to the RI's helmet and torso. But as rapid as his attack was, it paled in comparison to what a fully trained Ranger could do. The RI absorbed the blows, allowing Kitai to take his best shot. Then at one point he ducked backward, and Kitai missed clean. Before he could recover, the RI went low to the ground, sweeping Kitai's legs from under him. Down went Kitai again.

"You're out," the RI informed him. "You're out."

Like hell I am.

Once again he started to stagger to his feet. He did it with less certainty than he had earlier, but there was still strength and determination in his deportment.

Unfortunately for Kitai, the patience of the RI had been exhausted.

As a result, before Kitai could fully bring himself upright again, the RI slammed his foot forward and caught him on the chin. Kitai let out a startled grunt as he hit the ground a third time, and this time he didn't stand up. Not because he wasn't trying; he most definitely was. But the RI, having tired of the battle with him, put his foot on Kitai's neck. Even then, Kitai didn't immediately give up, instead bringing his hands around to start prying at the foot.

"You! Are! *Out!*" The sound of the RI's voice made it very clear that if Kitai continued to battle him, he would increase the pressure of the foot on his throat. The best-case scenario would impede Kitai's breathing. The worst-case scenario, depending on the RI's mood—which didn't seem especially generous at that moment—was that Kitai wouldn't be able to breathe at all, ever again.

Worst of all, the rest of the team had gathered around, breaking formation as they were intrigued by the entertaining vision of Kitai struggling for air. For the first time Kitai was actually feeling self-conscious. He stopped struggling and put up both hands in a submissive fashion.

Even then, the RI was still obviously pissed off over Kitai's aggressiveness. He glanced around at the rest of the cadets and said sharply, "All of you! Out!"

Just like that, the exercise was over. The rest of the cadets headed out toward the next one, removing their helmets as they did so. All of them relaxed, chatting with one another. No one bothered to speak to Kitai or even help him up. Bo gave him a single annoyed glance and then shook his head.

Kitai sat up, rubbed his throat, and coughed a few times. It restored his breath as he got to his feet, and then he set out after the others. They continued to ignore him. He continued to be convinced that they were jealous of his aggressiveness and determination. Well, that was fine. The bottom line was that the people in charge would know who and what they were dealing with. They would see his abilities for what they were and praise him accordingly.

In the end, that was all that mattered.

iii

The rock face was a pleasant diversion for Bo.

He'd climbed this particular obstacle a number of times in the past and was utterly confident in his ability to handle it without a problem. The thing towered nearly two hundred meters in the air, but Bo knew the best way up and was certain that no one in the troop could cover it as quickly or with as much assurance as he did.

And "no one" most definitely included Kitai Raige.

Bo didn't have any strong feelings against Raige. In point of fact, deep down he actually kind of admired the kid. Not that he would admit it, of course. That simply wasn't how it was done. But there was a great deal to admire about Kitai Raige in terms of how he handled himself and his determination to be first at everything.

With any luck, Kitai would outgrow that mind-set. Surviving as a member of the Rangers was about so much more than who finished first and second. Surviving meant getting through to the end of the day and still being in one piece. Over time, Kitai would learn that and potentially be a valuable member of the Corps.

Assuming they let him into the Corps, of course. That was by no means certain. Not if Kitai kept having the mini-breakdowns that he was experiencing during these tests.

Well, that was Kitai's problem, not Bo's. Bo, for his part, had to focus on the rock wall.

The harness around his chest provided the additional support and certainty required for climbing something such as this. It was secured into ropes that had been set into the wall ages ago. It wasn't as if Bo really felt he needed them. But they were there and they offered security, so why the hell shouldn't he take advantage of them?

Suddenly he heard something coming up below him, moving much more quickly than he would have thought. Given the speed at which he was moving, it was hard for him to think who could possibly be catching up with him.

He looked down and could actually feel his heart tightening in his chest.

It was Kitai. Of *course* it was Kitai. Even more alarming, he was free climbing. Ignoring the drop that awaited him if he lost his grip, Kitai was practically sprinting up the rock face.

"Cadet!" Bo shouted down to him. "Click into harness!"

Kitai was gaining on him. "Slows me down!" he shot back.

Bo tried to redouble his efforts, but it was no use. Kitai shot right past him. It was nothing short of astounding to Bo. Moments earlier he had been in the lead; now he was behind Kitai and fading fast. Even the part of him that warned against worrying about such things as finishing first was losing its dominance. His inner frustration and sense of pride drove him to try to pick up the pace so he could overtake Kitai once more.

It didn't happen, didn't even come close.

Instead he watched.

Kitai had reached a point near the very top of the peak. He was on a six-centimeter ledge just below with a face that tilted out by more than ninety degrees into space. That should have caused some hesitation on Kitai's part. He was, after all, facing every climber's greatest fear: commitment to the void. Usually such a move required one to take long moments to prepare oneself.

Not Kitai. Without the slightest hesitation, he swung himself out, dangling almost two hundred meters above the canyon below. Having insufficient speed for his first arc, he swung back and forth again and then a third time. The third one did the job, providing enough momentum for him to throw himself up and over and land atop the ridge upside down.

Quickly he scrambled up and around so that he was standing properly on the top of the ridge. He stood there with his arms spread wide, and Bo could distantly hear something. It took him a few moments to realize what it was. Kitai was making *aaaahhhhh* sounds as if a vast audience were watching him and cheering his achievements.

Oh, that little punk, Bo thought as he clambered the rest of the way.

Kitai was still making the noises of a thrilled crowd when Bo finally joined him atop the ledge. "That was stupid," Bo informed him, although he was certain that Kitai wouldn't give a damn what he had to say.

He turned out to be quite correct. "They don't give statues for being scared."

"Yeah, but they do give plenty of headstones for being dead!"

Kitai simply grinned as he clipped himself into a futuristic zip line. Bo morbidly wondered whether Kitai might, upon reconsideration, simply toss aside the zip line and just throw himself off the top of the ridge on the assumption that somehow he would float down on waves of his own greatness.

He was destined to be disappointed, because Kitai finished clipping himself in before leaping off the ridge. The zip line drew taut, and Kitai was off on his buzz toward the ground far below. Bo clipped onto the line and leaped off as well.

As they descended toward the ground, Bo couldn't help noticing all the sights of Nova Prime spread out before him: undulating structures in the canyon, windmill towers and waterwheels making use of the environmentally sound energies that Nova Prime provided them. In the distance there were ships ready to take off, heading toward any number of destinations within the solar system and beyond.

Not bad. Considering we arrived here centuries ago with the contents of the arks and that was all, this is definitely not bad. An appreciable testimony to the cleverness of humanity.

From below him, he heard Kitai giving out a loud war whoop that celebrated nothing else but the speed with which he was heading toward the ground.

Kid never pays attention to anything around him, and he doesn't even realize it. That's going to cost him. Cost him a lot.

Over the remaining twenty minutes, the rest of the Ranger cadets, one by one, came sliding down the zip line. It was the last endeavor of the day, and Bo knew that the next day, the results would be delivered. He was feeling fairly confident that he would score high enough to move on. And he had faith in 80 percent of the other cadets.

He just couldn't make his mind up about Kitai.

As the remaining Rangers gathered, Kitai made no effort to approach any of them. He stayed off to the side, stretching and then doing push-ups. Bo simply shook his head. He couldn't recall seeing anyone quite like Kitai Raige before. It made him wonder if Kitai's father had been anything like this when he was Kitai's age. He almost asked but then remembered that Kitai wasn't much for talking about his father except in the most reverent terms, and so an honest discussion about what his father was like seemed to be out of the question.

Kitai finished his push-ups and then, without sitting up, flopped back against a small rocky projection. His breathing was completely under control. Then, with a wry smile, he tossed off a salute toward Bo. "Sorry about buzzing past you back there," he said, and pointed in the direction of the ridge. "Sometimes I get a little . . ." He shrugged, apparently unable to come up with the appropriate word to describe his behavior.

Obsessive? Competitive? Nuts?

Since none of the words Bo was coming up with seemed any better, he just shrugged. "Don't worry about it."

Kitai leaned forward, ready to talk business again. "You think everyone passed the VR?"

The VR was the Ventax Reactor test developed by Doctor Abigail Ventax decades earlier. It sensed degrees of fear that human beings experienced under conditions such as the tests the cadets had undergone. The would-be Rangers had been monitored scrupulously the entire time.

"Everyone?" Bo snorted derisively at the notion. "Try 'anyone' and I'm pretty sure the answer is no."

Kitai stared at Bo in shock. "Wait. *You* didn't?"

Shaking his head, Bo said with a clear air of disgust and discomfort, "Spiders."

It had been during one of their high-speed chases through a cave. Everything had been going fine right up until Bo had charged through what turned out to be an entire mass of spiderwebs. He'd let out a startled gasp, which had only succeeded in making him inhale one of the webs. Then he had spent thirty seconds coughing violently to expel it from his lungs.

"I hate spiders," he admitted, and by coincidence, Kitai said the exact same thing at the exact same time. They looked at each other in mild surprise. Then they bumped elbows in a sign of camaraderie. It was an odd feeling for Bo, and he suspected that it felt the same for Kitai.

But hey . . . spiders. What could you do about spiders? "What was the point of spiders? What function?" Bo asked.

The arks that had carried humanity to Nova Prime had transported genetic samples of every species on Earth. Couldn't they have left out the arachnid family?

"I just don't get it," Bo said in frustration.

Kitai was just about to respond when a female voice interrupted them: "I heard they captured an Ursa."

Both Kitai's and Bo's heads snapped around in response to that. The speaker had been Rayna. On the face of it, Rayna seemed an even less likely Ranger than Kitai considering that she was half a head shorter than he. But Rayna was extremely intelligent and a formidable hand-to-hand combatant. Bo had great respect for her, and so did Kitai. When she suddenly announced that an Ursa had been captured, naturally that was going to get immediate attention.

Killing Ursa was not an uncommon situation on Nova Prime. It wasn't an easy undertaking by any means, but it had happened enough times. Capturing one alive, however, was definitely unusual. A number of other cadets had overheard Rayna's pronouncement, and they approached her to hear what she had to say.

There were numerous cries of "No way!" and "You're kidding!" and "Are you sure?"

Rayna simply nodded her head, her arms folded. "Absolutely," she said. "Heard it reported over the naviband." She tapped the communications device strapped to her wrist. "You guys should pay attention to these things."

"Who?" Kitai asked. "Who captured it?"

"Who do you think? The Ghosts," she said.

Kitai nodded, feeling slightly foolish. Any cadet worth his salt knew that when an Ursa was sighted, at least one Ghost was always called upon to dispatch it.

Rayna continued: "And they're going to move it to someplace they can study it."

"Ghosts. You mean like Kit's dad?" said Bo.

"Maybe him. Or somebody like him. It was out in the jungle somewhere. Your dad out in the jungle somewhere, Kitai?" Rayna asked.

Abruptly a silence descended over them. They collectively waited for Kitai to respond.

It was as if the utterly confident, overly aggressive Kitai Raige had vanished altogether. Instead, for a few moments, he just looked flat-out uncertain about anything and everything. Then he cleared his throat and in a manner that seemed far too faked to be anything legitimate said with an air of forced offhandedness, "Not sure. I know he's coming home tomorrow. I'll ask him then."

"What's that like?" asked one of the Rangers.

Kitai stared at him in confusion. "What's what like?"

"You know! Having the Original Ghost as your father!"

"It's great," Kitai replied. "He's a great guy. It's all great."

The cadets glanced at one another, and several snickered. Before the question could be pushed any further, one of the RIs emerged from the nearby makeshift headquarters that had been thrown together. "Tomorrow, eleven hundred hours at Ranger headquarters. You will be given the results then." That was his entire pronouncement on the subject. He turned on his heel and walked away.

Kitai took the opportunity to get the hell out of there. Rayna even called after him, but he ignored her. The Ranger cadet who previously couldn't get enough of talking about such subjects as himself now seemed extremely dedicated to the notion of putting as much distance between himself and his fellow cadets as possible.

Bo didn't know whether to find that amusing or just sad.

iv

Kitai stretched out on the hammock in his bedroom that evening, slowly turning the pages of his book.

His. Book.

It was something of a rarity, this novel of his. Printed in the twenty-first century, long before the Earth was abandoned, it was an ancient story about a man obsessed with a whale named Moby Dick. Not very many of the books had been made, and this rare copy had floated from hand to hand over the centuries, working its way into the Raige family via Senshi, where it had remained ever since. Kitai had been fortunate enough to get his hands on it.

He had been reading it over the last few nights. It hadn't been an easy endeavor. Someone had said to him that by the time he was finished with the novel, he would know far more about hunting whales than he would ever need to know. About a third of the way through the book, he'd come to the conclusion that that assessment was an accurate one.

He heard his mother's feet approaching his room. She sounded like she was trudging, which didn't surprise Kitai in the least. At least he'd been done with his day before the afternoon was over. His mother's getting home fairly early was something of a rarity.

Moments later his mother appeared, and she looked utterly worn out. She had dust on her coat. Her exhaustion was reflected in her eyes, but she visibly pushed it aside so that she could speak to her son. "Hey there, honey. Sorry I'm late. Do you need—"

"Something to eat?" He shook his head. "Nah. Ate already. You okay?"

"A lot of spikes today," she said by way of explanation. "We had a lot of orographic uplifts." She paused and then said with mild challenge, "What are orographic uplifts?"

Kitai was ready simply because not being ready wasn't an option. "The vertical forcing of air by terrain features like mountains."

She nodded approvingly. "Good. One day when you're done running around and hitting things, you'll take over the turbine research division for me."

He smiled humorlessly at that. "Sure, Mom."

She returned the smile because they both knew she wasn't serious. For Kitai, his career as a Ranger was a given. Only the specifics of how long were still up in the air. "How'd the test go?"

"I'll find out tomorrow." He kept up a deadpan expression for as long as he could, but then a smile crawled across his face that he was unable to hold back.

His mother couldn't help seeing it. "Looks to me like you're confident about how you did."

"It's just . . . it'll be great when I tell the general I got into the Ranger program on Senshi's birthday. That'll be great, right?"

"Not everyone gets into the Ranger program on their first try."

"Yeah, but those guys are bums," Kitai said dismissively.

She smiled at that. "Yes," she said with soft assurance. "He'll be happy." Then she noticed the book in his hand. "When did you start reading that?"

"I'm trying to get done before the general gets home."

Kitai nodded, sure that if he were a newly named Ranger, that alone would be enough to prompt his father to hang around, at least for a while. He tapped the book. "There are lines underlined. Does that mean the general and Senshi liked these parts?"

"I don't know."

"Maybe I should memorize one. Do you think he'd like that?"

"I think he'll like the fact that you're reading the book."

"Are we doing a cake?" he suddenly said, shifting subjects.

"We're not doing a cake. We'll just be together." After a moment's silence, she slapped her legs, causing a bit of dirt to rise up. "I'm going to wash off all this dust. I've been on the ridge all day."

"Mom . . . ?"

She'd been about to stand, but something in his voice caught her. She focused her attention on him. It took him a few moments to find the words, and even then she didn't fully understand at first.

"What was it like when Dad became the first? How did he do it?"

"The first?" Initially she stared at him without comprehension. But then she understood. "Oh. You mean the—"

"The first Ghost, yeah. How did he do it? I've tried looking it up, and I haven't found anything. It's all just . . . vague."

"How vague?"

He licked his lips, collecting his thoughts. "Well . . . it's just that everyone knows that the Ursa don't have any eyes. That they find us through sense of smell. And what they smell is our fear. It's how they work. They track us through fear. They hunt us through fear. Everything is fear with them. And the Rangers go out there and do everything they can to control their fear, but it's almost impossible.

"Ursa are monsters, and they come at you with everything they've got. And they've got a lot. Six legs, teeth, paralytic venom . . . everything. It's almost impossible to go up against one of them and be totally unafraid. But Dad did it. I mean . . . he just, you know, he did it. He did it when no one else in the history of humanity had done it. And they called him a Ghost. The first one ever. So I'd just kind of like to know how it was that first time. How he did it."

"Honey . . ."

He realized she wasn't looking at him. Instead she seemed to be staring off into space, as if her mind had partly checked out. Kitai expected that she was putting together her recollections of that moment.

For a surprisingly long time, she said nothing at all. Then, finally: "Have you ever tried asking him yourself?"

"Yeah. He, uh . . ." Kitai shrugged. "He would just shrug. And he'd just say that fear was something that could be controlled, and he just, you know . . . managed it. But he's never gone into any detail beyond that, and I . . ."

"Stopped asking."

"Yeah."

She stroked his short hair as she sighed. "Okay, well . . . so did I. Maybe he'll tell you someday."

Kitai nodded but said nothing more. There didn't seem to be much point. If there was one thing Kitai had learned after all this time, it was that everything having to do with his father fell into the realm of "maybe" and "someday." The problem was that Kitai couldn't decide if he wanted to be there when the maybe or the someday actually happened.

Kitai's father stared at him. Just stared.

Kitai took the opportunity to practice his attitudes. At first he indulged himself with a huge smile, but then he decided that it made him look too smug, and so he changed it for something extremely modest. After that, he tried an expression in between. All during the smile time, he practiced different oral sentiments ranging from "I knew I had it the entire time" to "I think they were being generous" and countless other statements as well. The whole time, Kitai's father maintained his hard, unmoving expression.

"Raige! Move it!"

He nodded to no one in particular and turned in the direction of Bo, who was shouting over to him from the elevators. His father remained right where he was, which was hardly unusual: He wasn't really there. Instead it was his image, a frieze carved into the wall of him along with six other people. They were collectively the seven Ghosts in the history of the Rangers. His father, Cypher Raige, had been the first, and over time six others had developed the ghosting technique as well. Kitai wondered if he likewise would develop the ability. *One thing at a time. First you become a Ranger. Let everything else work out after that.*

He left his father carved in stone and joined the other cadets in the elevator. Moments later they were heading down into the bowels of Ranger headquarters. There was little discussion or banter among the cadets. All of them were understandably wrapped up in their individual thoughts, which were, as it happened, all exactly the same: *Did I make it?*

Kitai glanced around at those standing near him. Every one of them looked nervous. Kitai tried to hide his confidence from them. All it would do was irritate them.

Minutes later the elevator delivered them to their destination: a series of offices in the tallest section of the HQ. The higher up you were, the more vital the offices. The view of the city from these levels was said to be spectacular and one of the perks of command.

There were no stools or benches of any kind in the hallway outside Commander Velan's office. It was Velan's job to oversee the development of cadets into Rangers, and his was the final word on whether one qualified to make that jump. Kitai was utterly confident in Velan's decision-making abilities. Velan had a keen eye for talent, and Kitai was certain that he would have had no trouble seeing Kitai's capabilities despite the attempts by others to try to deter or impede them.

Three other cadets were called in before Kitai. He stood in place, leaning slightly against the wall for support. No one spoke save whenever a cadet emerged from Velan's office. In this instance, each of the three who emerged one by one did so with a C-10 model of a cutlass in his hand. That meant, of course, that they had passed, and each was greeted with quiet congratulations from the others. Hands were shaken, backs were patted. Kitai did the same thing as the others, welcoming them into the fold of Nova Prime's planetary protectors. It was odd, of course, because the people who were welcoming them were hoping that they would have the same bounty handed to them.

"Raige!" came Velan's sharp voice from within his office. Kitai promptly snapped to attention, taking in a deep breath and letting it out slowly. There was no doubt in his mind that he was going to be coming out with his own C-10, but that didn't mean he couldn't be humble about it.

He entered as the door closed behind him. Kitai stood at full attention, chin snapped forward, eyes leveled on Velan, who was seated behind his desk. Velan was glancing at some holographic material Kitai took to be written reports on his performance from the previous day.

"Your test scores were very impressive," Velan said. "You've got a Ranger's mind. No doubt about that."

It was a huge strain for Kitai not to smile broadly. He had expected nothing less, and it was good that the Rangers who had been doing the scoring had seen that in him. It was indeed the only thing that had concerned him: that they'd be so annoyed by his determination and skills that they might try to sink him just out of hostility. He realized he should have known better. That was simply not how Rangers operated, and he would be sure to remember that—

"But I'm not advancing you this year."

Kitai felt as if the world had suddenly slipped out from underneath him, leaving him in an endless headlong free fall. The words hit him again one at a time like stones, the two heaviest and most painful of which were *not* and *advancing*.

How was it possible? He almost asked Velan to repeat himself—*almost*. But somehow he stopped short of that.

He was so stunned that he did not even see the compassion in Velan's face. There was no room in Kitai's world for compassion. All he cared about was accomplishing his goals, and here Velan was calmly smashing them to pieces.

Everything else that he wanted to do in his life, up to and most important making his father happy, hinged on his becoming a Ranger. And here Velan was sitting there calm as you please after telling him what a fine Ranger he would make and informing him that he wasn't putting him through? It was insane. It made no sense at all!

"You take unnecessary risks," Velan continued.

Whether he was aware of the pounding shock and rage going through Kitai's head was unknown to Kitai. In fact, it wouldn't have mattered even if he had known. Velan had a point of view, and he was going to make it clear. "You are emotionally unpredictable. You have improper threat assessment, and you confuse courage with recklessness, which at the end of the day is just a far more dangerous way of being scared. You may, of course, try again next year."

Try again next year?! Spend another year's worth of his time taking the same courses, the same preliminary tests, so he could wind up failing again? *This makes no sense! It's ridiculous! How can—?*

Kitai's inner turmoil was, of course, of no relevance to Velan. Having delivered the news that had just destroyed Kitai's day and possibly his entire life, the commander simply said, "Dismissed." With a casual sweep of his hand, he pushed the holographic file with Kitai's information out of his view and swung the next one out so that he could inspect it. He wasn't even bothering to look at Kitai anymore. He had pushed Kitai's information and achievements and life casually aside and moved on to the next cadet.

Velan looked up and blinked in mild surprise when he saw that Kitai was still standing right where he'd been, not having moved a muscle. There was no anger in Velan's face. He simply appeared mildly confused that Kitai was still standing there.

Fighting the urge to hyperventilate and only partly succeeding, Kitai nearly shouted as he said, *"Sir! Permission to address the commander, sir!"*

"Denied." There was nothing condemning or judgmental in his response. He was simply a man with a lot to do, and he saw no reason to waste time in a pointless discussion with a wannabe Ranger.

It was as if Kitai didn't even hear him. As if Velan hadn't denied him the chance to speak because who in his right mind would do so? He proceeded to continue talking in the exact same volume as he had before.

"Sir, I am dedicated, have studied and consistently displayed conduct becoming of a Ranger, sir! I request that the commander reconsider his assessment, sir!"

Velan stared at him with utter incredulity. Disobeying a direct order, which Kitai had just done by speaking to him, was grounds for pretty much anything Velan wanted to do in response, up to and including banishing him from the Ranger program forever. In one shot, Kitai was risking throwing away the entire future that he thought he was fighting for.

Then Velan's face softened just a bit. "I understand what it's like to see someone die. I know what that does to you."

Kitai stiffened. It was the equivalent of Velan smacking him across the face with a two-by-four. It stopped him cold, and Velan was able to continue uninterrupted.

"I've been your father's friend for a long time, Raige. Your friend as well, although you may not know it. I know what the loss of your sister was like for him and you and your mother. And I know that you expressed no interest in being a Ranger until after her death. You're trying to . . . no. Forget it." He paused. "I'm not going to tell you what you think because you already know that. What I am telling you is this: You're rushing your way into a situation that you are not, in my opinion, emotionally ready for. If I endorsed your moving ahead, it would be catastrophic, and your parents would have to face the rest of their lives with no children at all. I will not do that to them, and I certainly won't do it to you. Do you understand?"

Kitai did everything he could to hold back the tears. He steadied himself, fighting to bring himself under control. When he spoke again, he had to fight to get out every single sentence. His words were of no relevance to the decision made as to whether he should be a Ranger. He knew that for certain. Yet they were the only words he had left and, in addition, the only ones that really mattered to him.

"Sir"—his voice was barely above a whisper—"my

father is returning home tonight. Today's a special day for our family. I haven't seen him . . . and I *have* to be able to tell him that I have advanced to Phase 2. I've got to be able to tell him that I am a Ranger, sir."

Velan's face didn't move a centimeter. He simply stared at him for what seemed the longest few moments of Kitai's life. During those few seconds, it seemed to Kitai that anything was possible.

He was wrong, as it turned out.

"You tell your father that I said 'Welcome home.'"

Kitai couldn't believe it. How could Velan be doing this to him? He'd admitted that Kitai had everything it took to be a top Ranger. So he had some impulse-control problems. So what? If he moved on to Phase 2, certainly that was something that could be attended to at that point. Why deprive him of his move forward? What could he possibly—?

Velan's eyebrows knit, and there was now a darkness in his eyes. He was clearly displeased over Kitai's refusal to accept his decision, and his next words underscored it. "Your lessons in discipline begin right now. You may leave this room with dignity and decorum befitting a cadet. Or you may leave under escort. Your choice."

For half a beat, Kitai actually considered the latter. Being dragged out shouting over the way he was being treated . . .

But that was as far as he got in his thoughts. If that was really how he exited the room, being hauled out by Ranger troopers, he was effectively finished. All anyone would spend the rest of the day talking about was "Did you hear? Kitai Raige was dragged out kicking and screaming because he didn't have what it took. What a sap. What a fool." He would be done. That was simply not a public image that he could reasonably walk back.

"Sir, yes, sir," was all he said. Then he turned on his heel and walked out.

He emerged into the outer lobby to the questioning looks of the others. Then they noticed that he wasn't carrying a C-10, and that answered the first of their questions. Before they could ask any others, or offer consolation, or perhaps even revel in his failure, Kitai was across the hall and in one of the elevators. The door slid shut, and it was only once he was alone and on his way upward that the barely withheld tears broke free of his mental barrier and rolled down his cheeks unfettered.

The sense of tension could be felt rising with every block as Skyler Raige II neared the United Nations' thirty-nine-floor secretariat building on Manhattan's East Side. People who normally walked fast in New York City were walking faster, their shoulders hunched, ignoring everyone around them. Their steps had purpose, but they also were radiating fear.

Raige noticed how many storefronts were boarded up; some that were open had signs indicating a list of items that were currently out of stock. Sanitation also seemed to be taking it easy as the spring breeze coming in from the river whipped debris into the air. There was an unpleasant odor, and he blinked a few times as grit tried to blind him.

The Ranger was uncertain why he had been summoned to the office of the United Nations' secretary general, but he was a soldier and followed orders. His appointment was for ten-thirty in the morning, and Raige, spit-polished to perfection, had arrived from the United Ranger Corps base in Germany just hours earlier. He was tired and fueled solely by his third cup of coffee, but there was enough adrenaline pumping through his system to keep him alert for the impending conversation.

For the last nine years, he had served as a Ranger, seeing parts of the world he had only read about in school, never imagining he would be in Algiers, Sudan, Brazzaville, Portugal, and Germany in the same calendar year. His jacket was beginning to resemble a Michelin guidebook, and he regretted being able to see only the seedier parts of countries the guidebooks tended to omit. Still, he enjoyed sampling the local fare when time allowed; anything was better than the MREs, or Meals Ready to Eat, he was consuming en route to and from fronts.

He prided himself on his adaptability, adjusting from culture to culture with ease. Raige found himself making friends everywhere he went, playing endless rounds of soccer or stickball with the kids who usually flocked around the arriving Rangers, hoping for money or food or both. Rather than disappoint them, he shared his rations and played with them, cajoling many of the others to join in to even out the sides.

He commanded men and women into battle, which usually consisted of quelling food riots or protests against governments that were forced to ration as the planet suffered on many—too many—ecological fronts.

Now he'd been asked to meet with the secretary general. When he received the orders in Germany, his CO gave him a quizzical look, seemingly jealous, while everyone else razzed him about getting a trip home.

The summons concerned him, but he flushed the issue from his mind, taking in the decor. The place needed paint and a new carpet. In fact, for a prestigious office it was downright worn-out and in need of a massive overhaul. Still, there were larger issues to worry about and money was growing scarce as more and more resources were being poured into the ark programs. Construction was scheduled to begin in just a few months, and he suspected that was why he had been summoned: to discuss security procedures when work began in the Sahara. Still, he was just a sergeant; what made him so special?

A plump Asian aide stepped from behind a closed door and gestured for Raige to join him.

"Takeo Sato," the man said, shaking Raige's hand with a single pump. "We're running a little late, but please come with me."

Raige entered the larger office of the secretary general, which needed refurbishment, as did the rest of the place. Of course, Constantine Lider had other things to concern himself with, and he struck Raige as the kind of man who didn't notice his surroundings. He had liked Lider's strenuous efforts to take Project Next Generation's recommendations and make them a reality, ramming some of the less popular decisions through the UN. Of course, he had the full might of the Security Council behind him, and there was plenty of arm-twisting and outright threatening to get everyone, down to the last rogue state, on board.

"May I get you a drink? Some tea, perhaps?"

"Just water will be fine," Raige said. He was handed a chilled bottle from a well-concealed minifridge and appreciatively slaked his thirst. The rising global temperatures, coupled with the plane's dry air, made him feel constantly thirsty. The cool liquid felt terrific going down and helped steady him.

Before he could chug the whole bottle, a side door opened and Lider strode in, his hand already outstretched. He had gone entirely gray since taking office and appeared to have lost weight without having his suits taken in, making him appear gaunt. He looked like a man in desperate need of a weekend away, not that he had the time for such an indulgence. There was a planet to save, after all. Still, there was plenty of life in his eyes and the grin was broad.

"So glad to meet you, Sergeant Major," Lider said, his German accent clear.

"A pleasure," Raige replied, shaking the large hand, noting the strength it still possessed.

"How is it in Germany?"

"Pretty much as you left it, sir," Raige said. "They're restless but recognize their options are increasingly limited."

"I wish we could properly communicate that to the less educated of this world. There are still over two billion illiterate people, and they operate strictly by rumor and word of mouth. That's the chief cause of the panic, I fear. I wish we could do more."

Lider gestured them to comfortably appointed straight-backed chairs surrounding a small blond wood conference table. Atop it were tablets with maps already lit up, most showing hot spots in Europe. Raige sat and continued to wonder what he was doing there.

"Sergeant, the coming decade may well be the final one for all of us on Earth," Lider said. His tone dropped from friendly to deadly serious. "We're gathering the supplies we need to begin the largest construction project ever undertaken. Everything we're doing right now is on an unprecedented scale. In some cases, we have the material ready since it can be repurposed from one project to another. In other cases, we are still short-handed, and that includes the Rangers."

Raige knew that four years earlier Lider had ramped up recruitment, trying to reach the 1-million-man threshold sooner rather than later. They were still far short, but just about every able-bodied, soldier-worthy man and woman was being wooed to the Rangers. The promise of regular food and clothing was all the enticement some needed, whereas others wanted hard cash, refusing to believe it would soon be worthless. But Lider was right: The literacy and educational levels were a drag on training as remedial courses were added to the regimen, slowing down readiness for deployment.

"How are the troops?"

"I can't speak for all of them, sir, but my squad in Germany is tired. We've been regularly deployed with barely seventy-two hours to rest and recharge."

"Is burnout going to be a problem?"

"I think we need to schedule more R&R for the men," Raige replied. He began to wonder where the questioning was going. Were things already so bad that they'd be pushed to the limit of endurance?

"Are you well armed enough?"

"It's largely riot gear, which is designed for hard

knocks. Thankfully, our rifles and ammunition are less frequently needed."

"How's the new foam working out?"

"It's hell on the uniforms but really effective at slowing down the rioters," Raige admitted. The foam contained a mild sedative that was absorbed through the skin and helped quell the attackers. Though controversial at first, it was the most humane way of dealing with people when language and cultural differences inflamed problems.

"Good to hear, although I doubt the comptroller will appreciate the higher cleaning bills." He said it with a smile. He was joking, trying to ease whatever tension was in the air, but he looked as tired and worn as Raige.

"Things are only going to get rougher, Sergeant. We've pushed this planet to its breaking point. We just need to hold on until we can send some of us into space." Raige knew that Project Next Gen had been founded years before to find a way to preserve life beyond Earth. They'd found a world light-years away and were racing the ecological clock to build the arks that were their last hope.

"How many do you think will make it?"

"Current planning is for ten arks using the Lightstream engines, each carrying about 125,000 people plus fish, birds, animals, plant life, and supplies. So, 1.25 million people out of nearly 12 billion."

Raige was stunned by the small number despite the enormity of the project. He knew there was no way to save everyone, but that number for the first time in his life sounded woefully tiny.

"Your family is no stranger to those engines, are they?" Lider asked, accepting the tea Sato brought him. Without asking, Sato handed Raige a second bottle of water and then vanished out of sight.

"Yes, sir. My great-great-great grandfather was there at the beginning," Raige said.

Lider nodded and asked, "What do you know of his work?"

"Growing up, we were all taught how he was a scientist at a Russian site where a starship apparently crashed," he said, knowing how bizarre that sounded.

"Did it concern you that there is evidence of life beyond Earth?"

"I believe in the Bible, sir, but also accept that the universe is really too large for us to be the only ones."

Lider nodded, sipping his tea, savoring the peaceful moment. "Good to know."

"Thomas Raige, Viktor's son, came over and seemingly started a dynasty," Lider continued with a slight smile. "You've had aunts, uncles, cousins crawling all over the LST development. Now you're in line to continue that legacy."

Raige nodded in confirmation. He knew that Viktor Radoslav was a scientist at the time, and his son, Thomas, who was renamed Raige when he immigrated to the United States, continued the research. They were part of a team, sworn to secrecy about the alien discoveries. It was discussed only among the elders of the family, and where other families had confirmations or bar mitzvahs to mark the rite of passage, members of the extended Raige family were entrusted with this astonishing truth. He vaguely knew of the various Raiges who either helped protect its secrecy or plumbed the alien secrets.

"In fact, your own father flew some of the Lightstream experimental shuttles for NASA before becoming a private pilot," Lider continued. Raige was impressed that a man with this much on his mind could conjure up such details without a briefing report. That told him a lot about how serious this conversation was. The secretary general wouldn't have boned up on his life and background if this wasn't about something huge.

"His sister, your aunt Sarah, was once director of homeland security and fiercely guarded the Lightstream Project, cherishing it as both a family and a national treasure," Lider added with a small smile. "After all, the LST tech was actually owned globally given how many people from different countries had contributed to its development since its discovery in 1908."

Lider continued his questioning. "So tell me, if you knew all about the legacy, what led you to the military?"

"Truth be told, sir, I wasn't born with that particular scientific aptitude. I can't sit in a lab and do research, and if we're being honest here, I am not much for great heights," Raige said.

"Which leaves out flying," Lider said, nodding. "So you decided to enlist and see the world."

"More like try to save it from itself," Raige said. "Of course, once I filed the data work, I was shuffled over to the Rangers."

"True. By then we were screening heavily to find promising recruits, and now look at you, nine years in, an impressive rank and record," the secretary general said with a father's pride. "The field promotion in Portugal, for example. Tell me about that."

"You obviously read the report, sir. An extremist group was threatening a port with famine relief supplies destined for Morocco. They had booby-trapped the ships and the port and jammed the radio frequencies. While we negotiated for the release of the crews, I was sent in with a team to liberate the port. When my chief officer was shot down, I began issuing orders, and we successfully took the port. I then sent frogmen into the sea to disarm the ships."

"All the while, the negotiations continued," Lider said.

"Politicians can talk all they want, and we took advantage of the stalling."

"Loss of life?"

"On our side, just my CO, Sergeant Conway. On their side, two dozen."

"Impressive work."

"Thank you, sir," Raige said, suddenly feeling impatient, wanting the interrogation to end and for Lider to move on to the point.

"Are you hoping to be placed on an ark and leave this world behind?"

Was this what it was about, a posting on an ark? Couldn't be; the SG was too busy for that.

"It'd be nice, but I'm no one special, just a grunt trying his best," Raige said.

"You sound humble, but you come from a line that is anything but. In fact, your lineage is what brought you to my attention. You serve the Rangers and the world, but there's a more personal stake at work here, too. You want Lightstream to work and save us all, don't you?"

"Well, save as many as we can, yes, sir," he said.

"You have an impressive mix of credentials and glowing reports from General Rodgers, Colonel Mishkin, and Senator McCluskey. I've seen footage of you at work and studied your file for days," Lider admitted.

That didn't exactly surprise Raige, but it did fuel his curiosity and make him feel antsy. He'd been sitting long enough.

"Everything we do at the UN, at Project Next Generation, and with the Rangers has to work on multiple levels. We have to move things forward, protect the project to save humankind from itself, and we have to send out a constant stream of signals that we have their best interests at heart. We have to, in short, make the wisest choices, ignoring all the old rules and protocols. Frankly, I'm likely to be the last secretary general, and I don't have to worry about a legacy or election. I can act freely and intend to do that right now."

Lider stood, and Raige matched his action.

"Skyler, I intend to make the United Ranger Corps a fully independent body, answerable to no one. The primary goal remains to preserve humanity. That mission objective will not change until the last ark leaves Earth's orbit. Each one will carry Rangers to keep the peace for the next hundred years until the arks arrive at Nova Prime. From this moment forward, it needs a face the people can trust. It also needs a leader. I've created the post of Supreme Commander and would like you to accept this assignment."

Raige's jaw fell open. His legs trembled, and he gripped the armrests on the chair to stay upright. Supreme Commander was a powerful title. But he was just twenty-nine; how could he command a global operation, ordering people nearly twice his age to fight? Surely there had to be other, more experienced and qualified senior officers.

"Sir?"

"The Raiges have been caretakers of the LST tech for over a century, and it needs a Raige now to ensure it can do what we pray it can do. I need a strong, youthful, and, in your case, handsome face for the Rangers. We need to project confidence in having a future, so we're skipping a few generations of senior officers. The Rangers have been asked to do some difficult tasks, and now they are going to be asked to do some pretty impossible things over the next few years. It means the Rangers will be protecting those selected to leave Earth and also those who are being consigned to a fairly grisly death. It means protecting the transport ships from workers who understand they are building a means of escape for others. This job offer comes with no guarantee you yourself will be placed on an ark. I know it's a lot to ask someone so young, but trust me, this was not a choice hastily made."

Raige's mind was awhirl with fears, concerns, plans, hopes, and a certain elation at the recognition. His parents and family would be delighted as they always wanted him to be part of the "family business" and here he was, charged with protecting it.

"Thank you, sir. Where will the Corps be based? What is the command structure intended to be without UN oversight?"

"Good questions," Lider said, a twinkle in his tired eyes. "Does this mean you accept?"

"It is a huge honor, sir. And a powerful responsibility.

But how could I possibly refuse the secretary general, speaking essentially for the world?"

"I'll take that as a yes," Lider said, extending his hand.

Raige hesitated for a moment, the enormity of the next instant looming large in his mind. His heart was pounding, and he struggled for control. Finally, the hand crossed the short distance and sealed the deal. He had walked in a sergeant major and was about to walk out a commander, no, a Supreme Commander, something unheard of.

"Sato will take you next door to run through the schedule. We announce your promotion at eight tonight, and as of 12:01 a.m., you take charge. You will see he was most thorough and left half an hour for you to call your parents."

They really had all the bases covered. His agreeing had been a foregone conclusion, and if he had said no, he would have been kept in the room until that was turned into an affirmative.

Raige stepped out of the office, his mind racing with ideas, questions, concerns, and a rising sense of excitement. This had tremendous possibilities, and he had a few years to shape the Rangers for the next hundred years or more. Clearly, the opportunities meant his final years on Earth would be good, productive ones.

No sooner did Raige leave the room than Lider was confronted by a figure who had used the side door. Clearly, Damian Kincaid had been eavesdropping on the conversation and was furious. The red-faced man was four centimeters or so taller than Lider and cut an imposing figure, looming large in the room. He was wearing an expensive suit, and his shoes were polished to a high sheen; he clearly cared more about his appearance than his superior did. Kincaid had been one of his security advisors, and although Lider knew the man disapproved of his choice, he was just now getting a sense of *how* upset he was.

"You fool!"

"That is no way to speak to your boss," Lider said, slumping in his chair, ceding the room's domination to Kincaid. The man tended to go for large gestures, speaking with his hands, making faces when he couldn't speak out. Now he was letting it all hang out, and Lider steeled himself for the harangue.

"He's an inexperienced kid!" Kincaid said loudly.

"We've covered that. His record is exemplary, with more action than those with twice the seniority," Lider reminded him.

"Like that's going to matter in the months ahead! We're about to go straight to hell and need an experienced hand running that operation," Kincaid said, dropping his voice just a notch below a bellow.

"At least we agree on cutting it loose," Lider said, wishing he had a call from some world leader. *Any* world leader. "Supreme Commander is as much logistics as public relations. He's young, good-looking, and a war hero. He will project that confident image we need to keep selling the world that this is our best course of action. He'll surround himself with experienced hands, but he needs to be the public face."

Kincaid exhaled in frustration.

"Damian, you were outvoted. And now you're trying to spread your sour grapes over my carpet. I should think you know better than this. Skyler Raige has everything we want and need for the role. He's what the Security Council wanted when I said it was time for the Rangers to be independent. He's a youthful, vigorous presence. He has demonstrated an innate understanding of people, making him an ideal leader. Best, he'll be a calming force when everyone else, yourself included, is shrieking at the top of their lungs."

Lider had said similar words days earlier when the final vote had been taken and Kincaid was one of several who remained adamant that someone with more experience was required. But as Kincaid himself had just pointed out, everyone was headed into uncharted territory. Experience or additional years were not really a measure.

"We formed the Rangers in 2052 when it was clear we needed a global force. We've been training them for less than fifteen years. Who will really have more than Raige's nine years' experience and service record? I challenged you to give me alternative qualified names, and you failed to find one better equipped. Why are you so opposed to him?"

Kincaid spun about, jabbing a finger in Lider's direction. "Because as we face total annihilation, I'd like us to have total faith in our leadership. He's not even thirty, and you're about to entrust him with the largest army this world has seen since the Roman Empire."

"Let me remind you, Damian, Alexander was barely thirty when he ruled much of the civilized world," Lider said. "Don't be so hung up on age as opposed to the man's character. He's proven himself."

"Is that what you'll tell the generals who now have to salute a kid?"

"If they can make an appointment and get into this room, yes, that is what I will tell them."

"I cannot abide the disrespect you're showing to the natural order of things," Kincaid said.

Lider had had enough. He rose and stared up at the younger, larger man. "The natural order was tossed out decades ago. We're making every effort to preserve a tiny sliver of this world, and we need everyone on board, headed in the same direction, pulling their own weight. Pick your cliché, but I need to move forward and not waste time this world no longer has on rehashing decisions the committee made.

"Either support Raige or get out of the way."

Kincaid let it all sink in and thought very carefully for maybe a second. "Fine, I'll get out of the way. While you're busy touting the kid, I'll be tendering my resignation, telling the media that you have squandered the Rangers' best chance for making a miracle happen."

With that, the man stormed from the office, taking all his pent-up energy with him.

Lider sank back into his seat, realizing he wasn't going to miss Kincaid. He was capable, sure, but he was far from a team player. What his former employee seemed to have missed was that, in Lider's mind, Raige was Earth's last chance for greatness.

1000 AE

Nova Prime

i

Hours after his conversation with Velan, Kitai finally had managed to clean up his face. He felt as if it had taken him days. He kept staring into the mirror, and all he could see was a vision of misery and frustration. He knew he wasn't wrong in thinking that, because when his mother had come home, she had taken one look at him and mutely opened her arms to him.

But he'd been ready for that. All he did was wave it off casually, as if the failure of his aspirations was simply another problem that would be dealt with in the course of time. Faia naturally did not believe that for a second, but she was stymied by his determined reluctance to discuss it. She folded her arms across her chest, stared at him for a few moments, and then said simply, "If you want to talk about it, I'll be happy to listen."

But he wasn't interested in discussing it. Instead, after showering and dressing for his father's arrival, he contented himself with staring out the window that enabled him to look out over the entire city. Many apartments within the structure had no actual windows. Instead, they had to settle for holograms that enabled them to see re-creations of different Nova Prime visuals. The dwellers there would swear that their view was better since they could change it at will, but Kitai was sure that they were just making excuses. Nothing was as good as seeing the real life of Nova Prime.

The twin suns were in the process of setting. This was

his favorite time of the day, when one sun was disappearing and the other was still in the sky. It dropped a gorgeous haze over the horizon and made him proud to be a resident of Nova Prime City.

Faia had arranged the food on the table already because she knew exactly how her husband liked things to be when he came home. She looked it over with satisfaction and then checked her watch. Her husband was running late. Her husband *never* ran late, and that was enough to tell her that someone *else* was running late and delaying her husband, and her husband was doubtless going to be complaining about it when he came home.

No reason she couldn't minimize his reasons for complaining when he came home. "Kitai, care to sit?"

He looked away from his view of the city and stared at her in confusion for a moment. Then he shrugged inwardly. If his mother wanted him seated, he'd be seated. He took his customary chair at the table, smoothing out the lines of his jacket. As he did so, Faia brought out the actual foodstuffs. Some lettuce from her garden to start, followed by baked sartori, a cowlike creature that was native to Nova Prime and widely grown in farms around the planet for eating purposes. Not the cheapest meal she could have put out, but worth it considering that her husband and Kitai's father had been gone for months.

He's always gone for months.

The bleak thought filtered through Kitai's mind, and he hated himself for even thinking about it, because when he dwelled on his father's lengthy absences for too long, he always started thinking about *why* his dad was away for so long. It could well have been the reason he always gave: business. And since his business involved protecting the people of Nova Prime, what was Kitai supposed to say in response to that?

I know the reason you're never around. It's because you can't stand to look at me because I can't cut it as a Ranger. Yes, that would definitely go over well.

Faia seated herself across from her son and folded her fingers. So that was what they were going to do? Just wait for his father to show up? This was going to be unbridled excitement.

"Want to talk about it?"

"No, Mom, I really don't," he informed her.

"Okay." She glanced toward the landing on the other side of the apartment. The veiled doors had been pulled aside, allowing a steady breeze to flow through. She licked the tip of her finger and held it up, gauging it. "Did you notice that? The wind shifted."

He nodded. "To the northwest." It wasn't an especially exciting topic to talk about, but at least discussing the weather took the two of them away from matters that could well prove disastrous if engaged in.

Then they both heard sounds at the front doorway. Immediately Faia got to her feet. Kitai followed suit. He smoothed his jacket and said, "How are my lines?"

"Your lines are perfect." She reached up and ran her hands along her face. "How are *my* lines?"

"Mom . . ."

She laughed lightly at that even as she moved across the living room to the front door. Kitai straightened his posture as Faia opened the door for his father.

Cypher Raige stood revealed in the doorway. He had two arms and two legs and his face was unscarred, so all that was good. He wore dress whites that only a Ghost could wear. His kit bag was slung over his shoulder, and there was some baggage behind him. Considering that Kitai only ever saw his father wearing his Ranger uniforms, part of him wondered what could be in all the suitcases. A *dozen* Ranger uniforms? Kitai had no idea.

His father was as tall and strong as Kitai remembered him. He had the same haircut as his son, with a triangular face and eyes that were cold and appraising rather than displaying any happiness over being back. That wasn't unusual, really. It was hard for Kitai to recall a time when his father genuinely displayed happiness over anything.

For a moment, neither parent said anything. Then Cypher tilted his head slightly. "Faia."

"Hi."

They didn't kiss. They never kissed, at least not when Kitai was around. God knows, he'd never discussed it with either of them. He'd just figured that Cypher felt it wasn't appropriate.

Cypher slid the kit bag off his shoulder, and his gaze shifted to Kitai, who was standing stiff and upright by the table. "You've grown," he said. Cypher then strolled forward, walking past Faia without another word, and stood there in front of his son, taking him in. Assessing him. Kitai stayed right where he was, staring straight forward, arms at his sides, legs stiff. Cypher slowly surveyed him, walking around him and studying him up and down. His voice flat, showing no emotion whatsoever, Cypher spoke as he rounded his son: "Your collar's ragged. You have a crease on your right pant leg but not your left. Fold crease." He took a moment to glance toward Faia with a silent accusation that clearly condemned her for letting Kitai get away with such a sloppy presentation before he continued. "Your jacket is improperly fastened. Before you present yourself for inspection, cadet, square yourself in the mirror. Is that understood?"

"Yes, sir."

Cypher continued staring at his stricken son for long moments and then finally allowed, "But this isn't an inspection."

It was, of course, Cypher's attempt to let his son off the hook, or at least that was how Kitai saw it. His father reached over and gave him an awkward pat on the back. Apparently he thought that made up for the stiff and formal greeting, as if it were all some big joke. Yet Kitai couldn't help but feel as if it were anything but that. As if he and Cypher both knew the truth of his criticisms and Cypher had simply softened it a bit to make up for it and fool his wife. Kitai suspected that she hadn't been deceived in the least.

Yeah. This is going to be a great night.

It took Kitai a couple of minutes to help his father get his suitcases inside. Opting to wait until after dinner to put his things away, Cypher took his customary seat at the head of the table, and they began eating. He turned to Kitai and asked the question Kitai had been dreading all day. "So, how were finals?"

Kitai didn't respond. He had no idea what to say.

The lack of response immediately prompted Cypher to put down his lacquered utensil. He appeared to know immediately that something was up. Having received no response from his son, he turned to his wife and said again, "How were finals?"

Faia had trouble replying. Clearly she was worried that she would be betraying something about which Kitai was sensitive. Part of Kitai almost prompted him to say nothing just to see how his mother would handle it, but he knew that would be inappropriate. He had to say it himself.

But he couldn't look at his father as he said it. Instead, he became very interested in the potatoes on his plate as he said in a low voice, "I wasn't advanced to Ranger."

Cypher didn't even hesitate. "Where do we look when we speak?"

Kitai shifted his eye contact to his father. "I was not advanced to Ranger."

"You were not advanced to Ranger . . . ?" Cypher leaned forward, waiting for the additional word that, clearly as far as he was concerned, Kitai should have remembered to say at the end. Kitai was so distracted that for a long moment he actually forgot. Then he recalled.

"I was not advanced to Ranger, *sir.*"

A long silence followed. Cypher simply stared at him, almost as if trying to recall who the hell he was. The quiet seemed to stretch to infinity. Kitai fought to keep his face impassive, as if he had simply relayed news about a single poor test rather than a decision that seemed capable of destroying the rest of his life.

Then Cypher, to Kitai's astonishment, shrugged. "That's all right. You're young." And he went back to eating.

Kitai couldn't quite believe it. *That's IT? From the minute I left Velan's office to now, I've been dreading your response, and all you do is say, "That's all right, you're young"?*

He knew on some level he should be incredibly grateful. But instead all he could think was that his father, the great Cypher Raige, really didn't give a damn what his son did or didn't do.

Bristling with barely contained anger, he said, "I ran the canyon eleven seconds faster than you did."

Cypher shrugged as if that meant nothing. "Well, if you were ready, Velan would've promoted you. He's a good man. Knows his stuff. You weren't ready." He shrugged and cut another piece of meat.

That was it. End of discussion, at least as far as Cypher was concerned. The man who expected nothing but success from himself—the man who had exhibited endless support for his daughter during her time as a Ranger—was indifferent to his son's inability to qualify. *Oh, well, maybe you'll do better next time.* That was the range of Cypher's response.

Kitai was left with nothing to say. Part of him thought, *He could have reamed you out! He could have done all the things you were afraid he'd do. Just be grateful and call it a day.*

There was indeed some merit to that. His father could have ripped him to shreds. Instead, he'd just taken it in stride. Kitai should have been happy for that.

Instead, all it did was reinforce his deepest, most secret belief. He was convinced that his father really didn't care about what he did or did not accomplish.

Kitai realized he was staring at his plate. Nothing else seemed to interest him. Finally he announced, "I'm not hungry. I'm going to my room."

Cypher's response was deathly quiet. "Are you asking me or telling me?"

I'm telling you.

"May I go to my room, sir?" He was already half out of his chair.

"Denied. Sit down."

Kitai paused a moment, fighting the impulse to get up and walk away anyway. Hell, not just get up. Run. Maybe that would get a serious reaction from him.

Instead he slowly sat down.

Then Faia spoke up. Her voice was flat and even and filled with quiet rage. "May *I* be excused, General?"

Cypher turned and looked at her in surprise. He'd just been in the middle of disciplining his son, the failure. He clearly was not expecting his wife to intervene.

Nor did she wait for him to respond. Without a word she pushed her chair back, stood, and then walked quietly away into the kitchen. That left Cypher and Kitai in a horrendously awkward situation, the two of them sitting there in uneasy silence while the empty chair seemed silently to accuse them of screwing things up.

"You're excused," Cypher finally said.

Upon hearing those words, Kitai was out of there like a shot, leaving Cypher alone with his feelings and his meal.

ii

The guest room. That was what Cypher had just entered. Indeed, if anyone had asked whose room it was, he or she simply would have been informed that it was the guest room, and that was all.

The problem was that both Cypher and Faia knew whose room it was. It was Cypher's room. On the infrequent days when Cypher was at home, it was where—most nights—he stayed. Faia slept in their bedroom, and Cypher slept here. Cypher wasn't even sure that Kitai was aware of it. If a boy assumes that his parents are sleeping together, why would he question the idea?

Cypher finished depositing his bag in the guest room and sat down in a chair for a few minutes to regain his strength.

My strength. Once upon a time I could have off-loaded it with one hand tied behind my back. Now I'm actually tired. He stretched his arms out to either side and winced at the pain in his shoulder. That would go away before too long, but the older he got, the more often he would feel unwanted pains and the slower they would be to depart.

He lay back on the bed and stared at the walls of the guest room. The walls provided the other aspect of the room, namely, that it was his shrine to Senshi.

The wall was made of smart fabric, and family pictures had been transferred to it. The images moved slowly but deliberately across the cloth. There was Senshi, from her birth right up to a photo that had been taken two days before her death. Her entire life laid out in a series of pictures. Normally they simply sat there unmoving. But when Cypher entered the room and said, "On," the pictures would start to unfurl their individual stories. There she would be, running and laughing, or picking up her father's cutlass for the first time, or singing some merry holiday song.

Each of the pictures had an icon next to it, and Cypher zeroed in, as he typically did, on an image of her in a Ranger uniform. It had been taken the day of her graduation from the academy, the day she became a full-fledged Ranger. He had been so proud of her that day. So proud. It was hard for him to believe that any parent had ever been prouder of a child.

Cypher reached toward the picture, and his finger touched the icon.

Instantly the picture obeyed, growing from the small image on the smart fabric wall to full size. He was no longer staring at a small, short film. Instead it had completely enveloped him. He was in the middle of a cheering crowd of people at the graduation, shouting and applauding not just for their own children but for the graduation of every single kid. Because they knew full well that every Ranger was a dedicated protector of Nova Prime and its people and thus deserved the cheers of every person in the crowd.

He glanced over to his right and saw Faia and himself sitting right where they were supposed to be. Kitai was in his mother's lap and had fallen sound asleep. Cypher supposed he couldn't blame him. There'd been a lot of talking and speeches before the actual pinning ceremony, and it had fried Kitai's abilities to stay awake past what his young age would allow.

Enveloped in the fake reality of that wonderful day, Cypher could only watch as any other ghost would watch. He had no means of actually interacting with anyone in the scene.

Senshi climbed up the steps to the platform as her name was called out. Her pin of service was attached to her uniform amid much applause and cheering. Senshi held her cutlass straight up then, twirling it several times in some mildly ornate maneuvers. She didn't do anything too fancy, not because she couldn't but because she didn't want to show up any of her fellow graduates.

Cypher and Faia had had their own recording equipment, but this footage had been taken by a Ranger cameraman who had then provided copies to everyone who was interested. Cypher was most definitely interested, and as he watched Senshi step down from the stage, he couldn't resist. He headed straight toward her, his arms open. He positioned himself so that Senshi was walking right toward him, and he threw open his arms to receive her.

She passed right through him like a specter, and he turned and watched as she went to her "real" parents behind him. Cypher of the past wrapped his arms around her, and Faia grinned and said wonderful things while the young Kitai continued to slumber in her arms. Senshi laughed at that, and she reached over and kissed her little brother on the head. He stirred a bit in his sleep but did not awaken.

They were together, and they were a family. A family that Cypher was able to remember only vaguely.

And the strangest thing of all was that when he had thought back on that wonderful day previously, he had forgotten that Kitai was even there. He'd just assumed that they'd gotten a babysitter for him.

Tears welled up in Cypher's eyes. He would never have allowed himself to be seen reacting in that manner outside this room, but inside it, he could react however he wished, as all around people cheered for the accomplishments of Senshi Raige and all the other Rangers.

iii

In her office, Faia was hunched over a table with holographic wind turbines. She had spent weeks building them to perfect scale, but she still didn't have the power supply linked in so that they would turn automatically. That didn't matter to her, though. After all, it wasn't as if wind blew automatically, either. Instead, she very carefully spun the turbines with her hand and then jotted down the information she was able to acquire. Low-tech it may have been, but the results she was receiving were as reliable as anything else she might accomplish.

Then she heard a soft footfall at the door. She turned in her chair, and Cypher was standing there with a small, pained smile on his face. She gazed into his eyes and saw no hint of the man who had treated his son with carefully maintained indifference at dinner.

"Look at that," she said, studying him carefully, tilting her head one way and then the other. "Yep. Cypher's back. General Raige had him hostage."

He crossed the room and sat down in a small chair beside her. He reached out tentatively, and she took his hand, squeezing it warmly. He sighed. It was as if he were relaxing right into her.

"I have a last mission to Iphitos. Flying tomorrow," he said. Iphitos was a small planet, one of six anchorages over in the Milky Way's next spiral arm. Residing there was not for the faint of heart. There was a colony of maybe a hundred or so people, and they were getting ready to see if Iphitos could be terraformed from a training facility and Ursa respository into something more welcoming to human habitation. They could just as easily have been attacked by the Skrel as Nova Prime had been so often over the centuries, but so far that hadn't happened. The general assumption was that the colony was simply so small that the Skrel hadn't taken any notice of it, the several million people residing on Nova Prime posing a far greater threat.

Faia frowned when he said that. "Last mission?"

"Yeah. You see . . . after it's completed, I'm announcing my retirement."

"Retirement?"

"That's it," Cypher said with a nod. "It's that time."

"No, it is most definitely not that time."

He blinked in astonishment. He'd forgotten that she often surprised him, and then he was surprised when she did it again.

He looked deeply into her eyes. "I want my family back. I want you back."

He reached into the inside of his jacket and pulled out a necklace. It was not one of the items of jewelry that were fashioned by Nova Prime artists. No, this was unquestionably antique jewelry from Earth. It was not only incredibly rare, it was also symbolic. Or at least as far as Cypher was concerned, it was.

But Faia simply stared at it. She allowed a small smile to acknowledge its significance and his good intentions, but otherwise she seemed indifferent to it. She stood stiffly as he attached the necklace around her slender throat and then nodded in the direction of Kitai's bedroom down the hallway. "That boy in there is trying to find you," she said. "He is . . . a feeling boy, he's an intuitive boy, and I . . . *Moby Dick*."

He stared at her in confusion. "What? What about it?"

"He watched you read that book with Senshi his entire life. He's reading that book now. He's reaching for you . . ."

"Well, how was I supposed to know that?"

"You didn't. You couldn't. Because you couldn't ask even something as simple as, 'So how are things going?' Cypher . . . don't get me wrong. I respect everything that you've done. But you have a son in there that you do not know. He is drowning. He thinks it's his fault, what happened to Senshi. He doesn't need a commanding officer. He needs a father."

Cypher spoke to her, his voice distant, as if he were speaking from another place and time. "We fight monsters. And before that, we learn how to fight them. And before that, we dream about fighting them. That is who we are, and it is my responsibility to instill *that* into that boy."

"Oh, look," Faia said drily. "The general's back."

"You're damn right he is."

She spoke without heat. There was no anger in her voice. Just sadness. "Let me make a prediction. When the general is old and no longer looks like his statue, the father is going to realize this is the exact moment he lost his son."

His face frozen in annoyance, he stood, turned, and walked out. As he did so, Faia glanced at her reflection on a screen, studying the necklace. Its cold stones shimmered like distant stars.

iv

Kitai was dressed in a sleeveless shirt and a pair of blue shorts. His uniform, the clothing that he valued above all else, was lying crumpled on the bed. Anyone could have taken a single glance at it and known that it had not been removed with any manner of care. He had simply ripped it off himself and thrown it onto the bed. When he was ready to go to sleep, he was fully prepared to just kick the damned thing off the bed and let it lie on the floor all night.

Then he heard a quick stepping of feet and looked up. Cypher was standing in the doorway, staring at him. His face was immobile, as if he had a hundred thoughts battering around in there and still hadn't decided what would be the best way to approach his son.

What was he going to discuss with Kitai? Was he going to shout at him about his failure? Was he going to unleash the true despot he had hiding inside him? Was he—

"Pack your bags," Cypher said. "You're coming with me to Iphitos. We depart at second sun."

Kitai blinked in confusion. Whatever it was that he had expected his father to say to him, this was most definitely not it.

But why? Why would he bring me to Iphitos? Is he planning on just leaving me there? What the—?

With that pronouncement, Cypher turned away and headed down the hallway without a word. That had been a command more than an invitation.

Kitai, alone again, did the only thing he could: pack.

United Ranger Corps Space Port

i

Kitai could not recall the last time he'd been to the Rangers' main hangar bay. It was the largest single structure in Nova Prime, cut deep into the mountain where the city stood. Ships of all sizes would tear out of there at seemingly random times. Sometimes they were at the command of the Rangers. Other times ships were flown out at the command of the Savant's science guild. Even the Primus, who was the head of the religious guild, had need for various ships, and whatever anyone required could be found at the main hangar bay.

Everywhere Kitai looked, he felt nothing but a relentless sense of wonder. At the moment, he was engaged in watching a transport ship being fueled. He wondered if it was the vessel his father and he were scheduled to take. He was mildly chagrined to admit even to himself that he hadn't the slightest clue why the ship was heading out to a colony world. But his father had said that was where they had to go, and if that was his dad's opinion, well, then, that was that.

Kitai was finding it difficult to believe the many swings his opinions of his father had gone through in the last twenty hours. First he'd been terrified of him. Then he'd become angry. And now he was grateful that his dad was taking him along on this adventure. So grateful, in fact, that he resisted asking what was going on. The fact that his father had thought of him at all, for whatever reason, was more than enough for him.

He had, though, taken it upon himself to see if he could get information out of his mother. But she had simply smiled in her enigmatic way and said softly, "If your dad wants to bring you along, then I suggest you go." That had been her entire opinion on the topic. Kitai hated to admit it, but that actually sounded pretty reasonable.

He glanced across the hangar to where he knew his parents were. He was astounded to see that they were embracing. The teen smiled in joyous amazement at that. It was no secret to him that his parents did not get along especially well, and it filled him with nothing but happiness to see them displaying genuine affection for each other.

Were the two of them managing to work things out? It was impossible for Kitai to know for certain, of course. Perhaps he would be able to ask his father at some point during this outing.

That was when Kitai noticed something that looked extremely unusual. It immediately snagged his attention.

Something was being loaded into the aft cargo ramp of a ship called the *Hesper*. The thing was big: about two meters tall and almost three meters long. It was a loading pod of some sort, organically grown in such a way that it looked like an oversized boulder.

"What is that . . . ?" he whispered.

"Guess you'll find out."

The voice that had spoken to him captivated him so thoroughly that he nearly jumped into the air. Clutching his chest, he let out a long sigh, and then he saw that it was Rayna. She smiled and waved to him. She was in her Ranger uniform, and he noticed that she had a cutlass strapped to her back.

Rayna had made it.

Eager to turn the topic away from the strange pod that had startled him so thoroughly, he nodded toward her weapon. "Congrats," he said.

"Hmmm. Oh. This." She chucked a thumb toward

the weapon on her back and shrugged. "Yeah, it's no big deal. You'll be next. Guaranteed."

"Whatever."

"Hey, *you* have no reason to complain," she objected. "I admit it: I'm jealous."

" 'Cause I get to do Lightstream travel?"

"Hell no. Not that. I'm jealous because you get to travel with your dad. He's hot."

"Riiiiight," Kitai said with repressed amusement.

ii

Cypher watched from a few yards away as Kitai studied the transport ship. He hated to admit it, but he found his son's attitude amusing. The general tried to remember the days when he'd first witnessed such modern-day miracles as spaceships and wondered whether he'd had the same degree of obvious enthusiasm. He couldn't recall himself being in that state of mind.

Lieutenant Alvarez approached. "Good morning, General," she said briskly, and then added, "Ma'am," to accommodate the fact that Faia was standing there as well. Then she shifted her attention back to Cypher. "Your ship had maintenance issues. We've got you on the *Hesper*, sir. Runway two-seven. It's only a class-B Ranger and cargo transport, but if you give me another hour . . ."

It didn't matter in the slightest to Cypher. One ship was pretty much like any other, and so he gave it no thought. "That will be fine, Lieutenant."

Alvarez smiled at that. "Yes, sir. Just between you and me, the boys on board are pretty excited to rub elbows with the OG. I'll see you on board, sir." She saluted, and Cypher briskly saluted back. Alvarez then headed off to make sure the ship was ready.

Faia looked at Cypher with curiosity. "OG?"

"The Original Ghost."

"Oh, right. Of course. How could I forget?"

He watched her warily, uncertain of whether his wife was kidding him. He noticed a look clouding her expression. Something close to doubt.

"It'll be fine," he said with a confidence he did not truly feel but firmly believed he had to display. If she wanted her husband to spend time with their son, that was what he was going to do even if not all of it made a whole lot of sense. He would speak with Kitai, and he would try to understand this remarkably sensitive boy he and his wife had brought into the world. Even if it killed him. Or Kitai. Or the both of them.

Suddenly there was a loud, nearly deafening bang behind them.

Instantly Cypher grabbed Faia's wrist and twisted so quickly that she barely knew what had happened. All she knew was that one moment she was facing Cypher, and the next he had pulled her behind him to provide her bodily protection. His cutlass was already in his hand, and he was making sure that Faia remained behind him while he determined where the threat had originated.

That answer came less than two seconds later. There was a worker on an overhead gantry making some minor revisions, and his wrench had slipped out of his hand. It had clattered to the floor only a few feet away from Cypher and Faia, and that was the noise to which he was reacting.

Cypher scowled at the worker, who called down, "Sorry!" Cypher, annoyed, made an irritated noise and then reached down for the fallen tool and tossed it back up without giving it further attention.

Cypher then looked back to Faia, about to ask her whether she was okay. He saw, however, that she was smiling up at him. She looked pleased and flattered, and it was only belatedly that Cypher realized the truth: She was flattered that he had automatically moved to shield her from perceived danger.

He released her then, muttering, "Sorry," since he actually felt a bit embarrassed to be seen acting in such a protective manner, especially when it wasn't necessary. Faia, for her part, reached up and removed the scarf she was wearing. To Cypher's surprise, she was wearing the necklace he had brought her the previous evening. It sparkled against her skin, and Cypher couldn't help smiling at the symbol it presented. It seemed to him that at least on the surface, he was going to be getting a second chance with his wife.

Assuming, of course, that everything went well with Kitai.

That brought Cypher back to worrying about his son. Because the truth was that he still had no truly clear idea how to discuss anything with the boy. Kitai was like a mystery to him and always had been. Cypher hugged his wife, enjoying the nearness, but his mind was still on Kitai. If his marriage depended on fixing his relationship with Kitai, this nearness he was feeling with Faia and the possible rebuilding of their relationship might be a complete fantasy.

He looked in Kitai's direction and saw to his surprise that the boy was engaged in conversation with a female Ranger. He nodded in their direction and said to Faia, "Who's that grown-up hitting on our kid?"

"Now, now," she said. "Go easy on him." Then, in a softer tone, she said, "Go make some good memories together. Come on." Not permitting him any opportunity to respond, she slid an arm around him and walked with him toward Rayna and Kitai. She dropped Cypher off with his son and his female Ranger friend. "Rayna. Good to see you again."

"You too, Mrs. Raige. Uhm," and Rayna inclined her head toward the control tower. "So . . . I'll watch you take off from the tower, okay?"

Rayna promptly headed off. Faia watched the way Kitai was regarding her and smiled inwardly. She reached over to him then and gave him a strong motherly hug. As she did so, she said in a low voice to Kitai, "Take it easy on your father. He's a little rusty."

She could see by Kitai's expression that he had no idea

what she was talking about. The perfection he ascribed to his father was tremendously amusing. Sometimes it served as a benefit, other times a flaw. She realized it was anybody's guess how it would turn out this time. "You understand what I'm saying, son?"

Clearly he did not, but he nodded. Then, with a final look at his mother and also Rayna's retreating figure, he started to head off after Cypher.

Before Cypher and Kitai could make it to the ship, they were both stopped in their tracks by an extremely loud voice from a ramp way overhead: *"Stand me up!"*

All hands approaching the vessel turned their attention to the speaker. It was a Ranger veteran, a man in a mag-lev chair being taken to a medical transport ship. The chair was hovering above the ground. There were two attendants with the man, one on either side of the chair, and they were looking at him in confusion.

"General Raige," said the Ranger, "I was on the plateau. You saved me and four others. And I just came from seeing my baby girl's face for the first time." Upon realizing that the attendants had not heard his command, he repeated it with greater force than before. *"Stand me up."*

"That's not necessary, Ranger," Cypher told him.

The Ranger ignored the words of his commander. Instead, in an even louder voice, he shouted, *"Damn it, stand me up!"*

The attendants had been the targets of all the shouting they were going to endure. They nodded to one another and, moving as one, helped the Ranger out of his chair. All of the support was on them, because the Ranger himself had none to provide. His heavily bandaged leg buckled; the other was missing completely. Standing up was a complete impossibility, yet through sheer willpower alone he managed to persuade his aides to get him on his feet. Once he was sufficiently erect, he raised his trembling hand and broke off a salute.

Cypher Raige immediately snapped to attention and saluted back. Kitai felt pure wonder there as he watched this random Ranger forcing others to bring him to his feet so that he could offer proper reverence. Kitai couldn't help wondering what it felt like to have Cypher look at you as an equal, not some academy washout.

Cypher then dropped his salute and walked over to the Ranger. The man's eyes were filled with tears, as overjoyed as he was to see the great Cypher Raige coming right up to him. Cypher whispered in his ear, calming him, and then gestured for the assistants to stand aside. He gripped the Ranger firmly, one hand holding each of the man's arms, and eased him into the chair. Then Cypher stepped back and tossed off a final salute. The Ranger returned it and then muttered to his escorts, "Okay. We can go now."

Kitai watched as the soldier was led to his medical transport. Then he hastened to catch up to his father. As they approached the ship together, he whispered to Cypher, "What did you say to him?"

"What he needed to hear."

He turned away from his son then and walked briskly toward what Kitai was now certain was their vessel.

It was, Kitai realized belatedly, the same vessel he'd seen them pushing the large pod into. He wondered briefly if perhaps the pod was the entire reason they were heading toward another world. Or was it simply a secondary mission? Perhaps even something as simple as an addition to a zoo collection? He didn't know for sure what any of this was about.

What he did know was that his father wasn't exactly in a state of mind to be particularly helpful in explaining things.

Well, that was nothing new.

iii

The seats that lined the passenger bay of the *Hesper* were relatively simple and unadorned. They stretched up one side of the corridor, allowing sufficient space on the other side for people to walk past. There were crisscrossed straps attached to every seat so that people could buckle and seat themselves.

There was an observation port in the wall opposite Kitai through which he could see Nova Prime dwindling to a small dot rather than the planet where he had dwelled his entire life. Within moments it would disappear into nothing and become simply another small bit of matter in the sky field behind him.

Cypher Raige was in the adjacent seat. He was paying no attention to Kitai at all. Instead he was scanning through what appeared to be a dossier on his smart fabric. He was paging through the holographic document slowly, one page at a time. Kitai had always been told that his father had an eidetic memory, and now he was seeing what appeared to be proof of that. Cypher seemed to be studying each page until he had it committed to memory and then turning to the next.

"I'm reading *Moby Dick*." The remark about Kitai's latest reading undertaking simply popped out of his mouth with no serious thought given to what he was actually saying.

"Your mother told me," Cypher said. He barely glanced at his son when he said it, continuing to go through the dossier one page at a time. Then he stopped, as if realizing that simply informing Kitai of his mother's knowledge was somehow an insufficient response. He lowered the dossier for a moment and said, "That's great." Or at least he tried to say it. Unfortunately, it sounded like a halfhearted attempt to avoid coming across as indifferent.

Before he could continue his less than sterling response, there was a low, sharp whistle from the intercom. The pilot's voice crackled over it, announcing the travel time remaining before they would arrive at Iphitos.

It was a general announcement intended for everyone on the vessel, but Cypher seemed to take it as addressed to him and him alone. The overhead lights were dimming, and instead of continuing the conversation about an ancient whale, Cypher said brusquely, "I'm gonna grab some rack. Recommend you do the same."

Before Kitai could say anything to the contrary, Cypher's head dropped back and his eyes closed. He was asleep in less than a minute. Kitai attempted to copy his father's behavior, but it didn't work. Long minutes passed, and Kitai simply sat there, eyes wide open, his brain working furiously. Sleep was simply not an option for him. Perhaps his father was accustomed enough to spaceflight that he could treat it like something to be endured rather than to be excited about. But Kitai simply didn't have that ability. He was so stoked by the fact that he was traveling through space that all he could do, even in the dimness of the corridor, was sit there with his eyes wide open in endless fascination with the vehicle in which he was riding.

Eventually the only thing left in the section was the sleeping sounds of the other Rangers. Kitai sat there long enough to convince himself that slumber was not going to be coming his way anytime soon. If that was to be the case, what possible advantage could be gained by just sitting there in the darkness?

Softly, softly—because he was positive that his father could hear anything and everything—Kitai unbuckled the belt that was restraining him. He gradually eased it off his chest and rose. The only thing that could be heard was the low hum of the ship and the gentle snoring of some of the sleeping Rangers. They all had their cutlasses with them, tucked across their chests or laps. If Kitai had even been thinking about trying to take one of them, he wouldn't have gotten away with it.

Instead he crept down the aisle, bypassing everyone as he made his way to the aft cargo hold. He figured that if that pod he'd spotted earlier was going to be kept anywhere, that was where it would be. But at the far end of the hallway he saw a large sign over the exit door that spelled out the parameters of where he could travel in a fairly explicit fashion: RESTRICTED AREA. DO NOT ENTER. HAZARDOUS CARGO.

The sign deterred him for exactly five seconds, time enough to look behind him and confirm that all the Rangers were still sound asleep. Then he darted under the sign and headed into the cargo hold.

In front of him was a small flight of metal stairs that led into the belly of the ship. The area was dark and creepy, and the only thing he could hear was the distant hum of the ship's engines. At the end of the narrow walkway a heavy mesh fabric was drawn, obscuring what lay behind it.

Kitai took a deep breath to steady the pounding of his heart and then released it slowly to calm himself. Then, ever so gingerly, he made his way toward the fabric. Finally, when he was within a meter or so of it, he tentatively reached out and gripped it. He remained that way for a few seconds and, when it garnered no reaction, pulled it aside a few centimeters and peeked beyond it.

Glancing through revealed only the ship's cavernous, dark, and mysterious cargo hold. The pod was definitely in there, but all he could get was glimpses of it. Nothing much beyond that.

He started to enter the hold area—that was when something reached out from the darkness and grabbed his arm. Kitai let out a startled gasp and tried to pull away, but he had no luck. Instead, the face of a gruff military officer shoved itself at him. Maintaining a hold on Kitai's arm, the man snarled practically into his face. "Can you *read*?"

Kitai said nothing, mostly because his throat had frozen up, removing any possibility of his producing any useful words.

The security chief looked to be in his mid-fifties. His face was round, the top of his head covered in a shock of red buzz-cut hair. "I said, can you read? There's a sign back there. Says 'AUTHORIZED PERSONNEL ONLY.' Why didn't you read *that*?"

Kitai took an unusual step: He didn't answer the

question. There was no point in responding to it, because it wasn't going to end well for him. He'd seen a sign, had ignored it, and had gotten caught. The only shot he had was to move past it and into something more pertinent to him.

"What's in there?" he said, pointing toward the pod.

"He wants to know what's in there!"

It seemed strange to Kitai that the security chief was talking to him in that manner, and then he realized that he was not in fact the addressee. Instead, there were several Rangers seated around a small table off to the side. They had a game in progress. Kitai, it appeared, was simply something else for them to play with.

One of the men said, "Might wanna go easy on him, Sarge. That's the Prime Commander's son right there."

This was clearly something unexpected and unknown to the security chief. He looked at Kitai as if seeing him for the first time. "You're Raige's kid?"

This provided Kitai with the bit of a lead that he required under the circumstances. They could do whatever they wanted with some random kid, but Cypher Raige's son was going to get special treatment, and they all knew it. Kitai even puffed out his chest slightly to give additional heft to his presence, and this time, when he said once more, "What's in there?" it carried more weight and conviction. Or at least he imagined it did.

Indeed, the sergeant's entire attitude toward Kitai appeared to change in a manner that benefited Kitai's interests. He dropped his voice to barely above a whisper like a carnival barker with something to hide. "You wanna see?" he asked conspiratorially.

"Yeah, I wanna see."

"Okay, then. All ya had to do was ask."

If Kitai had been giving any real thought to the situation, that might have tipped him off. But he was so curious that he completely ignored any cautions and advanced slowly toward the pod.

The security chief followed right behind him as Kitai drew closer. "So are you gonna tell me what's—"

"It's an *Ursa*."

Kitai stopped moving so abruptly that the security chief actually bumped into him. "An Ursa?" Kitai said cautiously.

"Yup."

"A dead one?"

"Nope."

That was when he remembered Rayna discussing how some Rangers had managed to capture an Ursa alive. At that point Kitai completely ceased moving forward. This was it. This was the Ursa the Rangers had captured. This was the closest he had been to one since . . . since Senshi.

"How . . . how did . . . where . . . ?" He made several different attempts to ask questions, and none of them quite worked.

The sergeant didn't display the slightest hint of amusement. Instead he spoke with the same fear that filled every molecule of Kitai's body. "This is one of three we caught. We're keeping all three on Iphitos, away from the civilian population. This one we call Viper. This one's the biggest and meanest." He paused and then said conspiratorially, "You want to see if you can ghost?"

The challenge promptly caught the interest of the men who were grouped around the table. Cards forgotten, they focused their attention on Kitai, who didn't notice. He was busy looking in fascination at the pod, which was motionless.

Clearly intending to assuage Kitai's concerns, the security chief went on, assuring him, "The pod is biostructural organic armor. She's strapped and suspended in a gel inside there." He pointed to a red line that circled the pod. "All you need to do is step over that red line around the pod. The gel doesn't allow smells at certain distances, but at that distance it can smell you."

Kitai eyed the red line surrounding the pod. There were no footprints on or near it. No one had come that close to the creature. That meant one thing beyond question: They were taking no chances with the monster.

"You're not scared, are you?"

Without giving his response any thought at all, Kitai immediately declared, "I'm not scared of anything."

It seemed that the Rangers indeed took him at his word. In a declaration of "Uhh rahh!" the Rangers tossed off a verbal salute to him, congratulating him on his bravery.

"Even if it imprints on you, you don't need to worry. She ain't getting out."

That froze Kitai for a moment. The concept of an Ursa imprinting on him was certainly daunting. Imprinting was one of an Ursa's major weapons. Once it imprinted on a person—fully locked onto their DNA essence—that individual became the Ursa's new target. The Ursa would proceed to attack its potential victim for . . . well, forever. Kitai wasn't entirely sure how thrilled he was about becoming the creature's number one priority chew toy, especially for that length of time.

But he pushed those concerns aside the best he could. He was being challenged by a group of Rangers; he couldn't just walk away from it as if it meant nothing. Or, even worse, openly display his fear. They'd roast him for that. He'd be a joke. He'd be the gutless son of the Original Ghost and an embarrassment to the Raige family legacy.

All he did was simply nod in acknowledgment of the situation.

The security chief promptly called out, "Ladies and gentlemen, the son of the OG is going to try to ghost. Place your bets!"

To Kitai's annoyance, they actually started throwing down money. He couldn't help noticing that there weren't any bets placed on his ability to pull it off. *I'll show them*, he thought in grim annoyance.

Slowly Kitai made his way to the rear of the organic pod. For the first time he was close enough to see that in the shell-like exterior of the pod, there were holes so that one could see in. But there didn't appear to be an Ursa or anything else inside. "I don't see anything," he said cautiously.

"Active camouflage," the security chief replied. "Photo-sensitive skin cells change color and texture to match its surroundings. It uncamouflages so it can frighten you. So you release more pheromones—they're crafty bastards."

It truly was insidious. Ursa required fear to find their targets, and so their method of attack was calculated to elicit as much fear as possible. Being virtually invisible allowed them to appear abruptly and terrify the crap out of their intended victims.

Kitai moved closer to the pod. He stopped a mere few centimeters away from crossing the red line.

The security chief wasn't making it any easier for him. "Ghosting is when you don't have a trace of fear in you. Good luck doing that. To ghost one must be so free from fear that you become invisible to the Ursa. Fear is territorial in your heart. It refuses to share space with any other virtues. You must force fear from your heart and replace it with any other virtue. It could be love or happiness or faith, but the virtue is specific to the individual and comes from the deepest part of that person.

"You get all that, cadet?" said the security chief. His voice was sardonic as he added, "Your dad wrote that helpful tidbit."

And there it was, unmistakable. The security chief wasn't screwing around anymore. He was putting it right out there: *You think you're on your dad's level? Let's see what you've got.*

Without hesitation, Kitai stepped defiantly over the red line surrounding the pod. If the security chief was startled by his audacity, he didn't show it. Instead his voice dropped to just above a whisper. "Most guys freeze—that's your cerebral cortex looking for an answer it doesn't have. Your blood is filling with adrenaline right now, whether you know it or not. Your heart's beating faster. It's getting a little harder to breathe . . . Your neurobiological system is telling you to run, but your knees are too weak to move, and it's too late, anyway—the pores on your skin have already opened up, secreting an imperceptible amount of pheromones into the air. And all you can think about is *when it's going to kill you*."

Kitai was standing centimeters from the pod, his eyes wide. There still wasn't any response from within, and he was beginning to wonder whether the Rangers had been screwing with him the entire time. Maybe there was nothing especially dangerous in the pod after all. He did not notice that even the Rangers looked surprised that his proximity wasn't eliciting a violent reaction from within.

Or maybe I'm ghosting. Maybe this is what it feels like. I'm actually doing it. Ghosting, just like my—

That was when the pod exploded with violent sounds and movement. The tension wires wrapped around the thing were suddenly strained by whatever the hell was smashing the pod from the inside. Despite the wires, the thing shook so violently that it seemed as if the creature within was going to tear it apart and come leaping straight out . . .

. . . at him.

Kitai had just enough time to see a flash of the monster's pale skin slamming up against the side of the pod, and then he leaped backward, letting out a very unghostlike scream of terror. However, his yelp of surprise was easily drowned out by the thunderous shriek of the beast within.

It was a noise Kitai had heard before. It had overwhelmed him years before when the monster tore apart his beloved sister while Kitai hid in the shelter she'd thrown together for him.

He lay against the wall behind him, gasping for air, desperately trying to shove his mental images of his sister's death back into the more remote sections of his brain.

The Rangers, of course, didn't know. All they knew was that he was the son of the Original Ghost, and he was now pressed flat against the wall, trembling with fear. Naturally they responded in the only way that seemed appropriate. They laughed collectively. The security chief called out, "He sees you, kid!"

And suddenly, just like that, the security chief was on his feet. Not only that, but his hand had snapped into a solid salute. The other Rangers were doing the exact same thing.

Their reaction made it painfully obvious to Kitai exactly what was happening and who was standing behind him. Only one person could have prompted that kind of reaction.

"Kitai," came the sharp voice of Cypher Raige from right behind him. "Back in your seat now." Without waiting for a response or an explanation, neither of which would have done much to calm him, he continued, "Rangers, go to Red Con 1."

The security chief blinked in surprise. Obviously he'd been expecting Cypher to rip into them for screwing around with his son. Putting them on an alert had probably never occurred to him. But he responded crisply, calling out, "Secure all cargo!"

His crew obeyed instantly. They were confident about the security of the Ursa, but there were other objects being transported as well, which required double-checking to make sure they weren't going anywhere.

Kitai had moved in silence when he'd traveled from his seat to the cargo hold. The way back required no quiet at all; he barreled as fast as he could to his seat. Before he could buckle in, Cypher was already behind him and saying briskly, "Under your seat there's a lifesuit. Put it on, now."

Kitai did as he was instructed. Even as he did so, however, he looked up questioningly and said, "What's going on?"

Cypher was clearly in no mood to respond. All he did was snap, "Full harness!"

"Yes, sir," Kitai replied. Whatever was transpiring around them, there was clearly no time to engage in conversation about it. His father clearly had greater problems on his mind than answering his son's questions, and for once Kitai totally understood.

Cypher didn't wait around to see if his son obeyed. He headed off down the corridor in the general direction of the cockpit. Kitai suspected that was where Cypher was going to wind up, and he already felt a bit better. There was no one he wanted overseeing things more than his father. With Cypher Raige in charge, no matter what was coming up, they would all be able to get past it.

iv

The pilot and navigator at the controls in the cockpit nodded when Cypher made his entrance. "Good evening, General," said the pilot, a tall and powerful man named Lewis. "Care to take the controls? Feel her out?"

There was no doubt in Cypher's mind that that was in fact the last thing Lewis wanted. Technically Cypher could indeed take control; he was the ranking officer present. But that wasn't going to do anyone any good. "Appreciate the offer, Captain. But it's been a while since I sat in that chair."

Lewis and the navigator, a longtime veteran named Bellman, both chuckled.

Cypher's tone then became steely calm. "What's the last known position of the closest asteroid storm?"

"We've plotted well around those storms, sir. Nothing to worry about," Lewis assured him.

Cypher spoke with total respect in his voice, but the order inherent in it was clear: "I'd like you to check again, Captain."

The pilot clearly didn't quite understand why he was being asked to recheck, but it wasn't his job to understand orders. Just obey them. He ran their immediate vicinity through the data banks. "Category 4 asteroid formation, two thousand km to starboard at plus-four-five declination. Bearing one-two-seven mark four."

"That's headed in our direction," Cypher said. There was not a trace of nervousness in his voice. He was simply trying to anticipate anything that could go wrong.

"Yes, sir," Bellman acknowledged. "But at that distance—"

"I detected graviton vibrations in the ship's hull," Cypher said. "A cat 4 storm's large enough to generate its own gravitational field, correct?"

"Yes, sir. But . . . you detected?" Bellman was staring at him in confusion. "How?"

The fact was that Cypher had felt it. A gentle vibration that had actually awakened him from his slumber. No one else would have noticed it, and even if anyone had, he would have given it no thought at all. A vibrating hull. So what? It was probably nothing.

Even Cypher thought that he might well be overreacting. In fact, he was certain that a straight answer to the navigator's question would garner nothing save puzzled looks and assurances that he was getting worked up over nothing. Having no desire to deal with any of that, he kept his reasons to himself. Instead, all he said was, "Graviton buildup could be a precursor to mass expansion. That storm could be on us in minutes."

"Sir," said Lewis, "if I may . . . Mass expansion is one in a million."

"Then let's just say I don't like those odds."

The pilot and navigator exchanged confused looks. But if that was how Cypher felt, it was their job to make sure that his worries were attended to.

Long moments passed, and then slowly the image of a huge, swirling storm pattern began to take shape on the screen. "Not loving those odds, either," Bellman said as the storm began to swirl even more widely.

"If we try to navigate out, the pull of our own graviton wake could set the thing off," Cypher said. "Just hold course . . . and let's hope I'm wrong."

The storm seemed to be holding its *own* course as the men kept their eyes on the cockpit readouts. Lewis, doing his best to keep everything stable, asked Cypher with forced casualness, "Just out of interest, sir . . . how often are you wrong?"

Without so much as cracking a smile, Cypher replied, "My wife would give an interesting answer to that question."

A long, excruciating silence followed. Only the digital chirping of the computers in the cockpit could be heard. Beyond the forward observation port there was only a star-pricked expanse of space.

Studying his instrumentation closely, the navigator called out, "Graviton count's decreasing. Eight hundred parts per million . . . Six hundred and fifty . . ."

Upon hearing that, the pilot exhaled in relief. With the graviton count diminishing, whatever danger they might have been in was sliding away. "Well, sir," he began to say, "there's a first time for every—"

That was when the asteroids, which hadn't even been factored into the calculations until that split second, made their presence known.

It was like being witness to a star going supernova. One instant the space in front of them was empty, and the next instant a massive wave of asteroid fragments was expanding in their direction. The icy chunks of rock were coming in so fast that there was no time for Lewis or Bellman to react. All they were able to do was cry out in shock as the asteroid field engulfed them, hitting them like a freight train. The ship shook violently as the rock storm pounded them, creating the kind of turbulence that moments before would have seemed unimaginable.

Cypher grabbed an overhead handhold to stay on his feet as Lewis wrestled with the control yoke. *"Turn into it! Match bearing!"* Cypher shouted, and the pilot did his best to obey.

But it was doing no good. The cockpit instruments went completely haywire, multiple alarms sounding as the ship tilted wildly out of control. Sizable asteroids continued to pummel the ship. The cockpit computer snapped on and announced, *"Caution, critical hull damage. Caution, main power failure."* It spoke in a simple, flat, even mildly pleasant monotone, as if the total catastrophe it was announcing were really nothing to get all that worked up about.

The tail of the ship suddenly was struck by a violent force. It swung the entire vessel around and continued to spin it several times. Lewis managed to slow the whirl eventually, but then he called out, "She's a dead stick! Engines one and two are off-line! We're losing her!"

At no time during the entire struggle did Cypher so much as blink. Instead he remained calm, certain, stern. If the pilot and navigator had ever wondered why Cypher was the Prime Commander, that answered the question. He stepped forward, placed a hand on the pilot's shoulder, and said, "Can you travel us out of here?"

Lewis turned his frightened gaze to Cypher. "Where?"

"The anchorage on Lycia. It's the closest."

On hearing that suggestion, the navigator reacted so negatively that it sounded as if his head was about to explode. *"Negative, sir! We cannot wormhole travel in the middle of this!"*

Cypher knew that technically speaking, the navigator was absolutely correct. Generating a miniature wormhole was a tricky enough endeavor under even the best of circumstances, and these were certainly not the best. But he saw no other option and suspected that if he'd taken the time to push Bellman on the topic, Bellman wouldn't have seen any other way out as well. He simply ordered, "Do it," just as another mammoth asteroid slammed into them, hitting them square.

That was all the incentive Bellman required. Hurriedly he started entering the coordinates online.

For a heartbeat, Cypher was taken out of the current

situation. He imagined his son, wearing the lifesuit by now, strapped securely into his seat, terrified over what was happening. Cypher had no idea why Kitai had been screwing around with an Ursa, nor did he care. All he cared about was that his son was very likely horrified by what was going on and he couldn't be there to try to talk him down. And there was nothing he could do about it right now.

He could only watch with an escalating sense of dread as the navigator worked with barely functioning equipment to accomplish what he'd been ordered to do. After what seemed an eternity, he called above the ruckus, "Coordinates for anchorage at Lycia locked in, but no confirmation signal, sir."

Cypher saw only one option. "Travel us now."

"Sir, without confirmation . . ."

He didn't want to hear it. "That's an order!" he shouted as he pulled out the extra jump seat from a compartment in the floor. He buckled the double strap harness over his shoulder as the pilot threw open the protective cover of a control lever. Lewis placed both hands on it as the ship listed toward another asteroid.

"We're hot!" Bellman shouted. *"Go, go!"*

There was yet another violent strike by an asteroid as Lewis slammed the emergency lever forward. Dark space began to grow outside as the wormhole generation began. Some asteroids that had been heading toward the ship were abruptly pulled away into the darkness, yanked clear of the vessel as the dark of space continued to widen all around it.

Then the wormhole snapped fully into existence, and the ship was slammed forward. Cypher had just managed to finish fastening his straps when he suddenly was shoved backward into his chair. He saw the pilot and navigator similarly being slapped around by the forces of space and time that converged on the vessel simultaneously.

Cypher glanced at the chronometer on his wrist. It had stopped dead. Then, for a few moments, it ran backward before it abruptly hammered forward again at five times the speed. Then they were in complete and utter blackness. It was as if all the light around them were being dragged forcibly into the wormhole along with them.

Kitai, was the only thing that went through Cypher's head at that moment. *Kitai, Kitai*—

And then they were out of it, just like that.

One moment they had been surrounded by the blackest and most featureless space that Cypher had ever seen, and then they were out of it.

But they were hardly out of trouble.

Cypher saw pieces of the ship hurtling past them in different directions. They had sustained all sorts of damage, and he hadn't the faintest idea if they were going to survive long enough to reach Lycia. Hell, for all he knew, they weren't anywhere near Lycia.

The pilot was apparently ahead of him. He struggled with the controls while the navigator scanned readouts that were continuing to fluctuate. "Can't get a star fix!" he shouted. "We are *way* off the grid."

"I still got nothing here," the pilot agreed. He struggled with the stick but could not get a proper response from the ship's guidance systems.

"Caution, life support failure," offered the cockpit computer with the same apparent indifference it had displayed before.

The navigator checked the specifics of what the computer was talking about. "Cabin pressure dropping," he agreed moments later. "Heavy damage to outer hull. Breach possible in middle cabin!"

The pilot had no interest in hearing about the bad shape the ship was in. He already knew that. What he needed to know now was what to do about it. "Find me something I can land on!"

Quickly the navigator combed immediate space, hoping against hope that there was something close enough to put down on. Seconds later, he managed to pull up a blue-green world on the holographic imager.

"I got something! Bearing three-four-zero by nine-five, range eighty-six thousand. Looks like a C class—nitrogen, oxygen, argon. Can't get a volumetric—"

At that moment, a wholly unknown voice recording sounded inside the cockpit. Apparently they had managed to trip some manner of space buoy that had been left there to issue an advisory against any vessels that were even considering landing on the blue-green world.

The advisory sounded throughout the cabin: *"Warning. This planet has been declared unfit for human habitation. Placed under class 1 quarantine by the Interplanetary Authority. Under penalty of law, do not attempt to land."*

The ship had turned just enough in its approach that Cypher was able to make out the world's details for the first time. The advisory buoy continued its warning; it obviously had been designed to keep doing so until the ship had turned around or was so far gone that any caution was hopeless. Cypher's eyes widened as more details of their likely target presented themselves. For a moment he thought he recognized it, but then he dismissed the notion as crazy.

Then he looked again and realized that it wasn't only not crazy, it was in fact damned likely.

"It's not possible . . ." he whispered.

"Repeat, do not attempt to land," the computer voice sounded.

"Shut up!" the navigator shouted as he, too, recognized where they were heading. Bellman then turned to Lewis and Cypher. "The computer might have defaulted back to a known demarcation point . . ."

At that moment Cypher didn't give a damn why it had happened. All he knew was that it had to *un*happen immediately. "Can you travel us again?"

"Negative, sir!" Lewis shouted as the ship bucked furiously all around him. "We either land there or we break apart out here."

There was absolutely no choice being provided them. His voice even, Cypher said, "Set her down," even as he unbuckled his jump seat and moved back toward the main cabin.

From behind him, the pilot was calling out, "Mayday, mayday, this is Hesper-Two-Niner-Niner heavy in distress! We took sustained damage from an asteroid storm and are going down with bingo power! Request immediate rescue, repeat, request immediate rescue!"

The radio provided nothing but static in response.

V

The main cabin was shaking so violently that Kitai was convinced the entire ship was going to break apart around him. He didn't know which was more terrifying: the sensation that the ship was about to blow apart or the fact that his father was nowhere around.

Part of him wanted to condemn his father for being somewhere other than next to his son, but he quickly dismissed any such notion. If the ship was in danger of falling apart, there was only one place his dad was going to be, needed to be: in the heart of it, trying to prevent it from happening.

Kitai had put the lifesuit on as he'd been instructed and also had donned an oxygen mask handed to him by a Ranger passing by. But none of that made any difference. It was obvious that the ship was badly injured and spiraling downward toward . . . what?

He twisted in his chair to get a glimpse out the observation port and perhaps see what they were heading for, but things were moving too quickly. He saw pieces of debris flying off the ship, bounding away into the unlit darkness, and felt a new swell of terror. As near as he could determine, they were heading toward nothing. They were just a spiraling cloud of debris with only complete destruction awaiting them.

Kitai saw that Rangers were endeavoring to reinforce the bulkhead area, whose warning lights were flashing above them. They passed the equipment back and forth effectively and moved with great precision.

I'm not doing any good sitting here. Chances are, I won't do any good on my feet, either. But at least I'll feel as if I'm contributing.

He began to unbuckle the straps that restrained him, and that was when he saw Cypher heading toward him, lurching violently from side to side as he went. Cypher paused only to take a mask a Ranger shoved at him so that he could be as safe as Kitai was. Kitai, however, already had unbuckled his strap and was halfway out of his seat.

Cypher didn't hesitate; he slammed Kitai back down into the seat. Kitai let out a startled grunt into his oxygen mask but quickly recovered himself. His father was back. That was all that mattered.

Suddenly there was a noise that sounded like a thousand bones breaking at once. The sound was so catastrophic that it drowned out all other noises. *What is that?* Kitai wondered.

Cypher froze for a long moment, looking around to try to see whence the noise had originated. Then he shook it off and refocused his attention on Kitai. He helped Kitai relock his belt and harness and pull them in tightly. Once he was satisfied that Kitai wasn't going to be going anywhere anytime soon, Cypher placed his own oxygen mask on his face.

Then Cypher and Kitai's eyes locked, and Cypher very slowly, very carefully, worked on restoring his son to a clear frame of mind. His face only inches away from Kitai, Cypher began breathing very steadily and very slowly. To try to get Kitai's breathing even, he raised and then lowered his hand with simple, quiet steadiness. Kitai copied him in the breathing manner, and felt the exercise was starting to calm him. Another five or ten seconds and Kitai was positive that everything was going to be just fine.

Everything seemed to happen all at once.

One moment Cypher was right there in front of Kitai,

urging him to breathe steadily, and the next moment he was gone. Just *gone*. Cypher was lifted up off his feet and propelled down the hallway and slammed into the far corner of the main cabin like a rag doll.

Kitai, his mouth covered by his mask, screamed as the winds howled around Cypher, banging him around mercilessly against the end of the corridor. Kitai realized for a moment, to his shock, that his father was actually holding on to something embedded in a wall, some extended rod, as the wind smashed against him. Then, a second later, it tore Cypher away from his grip and sent him hurtling out of Kitai's sight.

Kitai was tempted to unbuckle and go after him, but he realized that he would be a goner if he did. Despite the fact that it went against his instinct, Kitai stayed right where he was, continuing to scream for his father even as the ship shuddered from one end to the other.

He heard something tearing away and realized that the ship had snapped in half. *In half.* The entire cargo section had broken off and fallen away from the vessel.

Kitai considered what that meant. *My God, they're dead.*

He wanted his father back so that he could tell him and then realized Cypher Raige was probably dead as well. The way the wind had smashed him against the corridor, there seemed little to no chance that he possibly could have survived. At this moment Cypher Raige was a pounded mess of flesh, and Kitai probably was not going to last when they hit the ground, and poor Faia, his mother, was back on Nova Prime doing her job or perhaps relaxing at home or even sleeping, thinking that she was going to have her son and husband back within a few days.

But she wouldn't.

Kitai fought to remain conscious, but he was losing the ability to do so. The G-force rippling across his face proved to be too much. His eyes rolled slowly back and shut. One moment he was there, and the next darkness reached out for him. He hesitated only for an instant and then embraced the darkness, welcoming its hold on him. *I'm coming, Dad; I'm coming.* Those were his last conscious thoughts, and then he slumped into nothingness.

He never heard the ship crash.

Lily Carmichael is grasping her mother's hand, hoping not to get lost. Lily, fifteen, thinks herself about seven years too old to be holding her mother's hand, but there are literally hundreds of people ahead of them, all trying to move in an orderly fashion from the staging area to the actual platform that would grant them access to the *Espérer*, the rocket that promised them salvation.

"Where's your father?" her mother, Rebecca, asked, her voice filled with rising concern.

"I'm right here, Bec," her husband, Paul, yelled. He was always overly polite and as a result, there were now six people separating him from his wife and daughter. Lily knew this was all too typical of her dad, but she loved him for it.

"Catch up," Rebecca demanded, and he tried to thread his way through the moving mass. There were people jostling back and forth, raising the air of tension, mixing with the cool temperature.

Lily examined the dull silver bracelet around her thin wrist. Somehow it contained her entire life. Her name, height, weight, medical history, school transcripts, and other arcane data that would ensure her life would resume once the transport ship departed Earth. Every one of the teeming masses around her wore an identical bracelet, biometrically encoded for each passenger. The massive ship stood like a silent sentinel in its gantry. Liftoff was six hours away and not a moment too soon if you asked her.

"Finally made it," a voice said behind her. She glanced over her shoulder, and Lily saw an old woman, wrapped in what seemed to be three layers of outerwear, shuffling behind her. The arctic air was cool, but not so chilly that she needed so many clothes. Once aboard the ship, of course, such outerwear would be superfluous and stored away for their descendants.

"Made what?" the man next to her asked. He was brown-skinned and clearly a stranger to the woman, but he was making conversation, which was better than most of the people crushing them. There was a feeling of resignation and sadness that hung like a thick fog over the people. Lily, though, was more excited about the prospects ahead of her; that is, when she wasn't weepy about leaving others behind.

"Seven continents!" the woman declared and let out a laugh. "As soon as I received my notification that I made the cut, I booked a series of trips. I wanted to visit every continent while I still had the chance. Got here last night, making this the seventh."

"Impressive," the man replied in a deep voice that Lily liked. "Of course, that didn't leave much time for sightseeing." He sounded like an actor or pod commentator.

"What about you? How many you see?"

"Well," he said to fill the gap as he thought. "Born in Africa, studied in Europe, and took a vacation to Brazil, so that's three."

"And this makes four, not too bad," she said. "Corinne Levy."

"Glen Mosri," he replied.

The two chatted amiably as the line slowly fed them toward the ship. Their conversation was interrupted as Lily's father tried to squeeze by them. "Sorry. Excuse me. Trying to reach my family."

"Slow down, son," Mosri said. "They're not leaving without you."

"Sorry, there's some sort of problem behind us," the man said, still scanning the masses ahead of him.

"Right here, Dad," Lily said reassuringly.

"Oh, she's a pretty one," Corinne said, helping herself to a hunk of Lily's pale blond hair. She stroked it in a friendly way, and Lily let her even though it sort of creeped her out. She'd been feeling this way for the last few weeks; suddenly every little thing bothered her as they prepared to leave their home and come to Antarctica for The Departure.

Her family got word three years ago they were among the precious few selected to leave Earth aboard the ark program. A transport ship would carry them to a docking station just outside of Earth's atmosphere. There countless ships from every continent would form the six massive arks scheduled to leave the solar system behind and fly for a century to a new world. A new chance for humanity. Lily would be long dead before the ship arrived at the world they named Nova Prime. But her children or grandchildren would be alive and set foot on an alien world they would call home. The remainder of her life would be spent living on the *Denkyem*, whatever that meant. Her mother kept giving her the translation, but it never stuck in her head.

Paul finally caught up to them, craning his neck to see past Rebecca to ensure their two boys, Max and Zach, were in sight. He made a satisfied sound and fell into step beside his daughter.

"Caught you," he said.

"You would have found us eventually," Lily said.

"I know, but I want us together until we're settled. This is chaos."

"Actually," interrupted Mosri, "it seems as orderly as you can expect. No protestors, no panic, not much weeping and wailing."

Paul looked around once more, absorbing the sight of hundreds of men, women, and children, representing countless cultures and countries, all united for a chance at survival. Lily also took it all in, a sense of awe slowly replacing the discomfort she'd felt moments before.

"That's thanks to the Rangers, I think," Paul said. "They're everywhere. Good thing, too, there are others desperately trying to cut the line."

Lily saw the brown-uniformed men and women of the United Ranger Corps nearby. They stood at the edges of the gangway, spread out every few yards. The arrival of the Rangers more than a decade earlier meant a unified police force to ensure the ships got built and the selected passengers made it safely to the remote continent and aboard the transport ships.

"What got you the golden ticket?" Mosri asked.

"The what?" Lily asked

"Sorry, the invitation to join the exodus."

"Oh," Paul said, still sounding uncertain. "I'm a network engineer and my wife's a teacher."

"Secure roles, needed roles," Levy said. "I'm a botanist. They tell me I am running a hydroponics bay, and I can plant a whole square yard of whatever I please."

"Wow, that sounds great," Lily said, finally ready to join the conversation. "What about you?"

Mosri smiled and said, "I am a physicist. They want me working in the astrometrics section, studying this wormhole space."

"Maybe you can explain it to me, then," Lily prodded. "I know we're going faster than light, but how does that work?"

"Magic," Levy said, and laughed a little too loud for Lily's taste.

"Feels like magic, doesn't it," Mosri said, his voice dropping a notch, sounding like one of her teachers. "The Lightstream engines will warp the space around us. You see, the engines will generate a powerful wave that can compress space-time in front of the arks and expand space-time behind it."

"Space-time?"

Mosri laughed and paused to consider his answer. Lily shifted the backpack on her right shoulder, trying to find a more comfortable position for the weight. It felt far heavier than it was; her hopes, fears, and memories were packed in there, all weighing her down.

"Okay, you know about the three dimensions."

"Length, width, and depth," she said.

"Right. Now imagine space having three dimensions." He paused and Lily nodded, tucking a stray hair behind her left ear.

"Now scientists like me consider time having three dimensions as well. While space has dimensions that work side by side, time's dimensions happen one atop the other so space-time combines the two into a singular formula we use to calculate all sorts of things."

"You lost her," Paul said. "She's an artist." Lily made a face at her father.

"I bet she's going to see all sorts of new inspiration when we leave the system," Mosri said.

"So you're compressing the space in front of us," Lily said, trying to keep it all straight and refusing to let her father know how right he was. This was just more information than she was really ready to absorb, but it beat standing silent like so many of the others around them.

"Look, it's like the prow of a boat slicing through the water and creating a wake," he said. "Can you visualize that?"

"Sure," Lily replied. That was easy, especially since she loved going out on the family boat every summer. She was going to miss that—the warm sun, the gentle breeze, the sea water, things she would never experience again—so she tried to press the memories like flowers in a book for permanence.

"The arks will actually be floating in a bubble along the wave being generated, literally surfing through space at a speed faster than light relative to objects outside the bubble," Mosri concluded.

"Wow," Paul said. "That's the first time I heard anyone explain Lightstream in a way that makes sense."

"You're welcome, all part of the service," Mosri said.

"Yeah, thanks," Lily said. The boat imagery really

did help her sort of comprehend how they would travel in space. The idea that the trip would last a century, even at those speeds, boggled her mind.

"Mister . . ."

"Call me Glen," he said with a broad smile.

"I'm Lily," she said.

"Nice to meet you." They briefly shook hands.

"If we're traveling faster than the speed of light, and the arks will travel for a century, where exactly are we going?"

"Interesting question," he said. "We're living along the fringes of the Milky Way Galaxy, on one of the spiral arms. We're heading inward, toward the galactic center. I'd estimate we'd be about thirty-two parsecs from here when we get to Nova Prime."

A parsec, she recalled, was a measure for the speed of light, how far it would travel over one hundred years, and it still sounded like an impossible distance.

Lily then realized she was being spoken to, but her mind had wandered and she looked around wide-eyed to see who had addressed her.

"Sorry, ma'am," she said to Levy.

"So polite," the older woman said, winking at Paul. "Nice job."

"What were you asking me?"

"I asked about leaving home. Where were you?"

"Connecticut," she said.

"Was it hard?"

Was it hard having a chance to live when she knew everyone she left behind—grandmother, cousins, friends, teacher, priest, and so many others—were being left to die a horrible death? Was it hard knowing that her parents received death threats from the jealous neighbors when their carefully guarded secret was leaked?

Damned right it was hard.

It felt impossible. Their carefully weighed and measured belongings had to be shipped ahead, and they were expected in Antarctica within forty-eight hours of departure. In between there were hours spent filling out additional details on the Web, physicals at the military base up in Groton, and determining what they would take. Her dad drove everyone nuts trying to scan and digitize everything they owned—diplomas, schoolwork, family records, whatever. Her mom was a pack rat and had generations of family memorabilia and old print photos that she swore she would one day scan and organize. Now it was being done hastily and she, along with her brothers, were pressed into service.

Max's pal Lou was unable to keep the terrible secret and when word got out it was hard. There were tears. Lots of tears. Everyone was cozying up to her at home and at school. She got stares, and the family had to turn down requests for interviews. Everything about The Departure was being handled through Project Next Generation, and it was a hassle to gain permission to speak to the press so they routinely said no, ending the discussion.

Her friends, the boys and girls she grew up with, were upset. Why did she get to live and they to die? Some insisted on spending *lots* of time together, and boys begged her for sex, hoping she'd get pregnant and thinking they would have to let the new father come along. That was tough. She was just thirteen when they got word, and her changing body was just one more nuisance to deal with. Instead, Lily shut down, limiting her time with friends and keeping to the ones she knew and trusted the most.

The extended family wanted their share of the Carmichaels, too. A last chance to tell stories and give them their own mementos for scanning and preservation. Lily could just imagine how many terabytes of material were being collected from families around the world. In her global studies class, she knew there were still parts of Asia and Africa that lacked the technology for such preservation. How much was being lost?

"Yeah," she said, summing it all up in one word.

"I left behind an ex-husband, two adult children, and my dachshund. So, Lily, you're far from alone."

Lily looked at her with fresh eyes.

"Your own children?"

The woman nodded, her eyes starting to tear up. "One's a museum curator, the other's a hairdresser. Not exactly high demand jobs on a spaceship. We're the lucky ones."

Lily was tired of that phrase. She had been dubbed a "lucky one" ever since Lou spilled the secret, but despite being named a traveler, she didn't feel lucky. Instead, she felt incredibly sad. She was leaving behind friends and the future she had dreamed about. There was comfort in all five members of the family traveling together; it was incredibly difficult to say good-bye to so many and so often. There were endless parties, sleepovers, chat sessions, and more as the months became weeks then days. Her mom insisted the final week be as family-centric as possible, with just Nana, Paul's mother, visiting. This way they could hope to just slip away.

Their personal departure was anything but easy. A military transport, protected by three Rangers, arrived in the wee hours of the morning, waking up the neighborhood. As burly men in gray jumpsuits loaded their approved belongings in the rear, the family wandered the house, taking it all in one final time.

Paul shut the door behind them and automatically locked it, which seemed silly since no one was going to take the house. There was little sense for those left behind to move anywhere. There was no escaping the inevitable death that awaited those left behind.

Lily was raised knowing that Earth began rebelling against its inhabitants in the decades before she was born, prompting the plan to evacuate the planet. But despite the best planning by Project Next Generation, they kept losing time. There were now massive storms with great regularity. School was repeatedly being switched to online mode when it grew too dangerous to leave the house. There were shortages that had led to governments falling and people starving. Connecticut was a fortunate location, but even they felt the deprivation.

Creating the United Ranger Corps helped restore some confidence in the crazy scheme to save as much of mankind as was possible. The Rangers were established just when her older brother was little, but she could sense everyone around her exhaling, as if they had been bottling up all this tension and could finally let it out. Not that they were great wizards and could make things better, but they certainly allowed the arks to be built and they were there to make certain her family and all the others could get to ships stationed at various locations around the globe.

Flying over the frigid white land, she immersed herself in the sensations and sights, taking in its stark features and imagining what it must have been like before the shipbuilding began. She knew from her third-grade teacher that it had been the stuff of legend. Mrs. Griffin made it sound magical, but now it was like everywhere else: filled with trucks, rails, planes, and row after row of gantries where the various ships waited. There had been an orientation vid presentation when they arrived at the staging area in Florida before the Americans were taken away from their nation for the last time. A three-dimensional program showed how each transport ship would take up an orbital position, and then all would fly toward one another in a space ballet, coming together and slowing their momentum just enough so they could link up, forming the grand ark.

This odd celestial dance was going to take place five times, following the success of the *Exodus* launch. A few months before, it was the first to make this attempt and it went off flawlessly. She remembered watching it late one night, holding her breath. She lost count of the number of spacecraft that came together like one of Zach's toys and formed a colossal singular vessel. It wasn't pretty, but it worked. The *Exodus* successfully cruised to the edge of the solar system and back. The ship even fired up its Lightstream engine at the edge of the system to ensure all worked according to plan, and then it returned to near Earth orbit where it patiently waited for the other five to catch up.

Before the sun rose tomorrow, something like a thousand ships would start to launch. Within days they would form the arks, and the fleet would travel together. Earth would shrink on the viewscreens, diminishing in size but looming large in their hearts.

Lily felt her own eyes grow wet and hot, as the enormity of this moment settled over her.

She looked ahead, blinking away the tears, and saw the *Espérer* grow larger. They were nearing the entrance to the point where she could make out the Rangers at the entrance. Zach and Max were talking animatedly to the people around them, but her mother was silent, staring ahead, ignoring the conversation before and behind her.

Lily could not tell who this was hardest on. Everyone, she decided. There was no easy way to say good-bye to friends and family, knowing you were pretty much guaranteed a chance to live while they were all certain to die. Things had grown out of control the last year or so. Something about the planet's magnetic field collapsing and she supposed she could ask Mr. Mosri about it, but right now she just didn't seem to care. She couldn't fix it, couldn't save her Nana or Mrs. Levy's dachshund.

She couldn't save anyone.

There was a loud roar, many voices rising in volume and the sound of something breaking. All the heads turned to look behind them. Lily noticed how close they were to boarding and couldn't believe something was happening that might keep her and her family from salvation.

Lily was shoved, nearly losing her balance, as a lean

man in a rust-colored uniform rushed past her. He was accompanied by three others, and they cut a ragged path through the crowd of passengers. Craning her neck to see past them, Lily saw that one of the barricades had been breached and people were fighting to get into the queue.

The Rangers were not brandishing weapons, but instead were using their bodies to form a barrier, moving the interlopers back. She watched as the lean one was speaking gently to a couple, using words not weapons. Other Rangers came from both ends of the line and worked to keep a full-blown riot from breaking out. There were screams and shouts and more than a few wails of anguish. The teen girl couldn't help but feel sympathy for people who knew they were being condemned to an unpleasant death.

The lead Ranger waved his arms, creating space between those waiting to board and those attempting to join them. Flanked by the other Rangers, he spoke to the crowd, and, try as she might, she couldn't make out the words. Instead, her trained eye saw his body move. There was poise and confidence in his actions. He didn't make broad gestures but smaller, more intimate ones. They invited dialogue, not confrontation. She watched in fascination. Leading seemed to come so naturally to him. Rather than a riot, the crowd listened and understood and willingly returned to the other side of the barricade. As they moved, the Rangers picked up the sections that had been broken and hastily restored them in place.

As quickly and as suddenly as the breach occurred, it was over. Order was restored and the sound dropped in volume but didn't entirely vanish. There would continue to be complaints and protests until her family was safely aboard the ship. The Rangers made their way back to their posts, and those on line knew better than to applaud their efforts, further antagonizing those unlucky to be left on Earth.

Lily and her father turned around, their backs to the crowds, and continued to wait until processing resumed. There was a murmur behind her, and she turned to see the Rangers returning to their posts, led by the tall, handsome one.

"Are you all right?" he asked her, a gloved hand on her shoulder.

"Sure," she said.

"I have to apologize for bumping into you like that," he said.

"Well, you were in a rush," she said, shyly smiling at him, noticing his large brown eyes.

He chuckled at that. "You could say that. But I didn't intend on knocking you over, so I'm sorry."

"No problem."

"Welcome aboard," he said.

"Hi, I'm Lily" was all Lily could manage, and she cursed herself for feeling the blood rush through her cheeks.

"I'm Joseph Raige, one of the Rangers assigned to the ship," he said. "You know where you're going when you're on board?"

"Yes, I do. Thanks." Raige sounded familiar to Lily, and she asked, "Aren't you in charge or something?"

He shook his head, smiling all the way. "That's my cousin, Skyler, the Supreme Commander. I'm just a Ranger."

"Supreme Commander, that's where I heard the name," she said, more to herself than the Ranger.

"Yeah, Sky's in charge of the whole operation, and he can have it. Some of us are born leaders, some of us serve best as followers," he offered.

"You've got some sort of rank, right?"

He tapped the markings over his right breast. "Lieutenant," he said.

"Nice," was all she could manage. He had dimples and those brown eyes, the artist in her noted, and she felt herself blush.

"I have to get back to my post," he said, and moved ahead, nodding to several others.

Her mind wandered and suddenly her family was the next to board. They paused at the entrance, all shiny and new looking, and adorned with scattered decals with pictograms and numbers. Within the cleared passengers were heading for different platforms and elevators while Rangers stood guard, even inside the ship. She wondered if these were the ones coming along.

Lily stepped over the threshold, silently saying one final farewell to the life she had led. The next step would be the beginning of something new.

One by one, her family had their bracelets scanned, confirming one last time that they were who they were supposed to be. The scan matched the passengers' current weight against their required weight. That had been hard, maintaining a consistent weight to ensure the *Espérer* could properly lift off. Her dad had to swear off the Guinness, and her mom saved one final bottle of wine for the last night in the house. Zach and Max passed without a problem, and Mom turned out to be three pounds lighter, which made her smile for the first time in what seemed to be days.

Now Lily stood in front of the scanner, handing off her backpack to be weighed separately, as a technician checked the readout on a tablet. He nodded with approval and his eyes moved her along.

It was Raige, though, who handed the backpack over to Lily.

He smiled and said, "Here you go, Lily." He remembered her name! "We can chat later, if you'd like. I've got a pretty rich connection to this whole Lightstream business. But right now, everyone needs to keep moving. We're on schedule, and I'll be busted to Private if we fall behind."

She nodded, intrigued by his dimples and the idea that he'd want to speak with her again. Lily hurried to catch up to her mother, who had been watching with a fresh smile.

Lily took her hand once more, and they walked forward into an uncertain future. There was a flutter in her stomach, a warming feeling that spread up her chest and into her head. It was a comforting feeling, one she hadn't felt in a while.

She was feeling excited. The adventure of a lifetime, her lifetime, was getting under way.

1000 AE

Earth

i

The world returned to him bit by bit. That wasn't bad, actually. He hadn't expected the world to return to him at all.

First there was simply the blackness. All around him, so thorough that on some level Kitai was convinced that he was in fact dead.

Then he slowly became aware of his breathing. It seemed highly unlikely that he'd be dead if he was breathing. The slight hum of computers followed, and moments later, something even stranger: the humming of insects.

Insects? We've . . . landed?

Kitai slowly and nervously attempted to open his eyelids. It held a moment of fear for him, because if he couldn't in fact open his eyes, he was in some sort of bizarre in-between state: not dead, not alive.

His eyes opened.

Okay, well . . . that's a start.

The world around him was slanted. Not a lot; just enough to get his attention. The backs of the seats in front of him were tilted, and cords hung from the ceiling at angles.

Slowly Kitai tried to sit up. He had no luck, and it was only after a few moments of near panic that he remembered he was double harnessed into the seat. His fingers fumbled slowly with the buckles. He felt as if it took him hours to undo them, though it actually took less than a minute. Technically he was in shock, but he wasn't capable of understanding that. He just felt unsteady and groggy.

He noticed that some of the observation ports had been broken open. Reflexively he braced himself, certain that he was going to be sucked right through the window. It was only when he saw shafts of daylight streaming through the windows that he remembered that they'd landed. Kitai was having trouble recalling various statuses. Dead, alive, dead, landed, still in space, still hurtling forward—he had to remind himself actively from one moment to the next what his personal situation was.

Tentatively, *very* tentatively, he started to pull off his oxygen mask. He wasn't really thinking when he did that. It was simply an obstruction that he wanted gone from his face. He wasn't even consciously considering what its basic purpose was.

Yet he received a very swift reminder as he gasped, finding it extremely difficult to breathe. He held the mask up, looking at it incomprehensibly, as a digital readout blinked on it: LOW OXYGEN: 15%. CAUTION.

This was all Kitai required to jog his memory, to make him remember that he needed to keep the mask on his face. Quickly he fastened it back into position and sat there a few more moments, gratefully breathing in lungfuls of air. *Right. Air mask. Need the air mask. Remember that.* Once he was certain that he liked the positioning of the mask, he clambered out of the tilted seat and moved into the aisle.

His first confrontation with mortality came a few seconds later, when he saw a body tangled between seats. It was twisted and contorted in a position that left no question in Kitai's mind that he was looking at a corpse. Yet still he could not take his eyes off him. After a moment, he realized who it was: the Ranger who had placed the oxygen mask on him.

Now he was dead. First alive, then dead.

Kitai's eyes were huge and terrified. There was no reason for him to worry about repressing his reactions because there was no one there to see them.

Dad . . . have to find Dad . . .

Slowly, tentatively, he started moving up the aisle. There was another body to his left, crushed under a section of the ship. He ignored it. If he just stopped and stared at every dead body he spotted, he might simply collapse and let the gravity of his situation immobilize him. He was faced with the reality that he might do well to lie down and die himself just because he had no business being alive. But on the off chance that his father was somewhere in this disaster, waiting for his help, Kitai was not going to deal with the situation by lying down and collapsing.

He made his way down the hallway until he got to a section that led to the cockpit. The door was sealed shut. All around him was debris from different sections of the ship. It had been tossed around enough in space for everything within to come apart and scatter itself throughout the vessel. And that was without looking outside to see where the rest of the ship had scattered.

It was only at that point that Kitai had an awful realization.

The Ursa. Its pod had been one of the things that had struck the planet's surface. The chances were that the creature inside it had not survived.

But what if it *had . . . ?*

As quickly as he could, Kitai pushed all such concerns away. Dwelling for any period of time on such disastrous possibilities was simply not going to do him any good.

Suddenly he was startled by a loud, ear-piercing screech of noise that came from everywhere at once. A loud series of beeps echoed throughout the area. He couldn't even begin to discern where it was coming from, until he looked behind himself and saw the air lock doors grinding together in the passenger section.

He'd gone right by that part of the ship, taking no notice of the body that was wedged into the opening.

The lifeless corpse had been shoved out of the cabin, but his arm must have gotten stuck in the doors, preventing them from closing. Slowly Kitai advanced, seeing something tattooed on the man's arm. Of all the stupid things to notice, a written word on a man's arm was what caught Kitai's attention.

It was the word *Anna*. The doors continued to try to close on it, obviously out of whack since the obstructing arm would have made them cease closing under ordinary circumstances. Since the doors were functioning improperly, they kept rolling open and closed, open and closed, trying to seal despite the arm that would not give way.

"Remove obstruction," a computer voice began repeating. *"Remove obstruction. Remove obstruction."*

Kitai continued to watch, transfixed and horrified. He felt as if he couldn't just walk away and leave the imprisoned arm behind. But he likewise couldn't bring himself to touch it.

Finally he hit on a compromise. Carefully, worried he might step on something or, even worse, someone else, he moved over to the arm. Slow and timidly, he extended his foot, hesitated, then sheepishly lifted the arm with his boot. He gingerly nudged it back with his foot through the door onto the other side, allowing the door to slide shut with a thud and a suction sound. Air started blowing hard through the vents, and a tinny computer voice announced, *"Repressurizing complete."*

Tentatively, Kitai removed his respirator mask. This time, with an air supply around him, he was able to breathe steadily.

There was an opening in the wall that looked into an adjacent corridor. Kitai peered through it, not thinking he was going to see anything of any use.

There was another human arm there, and at first it didn't register on Kitai as anything more than another piece of a person. That was all he thought about it until it suddenly dawned on him that its hand looked like his father's.

Instantly Kitai rushed through the opening and lifted the first piece of debris he could get to. He was preparing himself for the vast likelihood that he was wrong, that the man who was buried under the rubble was simply another stranger.

The moment he pulled away the debris, however, he gasped aloud—and looked down at the battered body of Cypher Raige. His eyes were closed, and his breathing was at best erratic. However, the fact that he was breathing at all was a huge relief to Kitai. He felt that as long as Cypher was still alive in any way, shape, or form, he himself had a solid chance of surviving. That was, admittedly, a hugely selfish reason for being glad that his father was still alive.

A large broken section of the ship was lying across Cypher's legs. Kitai tried to lift it clear of him. It didn't budge. *Unacceptable,* Kitai thought, and started working on another plan.

He looked around and in short order discovered a long metal rod that had fallen from the ceiling. With an effort, he wedged it between the floor and the debris. Then he set his jaw, positioned his feet, and pushed with all his strength. At first he thought he wasn't equal to the task. But then slowly, miraculously, the broken section of ship lifted off his father's legs.

Kitai wasn't strong enough to clear it all in one shot. It took several prolonged efforts as he continued slowly but steadily to pivot the debris clear. Finally, after what seemed like endless straining, when every muscle in his upper body felt like it was on fire, he managed to tip the debris so that it fell away from Cypher and hit the deck with a dangerously loud slam. The ship echoed and shuddered with the impact.

Kitai knelt next to his father. Cypher's mask was still on his face, slightly fogged with his breathing.

Kitai realized that he no longer had any idea what he should do. He had discovered his father, learned that he was still alive, and done everything he could to maintain that situation. But he had run out of ideas. His father was unconscious. What was he supposed to do about that? Yell at him until he was forced awake? How would that help?

Kitai felt his face getting wet and didn't understand why that was happening. He reached up and touched it and came to the slow realization that he was crying. He was so mentally disconnected from his body that it took him several moments to put it together. Once he realized what the wetness was, he lost all semblance of self-control and began sobbing openly. *Got to get under control*, he thought, but he failed utterly.

He continued crying that way, in huge heaving sobs, until slumber overtook him.

ii

The first thing Cypher Raige became aware of was the presence of his son next to him. Kitai's eyes were closed, and his chest was slowly rising and falling. Cypher was unsure where his son had come from before he remembered that he had brought Kitai along on this . . . this disaster.

Then it took him a few more moments to assemble what had just happened: the asteroids, the wormhole, the shattering of the ship, and the crash landing in the one place that no human in his right mind wanted to be.

Cypher noticed that Kitai didn't have a mask on anymore, but he didn't seem to have any trouble breathing. Frowning, Cypher removed his own mask. *No problem,* he thought, sampling one deep breath after another.

First things first.

He gently shook Kitai, uncertain of what sort of response he was going to receive. His son woke up slowly at first, but then he saw his father's calm gaze and snapped fully awake.

Before Kitai could say anything to his father, Cypher's face conveyed a message of all business. "Let me see you," he said. His voice sounded raspy, but he had to examine matters one at a time. "Can you stand?"

Kitai nodded and slowly got to his feet. Okay. Good start. "Evaluate yourself," Cypher said briskly.

Kitai proceeded to do exactly what he'd been ordered to do. Slowly and systematically, he started checking his joints. He rolled his wrists, flexed his elbows, rotated his shoulders and neck. He was moving with slow confidence, so much so that Cypher was convinced of his son's wholeness even before he finished testing his knees and legs.

"Good to go," Kitai said. "Fully functional."

That wasn't enough for Cypher. "Turn around."

Kitai probably didn't think he needed to do so, but Cypher wasn't in the mood to worry about what he thought at the moment. Kitai said nothing but turned slowly in a circle until Cypher satisfied himself that he was indeed fully functional.

"Confirm the Ursa is contained," Cypher said.

At that order, Kitai's confidence seemed to evaporate. When he first spoke in reply, his voice trembled slightly and he obviously had to fight to bring it under control. "It's gone," he said slowly. "The whole back of the ship is gone."

This was not news that Cypher welcomed. Unwilling to accept it purely on the basis of what his son was telling him, he raised his voice and shouted, *"Rangers! Count off!"*

No one responded to the general's order. There was simply a deathly silence.

"Most of them were in the back when the tail broke off," Kitai said slowly.

Cypher absorbed the news. This was the worst possible report he could have received . . . except for the fact that the Ursa was nowhere close. The last thing they needed was to have the creature escape from its pod and hunt them down.

Cypher had shown up in the cargo bay just in time to see the damned thing locking onto his son. If they had landed safely at their destination, it wouldn't have been a big deal. But because of where they had landed and the circumstances that faced them, it was a *huge* deal. Of course, if the rear section of the ship had landed nowhere near—maybe, in fact, hundreds or even thousands of kilometers away—the Ursa would be one less thing for Cypher to worry about.

At least for now.

Cypher noted that his body was unobstructed. That was a positive sign. At least he didn't have ship debris all over him.

But that positive appraisal of the situation lasted for about as long as it took Cypher to try to stand. Kitai tried to shout a warning, but it was too late. The moment Cypher tried to get up, he let out an earsplitting cry of pain. It was obvious that he couldn't apply any weight to either leg. He was effectively crippled; neither leg was going to function.

He collapsed back onto the floor as Kitai shouted for him to lie still. *"I know, I know!"* Cypher shouted back, mentally scolding himself for allowing pain to overcome him that way. It took him a few seconds more to compose himself fully and assess the damage he had sustained. In the meantime he lay there unmoving, the seconds stretching out until he was done. He was hardly thrilled with what he came up with.

I'm in bad shape, he thought. *Very bad.*

He looked up and saw where they were in relation to the rest of the vessel. "The cockpit is directly above us. Go. Now."

Kitai hesitated. It was obvious that he wasn't thrilled about the prospect of leaving his father. Cypher didn't know why and didn't really care. Whether Kitai was worried that Cypher would lapse back into unconsciousness or was simply afraid to leave his source of confidence, it didn't matter.

Cypher needed him to climb up into the cockpit and get a handle on the situation there. End of story. "Go,

Kitai," he said. Kitai stood reluctantly but did as he was told.

iii

There was a ladder well down the hallway, and Kitai headed for it. He had no idea why Cypher had insisted that he make it to the cockpit, but that fact didn't stop him. Whatever reason Cypher had for asking him to do something, Kitai would do it. Cypher Raige wasn't in the habit of making arbitrary requests. If he wanted it done, he had a valid reason. Period.

When Kitai reached the ladder, he clambered up into the cockpit. He suspected he wasn't going to be thrilled by what he saw there. He was correct. There were two people in the cockpit—he took them to be the pilot and the navigator—both of them dead. Some sort of structural beam had detached from overhead, falling on them and crushing them in their chairs. There were emergency lights blinking steadily everywhere.

Adjoining the cockpit was the avionics room. Much of the equipment in there was still lit up and blinking. Kitai moved to a control panel on the wall and tried to determine whether the panel was functioning well enough to give him some degree of control.

He heard his father's voice, raised so that Kitai could make it out. "Go to the control board," Cypher told him. "In front of the left seat. Top row, fourth from the right. Activate exterior motion sensors."

Kitai tried to touch the panel, but he wasn't able to—his hands were shaking too violently. He realized immediately what the problem was: He was shaking because he'd survived. Survivor's guilt; that was what it was.

He tried to tell himself that he had no business being shaken by the fact that he'd survived. Nor was he going to do his father any good by being terrified simply because he had lived. That was a good thing, not a bad thing.

Kitai clamped his hands together to get them to stop shaking. He took a deep breath and let it out to compose himself. After a few moments he tried again, finding the screen labeled "EXTERIOR MOTION SENSORS." His fingers still were shaking, but he got the result he wanted.

"MOTION SENSORS ACTIVATED" appeared on the screen.

"Check," Kitai slowly managed to say in a calm voice, as if this had been the simplest and least demanding undertaking in the history of humankind.

Cypher did not hesitate to continue. "Over your right shoulder where you just came through . . . there is a utility compartment. Go through it. There is an emergency beacon. Rounded silver top like a saucer, tapers at the bottom. We need it to send a distress signal. Bring it to me."

Kitai followed his father's instructions. The communication rack had been damaged, which did not surprise him in the least. Considering the pounding the ship had taken upon entering wherever the hell they had wound up, Kitai would have been astounded to find *anything* intact. Nevertheless, he managed to find the emergency beacon. He picked it up and turned it over in his hands; the bottom of it had been crushed.

Figures.

Disappointed, Kitai climbed down from the cockpit and brought it to his father. As he handed it over, he said in a voice kept deliberately low to hide his emotions, "I don't think it works."

Cypher made that determination quickly by trying to switch it on. Nothing. The activity light remained off. Quickly Cypher detached and examined the mangled lower section of the beacon.

Kitai didn't know any of the construction details of the device, but seeing Cypher's expression told him how completely screwed they were. For just a heartbeat he saw despair in his father's face. But just as quickly as it appeared, it vanished. Cypher Raige was not someone who gave in to despair, and he certainly wouldn't do so with anyone watching, much less his son.

Cypher didn't say anything for a few long seconds. Then, still studying the beacon in his hands, he said, "Kitai, my left shoulder is dislocated. Come here."

Dislocated? Kitai thought. *Oh, God. You've got to be kidding me.*

Cypher was already positioning himself flat on his back, his face unreadable. He then took Kitai's left foot and placed it on his shoulder. "Take my wrist with both hands."

Kitai's stomach muscles clenched. "Wait . . . Dad, wait—!"

Cypher ignored his son's obvious concern. "You need to pull as hard as you can."

No, I can't. You can't ask this of me. You—

Even as all his protests rampaged through his head, Kitai knew there was no point in offering any of them aloud. They all boiled down to the same thing: *Dad, please don't make me do this. I know you're in huge amounts of pain right now, but pulling on your arm really hard is more than I can take.*

And that was unacceptable. Kitai had to do what he had to do.

He took hold of his father's wrist, grasped it as tightly as he could, and mouthed, "One . . . two . . ." before pulling as hard as he could, his muscles straining.

Cypher screamed in agony.

It was such a horrifying noise that it jolted his arm right out of Kitai's grasp. Kitai fell backward and lay there, terrified, as Cypher spent long seconds gasping for breath. As soon as he had air in his lungs, Cypher said with grim determination, "We didn't get it. We didn't get it."

A pit opened in Kitai's stomach.

"*One more!*" Cypher insisted. "Pull harder, cadet. I've been through worse."

Kitai picked himself up. He had no choice in the matter.

Kitai braced himself as he held his father's wrist. He was going to do it this time. He *had* to.

This time it was Cypher who did the counting, and he did so out loud. "One," he said, looking steadily into Kitai's eyes. "Two." And then, unhesitatingly, without the least hint of the pain he had to be anticipating, "Three."

Kitai leaned back and pulled for all he was worth. The cracking sound in his father's shoulder was awful, like stones grinding together. But worst of all was the long bellow of agony that escaped from Cypher's lips.

It came from a place so deep inside that Kitai didn't even want to think about it, and it echoed through what remained of the ruined ship for what seemed like an impossibly long time.

By the time it was over, Kitai was sure it was his *own* pain. It took him a moment to remember that it wasn't, to separate himself from it, and to look up into his father's face to see if his effort had done any good.

Gasping for air as if he had run a sprint, Cypher tested his shoulder. He revolved his arm in its socket— not exactly all the way, but most of it. The movement made him wince, but not as much as Kitai would have thought.

"You got it," Cypher breathed, sweat streaking down the side of his face in rivulets. "You got it." He swallowed and looked around. "We need to get me into the cockpit." He frowned, no doubt trying to figure out how that could be done. Then a solution seemed to come to him. "There's a cargo loader at the rear."

Kitai nodded, but he was too wrung out to absorb what Cypher had said. It took him a moment to lock in on the words. *Cockpit. Cargo loader.*

Got to move . . .

And he did. He half walked, half crawled in the direction of the loader, glad that he had eased his father's pain—and even gladder that he wouldn't have to pull on Cypher's arm a *third* time.

Cypher watched his son move down the length of the ship toward what was left of its aft quarters. He wished he had time to reflect on how hard it had been for the boy to do what he had done and how proud he was of Kitai for doing it.

But he didn't, because it was only the beginning of what was in store for both of them. Pain, hardship, sacrifice . . . when it came to such things, they hadn't even scratched the surface.

Clenching his jaw, Cypher propped himself up on his good elbow and assessed the damage to the ship. The hull was twisted like a double helix, completely useless for the purpose of transportation.

All things considered, it was a one-in-a-million shot that either he or Kitai would have survived the crash. A statistical aberration of the highest order but one he was surely grateful for.

Unfortunately, it wasn't just the ship that had been twisted, maybe beyond any hope of repair. It was also Cypher himself.

He looked down at his left leg and saw what he had kept Kitai too busy to notice: Blood had soaked through his pants, leaving a crimson stain that was spreading with each passing minute. And it wasn't just his left leg that had been damaged, because he couldn't turn his right ankle without a bolt of fire shooting up his leg.

I've done it now, he thought. *I have most assuredly done it now.*

iv

Kitai lowered the flatbed of the cargo loader—a hydraulic machine on a set of four tough wheels—next to his father. Cypher looked impatient as he watched the thing descend beside him. But then, he *always* looked a little impatient, as if he had something more important to do somewhere else.

It was dark outside. *Night.* The ship's observation ports had frozen over with ice.

Must be cold out there, Kitai thought. Much colder than anyplace he had ever visited on Nova Prime. Fortunately, it wasn't cold inside the cabin. There was at least *that* to be thankful for.

Kitai extended a small ramp from the end of the loader to the ground. Then he hit a button, and the ramp started to move like a conveyor belt. He looked at his father, who was bracing his arms at his sides. He didn't look happy about being so helpless.

The first step was for Kitai to lift Cypher's leg and place it on the ramp. Even the slightest touch made Cypher wince, and so Kitai was as gentle as he could be. As the belt started to drag his father's leg, Kitai lifted the other leg and put it beside the first one. Then Cypher jockeyed his upper body around until that was on the belt as well.

As Kitai looked on, the belt moved Cypher up until he was on the flatbed at the top of the loader. *Mission accomplished.*

But it also underlined how badly Cypher had been hurt. There was blood from his legs on the ramp and also on Kitai's hands, and the effort of sliding himself onto the loader had left Cypher exhausted.

It was jarring to think that his father could be broken like any other human being. Cypher had always been bigger than life to Kitai. More than a hero.

And now he needs help from somebody like me.

He pressed a button, and the elevator began to rise. He craned his neck to watch his father as he ascended.

Cypher called down to him. "Inventory. Full assets. Now."

Because I'm just standing around gawking. I get it. "On it," Kitai said.

Occupying the space where the ship's navigator sat—or, rather, *would* be sitting if the navigator were still alive—Cypher considered the portion of the pilot's control panel that hadn't been wrecked in the crash.

He needed to access the panel despite the damage to his left leg. With that in mind, he manipulated the cargo loader's controls, using the machine like an adjustable gurney. Little by little he tilted himself forward until he was sitting upright. Then he propped his leg on the console beside him.

That done, Cypher placed his palm on a terminal to activate the cockpit computers. The initial burst of power gave him hope that he and Kitai might get out of this spot after all.

A hologram flashed in front of him: IDENTITY VERIFIED: GENERAL CYPHER RAIGE.

Having recognized him, the computers booted up with a soft hum. He tapped out a command, and a holographic display appeared over the panel, spitting out initial readings: MAIN CABIN BREACH . . . SELF-SEALING IN PROGRESS . . . TRANSPORT SHIP . . . CONDITION CRITICAL.

Cypher glanced at the recorder on the other side of the cockpit. Then he spoke and watched voice waves undulate on one of the monitors, indicating that the recorder was doing its job.

"General Cypher Raige," he said. "First quarter Earth day. Crash-landed."

V

Kitai dragged the navigator's inert form along the deck and tried as hard as he could not to acknowledge the fact that he was pulling a corpse.

Unfortunately, it wasn't the first corpse he had hauled that way since the crash. *But it's the last.* His back was sore from the effort since each of the bodies he had dragged had outweighed him, but he wasn't complaining.

It could have been worse. It could have been me *that died in the crash.*

When he reached an open hatch, he stopped. Clouds of cold white vapor rose from the opening. A sign beside it read "NITRO STORAGE CONTAINER."

They were Rangers, the navigator and the others. It was only right that their bodies be preserved. That way, when someone from Nova Prime found the ship—or this part of it, anyway—the dead could be transported back to the world of their birth and given a decent burial. Not to mention the fact that a decomposing corpse could attract predators and maybe even an Ursa.

As gently as he could, Kitai deposited the navigator into the container below. The man looked more like a statue than someone who had been alive not too long ago. With a shiver of revulsion, Kitai swung the hatch door closed.

And what about me and Dad? he wondered. *If we don't make it, who will preserve* our *bodies?* Again he shuddered.

Supplies, he thought, putting the hatch and all thoughts of its contents behind him. *Forget the bodies. Got to get supplies.*

Little by little, he lugged everything he found back to the cockpit, where Cypher was waiting for him. Before long, he had built up a considerable pile. That was a good thing, he supposed.

The bloodstain on Cypher's leg was a bad one, and it was spreading. Worse, it was dripping onto the floor. Kitai had noticed it earlier—he couldn't help it—though his father had seemed to want to distract him from the sight.

"That's it," Kitai said, placing a med-kit and Cypher's personal kit bag beside the pile. He was mentally and physically drained, more so than he had realized when he'd been busy collecting everything. How long had it been since the crash? He had no idea, no idea at all.

His mind was even more tired than his body. The

things he had seen in the last few hours, the things he had done . . . he wanted to forget them, pretend they had never happened. But they had. His father's injuries, for instance. They weren't going to go away. They were real. And Kitai wondered if he would have to deal with them.

"I need you to focus right now," Cypher said, bringing Kitai out of his reverie. "Assets?"

One shell-shocked teenager. One badly damaged Prime Commander, Kitai thought.

"Cadet?" Cypher said calmly. "I need an accounting of our assets."

Kitai struggled to focus. He looked to the pile of supplies in front of him, aware that his father was studying every nuance of his body language: every facial twitch, every stutter, everything. After all, that was what he did. It was what made him who he was.

"Four bodies," Kitai reported. "I put them in the nitro compartment. Radio nonoperational." That had been a disappointment, of course. "Four Ranger packs. Cabin pressure stable." *What else? Oh, yeah* . . . "Five— no, six cutlasses. One emergency med-kit. And I got your bag from the troop bay."

Was that it? He thought it was. Not that it seemed to matter to his father. Cypher had turned away before Kitai had finished his list and begun manipulating the cockpit controls. Suddenly, a holographic image of a landscape rose over the console. It was formed by thousands of wavy lines. And there was a marker blinking on the holographic landscape.

Cypher stared at the blinking marker, his expression grim, for a long time. Finally, he turned to Kitai and said, "Hand me the med-kit. Ranger pack."

Kitai didn't know why his father needed those things, but he moved to comply. Picking up the med-kit and the Ranger pack, he gave them to Cypher, who placed them in his lap. Then he took his son's wrist, turned it over, and activated the naviband on Kitai's lifesuit.

Instantly, lines of data crawled around the naviband,

creating what looked like a holographic bracelet. Kitai had never seen a naviband do such a thing before.

At the same time, the monitor to Cypher's right filled with a cascade of numbers and graphs, all of which matched those on Kitai's naviband. It took Kitai a moment to realize what his father was doing: syncing the band with the cockpit's computers.

But why? Kitai felt panic creeping back into his bones.

"Cadet," Cypher said, "center yourself."

Kitai did so. Slowly, he became calm again. Cypher seemed satisfied. Sitting back, he looked into Kitai's eyes, and Kitai looked back. The weight of their predicament hung between them, a shared burden.

Then Cypher began to speak. "The emergency beacon you brought me will fire a distress signal deep into space."

Kitai nodded. But it seemed to him that his father was speaking to himself as much as to his son, trying to cut through the haze of his pain by thinking out loud.

"But it's damaged," Cypher said.

"There is another one in the tail section of our ship."

Kitai's heart fell. The tail section was gone, and more than likely, the beacon was gone, too. But Cypher didn't seem daunted by what he had learned. If anything, he seemed intrigued.

As Kitai watched, his father manipulated the controls and altered the holographic landscape. In the grainy computerized image, Kitai could make out mountain ranges, rivers, valleys, forests, deserts, small storm patterns, animals, birds, and so on.

Cypher pointed to the screen. "This is us *here*. I can't get an accurate reading, but the tail is somewhere in *this* area, approximately one hundred kilometers from here." He glanced at his son. "We need that beacon."

Kitai considered what his father was saying. One hundred kilometers . . .

"Kitai," Cypher said in measured tones, "my legs are broken. One very badly. You are going to retrieve that beacon or we are going to die. Do you understand?"

Kitai nodded his head. "Yes." He felt tears welling in his eyes and wiped them away and awaited his orders.

Cypher opened a small black medical case marked UNIVERSAL AIR FILTRATION GEL—EMERGENCY USE ONLY. Inside, there were six vials sitting side by side.

"You have air filtration inhalers," said Cypher. He removed one of the vials. "You need to take one now. The fluid will coat your lungs, increase your oxygen extraction, and allow you to breathe comfortably in the atmosphere."

Cypher demonstrated how to use the inhaler. Kitai watched carefully. Then he placed the vial to his lips, pressed the release, and inhaled deeply. He had expected the air in the vial to be tasteless at best, but it wasn't. It was sweet, like the air in the mountains back on Nova Prime just before first sun.

"You have six vials," Cypher said. "At your weight, that should be twenty to twenty-four hours each. That's more than enough."

Next, Cypher helped Kitai with his naviband. A digital map appeared as a hologram above Kitai's wrist.

"Your lifesuit and backpack are equipped with digital and virtual imaging," Cypher noted. "So I will be able to see everything you see *and* what you don't see."

Kitai took comfort from that more than from anything else. Equipment was great; it was reassuring. But knowing that his father would have access to everything he saw was ten times *more* reassuring.

Cypher picked up the Ranger pack and placed it on Kitai's back. Then he turned his son around so that his backpack camera was facing Cypher. Turning so that he could access his console, he tapped a control, and a monitor in front of Kitai came alive. Kitai could see Cypher's face on the screen, its eyes looking into him the way his father's *real* eyes did.

On the monitor, Cypher said, "I will guide you." He tapped the same control to shut down the monitor. Then he turned Kitai around to face him.

"It will be like I'm right there." He looked Kitai up and down for a moment. Then he said, "Take my cutlass."

He picked it up and held it out to his son. Kitai looked at it, a little stunned. It was his father's cutlass. The one he had used to fight and kill Ursa, the one that never left his side.

And he was handing it over to Kitai.

That, more than anything else, brought home the gravity of the situation. If Cypher was entrusting his son with his most prized possession, it was because he wanted to give Kitai every advantage he could.

"Go on," Cypher said, "take it. C-40. The full twenty-two configurations."

Not just the ones Kitai had used as a cadet—pike and hook and blade and so on—but every possible cutlass form the Savant's engineers could come up with. Only the most skilled and experienced Rangers were given the C-40. And now, despite his fledgling skills and his utter lack of experience, he had one, too.

Kitai felt the weight of the cutlass in his hands. It was heavier than the ones he had practiced with as a cadet. It even *looked* big.

He looked up at his father. Cypher could have comforted him. But true to form, he went in the other direction, underscoring the magnitude of Kitai's task.

"This is not training," he said. "The threats you will be facing are *real*. Every single decision you make will be life or death. This is a class 1 quarantined planet. Everything on this planet has evolved to kill humans." A beat. "Do you know where we are?"

Where? Nowhere near home, that was for sure. Nowhere near the planet of Kitai's birth.

"No, sir," the cadet said.

Cypher frowned. "This is Earth, Kitai."

Earth? As in the world that gave birth to humanity but faltered under the lash of humanity's abuse? *That* Earth?

Kitai often had wondered what it would be like to

walk the surface of the world his distant ancestors had walked. Lots of kids had wondered about that. Now he would have the chance. But there was a danger beyond the ones his father had outlined, one that had been in the back of Kitai's mind.

"The Ursa?" he asked.

Saying the words out loud made them seem even worse, made it seem as if the creature were right outside. Kitai saw his father's eyes narrow.

"There are three possibilities," Cypher said. "The first and most likely is that it died in the crash. The second and less likely is that it is injured very badly and still contained."

Kitai would have signed up for either one. He would have done so in a heartbeat.

"And the third and least likely," Cypher concluded, "is that it is out."

The words hung in the air between Kitai and his father. Cypher had said that was the least likely scenario, but he hadn't ruled it out completely. He *couldn't*.

"We will proceed," Cypher continued, "in anticipation of the worst-case scenario. Every movement will be under protocol: escape and evade. If he's out there, I will see him long before he gets anywhere near you."

Kitai nodded. *Escape and evade*. What else was he going to do? Fight the Ursa on his own?

"Don't get ahead of yourself," Cypher said. "Do everything I say and we will survive."

And that was it. There was nothing left to say. For a moment, Kitai and his father just looked at each other. The cadet looked down at his cutlass, felt the weight of his pack on his back. He was a Ranger, outwardly at least, and he had a mission to carry out. But he wasn't *just* a Ranger, and the man with the broken legs sitting in front of him wasn't *just* his commanding officer.

Surprising himself, Kitai wrapped his father in a hug.

He could barely get his arms around his father's broad shoulders, but it didn't matter. Kitai hugged him hard and for a long time. And Cypher hugged him back. After all, it might be the last time they had a chance to do it.

Finally Kitai's father said, "Time's wasting. And we've got a lot to do."

Kitai let go of Cypher. Then he stood up and snapped his cutlass onto the magnetic plate on his backpack.

He took a last look at his father, managed a weak military turn, and left the cockpit. In a way, it was the scariest thing he had ever done.

But in another way, a way he hadn't expected, it was *exciting*.

VI

Kitai stood in the little gangway between two air lock doors. Outside the outer door, the ice was melting as the warmth of the sun's first rays started penetrating the darkness.

Just one sun, Kitai thought. *Weird.*

He turned over his wrist, activating his naviband and its many holographic layers, and said, "Can you hear me, Dad? Over."

There was the briefest of pauses. Then Cypher's voice came through clear and crisp: *"Copy."*

Good, Kitai thought.

There was so much he didn't know about this place. He looked around warily. So much. And from what his father had said, all of it was deadly. Experimentally, he tapped a combination on the handle of his cutlass. Instantly, one end transformed itself into a large curved blade—a blade that, if not for the protection afforded Kitai by his lifesuit, would have cut a nice gash in his arm.

Idiot, he thought, shaken by the near miss. *Until you know what you're doing, don't do it.* He retracted the blade end of the cutlass and tapped in a different pattern, one with which he was more familiar. In the next breath, the cutlass's fiber ends extended outward until the weapon was a couple of meters long.

That's better, he thought.

Taking a deep breath, he exited the torn end of the ship into a rocky ravine. A moment later, the hatch door closed behind him. As he jumped down to the ground, he saw more Rangers—dead like all the others—hanging from the straps of their seats. Kitai sighed. He thought he had seen the last of the corpses. The sight of so much death made his heart pound again.

"Kitai," his father's voice said, "take a knee."

Kitai knelt as he was told.

"I want you to take your time," said his father. "Acclimate yourself to the environment. Root yourself in this present moment. Tell me any- and everything. No matter how inconsequential it may seem. Everything you see, hear, smell, how you feel. Over."

Kitai could see daylight above, past the walls of the ravine. He was breathing heavily. "My body feels heavier."

"Very good," Cypher said. "The gravitational pull on this planet is slightly different than at home."

Beat by beat, Kitai grew calm. He appraised the distance to the top of the ravine walls. "It's about sixty meters to the top."

"Okay," Cypher said. "Get going."

"Roger," Kitai said.

Cautiously, Kitai began to climb, paying close attention to each placement of his hand or foot. This wasn't any different from standard rock-climbing walls back home, he realized, and he had climbed those rocks a thousand times.

It wasn't long before he reached the top. As he found purchase for his left hand, he felt something tickle. His right. When he looked to see what it was, he found a huge multicolored tarantula sitting on his hand.

"Aahhhhh!" he yelled, unable to control himself, and flung the creature from his hand. But in doing so, he lost his balance and slid a meter down the side of the ravine before catching himself. He looked down and shook his head. It could have been worse.

"What happened?" his father asked over their communication link.

Kitai took a deep breath and regained his grip. "You didn't see that? I thought—"

"What's your SitRep? Your vitals spiked. I say again— what is your situation report? What happened?"

"No change," Kitai said, a little embarrassed. "I slipped. I'm good to go." Then, to make it sound plausible: "There's condensation on the stones. I'm fine."

That seemed to appease Cypher. In any case, he didn't demand any more information. Kitai continued his ascent until he reached the top of the ravine. Even before he pulled himself out, he saw the glorious confusion of colors in the eastern sky. Purple, orange, fuchsia. He had never seen anything like it. Back on Nova Prime, there were sunsets, but they were mainly crimson and gold. These colors were new to him.

Mesmerized by them, he emerged onto what appeared to be an elevated plateau. He shaded his eyes. This sun was bigger than the ones he could see from the surface of his homeworld. Was there another one right behind it? Or was it on its own?

Funny . . . he had studied Earth but couldn't remember something as simple as how many moons it had. Then again, he would have considered that a pretty useless piece of information. When would he ever get a chance to use it?

Yeah, he thought. *When?*

All around him, plants and animals were waking up. He could hear the melodic morning calls of eagles majestically soaring overhead. Off in the distance, maybe a kilometer away, hundreds of buffalo roamed the plain. Well, they resembled the buffalo back home, but these seemed larger, bulkier in front. So much life. Kitai wasn't used to it. Back on Nova Prime, he had grown up in the desert. This was noisy, full of smells, full of shapes and colors he had never imagined. The spectacle took his breath away.

Abruptly, Cypher's voice came through Kitai's naviband: "There's an escarpment where two Earth continents collided. Looks like it could be a waterfall. It's at about forty-five kilometers. We'll call that our midway checkpoint."

Kitai absorbed the information. Back on Nova Prime, forty-five kilometers wasn't so much. A day's run for the colony's best long-distance athletes.

"There's no way you can return after that point," Cypher advised him soberly. "We'll assess rations and reevaluate when you get there. But let's break it into sections."

A moment later, Kitai's naviband produced a new hologram, one that his father must have generated. It was a map with an icon for Kitai and a large grouping of trees to the north of him. As Kitai watched, a line appeared and connected him to the trees.

"First leg," Cypher said, "is twenty kilometers to the mouth of the north forest. Let's take it easy. Set chronometer for 180 minutes. Over."

"One hundred eighty minutes?" Kitai said. "That's not right. I can do 10K in *fifty* minutes. You'll see."

Kitai began a light jog. That was all it would take, after all.

"I might even do it in under forty minutes," he said. "Over."

He listened for a response from his father, but he didn't get one. Concerned, Kitai slowed down.

"Dad?" he said. "Do you copy? Over."

Still no response. Kitai came to a stop.

"Dad, do you read me? Over."

Nothing but the sighing of the wind.

"Dad, do you copy? Are you there?" Kitai asked, panic setting in. After all, Cypher had been in bad shape. What if one of his organs had given out?

Damn, Kitai thought, and ran back toward the ship.

He hoped desperately that his father was still alive when he got there.

"Dad," he said, "I'm coming back!"

"No need," came the almost casual response through Kitai's naviband. "You just go ahead."

Kitai stopped in his tracks. "Huh?" He didn't get it.

"Seems to me that you're in charge of this mission. And in my limited military experience, when two people are in command, everybody dies. So I will defer to your leadership, cadet."

"Dad," said Kitai, "I was just saying—"

"What is my name?" Cypher barked unexpectedly over the comm link.

Kitai was confused. "I don't know what you mean."

"What is my name?" Cypher demanded.

Kitai swallowed. "General Cypher Raige."

"And who am I?"

"Prime Commander of the United Ranger Corps."

"You're goddamned right! And from this second forward, you will refer to me as sir, Commander, or General! You will follow my every command without question or hesitation. Am I crystal clear, cadet?"

Kitai's head was spinning. His father had never been this angry with him before. Without thinking about it, he came to attention.

"Sir, yes, sir!" he snapped.

A moment of silence—but only a moment. Then Cypher said, "Now at H plus 180 I need you at that forest. Set your chronometer."

"Sir, yes, sir!" Kitai responded.

He could hear his father speaking in the cockpit—but not to him. Evidently, he was speaking to the cockpit recorder.

"General Cypher Raige. Beginning probe search to confirm Ursa is not released."

Kitai waited.

"You may proceed," the general said.

Kitai set his chronometer and began to walk with no idea of what dangers—if any—lay ahead.

vii

Cypher was pleased with the way his son had responded. He had commanded many men in combat, and he knew that they needed different things from their superiors at different times. Just then, Kitai needed a firm hand, and Cypher gave it to him.

But he couldn't just send his son off across unknown territory. He had to give the kid some help. With that thought in mind, he deployed a probe-cluster projectile.

If he had been outside the ship, he would have seen it shoot straight up, out of the ravine and into the sky. He would have seen it rise higher and higher, as it was rising on his monitor, and then—once it reached the requisite altitude—explode. But not in a self-destructive explosion. It would be an explosion that produced dozens of separate probes and sent them flying vast distances from one another.

As they vectored back toward Earth, Cypher's monitors filled to the brim with the images the probes sent back to him. And it wasn't just images they transmitted. It was telemetry as well, including information on the curvature of Earth, topographical details, and so on.

One probe was lost in an ionic cloud, which appeared as a floating mass of white noise. Another slammed into an ocean, sending back data on undersea life. Yet another burrowed into the earth, revealing soil, weather, and erosion data. A fourth crashed in a copse of trees and went to black, and a fifth floated over packs of animals, thousands of them.

Cypher flipped through the images the probes sent back to him. And the more he did so, the more he came to appreciate the tremendous variety of life on Earth.

All of it deadly.

Periodically, he switched to the image that showed his son's progress from Kitai's point of view. As time wore on, Kitai reached a series of pastures that seemed to go on forever. Then he followed a ridge that looked down into a lush valley with a profusion of leafy green plants and wildflowers. Mentally, he began composing a report on the planet for the Primus and the Savant, evaluating its condition and making recommendations for the future. After all, if he got here, so could others. And they needed to be prepared.

Cypher studied the numbers floating over the pilot's control board. "I estimate H-plus-four days to reach the tail," he told Kitai. "Use your naviband. Stay on azimuth. The temperatures on this planet fluctuate dramatically daily, and most of the planet freezes over at night."

"Sir, yes, sir!" came the response.

Cypher manipulated the hologram of the terrain in his son's vicinity. There were areas demarcated by deep red lines. He understood what they meant. "There are hot spots," he informed Kitai. "Geothermal nodes between here and the tail that will keep you warm during the freeze-over. You must reach one of these nodes each evening before nightfall. Over."

"Copy," Kitai said.

As he looked up to either side of him, Cypher saw what Kitai saw. Clouds were moving over the mountains and fields like huge, ghostly spirits. "Standard operating procedure," Cypher said, "till I give you further instructions."

"Copy," Kitai said again.

Cypher looked down at his legs. The floor around him was covered with a thin sheen of blood. *His* blood. And there was more dripping from his pants leg second by second, minute by minute. He reached for the med-kit Kitai had brought him and hit a control on the pilot's console. Instantly, the medical analysis holographic screen came up.

Cypher pulled a flat box out of the med-kit. Then he activated it and ran it over his legs. A light illuminated his legs wherever he performed a scan. At the same time, the holographic screen over the console erupted with biomedical data.

"Code five trauma to left leg," said the cockpit's computer voice. *"Situation critical. Arterial shunt recommended."*

Cypher accepted the news as calmly as he could. He reached out and touched the words *arterial shunt*, whereupon the holographic screen showed him a three-dimensional outline of a human body. He touched the outline, and it zoomed in on the left thigh, revealing a network of arteries and veins. One of the blood vessels had been severed.

The words *arterial shunt—explanation of procedure* appeared on the screen. They were followed by a coldly mechanical animated segment. In it, a scalpel appeared on the screen. Next, a dotted line on the thigh. As Cypher watched, the scalpel plunged into the flesh of the animated thigh. Cypher forced himself to watch the procedure. After all, he was going to have to carry it out on himself. There was no way he could survive otherwise. And if he didn't survive, neither would Kitai.

There was no decision to be made.

He looked into the med-kit. There was a cylinder inside marked "NARCOTIC." He held it close and read the side effects on the cylinder's side. It said, "IMPAIRED VISION, DIZZINESS, DROWSINESS." Cypher turned to the screen that showed him Kitai's moving point of view. It was critical that he continue to monitor that screen, that he do so with a clear head. All it would take was a momentary lapse in his vigilance and his son would be yet another casualty of their ill-fated crash.

With a sigh, he put the cylinder back in the med-kit untouched. *Too bad*, he thought. It would have been a lot easier if he could have used the narcotic. Suddenly, a wave of pain engulfed him. His leg was getting worse.

"Hey, Dad," someone said, "you there?"

He found himself remembering . . . He was in a trench back on Nova Prime, dressed in full battle gear. Not alone. There were other Rangers with him. They were enjoying a moment of peace. Senshi appeared on Cypher's naviband. He moved it into the shadows to see her better. She was young, not a Ranger yet. Sitting in the family apartment. Kitai, even younger, was playing in the background.

"Dad, you there?" she repeated.

Cypher smiled. "I'm here."

Senshi held up the old copy of *Moby Dick*. "A boy I know had this. It's a real book, from a museum. It's *Moby Dick*."

Cypher's head swam. "Mm hmm . . ."

"He said I could even hold on to it," said Senshi.

Hold on to . . . ? "Hold on to what?"

"The book, Dad."

She laughed. He managed a smile. She had that effect on him. Cypher stared at his daughter, so full of life and possibility, her future like a flower that barely had begun to bloom.

"Did they really kill these whales?" she asked.

"Yes," Cypher said. "For their oil. And they almost disappeared. Just before the age of carbon fuels . . ."

Then it wasn't Senshi he was talking to anymore. It was Kitai's voice he heard saying, "Dad, you there? Over. Dad?"

Cypher took a steadying breath against the pain, which was beginning to bring on delirium. He cleared his throat and collected himself before he spoke.

"Copy, cadet." He turned again to the holographic displays. "The Earth's rotational cycle is shorter than back home. You have six hours to reach the first geothermal site. Over."

Cypher imagined Kitai's expression as he absorbed the information. Then his son said, "Roger."

At that point, Kitai was moving through a valley, alongside a deep, jagged fissure in the ground. Rocks jutted up from the darkness below as if someone had cracked the surface of the Earth like an egg. The sun seemed very strong. Cypher checked his holographic display and confirmed it. *More* than very strong, he thought. *Deadly*, like everything else on the planet.

"Let's stay in the shade as much as possible," he advised. "Direct sunlight is intensely carcinogenic. You must limit exposure. Over."

"Roger that," Kitai said.

"The rain used to be acidic," Cypher noted, "but it doesn't seem to be a problem now."

Cypher checked his son's position vis-à-vis his objective. The kid was making good progress. But he needed to know the position of something else as well.

The Ursa.

Cypher checked some of the images he was receiving from his probes. Probe 11 showed him an animal he did not recognize but one that probably had evolved since the days when people still lived on this planet. The creature reared up on two legs and looked directly at the probe.

The computer sent Cypher information: *Giraffa camelopardalis*.

Cypher looked at the live image of the giraffe with awe. He had read about these long-necked beings, but they were extinct on Nova Prime. It was almost like seeing a live dinosaur. Then the giraffe swatted at the probe with its horned head and moved away.

More important, however, than what he saw was what he *didn't* see. He hit the cockpit recorder and said, "Probe cameras unable to detect signs of Ursa in the wild." *For now.*

viii

Kitai arrived at the mouth of a forested valley. Gorgeous views of green woodlands stretched out before him. He checked his naviband.

"Twenty kilometers, 184 minutes. Request breather, Da—" He caught himself. "Sir."

"Negative," Cypher said over the naviband. A pause. "You've got three hours to reach the hot spot. That's plenty of time. Hydrate now and keep moving."

Kitai swallowed his irritation, flipped up a hydration tube from his backpack, and drank. Then he moved deeper into the forest. As he progressed, the trees around him grew taller and taller. Over a hundred meters high, he estimated. They were wide, too, maybe seven meters in diameter. At that size, they blotted out most of the sunlight. Kitai had to move cautiously through the shadows, peering into the foliage every few steps.

Suddenly, he realized that his lifesuit had changed. It had become jet-black. *Harder, too.* And it had the kinds of bumps one might find on body armor. Concerned, he stopped walking and said to his father, "My suit's turned black. I like it, but I think it's something bad. Over."

"Your suit's made of smart fabric," came the reply. "It has motion sensors. I'm tracking a life-form moving near you from the west."

Kitai felt ice climb the rungs of his spine. When he spoke, he tried to keep the fear out of his voice. "The Ursa? Over."

"Negative. It's smaller. Biosigns read only a meter and a half long."

Kitai stood motionless. Behind him? Where was it?

He wasn't comforted by the word *only*. "*I'm* a meter and a half long! Over."

"It's closing rapidly from the west," Cypher told him. "Do not *move*! It is what it is. Relax. Get ready. Try to give me a visual."

Kitai wished he could give *himself* a visual. But if he wasn't allowed to move . . .

"Creatures on this planet have evolved from the ones we have on record because of radiation bursts," Cypher said as calmly and clinically as if he were lecturing a class of cadets. "It's at fifty meters, forty, thirty . . ."

Kitai found that his breath was coming in gasps.

"It's slowing down. Twenty . . . ten . . ."

Kitai balanced himself, trying to be as ready as he could be. He could hear plants snapping as the life-form got closer.

In a whisper, his father said, "It's right there, Kitai."

Where was *there*? Kitai bit back his panic and whispered back. "I don't see it! I don't see *anything*."

"Relax, cadet," Cypher said. "Recognize your power. This will be your creation."

Then Kitai *did* see it. It emerged slowly from the undergrowth: a small baboon-type creature. But like everything else on Earth, it seemed to have evolved. Its face was hauntingly human, but it walked on all fours.

"It's fine, Kitai," his father said. "Be still. Let it pass. Do not startle it."

Easy for you to say. Kitai picked up a rock and made a motion as if he meant to throw it at the creature. He could feel his pulse racing.

"Back up!" he yelled at the baboon creature.

It reacted with a loud screech.

"Don't do anything!" his father insisted, a note of anger in his voice. "Kitai, *no*!"

Kitai heard the words but continued to threaten the thing with the rock. He couldn't help it.

"Get the hell out of here!" he yelled.

"Kitai, *stop*! Over."

Kitai couldn't catch his breath. He was gasping like crazy. Unable to tolerate the presence of the baboon any longer, he threw the rock at it. It glanced off the creature, but it had the desired effect. With a last look at Kitai, it turned and left. But his breathing was out of control. Beads of sweat ran down both sides of his face. For a moment, between blinks, it felt like he was back in that box. A scared little boy. A coward.

Cypher studied his holographic readout. His son's vitals were spiking.

"You are creating this situation!" he insisted. "Be still. Over."

Suddenly, his monitor showed him something else to worry about. A cluster of dots—maybe fifteen of them—began moving toward Kitai. Moving *rapidly*.

"Damn it!" Cypher breathed. Then, louder so that his

son could hear him, "Cadet, get control of yourself! Listen to my instructions."

Despite everything, Kitai was pleased he had gotten rid of the baboon—until he heard a rustling and saw six more of the creatures blasting through the foliage. Screeching bloodcurdling war cries, they surrounded Kitai.

As he had been trained, he tapped a pattern into the handle of the cutlass. Instantly, the weapon shifted shape, but not into the one Kitai wanted. Instead, the fibers on the end of the cutlass retracted into the handle and disappeared. Panicked, he looked up at the baboons. *Try it again*, he thought, and tapped out another pattern.

This time the weapon did what he intended it to do: separate into two parts. The fibers flattened out at the ends, making two distinct batons. Kitai swung his new weapons in every direction, figuring that would drive the creatures back. But it didn't. They began charging and jumping backward, mimicking Kitai's moves. Before long, they were picking up sticks and clubs from the forest floor and using them to mimic the two ends of the cutlass.

"To your rear, cadet! Out to your rear!"

Through his gathering malaise, Kitai recognized the voice as his father's. He looked behind him and saw that there was indeed an opening. Using it, he escaped the circle of baboons and took off into the forest. But the creatures gave chase.

Kitai was feeling faint, but he couldn't let them catch him. He slashed and darted his way through the forest, trying to shake the creatures from his trail. Still, it seemed to him they were getting closer.

No, he thought, redoubling his effort. Instead of running around the rocks he encountered, he ran over them and launched himself over long stretches. He began putting more distance between himself and his pursuers.

But they switched tactics, too. They took to the trees.

And up there, among the thick, plentiful branches that blocked the sunlight, they were in their element.

He glanced back over his shoulder: The creatures were gaining on him again. They began snatching branches and large pinecones from the trees and hurling them at Kitai. And they were growing in number. If there were six of them before, there had to be fifty now, all swinging and jumping from branch to branch, throwing whatever they could find at him.

Suddenly, Kitai felt something hit him in the middle of his back hard enough to send him flying forward. But he didn't dare go down or they would have him, and so he let his fall turn into a forward roll and came up running again. No sooner was he on his feet than he heard his father's voice.

"Cross the river, cadet! I repeat, cross the river!"

What river? Kitai asked himself. Then he saw it up ahead. It wasn't *just* a river. It was a torrent punctuated with gouts of leaping white water. *It's going to be hard as hell to get across*, Kitai thought.

Then he realized: *That's the point.*

Looking back over his shoulder, he saw the baboon creatures advancing through the trees. He took just long enough to secure his cutlass to his back before he dived headlong into the roiling water. As he swam, he saw the surface of the river explode with a relentless barrage of tree branches. But none of them reached him.

Unfortunately, he had to come up for air. When he did, the creatures unleashed another volley. But Kitai dipped down deeply enough into the water to avoid this one, too. Finally, he reached the other shore. Wading out of the water as quickly as he could, he cast a single glance back to see if anything was coming at him. Nothing was. Then he continued his frantic flight.

"Cadet," said his father, "they are no longer in pursuit."

But Kitai didn't register his father's words. He barely noticed that his lifesuit was its normal rust color again.

"I say again, they are not following you. Over."

Kitai kept sprinting. He couldn't stop. He didn't *dare*.

"Cadet, you are not being followed! Kitai, you are running from nothing!"

There was a clearing up ahead. As Kitai reached it, he pulled his cutlass off his back and held it out in front of him. Then he made a 360-degree turn, prepared to fight anything in his vicinity.

"Put my damn cutlass away," his father said. "Take a knee, cadet."

Kitai forced himself to obey. But he still searched the edges of the clearing, looking for evidence of the baboons.

Cypher regarded the image of his son on his probe monitor. Kitai was wide-eyed, hyperventilating, frantic. The general *had* to get him to calm down.

Cypher rubbed his eyes. He was tired and getting more so. But he wasn't going to let fatigue stop him. Suddenly he heard a beeping sound. *Kitai's vital signs . . .* He checked the readout.

"Kitai," he said, "I need you to do a physical assessment. I'm showing rapid blood contamination. Are you cut?"

His son didn't respond. He looked shell-shocked, not at all like a Ranger cadet. Hell, he seemed like a child. And his lifesuit was fading to white. *Not good*, Cypher thought.

"Kitai," he said sternly, "I need you to do a physical evaluation. Are you bleeding? Over."

Slowly, ever so slowly, Kitai regained control of himself. Responding to his father's command, he began to check his body. Of course, the evaluation required him to stand up, but when he tried to do so, he looked unsteady.

Off balance, Cypher thought. "Kitai?"

"I'm dizzy," said the cadet.

"Check yourself!" Cypher insisted.

Kitai looked at his hands. On the back of his left hand there was something Cypher couldn't make out at first.

Then he zoomed in and saw what it was: some kind of leech. Or, rather, what leeches might have evolved into.

Repulsed by the sight of it, Kitai tore it off. But in doing so, he tore his skin. Instantly, a livid rash blossomed across the damaged skin. *It can't be allowed to spread*, Cypher thought. It had to be tended to immediately.

As calmly as he could, he said, "Your med-kit, Kitai."

His son snatched his pack off his back and fumbled around blindly in the med-kit. He looked worried. After all, he could see the rash, too. Kitai started to sway.

"I can't stand up . . ." Still, he managed to open the med-kit.

In a clear, measured voice, Cypher said, "You have to administer the antitoxin in sequence. Inject yourself with the clear liquid first. Do it now."

Kitai took the first hypodermic from the med-kit and popped off the protective cap. His hands were trembling.

"Dad," he said, ignoring his father's earlier admonitions to call him General or sir, "I can't see."

Cypher wanted to help his son, to administer the drugs himself. But he couldn't. He was sitting in the cockpit of a ruined ship, his legs broken, and Kitai was too far away.

"The poison is affecting your nervous system," he said instead. "Relax. Stay even."

Kitai fumbled with the needle—not once but twice. He stopped, looked up, looked around, his eyes dilated and swelling shut. Cypher could see his son's panic deepening. The veins of Kitai's hand began turning black.

"Dad," he pleaded, "please come help me. I can't see! Please come help me!"

"Stay even," Cypher said. "Inject yourself directly into the heart with the first stage now!"

Kitai took a deep breath, struggling to remove the top of his lifesuit. He couldn't control his fingers, which he couldn't see, and they shook from fear. He was running out of time and needed to do this quickly no matter how sick he felt. As he exposed his chest to the warm sun, it was hot to the touch and slick with sweat. He shook with increasing violence and just had to inject the anti-toxin. It sounded so simple, but he was shaking so hard. Finally, he gritted his teeth so hard that they hurt, grimaced, and finally stuck himself with the hypodermic squarely in the chest. Then he pressed the plunger.

"Now the second stage," Cypher said. "Hurry."

"Your left," Cypher told him. "To your left!"

Finally, Kitai's fingers seemed to find the second hypodermic. But by then, his eyes were swollen closed. His hands shaking, he removed the protective cap on the hypodermic. Then he stuck himself with it. But he couldn't press the plunger. His thumb looked like it was too swollen to move.

"I can't feel my hands!" Kitai groaned. "I can't—"

Suddenly, his eyes rolled back in his head. His eyes flickered. He fell to his knees, on the verge of losing consciousness.

Cypher got an idea. "Press it into the ground! Kitai, roll over on it and press it into the ground!"

For a moment, he didn't know if his son had heard him. Then, with a final effort, Kitai threw himself forward. The plunger on the hypodermic pressed against the ground as he slumped over. After that, his limp body lay motionless.

But had he pressed the plunger? Had the hypodermic released its payload into Kitai?

Cypher watched the holographic monitor. *Come on*, he thought. *Work, damn it*.

Then, ever so slowly, Kitai's blood contamination levels began to change, to decrease slowly. The red beeping lights turned to yellow, signaling the gradual return of his vital signs to normal. Cypher sat back, relieved. "Great work, cadet. Now you're going to have to lie there."

Of course, Kitai couldn't hear him. He was unconscious. But Cypher kept talking as if his son were still awake because it felt better than talking to himself.

"The parasite that stung you," he said, "has a paralyzing agent in its venom. You're just going to have to lie there for a little bit while the antitoxin does its job."

Cypher glanced at the feed from Kitai's backpack camera. It captured the grotesque doughiness of his badly swollen face. A single tear rolled from the corner of his misshapen eye. For Cypher, it was an excruciating experience. There was nothing he could do to help his son. *Nothing*. He thrived on control, insisted on control, but in this situation control eluded him.

Compared with the forest in which Kitai had collapsed, he looked pitifully small. And the sun, Cypher noticed, was starting to slip past its apex. Cypher glanced at his timer. It would take a while for the contents of the hypodermic to do their job, but Kitai didn't have forever.

As the sun dropped in the sky, approaching the horizon, the temperature began to drop as well. Cypher didn't like it. He could see plants withdrawing into themselves, closing up to conserve heat in anticipation of what would be a brutal nighttime chill.

But Kitai couldn't close up. He couldn't protect himself. And Cypher couldn't protect him, either. He could see that his son's face was getting better. The swelling was gone. But he still lay unconscious, his eyes closed, his lifesuit pale.

"Kitai," Cypher said.

No response. A gentle dusting of frost began to form on and around Kitai's weakened frame. Cypher wanted to wake him, needed to wake him. He could hear the wind howling around his son, see the edges of the furled leaves flutter ferociously.

"Kitai," he said again, "it's time to get up."

But Kitai's eyes remained closed.

Please, Cypher thought, looking at his son's beautiful

face. He prayed for anything, anything at all. A muscle twitch. A flicker of life.

"Kitai," he said more forcefully, "I want you to blink your eyes."

Suddenly, Cypher heard something over his comm link. It was faint, shallow, but there was no mistaking it. Kitai was breathing. *Breathing.*

It was a start. But there wasn't much time left. A tiny hint of ice showed up on the cadet's left eyebrow.

"Son," Cypher said, deeply concerned, "I need you to please blink your eyes."

Slowly, ever so slightly, Kitai did as he was asked. In a raspy voice, he said, "Hey, Dad."

He was looking directly into his backpack camera as he spoke. Cypher stared at the monitors and the bio-readings and exhaled a breath he hadn't known he was holding.

"That sucked," Kitai said. Looking a little unsteady, he got to his feet and began gathering his gear.

"That is correct," Cypher stated, always seeing things for what they were. "The temperature is dropping five degrees every ten minutes," he added, emphasizing the urgency of the situation. "You've got twelve kilometers to the hot spot."

Cypher checked Kitai's vitals. They were stable. As he watched, his son gathered his gear and got ready to go.

Reassuming his general mode, Cypher said, "Let's see that 'ten kilometers in fifty minutes' that you spoke about earlier, cadet."

Kitai set his naviband and turned to the north. "Sir, yes, sir," he said, but in a voice that betrayed how weak he must have felt from his ordeal. Still, he set out at a sprint over the rugged terrain ahead of him. All around him, there were signs of the deep freeze that would accompany the onset of darkness. Animals were scrambling underground. It began to snow, lightly for now.

"SitRep?" Cypher said.

"Ten mikes out," his son reported. "Good. All good."

Out there, maybe, Cypher thought.

ix

Inside the cockpit, it wasn't good at all. The words *arterial shunt* stared back at Cypher from the med screen. He pulled a long, narrow piece of tubing from the med-kit, then took out a thin surgical knife, leaving it positioned over his left thigh. Next he ripped open the side of his uniform pants, exposing the side of his leg. He could see the nasty gash there that was leaking all the blood. The holographic screen behind him displayed his arteries and veins. One blood vessel had been severed.

Cypher cast a quick glance at Kitai's camera view. It showed the cadet pelting through a snowy landscape that was getting snowier all the time. Kitai was doing all he could to enable them to survive. It was up to Cypher to do the same. Without fanfare, he plunged the thin surgical knife into the side of his leg.

It hurt like *hell*. There was nothing Cypher wanted more than to slip the knife back out again. But he didn't. Instead, he cut through the flesh of his leg, using the readout on the holographic display to guide him as he sought the end of the severed artery.

Finally, he pulled the knife out. But only for a moment. Then he drove the knife into his leg again, this time higher up on his thigh. Again the knife cut through tough muscle tissue until it reached the other severed end of his artery.

Only then did he withdraw the knife for good. By then he was shaking uncontrollably. He stared at a point in the distance and regained his composure for a moment. At the rate he was losing blood, he couldn't afford any more than that. Jaw clenched against the pain, he inserted the tubing into one of the incisions in his leg. He could see its progress on the holographic image behind him. As he fed the tubing into his leg, it slid toward the artery and then into it. As Cypher watched, the artery closed around the end of the tubing.

Cypher felt something feathery touch his cheek. It took him a moment to realize that it was a tear. He wasn't a robot after all. He could feel pain like anyone else. He just couldn't give in to it.

With shaking hands, he inserted the piece of tubing into the second incision. Again using the holographic display for guidance, he slipped the tube into the ragged end of the severed artery. This time the fit was less perfect. Cypher wiggled it, almost passing out from pain. His readout told him that the arterial shunt was 87 percent effective. Looking down, he saw that blood was flowing through the piece of tubing sticking out from his leg. He had repaired the damage, at least temporarily. It was good enough for the time being.

Cypher leaned his head back against the loader, focused on the screen showing his son's point of view, and struggled to remain conscious despite everything he had been through.

He could hear Kitai's voice as he ran. "Five mikes out." His voice was stronger now, more confident. "Who wasn't advanced to Ranger? Who was it? Watch him go. Watch him go."

Cypher stared, on the verge of losing consciousness. His eyes closed, opened, fluttered closed again. A memory came to him . . .

He was on a Ranger ship. It was dark. Someone was yelling, "Five mikes out!"

It was a drop captain. Cypher couldn't remember the guy's name, but he recalled being one of the Rangers waiting in the ship. He remembered, too, the piece of smart fabric in his hands. On the fabric was a face. *Senshi's* face. She was sitting at a table with a birthday cake in front of her. There were nineteen candles on the cake. Faia and Kitai, who was only eight at the time, looked on from the background.

Senshi held up the cake. "Dad," she said, "you help me."

"No," he told her as he sat among his fellow Rangers, "you go ahead. You blow."

"Come on, Dad," Senshi insisted with a grin. "Blow."

Cypher looked around at the other Rangers. They were watching him, making him self-conscious. "Now," he told Senshi, "you know there's no way I can actually do that from here."

"No," she said, full of faith, "I think you can."

Cypher sighed and addressed his wife. "Faia, why don't you step in here and help the girl?"

Faia came into the frame of the smart fabric and said, "You can do it."

"I know you can," Senshi added.

Cypher shot a glance over his shoulder. A Ranger was sitting there, stone-faced. Cypher turned back to the cake and Senshi's expectant face. Resigned to his fate, he leaned forward quickly and blew. As if by magic, the candles went out.

Suddenly Kitai leaned into the frame, laughing. It was he who had blown out the candles. Faia was laughing, too. So was Senshi. Cypher basked in the laughter. He smiled. "Happy nineteenth birthday, Senshi."

Just then, an alarm went off in the ship. The other Rangers turned to Cypher.

"I have to go," he told Senshi.

He tapped the piece of smart fabric, and it turned off. Sometimes it unsettled him, seeing his family vanish with one flick of his finger. All that he knew, gone in a flash. Then he tucked it away. All the Rangers in the ship stood, strapped on their gear, and looked to Cypher. The back of the ship began to open. Cypher stared at it. "Rangers," he called out, "in formation! Move!"

They moved.

"Hot spot one arrival," came a voice.

Cypher blinked away the memory and checked his son's camera. It showed him that Kitai had reached a geothermal node that was elevated from the landscape around it. Steam rose from the ground. Fallen trees were overgrown with moss. There was decay everywhere, the product of the place's warm, wet air.

"H-plus-forty-eight minutes!" Kitai announced, an unmistakable note of satisfaction in his voice.

Outside the geothermal zone, the forest was going into a deep, rapid freeze. Every tree in the vicinity was developing a thick skin of ice.

Kitai began to cough. "Sir," he said, seemingly hoping for a response from his father, "I made it. I'm here."

Ignoring his own condition, he checked his son's vital signs. They scrolled in front of him. "Make sure you have everything," he instructed Kitai. "Take your next inhaler. Your oxygen extraction is bottoming."

Dutifully, Kitai opened the med-kit. His father had gotten him this far. The last thing he was going to do was diverge from Cypher's instructions.

We're doing all right, Kitai thought. *Spacing out the oxygen. Had a little setback before, but I'll be calmer next time, smarter.* Then he saw something bad—very bad. Of the five oxygen vials left to him, two were broken. Quickly, he closed the case, hiding its contents from Cypher's view.

I don't have enough breathing fluid, he thought. *What am I going to do? How am I going to reach the tail section and the beacon if I don't have enough to breathe?*

"Use the next dose of breathing fluid," Cypher said.

Kitai strained not to cough. "I'm good, Dad. I don't need it right now."

Cypher watched his son, knowing that he was lying but refusing to berate him for it. "Okay," he said.

Finally Kitai coughed a deep cough, his chest making a hollow wheezing sound. He was starving for oxygen, no question about it. Still Cypher said nothing. He just watched and waited even though his son's struggles gradually were getting worse. Kitai's coughs became more brutal, driving home the sad but inescapable fact that human beings no longer could breathe the air of their homeworld.

To make things worse, the cockpit's medical computer displayed a graphic: ARTERIAL SHUNT 70% EFFECTIVE. Cypher was still getting blood, getting oxygen, but not as much as he had gotten before. Why?

Then he saw it on the holographic readout: His self-administered shunt was slipping on the ragged end, where the fit hadn't been perfect. Blood was escaping from it, running down to the floor. The medical computer advised him to commence transfusion. It told him he needed four units of O-positive.

But all he cared about, all he could hear, was Kitai's deep, racking coughs. All he could see was the pain on Kitai's face as he fought for air. It was a tough lesson, but one Kitai had to learn: *Listen to your father.*

X

Kitai dragged in breath after breath, each more difficult than the last. Finally, he couldn't stand it anymore. If he went without breathing for another minute, he would pass out. And that might be a disaster from which he couldn't come back. Finally, reluctantly, he administered the second vial of breathing fluid.

Instantly, he could feel the oxygen spread throughout his body, meeting his needs. His breathing slowed. His strength came back to him.

"Second dose of breathing fluid complete," he said. "Over."

"Count off remaining so you can keep track," his father said. "Over."

Kitai hated the idea of lying to his father. However, he had no choice. He couldn't take a chance on Cypher pulling the plug on the mission, especially when it was their only hope.

His face flushed with shame, Kitai replied, "Four vials remain, sir."

Just then, a pack of wolves slinked past him, seeking a warm spot against the frigid cold. A couple of deer lay down to go to sleep. Bison crowded in, side by side with jade-eyed tigers. Everyone had sought the same refuge. *Even insects*, Kitai thought. During the day, they might be bitter enemies, but at night, when their world froze over, they enjoyed a kind of truce.

Otherwise, none of them would survive.

Kitai saw a bunch of monkeys with bioluminescent eyes staring at him. He couldn't help staring back. Suddenly the sky opened up and unleashed a mighty downpour. Kitai ducked back into the musty hollow of a huge rotting tree, but it didn't keep him very dry.

Right in front of him, a bee struggled to free itself from a spiderweb. The more it moved, the more it sent a signal to the spider that had made the web. Suddenly, a spider bigger than Kitai's fist showed up and rushed down to claim the bee. But the bee wasn't defenseless. As the spider approached, it tried to sting its captor. Kitai watched the struggle, caught up in it. Lightning flashed as the bee tried to free itself, but to no avail. The spider just hung there, waiting. Finally, the bee got too tired to buzz its wings. But instead of moving in for the kill, the spider backed up. It looked confused.

Kitai supposed the spider couldn't find the bee unless it moved and sent a vibration through the strands of the web. The spider began testing each thread for its tension until it came upon the thread on which the bee was trapped. Suddenly, the spider made another charge. The bee flailed wildly, trying to escape from the thread that was holding it down. Meanwhile, the spider came in low, its venomous fangs visible.

Abruptly the bee went still again, ceasing to fight, and again the spider seemed to become confused. It backed up, testing the tension on the web threads until it located the bee again. By this time, the bee seemed exhausted. It barely struggled, tracking the spider circling across its web. Then the spider came in for the kill.

Suddenly the bee snapped to life and flew up despite the thread stuck to its leg. Attaining a position over the spider, it sank its stinger into the spider's soft exposed back. The spider twitched. Then the bee stung it again and again. The spider, poisoned with the bee's venom, moved slowly to the middle of its web. The bee took advantage of the respite to try to fly away. But the spider's thread held it in place. Finally the bee died, hanging from the thread.

Kitai watched it hang there. After what it had done, it seemed to deserve a better fate.

A question came to mind, something Kitai had meant to ask for a long time. "Dad . . . ?" he said. "Dad—"

He imagined his father awakening from a state of semiconsciousness, dealing with his injuries as best he could. For a moment, there was no response.

Then Kitai heard: "I'm here. SitRep?"

"How did you beat it?" he asked his father. "How did you first ghost? Tell me how you did it."

Cypher pictured his son, alone in an unfamiliar and hostile world. Afraid of what he could see—and especially of what he couldn't. Now more than ever he needed to hear this.

"I was at the original Nova Sea of Serenity," Cypher began matter-of-factly. "The settlements. I went out for a run. Alone. Something we are never supposed to do. An Ursa de-camos not more than a few meters away. I go for my cutlass, and it shoots its pincer right through my shoulder.

"Next thing I know, we're falling over the cliff. Falling thirty meters straight down into the river.

"We settle on the bottom. It's on top of me, but it's not moving. I realized it's trying to drown me. I start thinking, *I am going to die. I'm going to die.* I cannot believe this is how I'm going to die.

"I can see my blood bubbling up, mixing with the

sunlight shining through the water, and I think, *Wow, that's really pretty.*"

Kitai was amazed that his father could come to that conclusion at such a time. Hell, it amazed him that his father thought *anything* was pretty. It was a side of him Kitai hadn't seen before, or if he had seen it, it was so long ago that he didn't remember.

"Everything slows down, and I think to myself, *I wonder if an Ursa can hold its breath longer than a human?* And, I think of Faia. She was pregnant with you, and close, too. Half a moon's cycle away, maybe twenty-three days. She was so beautiful.

"And suddenly I knew one thing with perfect clarity, and it obliterated all other thoughts: There was no way I was gonna die before I'd met my son. Before I met *you*."

Kitai felt a lump grow in his throat. *Me?*

"I look around, and I see its pincer through my shoulder, and I decide I don't want that in there anymore. So I pull it out, and it lets me go, and more than that, I can tell it can't find me. It doesn't even know where to look.

"And it dawned on me: Fear is *not* real. The only place that fear can exist is in our thoughts of the future. It is a product of our imagination, causing us to fear things that do not at present and may not ever exist. That is near insanity, Kitai.

"Do not misunderstand me: Danger is very real, but fear is a choice.

"We are all telling ourselves a story. That day, mine changed."

Kitai thought about that: *We're all just telling ourselves a story.* It made sense, as if he had known it all his life and had just never had the words to express it.

Kitai looked around the geothermal zone and took in the sight of the animals all resting in close proximity to one another. He wished his father could see it, could see the majesty of it. *Maybe someday*, he thought. He sighed. It didn't look like he would get a lot of sleep that night.

And how could he, with his father's words still fresh on his mind? *If we're nothing more than the stories we tell ourselves . . . we can change the story, the way Dad did.*

And if the story changes, we do, too.

From the cockpit of the ruined ship, Cypher watched the geothermal zone flood with dawn light. Somewhere, Earth's sun was breaching the horizon.

Kitai, who had been drifting in and out of sleep as far as Cypher could tell, roused himself. He grabbed his gear and stood up.

"Fourteen kilometers from the falls," he said, giving his son an objective. "That's our halfway checkpoint. Over."

"Reading you," Kitai said.

He began his day's trek slowly and steadily. No doubt, he was feeling the weight of the immense distance he had to cover. And without any real sleep.

Cypher spared his leg a glance. The puddle of blood on the deck below it was growing, spreading. On the holographic readout in front of him, it said: "ARTERIAL SHUNT—58%. TRANSFUSION CRITICAL. 7 UNITS NEEDED." *Seven units*, Cypher thought. *Be lucky if I had even* one.

He turned off the screen. *I need to focus on my son*, he thought. And that, despite the pain and the worsening loss of blood, was what he did.

Kitai hacked his way through the forest with his cutlass, the end of which he had turned into a machete. It was hard work. The cutlass was light, but the leaves he was fighting his way through were tough and heavy. After a while, he paused and took a swig of water. Then he pulled a nutrition bar from his pack and ate it.

"Seven kilometers from the falls," his father said, as if to remind him that they didn't have time to stand around.

"Roger," Kitai said.

He balled up the wrapper from the nutrition bar and threw it on the ground. Then he began to walk away. But before he got very far, he stopped himself and went back for the wrapper. *Can't just leave it here,* he thought. *That's how we lost this planet in the first place.*

Except when Kitai bent down to grab the wrapper, a gust of wind blew it out of reach and carried it through the thick vegetation. He frowned. Then he made his way forward through the chest-high leaves and lunged. His hand closed around the wrapper, giving him a little thrill of accomplishment. But the feeling lasted only a moment because when he looked up, he saw a scene of unexpected devastation.

For a wide stretch in front of him, the forest had been trampled as if by a gargantuan foot. Trees had been ripped down. Baboon carcasses were lying everywhere, some of them torn in two. Kitai got the sense that a battle had taken place there. But with whom? And for what reason?

"What could do this?" he asked out loud, his voice sounding strange in the stillness.

He hadn't really expected a response. But he got one.

"Double-time it," his father said in a tone that left no room for disagreement. "We need to make it to the falls. Hurry!"

Kitai started walking again. Overhead, the wind rustled the forest canopy. It sounded like claws scampering along a rooftop. Suddenly, he heard a *boom.* Not knowing what it was, he crouched, his cutlass at the ready.

"Volcanic eruption," Cypher informed him. "Twenty kilometers east. There are volcanoes all over the planet now. You're fine. Keep moving."

Expelling a breath in relief, Kitai resumed his progress through the woods. For a while, it was uneventful. He liked it that way. Little by little, the ground underfoot began to rise. Then the rise became more pronounced, too steep to negotiate without some assistance.

Pausing for a second, Kitai tapped a combination into his cutlass. The handle separated into two pieces, the end fibers of which formed twin picks, each half a meter long. With them, he began to scale the hill. He was getting better with his father's cutlass. *Good thing*, he thought. There were plenty of things on this planet capable of killing him without his doing the job himself.

As Kitai climbed, he felt the fatigue of not having slept. But he couldn't let it slow him down. He had an objective to reach. Then he heard something in the forest behind him. Or he thought he did.

"Is there anything behind me?" he asked his father. "Over."

"Negative," Cypher told him.

Normally, Kitai would have trusted his father's observation, trusted it *implicitly*. But he couldn't shake the feeling that something was following him. He froze and cocked his head like a dog. Then he heard it: a sound. Like static in the distance.

"I hear something," he said emphatically. He listened some more. "I think it's water. A lot of it."

"You're close. Keep hustling," Cypher told him.

Kitai climbed faster, digging into energy reserves he didn't know he had. Whatever fatigue he had felt seemed to fade, at least for the moment. Abruptly, he came to the end of the foliage. Pushing aside the last of the leaves with his hands, he emerged onto a rocky ledge. The sound around him was deafening, the product of an immense waterfall that stretched in either direction as far as the eye could see. A thousand feet below, it crashed into a shallow basin and raised a thick white cloud of mist. Birds circled above it in flocks. Every so often they dived into the mist and came up with something in their beaks.

Beautiful, Kitai thought. It looked as if two continents had smashed into each other, one coast considerably higher than the other. No longer in need of the cutlass's help, he connected its two halves and tapped them with his fingertips. A moment later, they contracted into a single piece. Then he took that piece and snapped it to his back, where it stuck magnetically.

"Inventory your remaining supplies," his father said, bringing him back to reality.

Kitai began unloading his gear. As he did so, he described it to Cypher: "Roger. Food rations half available. Flares full. Med-kit half available. Breathing fluid—"

He bit his lip. Was he going to lie to his father again? *Yes*, he thought, though not without a considerable load of guilt.

"Breathing fluid—four vials available," Kitai reported.

"Why are you not showing me the case?" Cypher asked. "Let me see it."

Kitai swallowed. "What?"

"Show it to me now."

"Why?" he asked.

"Cadet, let me see the case."

This is it. There was no hiding the situation any longer.

Kitai held the case up where Cypher could see it. Only two vials were left. He waited for his father's response. And waited.

"I thought that I could make it, sir," he said finally.

No answer. Then Cypher said, "Abort mission. Return to the ship. That is an order."

For a split second, Kitai's mind flashed back to when Senshi put him in the glass box and told him not to come out. That, too, was an order, and she died.

"No, Dad. We, *I* can do it, I can, I don't need that many. I can get across with just two."

"You need a minimum of three inhalers to make it to

the *tail*; you have exhausted your resources," Cypher said, failing to keep the frustration and anger out of his voice.

"I can get across," Kitai insisted. "I can do it with just two, Dad."

His father was adamant. "This mission has reached abort criteria. I take full responsibility. You did your best; you have nothing more to prove. Now return to the ship."

Kitai hung his head in shame. His father was right. There was no way he could make it to the tail on the breathing fluid he had left. He looked out at the waterfall.

Unless . . .

"What was your mistake? Trusting me? Depending on me? Thinking that I could do this?"

There was no hesitation in his father's response. "I am giving you an order . . . to turn around and return to this ship."

I've got 80 percent, he thought to himself. *I could sky it.*

"You wouldn't give any other Ranger that order," he said to the air.

"You are not a Ranger, and I am giving *you* that order," his father snapped.

No, he wasn't a Ranger, but he knew what it took to be one. He had prepared so hard, including being able to use the lifesuit's aerial abilities.

"Come back to the ship, cadet."

But what good would that do? "You said we would both die if I didn't make it to the tail."

"An error in strategy on my part. I take full responsibility. Now, I gave you a direct order."

All his life, he had been in awe of his father. He would never even have considered disobeying a direct order from Cypher. *Until now.*

Kitai felt himself overcome by a wave of emotion. Everything he had always kept bottled up inside, everything he had wanted to say to his father. How it was *so* obvious that he didn't believe in his son. How the mere sight of Kitai made Cypher so ashamed, he stopped coming home.

Everything he felt, he was saying it now.

"What was I supposed to do?" he screamed. "What did you want me to do?! She gave me an order! She said no matter what, don't come out of that box! What was I supposed to do—just come out and die?"

"What do you think, cadet? What do you think you should have done? Because really that's all that matters."

There was a moment's silence before Cypher said again, "What do you think you should have done?"

Kitai walked up to the edge of the falls. He could see the mist, the birds rising from it and diving into it. He could hear the incredible roar of the water far, far below.

Kitai was boiling with fear, anger, and frustration. His reply was unguarded and came out with a rush. "And where were you? She called out for you; she called your name! And you weren't there 'cause you're *never* there! And you think I'm a coward? You're wrong! I'm not a coward! *You're* the coward!

"I'm. Not. A. Coward." Cypher stared at Kitai, at his son. What *was* he supposed to have done? He felt as if he had been hit with a rock—and by his own son. No one had ever said that out loud to him. He had thought it on his own many times, too many to count. But he could never admit it, never confront it, never face up to the truth that he hadn't been there when Senshi needed him most.

Kitai had been a boy, a small, frightened boy. *But what was* my *excuse?* Cypher asked himself. *Where was I when she needed someone to defend her from that Ursa?*

He felt himself falling as if from a great height into a dark, bottomless pit. *Where was* I?

He'd sworn an oath to the colony. An oath to the

Corps. That was why he had been away from home all the time, why he had never given enough of himself to his family.

Because of my oath.

Suddenly, his anger and his pain and his resentment were all spent. There was nothing left inside him but remorse.

Kitai stood above the falls, hyperventilating from the emotion of what his father had said to him and what he had said in return.

Then, before even *he* was sure he was going to do so, he turned, took two steps, and dived off the cliff.

For a single, sublime moment he hung there, arms outstretched, floating on an updraft of air. He had time to think about how peaceful it was, how completely and utterly serene. Then the ground flew up at him, a huge uprush of wind snatching sound away from his ears. His father yelled something, but he couldn't make it out.

At the same time, his lifesuit released fabric on either side from his leg to his outstretched arm, and he wasn't falling anymore. He was gliding, soaring like a bird. They really didn't teach this until Phase 2, but he had studied in advance, and boy, was he thankful that he'd cheated a bit. He glided lower, not into the water at the base of the falls but over it. Making adjustments in the positioning of his arms and legs, he changed direction and followed the flow of the river through the lush landscape below.

His lifesuit, he noticed, had turned black. Free-falling at an insane rate of speed, he slid past rock walls and over ledges, the wind pulling at the skin of his face like a G-force thrust. Then he heard his father yell at him again, and this time he could figure out what Cypher was saying. It was: "Kitai, you've got incoming; dive! Dive!"

For what? he wondered. Then he felt something hit him with bone-jarring force, sending him spinning out of control. As Kitai fought to regain control, he saw a massive birdlike creature—something that resembled a condor—circling around for another pass at him.

Food, Kitai thought. *It thinks I'm* food.

Reluctant to become a meal for the thing, Kitai pulled his arms in to his sides and pressed his legs together. The configuration allowed him to arrow through the air at top speed. But it didn't stop the predator from slamming into him a second time, its razor-sharp talons narrowly missing his face. The air knocked out of him, Kitai lost his discipline and went into a clumsy, head-over-heels free fall. The air rushed by him so quickly that it was hard for him to breathe. He felt himself begin to lose consciousness. Darkness ate at the edges of his vision.

"Kitai!"

Cypher watched from his place in the cockpit as the vicious-looking airborne predator banked in preparation for a third attempt on Kitai's life. He couldn't tell if his son was still conscious. All he could see for sure, through Kitai's camera, was that the monstrous creature was heading straight for his son, its cruelly curved beak wide open.

Irrationally, Cypher tried to get up. But he couldn't, and the pain of his attempt forced a scream from his throat. Through his terror and his agony, he stared at the holographic screen. The creature let out a blood-chilling screech as it attacked. Then it slammed straight into Kitai's camera, filling it with its bulk.

651 AE

Nova Prime

i

Vanessa Raige was running. She controlled her breathing and felt her leg muscles strain to gain speed. All around her, there was carnage as the Ursa carved a fresh scar onto the surface of Nova Prime. Their coming was unexpected, and their three-legged nature caught everyone by surprise. The first ones had been four-legged beasts, and this new breed appeared to be just as deadly.

None of that mattered right now.

Her naviband was vibrating on her wrist as a steady stream of messages and alerts came through.

She ignored them all.

Instead, Vanessa focused every ounce of strength she possessed on going faster, getting to the northwest medical center. Deep in her chest, she sensed that her brother needed her, and that trumped everything else. Hunter was the Prime Commander and also her twin, and either one dictated that she abandon everything to come to his aid.

She prayed she'd get there in time.

Once more the Skrel dropped three dozen Ursa on an unsuspecting populace. Once more the aliens eluded the satellite warning system and managed to deposit their payload without taking serious damage. Once more the people remained clueless as to why this was happening. All that mattered was killing them. Questions could wait.

Hunter's beautiful wife, Jennipher, was due any day

now, the next generation of Raiges to be brought into the world. Vanessa worried that Hunter's psychic alarm was about her and not the Ursa. In the worst of all possible worlds, it would involve both. The hospital was on the lowest level of the cliff, one of the earliest structures dug out after The Arrival and considered one of the safest and most secure facilities in the city. Considering its location and lack of external activity to attract the marauding beasts, she hoped none were in her way. Still, she grasped her cutlass in her right hand, running with it like a relay racer with no one to hand it off to.

Her breath was getting ragged as the meters faded under her boots. She was in sight of the hospital entrance, but reaching it meant jumping over a trail of bodies, trying not to slip on the blood that had yet to soak into the streets. It was a sight she wanted to forget, fighting the instinct to stop and check for survivors. Her heart said to help; her mind said the Ursa never left victims alive.

The screaming made her finally slow down. It was not just a single voice but a chorus of cries, all of them filled with pain or terror, a symphony of agony.

Through it all, she heard one defiant voice.

Hunter.

Emboldened by knowing her twin was still alive, she surged ahead and flicked the stud on the cutlass, turning it into a sword that would cut right through the Ursa. When they'd first arrived just under a century ago, it had taken some genius to figure out how to weaponize the F.E.N.I.X. technology. The cutlass could alter shape in a heartbeat, becoming the most versatile killing tool ever created. Powered by quantum-trapping energies, it reconfigured thousands of filaments into whatever the programming called for, and the C-10 model was able to become flat, a blade, or a hook. She favored the blade and practiced with it endlessly.

Now she was ready to slice through any creature that might stand between her and her family. If Hunter was in the hospital, Vanessa figured he was hurt. That or Jennipher had chosen a lousy time to give birth.

Slowing to assess the situation, she took in the doors torn from their hinges and the shredded smart fabric that provided power and shade. Bodies continued to litter the area, a grisly trail that pointed in the direction in which she needed to go.

As she neared it, Vanessa could start making out her brother's words. He was alternating between shouting orders and bellowing at the Ursa. An Ursa in the hospital was an absurd notion until she considered that the sightless beasts might be drawn by all that blood. She didn't really understand what made them work, and after the first attack the Savant's people had had little to go on but speculation. At the moment, she could recall none of the details, and frankly, they didn't matter. If she encountered the creature, she would stab and slash at it until the thing fell and threatened no one ever again.

Before she could enter the building, she heard additional footfalls and spared a look over her shoulder. To her surprise, eight or ten Rangers were falling into place behind her.

"Orders?" the nearest shouted.

"One stays out here to check the bodies," she said, barely slowing. "The rest of you, cutlasses out. Protect the people!"

The Rangers let out a piercing battle cry, a unifying sound that told the world they were here. They would die performing their job, which was to protect the rest of the populace. So far she knew that nearly one-third of the Ursa had been taken down, all thanks to the cutlass.

Vanessa charged through the entrance and silently gestured for two to split off to the left and two others to go down the right corridor. The sounds indicated that the real action was directly before her, and, careless of all else, she headed for the noise. Hunter could be heard, and that was her homing beacon.

Deeper into the cliff she ran, barely registering the lack of doctors, nurses, or patients. The evacuation had been fairly complete, and a tiny portion of her mind acknowledged the lack of corpses.

Finally, she jogged to her left at a juncture, the sound drawing her closer. But as she made the turn, she skidded to a stop. Directly before her was the Ursa, its gray hide and three-legged form obscured with drying blood and viscera.

The Ursa's stink assaulted her senses, but she blinked it away, trying to see past it. As it shifted to lunge forward, she could see Hunter, a bloody mess, trying to wave the cutlass with one arm. The other arm was missing.

"Hunter!" she called, trying to alert her brother and distract the Ursa in one word.

The beast was not dissuaded, making its leap and landing atop her brother, who cried out on impact. There was one leg pinning him to the ground; the other foreleg was raised to deliver a killing blow. The rear limb allowed it to balance with an odd grace.

Vanessa charged forward, her cutlass rearing back, and then it swung around, slicing the air before it met the rear leg joint. The blade bit deeply through the hide, and a black liquid—its blood, she hoped—seeped out. All the human sounds were drowned out by the wounded yell coming from the creature. The unearthly sound made her wince and squeeze her eyes shut. It whirled about, struggling with its balance, and opened its sharp-toothed maw wide.

The Ranger stood her ground, keeping her mind focused on the beast while her heart switched signals. She knew the Ursa had mortally wounded Hunter and she could feel his suffering, but she had to ignore it. Instead, she had to kill the Ursa, the only way she could reach Hunter and try to save him.

Vanessa suspected an injured Ursa was worse than a healthy one, and so she wanted to make this kill a quick one. The width of the corridor meant the Rangers behind her could not come to her aid; instead they watched, a silent Greek chorus.

The Ursa righted itself, bellowing all the way, hurting her ears. As it positioned itself, she saw Hunter sprawled in his own blood. A red tide of anger swept over her, and she gripped the cutlass with both hands, pulling it back. Then she charged and lunged with the cutlass. For its part, the Ursa roared and tried to swat her with its right foreleg. Instead, it faltered and dipped low, letting her thrust go right behind its head, cutting deep into the body. She felt it easing through skin and veins into bone.

Bodily fluids gushed from the wound, and the Ursa dropped dead before Vanessa.

The Rangers behind her let out a singular whoop and then began moving toward her. Vanessa, though, leaped over her kill and dropped to her knees before Hunter's body.

She was too late. Her brother had stopped breathing some time before, and his eyes were fixed; his expression was one of unimaginable pain.

Hot tears fell from her face, rolling down her cheeks and dripping onto his body, merging with the blood that covered the Ranger emblem. Before she could decide what to do next, she caught a fresh sound. It was weak, more a whimper than anything else, and was detectable only because all the other screaming finally had ceased. She held up a hand, putting her fellow Rangers on hold as she concentrated. It came from beyond her brother's body, in one of the patient rooms: someone who had not been evacuated.

Once again, her body told her what she feared to know.

Hunter was here for Jennipher.

She rushed forward and walked into the first room on the left to find a mess. Jennipher, still linked to various monitors, was on the floor, covered in blood and other fluids. She arched her back as a contraction convulsed her body.

She was alive!

Labor meant the baby was also still alive and ready to enter the world. Part of Vanessa wished the baby would stay in the womb, where it would be safe and warm, protected and loved.

The baby, though, had other ideas and was coming. As Vanessa moved toward the feet, she could see the baby's shape, well into the birth canal.

"Jennipher, it's Vanessa! Talk to me!"

Jennipher didn't respond. At best, she was unconscious. At worst, the Ursa had gotten to her and she was dying.

A Ranger's field training did not include anything about delivering babies, and so Vanessa had to go with whatever she had learned from her mother, Paige. Looking about frantically, she spotted some blankets and what looked like the remains of a towel. They would have to do.

"Hey, you!" she shouted at the first Ranger looming awkwardly in the doorway. "Go find me clean blankets or cloths or something sterile."

At the man behind him she shouted, "And you, go find a doctor or a nurse or both. Now!"

She turned her attention to Jennipher, who was having another contraction already. They were coming fast, which meant the birth, already in progress, could not be delayed. Carefully, she spread the blanket under Jennipher's head, then took the cleanest towel to try to rub her hands clean of blood and gore.

"Push, Jennipher," she called. There was no response. Without the mother intentionally pushing, the birth was going to be more complicated.

"Come on, baby; come to your aunt Vanessa," she cooed, regardless of how silly she sounded to herself. "Keep pushing, Jennipher. If you can hear me at all, keep pushing and let's get your son into the world."

There has to be a doctor nearby. Where is he?

A shrill sound alerted her to a new problem. She glanced over her shoulder, and her eyes went wide as she saw the mother's respiration rate and blood pressure dropping with every beep. Jennipher was dying.

A secondary system monitoring the baby also had shifted from green to red, indicating that the baby was now in distress.

Without proper medical training she had no choice but to try to save the baby any way possible. Her head swiveled around the small, blood-spattered room to try to see where there might be tools. Panic was welling up within her as the enormity of the situation was becoming evident. Hunter dead. Jennipher dead. The Ursa dead. She'd be damned if the baby joined the list.

Just then, a hand reached over her shoulder and gave her a blade. She looked up and saw one of the remaining Rangers, a woman she didn't know. Vanessa nodded and took a deep breath.

"There's a holographic display over the bed. Turn it on," she commanded.

The other Ranger complied, and then Vanessa called out, "Display cesarian section protocols." Obediently, the hologram appeared over her sister-in-law's body and step by step showed Vanessa where to cut and how to deliver the baby. The first Ranger returned with a meter's worth of towels and blankets. The female Ranger grabbed a few and went to work, assisting Vanessa.

No one said a word, and so the only sounds were from the displays and the gentle, slightly accented voice of the computer.

With every centimeter, Vanessa kept waiting for a doctor or nurse to walk in and take over. Instead, she had to keep raising her eyes to follow the holographic tutorial. This was no way to bring new life into the world, but she continued as cautiously as she could. It felt horribly disrespectful to be slicing into her sister-in-law and then reaching into the body, but really, what choice did she have? Her nephew needed to be saved, and she'd be damned if she'd fail again.

There! The baby could be safely lifted upward, the

umbilical cord trailing back into the womb. The tiny figure was covered in white and blue and red stuff she couldn't name, but it had yet to cry. Hell, if it were her, she'd be wailing the moment she felt the cool air.

A fresh pair of shears was placed in her hand, and she cut the cord and then wrapped the baby tight. Peering into the tiny face, Vanessa willed it to breathe, to cry, to show some sign of life. One eye opened, unfocused, and then the other. The mouth parted, and first there was a gasp of air and then a whimper. The whimper repeated and turned into the cry she expected.

Fresh tears obscured her vision, and the other Ranger carefully took the baby from her and brought it to the nearby diagnostic monitor.

The baby was born: an orphan in a world still at war.

ii

General Gustav Hawkins was looking forward to retirement. He had done his service to the Rangers and was ready to go fishing with his grandchildren. He last saw action over a decade before, earning him a promotion and the post of overseeing the Rangers in the twin city. He was capable and maintained readiness, taking pride in exceeding his recruitment numbers every year. When he woke up that morning, he found himself dreading putting on his uniform and traveling from New Earth City across the desert to Nova Prime City.

That morning, for the first time in memory, Nova Prime was absent leadership.

The minute Hawkins heard PC Hunter Raige was killed, he knew that the job was his if he wanted it, and deep down he knew he *didn't* want it. If offered, he'd have little choice but to accept so he strode into the great hall for the emergency session with one mission in mind: Find someone else to take the post.

What he didn't anticipate was the total vacuum that

awaited him, with all three world leaders now dead. Instead of meeting with Primus Ione Kincaid and Savant Sinead O'Brien, he was seated opposite the Primus's second in command, Crucible Maria Pryor, and the Savant's number two, Tribune Suraj Gurang. They looked as bewildered and lost as he felt and clearly were not prepared for the meeting. He couldn't blame them; they were younger and less experienced and were still mourning their superiors.

The Crucible opened the meeting with a prayer and a short memorial to the Primus, then took her seat and gazed at the tabletop. Hawkins at least had had the foresight to have his own number two prepare a rough agenda.

Gurang, thirtyish, with dark hair and brooding eyes, had been working as the Savant's Tribune for two years, and Hawkins recalled seeing his name on numerous reports. He had been a physicist, working on improvements to the cutlass, and so he showed sympathy for the Rangers' needs. That was a good thing.

Crucible Pryor, though, was also nearing retirement and was clearly there to serve the Primus, not succeed her.

With Hunter dead, that left Vanessa, but she had been a Ranger for just eight years. Was that enough to elevate her to such a role? He barely knew the woman, having met her only at a handful of functions. Still, she had a reputation, including that of killing the Ursa that had murdered her brother and then delivering her nephew. Pretty gutsy in Hawkins's estimation, but that was during a crisis. What about during peacetime? Of course, the lack of leadership was a different sort of crisis, so maybe this was her time after all.

"Nature abhors a vacuum," Gurang said, causing Hawkins to inwardly wince at the reminder, "and our own committee is reviewing suitable candidates to replace our Savant."

"No obvious candidates? She was running that place

for nearly thirty years, so somebody had to pop up," Hawkins said.

Gurang stared at the tabletop. "We didn't anticipate needing to replace her so quickly."

Hawkins swiveled about, facing the Crucible. "And what about your team? After Primus Bernardo made it to 101, Kincaid decided to go for the shortest record?"

Pryor didn't meet his gaze and quietly answered, "She was focused on fighting Ressler's Disease and as such did not like to dwell on life after her passing."

"So she just left you high and dry?"

Pryor stiffened at Hawkins's casual approach toward the holy order. She refused to look his way and was acting a little too high and mighty for his taste.

"How do you guys pick your successor?" Hawkins continued.

"We . . . have a holy congress and weigh each candidate's value. Many are qualified, but few choose to serve in such an august position. This is not something done in a hurry."

"Well"—he paused and looked at Gurang—"if you don't pick someone soon, running this world will fall to us. I can't speak for the Citadel or the Mirador, but I know the Rangers could benefit from someone better equipped to lead."

"And what of the people, General? What do they need?"

"A triumvirate to rally around, a trio of leaders they can place their confidence in. They need faces to see on the screens and on the streets. We need to rebuild not just structurally but also to rebuild faith and trust. If you think about it, we failed. All of us. The Savant's satellites were easily circumvented—again—and the Primus was so busy hiding her illness, she wasn't there when we needed her guidance. The Rangers couldn't take the Ursa down fast enough, weren't anticipating a three-legged version. We let the people down, and now we have to build that back up, put a fresh bandage over the wounds left behind."

"Most important, it needs to be done quickly," Gurang added. "The media has already concluded that the Savant's passing leaves us adrift. The people are mourning and worn; they need something to rally behind, and that's this government."

"Well said," Hawkins began. "You want the job?"

"Heavens, no. I have other things I prefer to devote my time to," he said defensively.

"So we're back at the beginning. We need leaders in all three divisions and need them fast," Pryor said.

"May I make a suggestion?" Hawkins rose and tapped a control on the panel before his seat. Appearing before the Crucible and the Tribune were images of Vanessa Raige along with her duty jacket. Both scanned the data as the General paced around the room, warming up to his topic.

"We need leadership sooner than we're comfortable with. What about an interim leader?"

The Crucible nodded in agreement, her eyes still reviewing the findings. "Yes, we might be able to name a pro tem Primus. It's never been done, but the guidelines do not prohibit it."

"You said 'leader.' *Singular*," Gurang said.

"Good catch," Hawkins said. "Yes, I am proposing something radical. As you will see in her profile, Ranger Raige is deeply religious and respectful of the Citadel. She also has amazing science scores. She understands all three branches of government and has proved herself in the field. The best thing about her is her name."

"Raige."

"Yes, Crucible. She's a Raige, one of a long line that has become a part of the planet's lifeblood. Who better to rally around than a Raige in our hour of need? Make her interim everything for a year and let us rebuild and reorganize."

"No," the woman said. "She is not trained in our ways."

"But you are," Hawkins said. "Guide her. Let Vanessa bring her skills to your operation, and that gives you time to select someone appropriate to continue Primus Kincaid's work."

"Six months," Gurang said. "We'll have someone picked long before that, but it gives us time to prepare and make this a smooth transition. It gives Raige a chance to get all three branches back in working order."

"I can live with that; can you?" He stared intently at the Crucible, who wrinkled her brow in concentration.

"If I say no, you still outvote me two to one. But for the sake of the people, I will make it unanimous. There can be no clue we disagreed. Now is not the time for dissension."

iii

"Ah, Commander Raige. Do you know Crucible Pryor or Tribune Gurang?"

Vanessa shook her head, meeting their eyes briefly, and then scanned the room, wondering where everyone else might be. She could have been called in for a specific mission, but she couldn't imagine what area of expertise she alone possessed. Finally, she mentally gave in and just went with the flow.

"Tell me, my dear, why did you not become an augur?" Pryor asked.

"I believe, Crucible, but felt my path was with the Rangers."

"The family business, as it were," Hawkins added.

"I had ancestors in the augury," she admitted. That earned her an approving smile from Pryor.

"It's the family we're here to speak with you about," Hawkins continued. "The people hold the Raiges in high esteem. You might say they are the first family of Nova Prime."

"You might say that, but we don't," Vanessa said defensively. "There are many other families that have long, rich histories. Like the Kincaids."

"But none with your history," Gurang interrupted.

"Granted. How can the family help?"

"My dear, we're facing terrible times. You know that there was no clear line of succession for the Rangers. It appears all three divisions of the planetary government are in disarray. It's certainly not a legacy our departed would have imagined leaving, but it is the truth. We need to quickly show the people the government still functions."

Raige turned as Hawkins continued where Gurang had left off. "We need to do this quickly and focus on the reconstruction, not the leadership. To do that, we need to buy time for all three divisions to reorganize and rebuild. To accomplish this, we need a singular face and voice to lead the people. We're offering you the chance to help your people. Lead us, lead all three divisions, for a period of six months."

Vanessa was stunned. She expected assignments, commendations, maybe a promotion. But being put in charge of the planet? Her best friend and fellow Ranger, O'Shea, would flip.

"General, you know I have just accepted my nephew, the PC's son, into my house. He has to be my priority," she began.

"He will benefit from a stable home and a stable planet," Pryor said. "Right now, we have a world in need of a symbol of unity. That, my dear, means we need a Raige. You."

Her mind was whirling. Questions kept forming, but so were ideas. Gaps she had noticed that needed sorting, improved communications between divisions. Suddenly, possibilities were outnumbering objections. But a dark memory lingered. There hadn't been a singular leader of the people in centuries, and the last time that had happened, it hadn't ended well.

Vanessa turned away from the trio of expectant faces and tried to sort her thoughts. She noted that the first sun was setting, painting the horizon in red and gold. She studied the window, and for a moment she thought she saw Hunter's face staring back at her from the reflection. He was smiling, flashing her a thumbs-up the way he did as a kid before she did something monumentally stupid. It made her smile. It also made her heart ache.

He wanted her to take it. To do the family proud.

"I can't say yes before I speak with Trent. You have to give me that."

"Agreed," Hawkins said. "You have until tomorrow. We need you. Yes, so does your baby, but you're about to inherit more on-call babysitters than you can count."

Vanessa's husband, Trent, was playing with Lorenzo, who was gurgling high over his head. He was young, but it was clear he'd have eyes like his father, Hunter. Vanessa watched them contentedly playing and was happy they could provide the infant a safe haven.

"Hey," she said, entering the room. He angled the baby toward her, using his hand to make Lorenzo "wave" at his mother.

She walked over, leaned down, kissed Trent on the forehead, and took Lorenzo into her arms. If she took the post, moments like this would grow fewer and fewer just as she was getting used to thinking of the baby as her son.

"Trouble?" He followed her into the baby's nursery, which just a week ago was a workout room. There remained a faint aroma of sweat that Trent needed to address but first things first. She was changing Lorenzo's diaper, powdering his skin and cooing over him. Finished, she swaddled him in a bright red, blue, and yellow blanket.

"Not exactly," she said, accepting the bottle Trent offered her. "Comm chatter appears surprisingly quiet."

"Admit it, you like when things are slightly off the rails," he said. "But there's something going on, otherwise you wouldn't have been called in."

"Yeah, there was a meeting," she said, uncertain how to broach the topic. She mentally reviewed a speech the entire way home, but now, with Trent and Lorenzo in the same room, it wasn't coming easily.

"We've built a pretty good life, haven't we?"

"Sure."

"We have friends, we go out, we do things," she said as she adjusted the bottle in her grip. Then she settled into a chair and fed Lorenzo. It felt wonderful. Peaceful and calm.

"Are you worried the baby will change all that?"

"Oh, he will. We won't go out as often, our social circle will change, especially when he begins classes. But I was ready to accept the responsibility."

"What are you getting at? You're being vague and not telling me about the meeting. Was it bad?"

"No, not bad at all. Kind of thrilling, actually. But it would mean changes. Lots of them."

Trent stepped closer, brow knitting in concern.

"Are you being reassigned?"

"I have an offer," she began.

"One of the new colonies?"

"No, here in the city," she said as her free hand stroked the baby's cheek. Lorenzo sucked away, oblivious to the growing tension in the room.

"Come on already, tell me what's going on."

"You know the family history. You know how the Raiges are forever intertwined with the Rangers. Well, that's being called into play."

"PC? You're kidding. Shouldn't Hawkins have the job?"

"More."

"What more? There's nothing more than the Prime Commander," Trent said.

"They want me to run the government and fix the planet. I'd oversee not only the Rangers but the Citadel and Mirador."

"That's crazy," he said. "A one-person PC, Savant, and Primus? That's unheard of."

"It's happened before, but it didn't turn out so well," she said, and reminded him of the disastrous man who assumed all three roles in 195 and took the overbearing title of Imperator.

"Really? I'd forgotten all about that."

"Well, they hadn't and want me to do the same, only better."

"But you're so young," he said. "Are you experienced enough to know how to fix the government?"

"They think I am," she said, placing the now-empty bottle atop the changing table. "It's an amazing offer."

"Did you accept?"

"I told them we had to talk so here we are, talking." She reached out and grasped his hand.

"A week ago we had one kind of life, and this last week we began something new and wonderful. Now I'm being asked to give it up and take on a monster responsibility. But I like our life. I love spending time with Lorenzo. That'd all change."

"For how long?" he asked.

"Six months, time enough for everybody to figure out who should really be running the planet."

"So, you'd just be a caretaker?"

"More than that, Trent. There are things that need fixing. There's rebuilding to do. People who died that need replacing, beyond our leaders. The list could be endless."

"And you have six months."

"Yeah."

"Sounds like you want to do this," he said, gripping her hands tightly within his.

"I love what we've built. I love our little family. But I am a Raige and we're built to protect all of Nova Prime. The people are our family, too, and they're hurting."

"I know. I know all about the Raiges and the way you're trained. Protecting runs in your family."

"But you're not happy."

"I worry about you. Emotionally, you've been through so much in such a short period of time. Taking this on will be crushing and you rarely rely on others, preferring to do things yourself. Looking after the planet is a huge responsibility, and I want my wife back when the six months are over. Will you be the same?"

She leaned over and kissed him.

"As long as I can come home to you and Lorenzo every night, I'll be just fine."

Carefully placing the baby between them, the couple embraced and she soaked it in. After all, she began wondering, just how many nights over the next six months would she actually have the luxury of coming home, finding either one still awake?

It was, though, just six months. And Hunter already told her to do it. He was speaking for the ancestors. She would do the job, without that damned title, and protect not only her family but all the families on Nova Prime.

It was in her blood.

1000 AE

Nova Prime

i

Faia Raige had been preparing dinner for herself, since the men in her life were away together, when she heard a knock at the door. For a moment, she wondered if she had extended an invitation to someone and forgotten. That would be unlike her. She was usually good at remembering such things.

Hearing the knock again, she wiped her hands with a cloth and went to answer the door. When she opened it, she saw two men she had never met before. There was something about them. They looked . . . official.

"Mrs. Raige?" the taller of them said.

"Yes. Can I help you?" Faia asked.

Then they told her what had happened. For a moment, they were just words. Then they sank in, and she began to scream. The men looked away. What could they do? They had torn her life open and ripped its heart out. What was there to do after that?

Years earlier, Faia had lost her daughter, Senshi. That was the most horrible thing she could ever have imagined, the most horrible pain she could ever have borne. But this . . .

This.

ii

Kitai felt a soft pecking at his cheek. *What . . . ?* He brushed it away with his hand, but it resumed a moment later. Finally, he opened his eyes to see where the pecking was coming from and found himself staring into the eyes of a tiny, newborn baby bird, close enough to nuzzle at him with its beak. Instinctively, Kitai jumped back and realized he was covered in something clear and viscous. He sucked in a breath and began wiping the stuff off his face. Only then did he pay attention to the patchwork of light and shadow around him and the intertwined branches picking shadows from the sunlight.

Where am I? he wondered.

Propping himself up, Kitai looked around. He was surrounded by eggs: not the kind he had known on Nova Prime but huge ones, each of them bigger than the baby bird. And they had all begun to crack.

As he watched, the birds inside them—dark, wet things—emerged from the eggs and spread their slick wings as if they would take flight. *A nest*, he realized. *I'm in a giant nest.* Kitai looked down. He could see through the bottom of the nest, where there were gaps in the branches. *If I'm in a nest*, he thought, *I must be in a tree.* He identified the biggest branch in the interwoven structure and traced it back to an enormous trunk. And there, sitting on the branch right next to the trunk, was a massive bird of prey, not unlike a condor except it was more than two meters tall if it was a centimeter. As Kitai looked on, his heart pounding, the bird opened its beak and spread its wings. They spanned a good five meters. Of course, he had seen that kind of wingspan before . . .

Just before the bird plucked him out of the sky.

It seemed to be standing guard at the base of the branch. Eyeing him. As what? Food for its newborn?

Kitai had no intention of serving that purpose. He looked around for his backpack and found it on the other side of the nest. It was torn in the corner, but his cutlass was still clipped to it. That was good. With the cutlass, he had a chance against the bird. He started moving toward the weapon slowly so as not to disturb the bird. All around him, its young continued to break free of their eggs. Finally, Kitai reached his gear.

But as he reached for it, he looked down through the gaps in the nest and saw a dark shape moving up the trunk of the tree. He couldn't tell what it was, but it looked enormous, even bigger than the adult bird. One of the newborn creatures moved toward Kitai. He extended his foot and pushed it away. It fell on its side so clumsily that it was funny.

But Kitai wasn't inclined to laugh. Not when the dark shape was still moving up the trunk below him. And *definitely* not when he saw a second shape drop onto his branch from above.

With trembling hands, he unclipped the cutlass from his pack. Then he tapped in a combination on its handle. Instantly the weapon extended to its full two-meter length, with one end featuring a sharp spear point and the other a flat blade. None too soon, either, because the limb on which the nest rested began to shake violently.

Suddenly, the adult bird went at the invader that had attacked from below. Kitai could see the intruder better now. Its fur was a burned gold. The body someplace between leopard and lion. It snarled and swiped at the bird, which spread its wings and took itself out of the leopard's range. But not *too* far. It still had a nest full of young to protect. As Kitai watched, it flew at the leopard and pecked at it with its razor-sharp beak.

This is my chance, he thought.

While the creatures were busy, he could slip out of the nest and make his way down through the branches of the tree. With luck, neither of them would notice his departure until it was too late to retrieve him. Kitai crawled to the edge of the nest, but before he could climb over it, he felt the branch shudder. Casting a glance over his shoulder, he saw another leopard appear on the end of the branch. Still others were scaling the trunk below him.

The cadet looked back at the newborns in the corner of the nest. They squawked at him. Kitai didn't know why, but he felt an obligation to defend them.

It was crazy. He had his own skin to look after, and his father's life depended on him, too. But he couldn't just leave the newborn birds to the mercy of the leopards. Moving back into the center of the nest, he stood in front of the younglings, his cutlass at the ready.

Suddenly a huge leopard paw erupted from between the branches of the nest, narrowly missing Kitai. It was the first of many. As Kitai watched, paws came up from the bottom of the nest here, there, and everywhere. One of them struck a newborn bird. The branches of the nest began to crack and break apart under the leopards' assault. Kitai used his spear point to stab at one of them. The leopard screamed as the weapon pierced its hide.

Then an entire section of the nest broke off from the main structure. The leopard clinging to it fell with it to the ground far below. Another section broke off. And another. Soon all that was left of the nest was the bowl-like shape in the center of it. Before Kitai could react, one of the leopards crawled over the edge and sank its claws into a newborn bird. The cadet stabbed the leopard with his cutlass and watched it retreat back over the edge of the nest.

But there were others climbing in from every direction. Kitai spun his cutlass, slicing one of the leopards' paws.

"Leave them alone!" he cried out.

Suddenly he wasn't alone in his efforts to defend the nest. The adult bird, which had engaged the first leopard creature, rose into the air with the leopard's hind leg in its beak. Then it dropped the leopard, which fell end over end until it hit the ground with a heavy thud.

Free now, the bird swooped in and snatched another leopard from behind. It dragged the leopard out of the nest and tossed it into the air, where it became another victim of the planet's gravity.

Meanwhile, one of the other leopard creatures reached a newborn bird. As it began mauling it, Kitai rushed forward and skewered the leopard's flank. The leopard writhed in pain and, still clutching the baby, plummeted over the side of the nest.

Kitai and the adult bird continued to fight off the leopards. By the time the last of the beasts was thrown to the ground, he was breathing hard and was drenched with sweat. He looked around and saw that none of the newborns remained in the nest. Their shells lay shattered and empty.

All for nothing? Kitai asked himself.

With a screech, the massive bird dived from the nest, no doubt in search of its young. *I've got to leave*, Kitai thought. But he stood there for a moment, the cutlass in his hand, wishing he could have saved at least *one* of the baby birds. Finally, he retracted the ends of the cutlass and snapped it back onto his pack. Then he donned the pack and started climbing down from the tree. It wasn't all that hard. There were plenty of branches and vines to hang on to. Finally, he landed on the ground.

That was when Kitai saw the bird through the foliage. She was standing amid the carcasses of her babies. As he looked on, she raised her head and screamed. He could hear pain in that sound. The pain of loss. It almost sounded human as it ripped through the forest.

Again the bird bowed her head and touched it to the lifeless newborns. Then she screamed again, this time even longer. Kitai recognized that sound, that sense of loss. He had felt it himself, after all. Everyone in his family had felt it. He watched a little longer. Then he left the bird behind in its misery, backed up into the jungle, and slipped away.

He hadn't gone far, however, before he realized that something was wrong. Abruptly, he checked his wrist and felt a fresh wave of panic when he saw the naviband was missing. It must have broken free when the leopard creature slashed at him. This was a new complication he really did not need.

"Come on, no!" Kitai cried out in frustration. The woods echoed his words back at him.

It was hard enough to traverse a treacherous landscape with all kinds of obstacles, both living and otherwise. But to do so without a working naviband . . . ? Kitai looked around. He was all alone, cut off from his father for good, and he had no idea how long he had until the sun went down.

Panicked, he ran through the dense jungle ahead of him, crashing through branches, trying to gain altitude to catch the sun before it vanished. He ran so fast, so desperately, that he was out in the open on a high plateau before he knew it. Skidding to a halt, Kitai saw that he was in the midst of ancient ruins. *A dam*, he thought. He had never seen one before, though he had read about them.

Suddenly, a shadow passed over him. He looked up and saw the condorlike bird in the sky, clipping the tops of trees, flying recklessly, almost angrily. It was a scary sight. Was it trying to hurt itself because it had allowed its young to be killed? Was it feeling guilt? Sadness?

It's a bird, Kitai reminded himself. But it wasn't like the birds he had known all his life on Nova Prime. It had evolved in the time since humankind had left the planet. As he thought that, the bird rocketed straight up toward the sun. *Angry. Definitely angry.*

But Kitai had more to worry about than the condor creature. He could see his breath starting to freeze in the air. The temperature was dropping rapidly. The bird might have the luxury to run wild, to let her emotions get the best of her. *But I don't. Not if I'm going to live through the night.*

Kitai steadied himself, took control. He wasn't going to panic, wasn't going to let his emotions get in the way. He was going to keep a cool head no matter what. He was tired. He was lost. But it was going to be all right. Figuring the bird would know where to find a warm spot, he took off after her.

It wasn't easy keeping up with something that could fly, but he did his best. Sprinting through the jungle, he moved toward what he hoped was a geothermal zone or at least some kind of shelter. All the while, the sun dropped through the sky like a stone.

iii

Cypher, trapped in the ship's cockpit, felt a wave of panic wash over his battered body as the connection with the naviband was terminated abruptly. Something had happened to the device or, worse, to his son. Furiously his fingers tapped controls, checked probe after probe. Images blasted at him—of mountains, of jungles, of beaches—but Kitai was nowhere to be seen.

He has to be somewhere, Cypher thought. "Come on," he said out loud, his voice cracking with the strain. "Where are you?" He scanned a stretch of plains covered with herds of evolved bison, clefts full of twisted foliage, a rushing river that churned through a pine forest. But try as he might, he couldn't come up with a sign of his son.

Please, he thought, *be alive. Be alive . . .*

As Kitai ran through the jungle, the plants on either side of him began to close up on themselves. The world was frosting over again. Kitai looked left and right for shelter but didn't see a single possibility. Then he caught a glimpse of a small hoglike creature running just in front of him. As far as he could tell, the hoglike thing didn't seem worried or lost. It seemed to know exactly where it was going.

Bereft of any other viable options, he decided to follow it. It wasn't easy. He had to use all his quickness and agility, scramble under bushes and leap over piles of rocks, swing around tree trunks and crash his way through branches heavy with leaves. Finally, Kitai saw the creature burrow into a hole in the ground. A moment later, three smaller specimens of the same species followed it.

The ice was like a tide, crackling its way across the landscape in his direction. In a matter of seconds, it would be on top of him. Kitai didn't hesitate. He tried to dive into the creatures' hole. Unfortunately, he was a lot bigger than they were. As the frost crept over him, he picked up a flat stone and used it to start digging to make the hole bigger. His fingers growing colder by the moment, he dug for all he was worth. Finally, the hole was big enough. Just in time, Kitai slid his body into it.

He thought he would find a hollow where he could curl up with the hog creatures. Instead, he started sliding along something slick and wet. Not just a little, either. He must have slid ten meters before he came to something soft and grassy. Not that Kitai could see down there. He was just going by the way it felt.

Need light, he thought, and hit an area on his lifesuit. Instantly a section of the suit lit up, dispelling the darkness, and he saw that the hog hole was actually a cave with smooth stone walls. Kitai moved between them. The light from his suit illuminated the stone surfaces, revealing a collection of beautifully colored cave paintings. One of them showed herds of bison. Another showed flocks of birds. Still another showed a primitive hunt.

Kitai wondered how old the paintings were. Many thousands of years, no doubt. A particular painting caught his attention. It showed a man, sleeping apparently, surrounded by different animals.

Despite the crudeness of the technique, there was a beauty and a majesty to the place. As he caught his breath, he admired everything around him, appreciated it for what it was: a window into the way the first men looked at their world. Down below the cave, which was really just a slanted pocket in the earth, a tiny rivulet of lava could be seen moving in the darkness. Kitai nodded to himself. *That's where the warmth is coming from.*

Suddenly, he heard a noise, a scratching sound. Following it to its source, he saw a snake emerge from a seam in the cave wall. As he watched, it spread the skin on either side of its body into what looked like wings. Then it rose up and floated through the cave.

Kitai shrank from it, pressing himself as far back into the stone wall as he could. But the snake didn't seem to take an interest in him. Instead it landed on a rodent that was scurrying in the darkness. With blinding speed, the snake coiled itself around the rodent and crushed the life out of it. Then it flew away with the limp little carcass.

Kitai moved closer to the warmth of the lava thread. His cutlass at the ready, he found a good spot and hunkered down. Finally, he could rest his body. But it wasn't so easy to rest his mind. He had to remain watchful there, like anywhere else on Earth. It became harder when the light from his lifesuit dimmed and went out.

Delirious, Cypher continued to search his probe cameras for a glimpse of Kitai. But as many probes as he checked, over and over again, he didn't see a thing. Not even a hint that Kitai was still alive. Then Cypher saw him—or thought he did. But no. It was just that he wanted to see Kitai so badly, he convinced himself for a second that he had.

I've lost him, Cypher thought. *Lost him.* And he cracked. The weight of it, everything he had been through—everything he had put his son through—was too much for him. He had sacrificed both of his children on the Raige altar of pride and service.

He fought the collapse and turned back to the search for his boy. "Come on," he whispered fervently, "come on! Where are you?"

It was no use.

Reluctantly, his fist shaking, he hit the stud that activated the cockpit recorder. "General Cypher Raige," he groaned. "The mission with Cadet Kitai Raige was a failure. I—"

He tried to go on, but he couldn't. With a sigh, he looked down at his tortured legs, at the blood running down them and collecting on the deck. When he looked up again, his tone was different. Softer. More human. "This is a message for my wife.

"Faia, I have lost our son."

She would find that shocking, no doubt. How could the general not know what to do?

But Cypher didn't feel like the general anymore. He felt helpless, unable to help his son or even himself. His eyes, the eyes of a father, began to fill with tears.

Kitai didn't know when light began to filter into the cave. After another sleepless night, time blurs into one endless mess. He realized that he could see without the help of his suit. His cutlass sat on the ground beside him along with the rest of his gear. Only one vial of breathing fluid remained to him.

Kitai looked at the cave paintings and felt a spurt of inspiration. With the help of a rock, he drew a picture of his own—a huge map that covered an entire wall— and traced his journey step by step since he had left his father in the ship. When details became fuzzy, Kitai found himself hearing his father's voice in his head, guiding him as he labeled every location: *Dad. Baboons. River. Waterfalls. Nest. I am here, I think.* And finally, *Tail somewhere here* in a huge open area on the map.

As Kitai worked, he developed a plan.

He didn't stop until he saw the hog family start to leave the cave. He quickly gathered his things and followed them out into the sunlight. Once he emerged from the hole, the mother pig looked back at him as if to say "You're welcome."

He was still marveling at the creature's intelligence when a huge shadow fell over him. Shading his eyes and looking up, Kitai saw the mother condor creature circling overhead.

Why? Is it hungry? More than likely it was. He got a better grip on his cutlass and began walking south. As Kitai made his way through the jungle, he felt hollowed out. He hadn't slept well in the cave. After a while, he glanced up again and saw that the condor creature was still pacing him on the other side of some trees.

"Leave me alone!" he cried out.

But it didn't.

Finally, no longer content just to fly beside Kitai, it landed on a branch above him. Looking up, he could see it sitting there. There was no question in his mind that it was watching him. But the more he looked at it, the more he thought it looked listless rather than hungry. It seemed to him that it was still mourning its young. Still, it was a dangerous creature, and Kitai wanted to escape from it. But he couldn't. He was too spent. He lumbered along as best he could, keeping an eye on the bird all the while.

He was directly below the condor creature when the ground began to tremble. Kitai looked around, confused. What was going on? Moment by moment the sound grew louder, like boulders rolling down a hill, and the ground shook even more violently. Kitai's suit turned black and developed little bumps in its texture.

Suddenly a herd of six-foot-tall creatures burst from the foliage. They looked to Kitai like an evolved variety of okapi. He flung himself out of the way of the first creature but was instantly caught up in the stampede. One hit him as it came on and knocked him to his left; then another hit him and sent him to the ground.

Powerful hooves trampled the turf all around him, narrowly missing him.

The sound of the herd was deafening as Kitai struggled to his feet. But there was good news—he had an open lane up ahead, a lane free of the creatures. If he kept to it, he might be all right. Then he was hit again, a glancing blow. Unable to stop himself, he fell among the trampling hooves a second time. *That's it*, he thought. *I'm done.*

Suddenly, Kitai felt something grab him and jerk him into the air. Looking down, he realized he was rising above the okapi—and rising even more, the herd falling farther and farther below him. The okapi charged through the field, unrelenting. From this height, Kitai could see how green the landscape was. He could see how thoroughly the herd was trampling it.

But not me, he thought. *It's not trampling me.* He was safe. *Somehow.*

Kitai caught a glimpse of something metallic glinting in the distance, something human-made sticking out of the natural landscape. It made him wonder what it was for a second.

Then he fell toward the ground.

It rushed up at him faster than he thought he could handle. As he hit it, he tucked and rolled and by sheer luck missed a pair of colossal trees when he somersaulted between them. The next thing he knew, he had stopped, and unlikely as it seemed, he was still intact. Dazed, dizzy from the spinning he had done, he managed to get his feet underneath him. He looked around.

What happened? Kitai asked himself. One moment he was about to be crushed under all those hooves, and the next he was rising through the air. As he was wondering, he caught movement in the trees. Then he saw what had saved him from the okapi. The condorlike bird was sitting on a tree limb far above, looking down on him.

Kitai stared up at it, still shivering with adrenaline. His neck stiff from the fall, he moved it from side to side to alleviate the pain. To his surprise, the bird did the same thing. *Did I just see what I thought I saw?* he wondered. He stood still and stared up at the bird. Then he moved his head from side to side again, this time intentionally. And again the condorlike creature did the same thing. Kitai smiled and nodded his thanks. Clearly, the bird wasn't like the birds back on Nova Prime.

It was much more than that.

With that discovery in mind, he backpedaled slowly into the jungle, turned, and hurried on.

iv

Sometime later, Kitai approached the banks of a river. His lifesuit was rust once more. Exhausted, he dumped his gear on the ground. He fumbled with the breathing fluid case. For a moment, he thought he was going to pass out. Then he closed his fingers around the last vial. Kitai regarded it, knowing the significance of it. After it was done, there would be no more breathing fluid. *None.* But what choice did he have?

As his father had shown him, he accepted the contents of the last vial. Then he sat back. Even with the oxygen coursing through his bloodstream, he was bone-tired. It would be so easy for him to just give up. *So easy* . . .

As Kitai thought that, he saw a log float by on the river. He stared at it, and an idea came to him. He looked around and saw a group of fallen trees by the river's edge. He struggled to his feet, approached some long vines hanging from the trees, and started cutting them.

Before long, he had created a small raft made of fallen tree logs and lashed them together with the vines he had found. He pulled it to the edge of the river. Then he pushed it in and jumped on top of it. As the current caught the raft and pulled it along, Kitai saw that the water was teeming with life. He stood up in the center of the raft and used a long branch he had acquired as an oar.

He was so enthralled by the fish flitting through the water, in and out of the sunlight, that he almost missed something else: a forty-foot anaconda swimming lazily alongside the raft. Kitai tamped down his fear. He held his breath for what seemed like forever, hoping the snake wouldn't try to overturn the raft. Eventually, the thing passed him by.

He took a breath, let it out. Aside from the snake, the river was actually kind of peaceful. There was thick, lush jungle on either side of it, its leaves reaching out over the water. Kitai allowed himself to relax, to lie down on his back. The breathtaking landscape moved past him on either side.

Drained of energy, fatigued, he took the opportunity to close his eyes for the first time in nearly twenty-four hours. The sounds of life served as a haunting lullaby, the river rocking him to sleep. *No*, he thought. *Got to stay awake.* But he couldn't. Slowly but surely, he drifted off . . .

Then a hand touched him ever so gently, and he heard a feminine voice say, "Wake up."

Kitai opened his eyes and saw his sister, Senshi, sitting on the raft with him. Her hair hung to one side. Stroking his face gently, she said, "It's time for you to wake up."

He looked up and smiled at her. "Hey."

He wondered how it could be that she was with him in that moment on Earth. But he was too tired to question it. He just took in the welcome sight of her face, which he hadn't seen in a long time. Not since her death. Suddenly, he felt a pang of guilt.

"I was about to come out that day," he said.

His sister smiled and shook her head. "No, you weren't. But you did the right thing."

It felt good to hear her say that. But it didn't lift his burden, not entirely.

"Dad says I should have tried."

"He's just mad at himself," said Senshi. "That's all."

"Why couldn't you ghost?"

His sister stared down at him and touched his face again. "You're close right now."

"I am?" He was surprised that she would say that.

"Are you scared?" Senshi asked.

Was he?

"No," he decided. "I'm tired."

"That's good. You filled your heart with something else. Now you've got to get up."

Kitai looked up at her. "I memorized some of *Moby Dick*." He thought that would please her and convince her to stick around a little longer.

But all she did was repeat what she had said: "Kitai, get up."

Maybe she didn't believe him. Well, he would prove it to her. "'All that most maddens and torments,'" he said, quoting the book, "'all that stirs up the lees of things—'"

His sister took on a concerned look. "Kitai, wake up. It's time for you to wake up."

She was distracting him. Kitai covered his ears so that he could concentrate. "'All truth with malice in it—'"

Senshi said it again, this time with more urgency: "Kitai, *wake up*."

Ignoring her, he continued. "'All that cracks the sinews and cakes the brain—'"

His sister looked down as if resigned to the idea that Kitai wouldn't listen to her. Her hair hung in front of her face. Then she looked up suddenly, and when she did, her face was mangled and bleeding, just as it had been when the Ursa attacked her that day. Her eyes wide, she screamed in a voice full of fear and pain, *"Wake up!"*

Kitai snapped awake. Disoriented, he looked around. All around him, the jungle was freezing over. The river was already half frozen. The raft was propped up against a riverbank. Kitai cursed beneath his breath. The jungle was turning gray. The rough undersides of the plants had become a carapace against the cold. He had lost a critical amount of time. There was only one way he could make up for it. He got up and sprinted like crazy. But with every step, the temperature plummeted. The plants and trees around him turned a frigid white. Frost formed on his upper lip and on top of his head.

Still he kept moving, kept pumping his arms and legs. His lifesuit turned icy, but that didn't stop him. Then, up ahead, branches began snapping. Chunks of shrubbery flew about and fell to the ground. Kitai was shivering violently, his arms wrapped around himself, but he didn't dare go on until he saw what was causing the carnage.

Then he caught sight of it—up ahead, high in the trees, a bird like the one whose nest he had helped defend. Or *tried* to help defend. As he watched, the creature viciously broke off one leafy branch after another and let them fall to the ground.

Kitai wished he knew why.

At the same time, the jungle floor began to freeze. Kitai collapsed to his knees and fell forward. A moment later his face hit the hard, cold ground. He felt as if ice were forming on his eyelids. His face was cold, so cold. Everything in front of him became a blur. He got the vague impression of claws digging at the earth, of the jungle turning to ice, of his lifesuit turning from rust to deadly white. Then he saw a flurry of dark feathered wings, and came to the conclusion that the mammoth bird was coming to kill him.

My cutlass. If I can only get to my cutlass—

It was the last thing he thought before darkness closed down on him.

933 AE

Nova Prime

i

Brazil was the wettest month in Nova Prime City, although that wasn't saying much. The rainfall measured barely sixty millimeters, twice the average of most other months. It did help control the ever-present dust the light breeze usually spread, and there was a burst of color as flower gardens everywhere suddenly sprouted with new life.

Spring was certainly in the air, and it brought a rare smile to Khantun Timur Raige's face. With the mildly damp weather came the conclusion of another year of cadet training. By now, the latest round of War Games was concluding somewhere in the cliffs just outside the city. She had checked in a day before and silently observed as the Blue team appeared ready to triumph, but the overnight report showed the Red team had outmaneuvered them. If the Green team was smart, they'd let them fight it out and slip through to win.

Within weeks, there would be the graduation ceremony, and another few dozen Rangers would don their uniforms and get to work. It was one of her favorite times of year; the promise of greatness lingered in the air along with one of renewal and rededication to the ideals of mankind. It amazed her that it was nearly a millennium since her ancestors left Earth and started afresh. Despite unexpected adversity and a harsher than anticipated environment, they have grown strong. It fell to her, as Prime Commander, to keep them strong and the planet well defended.

Since assuming the office sixteen years earlier, almost every waking hour had been spent focused on making the planet battle ready, prepared, and wary. The last Ursa attack was back in the 880s so she felt another assault was coming over the next few decades. By now they were expected like the hundred-year weather events, and just like they had to construct buildings with storms and earthquakes in mind, so, too, did they have to ensure there were shelters for the growing population and that the satellite warning system was constantly maintained and enhanced. Defensive satellites had been deployed since the last attack, so the hope was to winnow the number of Skrel that dared come near Nova Prime. Such preparations were in disarray when she took the post from Nathan Kincaid, who never should have accepted the promotion in the first place. His five-year tenure was a mess, and when she was given the top job she made preparation her priority. It took time and effort, and more than a little cajoling of the Savant's comptroller general, but they managed.

When she took the job, becoming another in the long line of Raiges to hold the post, she wanted to prioritize the Rangers and her life. Knowing how all consuming the job was, she quickly arranged to have a child, never publicly disclosing who the father might be, so she would also know motherhood. Brom was born a healthy boy and grew up surrounded by the extended family, which helped raise him. Once that was ticked off her list, she made certain the Rangers would be her priority. This often meant Brom was brought to visit her after classes since she didn't frequently make time to return home. He'd do homework while she conducted meetings or as they toured the troops around the spreading number of communities. Now a teen, he was already eyeing his own application to the Rangers.

Raige focused on the plans for the anchorages, the safety valves that were finally constructed over the last century on inhabitable worlds found in the Carina–Sagittarius arm of the Milky Way Galaxy. Heliopolis was opened for use four years earlier, and she was scheduled to make an inspection tour later in the year. She had managed to visit Lycia and Iphitos but needed to arrange a grand tour of all six. Brom would learn much by seeing them all, she noted. Any one of the anchorages promised to offer refuge to the nearly five million inhabitants of Nova Prime, but the one thing they still lacked were enough ships to ferry them all, let alone the wildlife.

With Heliopolis now ticked off her endless list, she needed to meet with Savant Burch and with Tähtiin Industries' president Nelson Ben-Greiner. Plans for stockpiling the material and for rapid construction had to be the next priority. With the anchorage program at an end, for now, there should be plenty of manpower and resources available for the task. She paused in the shade of the seating area on the grand plaza and tapped in the note on her naviband.

Her last stop before entering Rangers headquarters was at her favorite street vendor, where she would enjoy a hot tea and the latest street gossip. Talking to Raj always made her feel a little more connected with what was on the minds of the people she was sworn to protect. In uniform, she so rarely had a chance to hear the unvarnished truth from the citizenry so she soaked up what she could from reliable sources, beginning most mornings with Raj.

"Here you go," he said, leaning over his teapot, which was simmering with something cinnamon-like. "It's just come in from the tea fermentators' guild, something new."

"I want my usual oolong," Raige complained, accepting the cup anyway.

"Try something new," he instructed. "Live a little."

"At least it smells good," she said, letting the aroma waft around her. "So, what's new?"

"That tea, for one," Raj said with a grin. He was

nearly seventy and had grown and sold tea his entire life, starting at a colony upriver but moving to the city when his children were adults. He'd been selling tea to Raige long before she was named PC and therefore was a trusted companion.

"The new performance of *Let Me Help* is supposed to be good. Mouly is said to be superb in the lead."

Raige grunted at that, not one for the arts, but if it was revived, she was glad to know a respected work from the last century was at least well done.

"There's been some talk that people want to permanently settle on Olympus," Raj said. "It's that Safe Movement talk all over again."

She nodded at the memory of the moment the first anchorage opened: There were requests by many to relocate and colonize. Right now, the anchorages were exploratory outposts and emergency evacuation points. The next spiral arm over was a more difficult move than hopping to the next continent. The proposal had bubbled up now and then, but the triumvirate leadership quickly shut down the discussion. Hope (or was it fear) springs eternal.

As a reward, she took a deep drink of the new tea, which had cooled enough. It had a nice, spicy taste, maybe too sweet for regular consumption but not bad at all.

"This is nice, thanks, Raj, but I'll be sticking with my usual," Raige told him and headed directly for the Rangers' base of operations. She hadn't gone more than three meters when her naviband buzzed and vibrated. A quick glance showed all red. Something major was happening.

She rushed inside, handing off the unfinished cup of tea to the security guard at the entrance, who snapped to attention the moment he spotted her.

Heading up to her office, wishing she could just be teleported there, the PC studied the incoming alert. The satellite system had detected Skrel ships approaching. They were early; she wasn't expecting them for some time. That in itself concerned her at the same time she was pleased the upgraded surveillance system actually worked and they now had some time to prepare.

Skipping her office, she went to the tactical command center where all the feeds were received and analyzed. As she entered, the lighting was already dim and there was an undercurrent of voices communicating with others. Holographic screens showed a map of the solar system with red lights denoting the satellites. Huge purple lights at the system's edge marked the Skrel. She counted at least six ships, maybe more.

"Situation?" she called.

Only then did the majority of the staff notice the PC was among them. Her adjutant, Lieutenant Strongbow, approached with a tablet gripped in both hands.

"They appeared on the screen ten minutes ago and are estimated to reach Nova Prime in three days, six hours, fourteen minutes."

"They're in a hurry," Raige said to the tall, trim brunette. Strongbow knew better than to try bantering and kept it to just the facts.

"The lead Skrel ship appears to be targeting and taking out any satellites in its path."

"Have we fired?"

"First one's coming into range shortly," Strongbow reported.

"Make it the main image," she snapped. Suddenly, a tactical map of the solar system flicked into existence, looming large over the room. Enough sensor data had come in to render a silhouette of the Skrel ship, resembling the ones that arrived almost seven hundred years earlier. Large, bulbous shapes up front, spikey tail sections with cables running loosely under the carriage. Without a Skrel corpse for reference, no one could estimate the scale or determine how many might be flying each ship. What worried Raige and the others was their firepower. How much had that improved since the Skrel's last attack?

"Fire at will," she ordered. Several voices acknowledged and then the waiting began.

Long minutes passed until the first F.E.N.I.X. missile was launched . . . and obliterated before it hit its target.

"That screws with our intelligence. Damn, I knew we needed warships," she said, not for the first time. While the last century saw a new generation of starships with upgraded Lightstream engines, they were designed for deep space and for the wormhole to the next spiral arm. All the resources went to them, and the anchorages, when her predecessors recognized they needed a fleet of fighters to keep the battle in space. Had the Varuna Squadron been supplied with such ships, the last iteration of Ursa would have been sucking vacuum. But resources, even after nearly a thousand years, remained carefully apportioned. The system had its share of asteroids to mine, but unlike the ones placidly orbiting Sol, they were tougher to tame and access. As a result, every scrap of ore had to be allocated.

"I have the Savant and Primus calling in," Strongbow said.

"I'll give a briefing once I have something to say," Khantun snapped. Any vestiges of her personable character were gone. She was now a focused warrior, readying for battle. The Prime Commander never asked her parents why they chose Khantun, meaning "Iron Queen," but she was determined to live up to the name.

For the next several minutes, with her eyes barely wavering from the purple dots—now confirmed as eight identical ships—the Prime Commander was briefed on speed, point of entry into the solar system, estimated angle of orbit, and speculation as to whether they brought the deadly beasts with them. Ruth Strongbow took notes and convened the command staff in the adjacent room. Meantime, leaves of absence had been canceled and every Ranger in uniform was put on alert. Following a well-practiced series of protocols over the last fifteen years, the Rangers were now checking all supplies, power packs, medical field kits, and, of course, their cutlasses. Tomorrow, the squadron would take to the air and begin around-the-clock patrols. The shelter alert would not sound until the Skrel were one day away, time enough to prepare but not long enough to panic and cause additional headaches.

Raige was pleased with the intelligence coming through as well as the projections. "Have these confirmed by the Savant," she instructed her adjutant. "I'll meet with the Savant and Primus in two hours. Have someone bring Brom to Mama Sam."

Strongbow acknowledged the orders and began by having the nearest Ranger collect the PC's son and deliver him to Samantha Raige, Khantun's mother. Once the teen was secured, Strongbow knew Raige's total focus could remain with the Rangers. Her father, Mark, was once the PC, but had been injured in the line of duty and was largely paralyzed. Brom was a strapping teen and could help with her father's care while Samantha could ensure the boy didn't do anything foolish.

The preparations were now under way, but the waiting for the Skrel to arrive would make everyone skittish. All except the Iron Queen. She would show them how it was done.

ii

Primus Jon Anderson was the perfect image for a pious man. He was tall, with a wizened face, and dark, bushy eyebrows that helped animate his expression. His salt-and-pepper beard extended nearly to his breastbone. Anderson carried a staff that had become synonymous with his office but hid a slight limp. His robes of office remained immaculate, and his hat gleamed in the sunlight.

Today, he looked like hell.

He hadn't slept in days nor, it appeared, had he

changed his robes or washed. The beard was a wild tangle, making him appear more savage than sage. There was a faint aroma of sweat rising from the heavy fabric that only added to the stale air in the council room. A plate of food sat uneaten before him and the cup of wine untouched. Had he not blinked now and then, Raige would have thought he had gone catatonic. He was getting pretty damned close.

Their counterpart, Savant Erich Burch, at least had put on a fresh lab coat and violet gloves. At least it looked like he had an hour or more of sleep.

The three leaders of Nova Prime sat in silence as around them holo screens displayed details of the devastation that began three days earlier. When it was clear the Skrel were on the attack, they departed their vulnerable council room and settled into a makeshift operation in a conference room near the Rangers' hangar bay, low enough in the cliff to be a hard target. It was close quarters, adding to the foul air, and bare of decoration, which matched her mood.

Khantun felt she had failed them all. She prepared the Rangers and the people for a fresh batch of Ursa, but was stunned when the eight ships entered the atmosphere and began blasting away with energy beams that packed explosive force.

It had taken over a day to realize there was a method to the constant back-and-forth flying being done by the Skrel. They were dropping incendiary devices all across the continent. The devices burrowed beneath the surface and were programmed to detonate when weight was placed on them. At first they thought animals were being shot from the sky, but it then became clear the animals were triggering the devices themselves. Savant Burch reported all it took was a few pounds of weight to be detected, and the device would explode with enough force to kill any living thing in a half-meter radius, which was deadly enough.

The dead were an unfathomable number.

"This defies everything we've experienced in centuries," Burch said.

"What do you mean?" Anderson asked.

"The Savant is referring to the fact that in 243 the Skrel were very selective about where they fired. Their targeting systems were incredibly, impossibly precise. It was always things we constructed. Or people. Or livestock. Never the planet itself."

"And did that happen the second time?" Anderson inquired.

"Yes," Burch answered, finally reengaging with the conversation. "In 350, they returned and took more shots at *us*. Not the planet. Your predecessor wrote a treatise speculating about why the planet was left unharmed. You should read it sometime."

"Ever since then, the Skrel have seen fit to come here, deposit the Ursa, avoid our cannon fire, and leave the atmosphere as quickly as possible," Khantun said. "This defies everything we have trained and prepared for."

"Your flyers lack the weaponry, don't they?"

"Yes, Primus. They were never designed to handle threats from outer space. Same with the Suijin Fleet. The Skrel ships never neared the waterways. I've had the ships stored out of target sighting and the crews redeployed."

She cursed herself for being caught by surprise, but really, how could she know they would choose to fire for the first time in six hundred years? Still, the Iron Queen was feeling beaten and it irritated her.

All available flying craft were being used to throw whatever weaponry they had at the eight ships that leisurely crisscrossed the continent, strafing New Earth City then picking off people who ignored the shelter order, thinking the smaller colony towns would not be targets. Tähtiinville, home to their spacecraft manufacturing, was a smoking ruin.

Everything had gone wrong. All her plans and preparations for over a decade had been useless. People were dying, the Skrel were winning, and this time they didn't need the Ursa.

"We need a weapon of mass destruction," she said.

"What about the F.E.N.I.X. bombs?" the Savant said, pushing his plate away.

"How many are left?"

Burch paused and consulted a readout on the display before him and held up four fingers.

"We're going to have little left but rocks to throw at them. Those we have plenty of, and it seems they will prove as effective," the Iron Queen grumbled. "What about the upgrades?" she demanded, refusing to appear weak, even if it was just the three of them in the room without any aides.

"We're working on them, but scaling up has proven difficult. No one has really looked at those schematics in decades. After all, those damn ships descend, drop, and leave, all too fast for the batteries to track them down."

"What are we doing about that?"

"I have my top people on it," he replied.

"This isn't working," the Primus said. "We're all going to die."

"I don't need you losing your faith, not when the people are looking to you for guidance," Raige said, her tone allowing no argument. "Your addresses to the shelters are giving them something to hold on to. It's the one thing you can give them that I cannot. That he cannot."

Raige was frustrated at the lack of a plan, at the lack of action. If she could, she'd don a jetpack, grab a cutlass, and go meet a Skrel ship in the skies over the city. Since the jetpack remained mired in the R&D branch of the Mirador, the Savant's headquarters and labs, she had little choice but to control things within her grasp.

She stabbed a control and spoke into the microphone. "This is the Prime Commander. Strongbow, send teams to the F.E.N.I.X. surface-to-air guns and have them ready to go again. Send a runner to the Mirador and get me eyes on the upgrades. Then round up the Defense Corps. Have them check shelter by shelter. Make sure we have people secure and safe. Medical emergencies are the only ones who have permission to leave a shelter. I want Defense Corps people teamed with Rangers to begin walking the streets. Those Skrel bombs bored into the ground, which means they left evidence. Find them, tag them, and keep moving. We'll figure out how to deactivate them later."

"Commander, it's Sykes. Strongbow is dead."

Raige was stunned. She blinked and sat back in her chair. "How?"

"She was bringing in fresh supplies from a warehouse when one of those bombs went off."

"When?"

"Last night."

Damn. Was she that wrapped up in the mission she missed her adjutant's presence for that long? In fact, did she ever get confirmation Brom made it to Mama Sam? He must have, she assured herself. Right now it was all about maintaining focus on the mission above all else, and the mission was far from done.

"Mourn later, Sergeant. Can you carry out those orders?"

"Affirmative."

"Execute. Congratulations, you're the new adjutant. When you have the orders carried out, change the duty rosters, grab Strongbow's materials, and carry on."

She turned her attention to the Primus.

"And I need you to keep the people calm. We're at that point in every battle when fear and rumormongering can undermine us as easily as a Skrel bomb."

Anderson nodded.

"This is overwhelming."

"I know, not something they can train you for. Are you up to this or not?"

"Do I have a choice?"

"Not really, but I do have a suggestion."

Raige studied the Primus's expression, trying to anticipate the question.

"Take over. Lead us all."

That was not what she expected.

"Now there's an idea. I can focus more on the F.E.N.I.X. tech work if I don't have all the other demands," Burch said.

"You do remember the last time one person controlled all three offices," Khantun said.

"Yes, it was at a time when we weren't prepared and needed a single leader to take us forward. If I recall, it was also a Raige. Your family seems to be built for leadership. So lead us," Burch said.

"Amen," the Primus added softly.

"The people will need to understand that I am in command. Me and no one else. So I will accept this, but as the Imperator."

Anderson stared at her in confusion.

"You don't remember your history, Anderson," Burch said. "Back around 200 AE, we had an Imperator, and it didn't end well for him. It's why the Prime Commander's ancestor refused the title when she took control. But I think we need that title now. Take it and wear it with pride."

The Iron Queen stood, looking each man in the eye. For the first time in hours if not days, there was certainty in their expressions. They wanted her to take control, to lead the people or die trying.

Tapping a control on the table, she said, "Computer, as of this moment, Khantun Timur Raige is no longer the Prime Commander."

"Acknowledged," the artificial intelligence replied.

"Effective immediately, Khantun Timur Raige will be listed as the Imperator. All Citadel and Mirador commands will now flow through Ranger protocols."

"Acknowledged," the computer repeated.

The Iron Queen was retired and in her place stood Nova Prime's Imperator, charged with protecting the people of Nova Prime and driving the Skrel from its skies.

Khantun moved closer to a holo display and watched one Skrel ship dip low over the city.

She grabbed a small device that remotely controlled the station. "This is Raige. Varuna flights Alpha and Gamma, converge on target over the northwest medical center. Target exhaust ports."

"Roger, Prime Commander," came a female voice. "Do we have confirmation on where that is exactly?"

"Use your thermal imagers to trace heat emissions. Target their hottest spots and fire at will."

"Acknowledged."

It had yet to be tried, but now was the time to be unorthodox. If the Skrel were going to play this game, she was here to win it. Silently, she studied the two purple blips registering the squads of flyers as they converged on the Skrel ship, which was moving into a position that would mean the medical center was destined for rubble.

The purple blips grew closer to the red at a remarkable rate.

Khantun caught herself holding her breath and forced herself to exhale through her nose. Deep breaths.

The purple blips touched the red dot and then the red winked off the screen.

"Target down," the female voice said.

"Good shooting," the Imperator told them.

Before she could redeploy them, her new adjutant entered the war room and handed her a tablet. Scrawled across the screen was a note from Brom, safely at Mama Sam's and asking innocently about a missing file. Khantun allowed herself a moment—just a moment—of relief.

Khantun's son was safe, and the planet would be, too.

1000 AE

Earth

i

The darkness inevitably gave way to light, and the sun began to rise above the horizon. Kitai was startled awake as he tried to move and felt constricted. He stretched and felt trapped under something. Panic forced his eyes open, and a ray of morning sunshine streaking through a gap in his binding nearly blinded him. He strained against whatever it was that confined him. Reduced to crawling, the teen moved toward the light and the promise of escape.

He was inside a leaf-covered ditch, piled high and thick, but still, he could escape. With both hands, he tugged at the leaves and tore through them, enlarging the gap, and finally crawled to his freedom. Regaining his footing, Kitai studied the sky for a moment, noting the thick clouds and brightening blue as the sun now was fully visible. He kept expecting a second sun to join it in the sky eventually, but that was back home and he was trapped here, on Earth.

He was distracted by watching his breathing condense into a mist, and he finally acknowledged how cool it was, although the sun was rapidly melting the thin coating of ice that covered everything. Slowly studying his surroundings, Kitai made a circle and was startled to see that atop the makeshift nest was the huge condor. This giant bird was now a friendly figure. He drew closer, tapping the still figure, and said, "Hey."

He tapped the bird a second time, adding, "Thanks."

But she did not respond. In fact, she didn't twitch in the cool air or appear to be breathing. With mounting horror, Kitai examined the protective bird and realized she had covered him in the nest and then kept him warm by sitting atop it, and rather than expose him to the elements, she'd sacrificed herself, freezing to death during the night.

Stunned, Kitai silently mourned her, appreciating the first act of kindness a resident of the planet had shown him. Although he wanted to say or do something to acknowledge her act, especially in the wake of her losing her chicks, he was at a loss for words. This was an entirely new experience atop all the others he'd had over the last few days. Worse, he didn't have time to spare. He turned and moved solemnly into the jungle.

His mind was a jumble of thoughts, overwhelmed by the condor's selfless act. His mind drifted to Senshi. He was helpless then, too, and someone died so that he could live. Maybe there was a difference between being a coward and being unafraid to accept help. Maybe there was strength in realizing and accepting that you're not alone.

He was also concerned about the amount of time and distance left to accomplish his mission, which made him worry about his injured and possibly dying father. It was overwhelming, but his father's image and stern countenance urged him to focus on the mission.

He studied the subtle trail and followed it, sweeping his eyes from side to side and making certain to keep his ears alert. The hunt continued as the sun rose higher, and he started to notice that his constant walking was beginning to take a toll on him. He could hear how labored his breathing was getting, but he was determined to go as far as possible before death could claim him. Soon the jungle thinned, and he was walking through grassland, squinting in the sunlight, wishing the lifesuit's backpack came with sunglasses. He admired the surroundings and the scattering of animals that moved back and forth, continuing to ignore his presence, for which he remained grateful.

The warm air dried him out, and he tried to clear his throat, but instead, he coughed. First it was a slight irritation, but then it grew worse, and soon he was hacking and feeling like hell. The breathing gel had run its course, and his system was clearing out the last of it. The coughing fit continued, and he had trouble catching his breath, worsening his difficulty. He stood, hands on his knees, coughing and dreading his condition.

One final racking cough sent him to his knees.

While close to the grass, he looked down, trying to catch his breath. All he saw was dirt and tall grass, but then, in his peripheral vision, he finally spotted something shiny, reflecting the noonday sun. Unable to rise, he crawled toward the object, feeling less like a Ranger and more like a two-year-old with a new toy.

As he neared the object, Kitai saw that the jagged off-white item was metallic with numbers stenciled on it. Holding it gently in his left hand, he studied it and saw that the word *Hesper* was on the half-meter-long piece of the ship.

With renewed energy, he stood, holding the debris that had given him hope. His efforts had not been wasted and he was nearing the mission's goal, and so he began to walk, then trot back toward the jungle. It wasn't long before he noted that his dwindling oxygen boost was costing him energy. He had little choice but to keep moving, but then he spotted another piece of the ship. Despite his lungs now feeling as if they were constricted, wrapped in plastic, he forged ahead with determination. His body, though, repeatedly signaled its distress by making him cough again and again. It was as if he were issuing a homing signal to predators: Come and get me.

Yet with each newly discovered piece of wreckage, he ignored it all and kept moving. The frequency of discovery increased, and he continued forward, each step and piece of debris punctuated with fresh coughing.

Pausing to catch his breath, which now hurt with each shallow lungful of air, he saw a wiry, strange-looking tree. Gnarled and old, the bark was flaking in spots where animals might have butted it to sharpen their antlers. It stretched in many directions and grew very tall indeed. Encouraged, Kitai leaped to the first limb and then scrambled aggressively up the branches until he was high enough to look over the dense jungle shrubbery. It hurt and he wanted to rest, but images of his dying father propelled him forward.

As he stopped his climb, he saw in the distance, atop a hill, the enormous tail of the ship. The once-proud ship now reflected the sunshine, a beacon of hope. Between it and Kitai, there was a scorched area of open flat terrain, a path to salvation. He grinned. Then he coughed, a reminder that time was running out.

Kitai lowered himself quickly, dropping the last few meters, and then, without pause, began jogging toward the path.

Each step was accompanied by a cough, and soon the movements were joined by a wheeze that hurt. He couldn't control it, and the sound grated against his ears. He felt like a sickly boy despite being in peak physical condition. Well, he *had* been that before the ship crashed. Now he felt like anything but a Ranger. What kept him moving was that every step brought him closer to the *Hesper* and its precious contents.

Working his way up the hill sapped the last of his energy reserves, reminding him of how hungry he had grown, and the wheezing made him thirsty. He wanted to rest but knew he dared not stop. He kept walking, and as he drew within a hundred meters of the wreck-age, he stumbled. Falling to the ground, he began the worst bout of coughing yet. Kitai couldn't breathe, couldn't catch his breath, and if it hurt before, it was excruciating now. Hands clutched his chest, unable to open the lifesuit, rip through skin and bone, to help his lungs find fresh air.

Choking, he steeled himself and reached down deep. He filled his mind with determination and raised his head, focusing only on the *Hesper*. One arm covering his mouth, he rose once more to his feet and stood. Certain he would not topple over, Kitai resumed his pilgrimage.

The ship loomed large in his vision, but Kitai had grown dizzy, his breath coming in torn strips. He felt hot without sweating, and his chest was heaving. He was out of options, out of luck, and so close to his target that he felt cheated of his victory.

On his knees, he moved among the debris, eyes desperately scanning for salvation. He grew desperate, hands getting cut on the sharp edges of torn, twisted metal. He needed one thing to survive, and it was proving elusive. The dizziness was affecting his vision, and he was certain he would pass out in moments. Light and dark merged, blurring his ability to see, and he found it difficult to remain steady. Thoughts of simply surrendering to the inevitable fought with his instinct for survival, but willpower could fight his body's physical needs for only so long.

As Kitai was about to topple over, his vision cleared enough to spot a damaged, shredded med-kit. Going more by touch than by sight, he rummaged through the remains of the kit until his fingers grazed a familiar object: an entire pack of the breathing gel. A final surge of adrenaline allowed him to open the packaging, although his fingers fumbled badly. Awkwardly, he grabbed the inhaler and placed it over his lips.

Almost instantly, his lungs stopped aching. He could draw a breath without pain or wheezing. It felt terrific.

As his body adjusted to being normal once more, he ingested a second dose. Too exhausted to do much more than breathe, Kitai fell onto his back, taking in deep lungfuls of air, enjoying every one of them. And then, like a chill in winter, it dawned on him: He was sitting in the spot the Ursa pod once had occupied.

If the Ursa wasn't here . . . *where was it?*

ii

Cypher Raige had had better days. Slumped in his chair, he dimly recognized that he was delirious. Images of his career played before his mind like an entertainment vid. Great battles, tremendous loss, and everywhere he looked, the Ursa were scuttling across *his* planet. No matter how many he killed, there were more. They were shredding Rangers, crawling through his family's windows. One killed his daughter. There was blood everywhere.

He continued to feel helpless and alone, uncertain if Kitai was alive or dead. He desperately wanted to believe the boy was still on the mission, but the odds were stacked high against them both.

What Raige could not see was the medical screen's readouts indicating how much blood he had lost. A red warning light indicated that blood transfusions were needed. Another readout showed that his potassium, creatinine, blood urea nitrogen, and myoglobin levels were off the normal charts. Warning lights flashed, summoning medical assistance that was not forthcoming.

Yet another screen Cypher could not see indicated that the arterial shunt had failed completely. The computer offered one final option: IMMEDIATE MEDICAL TRANSPORT.

With half-open eyes, Cypher roused himself from the images of war at home to see the battle his body was waging—and losing—against death. He saw the alert for transport and thought that was a lovely idea. Completely impossible but a nice idea nonetheless.

His only hope remained in the hands of his teenage son, far from him on the quarantined planet Earth, searching for the proverbial needle in a haystack. Cypher found himself drifting, remembering Kitai as a boy.

Suddenly, Cypher was in the old apartment again. Three-year-old Kitai was marching around in his pajamas and his father's huge boots, struggling to hold Cypher's cutlass.

"Those lines are tight, son," Cypher said approvingly.

Kitai beamed with pride. As Faia captured the scene with her camera, Kitai hugged his father.

Cypher hugged him back. "And now it's time for one junior officer to head off to bed."

"Noooo—" Kitai protested.

"That's a direct order from a superior officer, son," Cypher told him.

The little boy straightened up and gave him a salute. Cypher leaned down and talked seriously to his son.

"We never disobey an order," he told Kitai. "Not at home, not when deployed."

"Yes, sir!" Kitai snapped.

"And give your mother a kiss, tell her you love her." He cast a glance at his wife. "One day I'm just going to be 'Kitai's dad.'"

One day, Cypher thought as he sat there in the cockpit of a ruined ship and watched his son suffocate in the oxygen-poor air. His son was a Raige. Possibly the last in the family line, but he was a Raige. And a Raige never gave up.

So he would not—*could not*—give up on Kitai.

iii

Refreshed but still hungry, Kitai rose to his feet and continued his search through the wreckage to find the homing beacon that would summon help and save his father's life. His father had explained exactly where to look and there were pictograms on the sides of various stations, and so he knew the exact size and shape of the space where the homing beacon should be. But there was so much twisted, torn metal and material that he began to doubt anything was where it should be.

Moving around, he allowed himself to take in the remains, missing the crew members who had plunged to their deaths. Against a far wall, he spotted a set of cutlasses, the C-40 model that he coveted using.

The one he had taken from the forward portion of the crippled ship, his father's own weapon, was gone. Either lost in the stampede or jarred lose as the condorlike creature dragged him to safety. But that speculation didn't matter now. Kitai grabbed a fresh weapon, checked it for damage, and affixed it to his backpack.

Having the weapon reminded him that it had been created to deal with the Ursa and that he had yet to verify what had become of the one the ship had been carrying.

He walked with purpose toward chunks of debris farther from the tail and soon found the pod that once had fascinated him in the cargo hold. Resting on its side, it sat crushing large fronded plants.

He snapped the cutlass to life, and it extended to its three-meter length, a soft hum filling the quiet, cooling air. The yellowish pod that had once contained the captured Ursa that the security chief had named Viper was shattered. The gel that inhibited the Ursa's pheromone-locking ability was splashed everywhere. Pieces of the organic shell were strewn about, as were the binding straps, which lay on the ground.

There was no sign of the Ursa's corpse.

That was very bad, and Kitai backed away from the damaged pod, weighing his options. First was the original mission target: the homing beacon.

It took time, and he felt each passing minute weigh on him, but he was methodical in working deeper into the remains of the *Hesper* and was rewarded with the section of hull where the beacon was stored. Surprisingly, it was intact in its cubby, unlike its twin, and he snapped it free. To be certain it would work, he backed out of the ship and into the clear space the crash had created. As he moved, he thumbed it to life and was delighted to hear the whir of the beacon cycling to life.

Cypher was nodding his head, his mind filled with images of home. He was there, out of uniform and in casual clothes he didn't recognize. He and Kitai were sitting at the table, the remains of a meal between them. Faia was nowhere to be seen, but he missed her; that he was sure of.

The two obviously had been talking for some time, and he watched himself lean forward, a comforting hand coming down atop Kitai's right forearm.

"Now listen to me," he told his son.

Kitai stared at him blankly.

"Are you listening to me?" he asked in a tone he didn't like hearing. He cleared his throat, and when he spoke again, it was low and forceful, making it clear that his meaning was unambiguous.

"You are not responsible when your father is not home."

He nodded to himself because Kitai was not arguing but listening intently.

"You may have felt like I was angry at you, and maybe I was. But that was wrong."

He nodded once more. Cypher was getting through to the boy.

"You were a child. I should have been there. You were right. I was a coward for being away from you guys for so long."

Kitai finally opened his mouth to reply, but rather than words, he emitted a beep.

His son didn't beep.

What was happening?

Forcing open his eyes, which were stinging from salty sweat, Raige noticed the secondary screen that was monitoring Kitai's vitals. A steady beep was a welcome sound and gave the gravely ill man a point of focus. The peaks and valleys of a steady, healthy heartbeat were reason to remain hopeful.

Somehow, Kitai was still alive!

Then, from the speaker nearby: "Dad . . . are you there?"

It sounded like Kitai, but Cypher was having trouble focusing. He felt like he could not take a deep breath, just shallow, rapid ones. That wasn't good. Shaking it off, he looked at the monitors and then spotted a grainy image of his son's face flickering on the screen. *That's odd*, he thought. *The signal should be clear.* The shaking stopped as his son steadied the backpack's built-in camera. It was Kitai for certain.

"Dad?"

Cypher didn't respond, couldn't respond. He lacked the strength. But his hearing was working just fine, and his son's voice was most welcome.

"Dad, I made it to the tail. Over."

The tail? Kitai made it to the tail? Was this more of the hallucination? He blinked. His son's grainy face remained in place. The expression had gone from happy to serious as no response was forthcoming. Clearing his throat took an effort, but finally Raige said, "Are . . . are you okay? Over."

"Dad? Are you there? Over."

That was odd. He had heard his own words; why hadn't Kitai?

"Kitai?"

"Dad, I made it to the tail. Are you there?"

Of course he was. Where else would he be without both legs in working order? "I'm here!" he said.

"Dad, please copy."

Cypher tried one more time: "I copy."

That seemed to work, and Kitai's face looked relieved. "It's Kitai. I made it."

The exchange seemed to recharge Raige somewhat, chasing away the nightmare images. "There's something wrong with the signal, Kitai."

". . . Dad." Yes, the static was going to make this conversation nearly impossible. "Dad, you're still there, right? Can you hear me? Over." His son was looking on the verge of panic, and that would not do.

Raising his voice, hoping he could punch through the static by sheer will, Cypher said, "Kitai! I swear to you I'm here!"

His will failed him as Kitai repeated, "Dad, please. The Ursa is not contained. Do you copy?"

Cypher realized that while he could hear his son, Kitai was effectively deaf to his words. There was no way he could guide and assist the teen, which anguished the general.

"No," escaped from Cypher's lips. *It's hunting him.* Frustration energized him, and a flat hand slammed the console, the age-old remedy for balky equipment. Nothing changed.

By the time Kitai made his way outside toward the already setting sun, the homing beacon signaled that it was ready for use. Even if he couldn't talk to his dad, he could save him. He was still alive, and now he had the beacon. Help would be coming. Of course, there was some thirty-two parsecs separating Nova Prime from Earth, but still, help would save his father.

There was no use sitting in the tail section futilely trying to converse with his injured father. Instead, he clicked off the naviband he had retrieved from a fallen Ranger half-buried in the wreckage and put on his backpack. The clouds were thick, obscuring some of the sunlight, but clouds meant nothing to the homing beacon that would traverse the stars. Standing away from the wreckage, he held the beacon high over his head and activated the device. The rounded upper section rose from the base and winked to life. The horseshoe-shaped display indicated it was fully charged and ready to transmit.

Kitai took a deep breath—which still felt great—and fired the device.

He waited for confirmation that the signal had been sent but was greeted with silence. Lowering his arm, he studied the device, and right above the red light in the center were the words *signal interference*.

Within the forward section of the *Hesper*, Cypher watched the readouts and was disheartened to see the words *signal interference* flash repeatedly. He was frustrated and angered that this was happening, but while he had the energy and focus, he would be damned if he'd just sit there doing nothing to help. His fingers stabbed at the command controls near him, and a holographic map appeared. The dozens of flying probes continued to transmit signals that the computer assembled into a three-dimensional relief map of the topography where Kitai stood. He narrowed the focus and spotted a mountain shape just past the blinking dot that represented his last best hope.

Another adjustment was made, and the image was now that of his son. Kitai looked fit and whole, which pleased Cypher, but then he saw the boy throw his backpack away from him. He moved about, arms flailing and mouth wide open, screaming words Cypher could not hear. If anything, it reminded him of the temper tantrums Kitai had had when he was a toddler. Cypher knew he couldn't stop the useless behavior even if he understood it, but he still whispered, "Take a knee, cadet."

The words were not heard, and now Kitai was swing-

ing the fully extended cutlass without grace. It was just
blind rage and anger fueling him as he cut away pieces
of the tail section. He whipped the weapon about his
body and let it cut deeply into a panel that still had
power, emitting a shower of sparks. He moved away
and continued to shout and smack the ship and breathe
hard until the rage that roiled within him had been exhausted.

Kitai lowered the weapon. Cypher watched in fascination as his son expelled the last of the frustration and,
on his own, took a knee. Nodding to himself, the general was pleased. Wiping away the tears that stained his
cheeks, Kitai needed a new plan. Something was preventing the homing beacon from working, and every
minute wasted meant the sun was lowering, the Ursa
was prowling, and his father was dying. He didn't have
time for such outbursts and felt bad about his behavior,
thankful his father wasn't there to witness it.

Satisfied that his son had regained control, Cypher
focused on the problem at hand. The computer's diag-
nostics confirmed his fears, and he said aloud to himself, "There is an ionic layer in the atmosphere above
your current position. It creates electrical interference.
That's why the beacon isn't firing.

"You must be above the ionic layer before you fire the
beacon, Kitai." Cypher knew his son couldn't hear him,
but he kept talking anyway.

Cypher watched helplessly as Kitai once more studied
the homing beacon. The teen then looked upward,
studying his surroundings, including the thick clouds.

"That's it. You got it," he said to the holographic
image of his son.

"You should see a black mountain in the distance,
directly to the north. The mountain's peak is above the
ionic layer. Fire the emergency beacon there.

"Please see it . . . the top of the mountain . . . to your
north."

Cypher stopped talking, exhausted. He silently watched
the image, mentally urging his son to succeed. Slowly,

Kitai continued to turn in a complete circle, examining the situation and forming a plan. Then he spotted the mountain, studying it for a long beat before rising and moving toward it.

Cypher felt tears welling up and blinked them away. "Good boy . . . Good boy . . ."

1000 AE

Earth

i

Kitai had broken into a sprint, heading for the higher mountain and a chance for success. He pushed aside his growing hunger and instead studied the black mountain. His studies had taught him that such markings indicated it was a volcano, simmering. Dad had warned him the planet had many active volcanoes, and so he was glad this one was quiet. Its rough terrain would give him plenty of traction, making the climbing easier. There were no animals or birds nearby, and that meant he could focus entirely on the target. His Ranger training was coming back to him, and he would show Velan and Bo and Rayna. He was every bit a Ranger.

His run was interrupted abruptly when he came across the body of a leopard. It was not just lying before him on the ground but instead hanging from a tree, partly blocking his path. No wonder there were no other animals around. His mind also warned him of what could possibly have hung the carcass. Forcing that image from his mind, he kept moving.

Not long afterward, though, he came to a complete stop as he took in the sight of an entire pack of hyenas also hanging in the trees, almost in a straight line. This was not the work of some random predator higher up the food chain. They appeared to have been dead for some time. The Ursa was setting a trap, trying to rile up Kitai's fear. And it was working.

He reached the base of the coal-black mountain without further incident, which was just fine by him. He forced himself to study the area before taking in the magnificent sight. There were hundreds of tiny lava rivers charging down the ebony slopes. Maybe it wasn't so dormant after all.

Leaving the jungle behind for good, he hoped, he was stopped by a sound. He looked over his shoulder but saw nothing. Still, his flight-or-fight instincts said this was a good time for a jog. He kicked into high gear and began running up the black slope of the mountain.

Kilometers away, something made the motion sensor screen wake up and command Cypher's attention. A new dot was moving toward Kitai's blinking dot. There was no guessing what it could be, but without confirmation he merely told the holo image, "I have something moving toward you from the west . . . It has found you." Like a good coach, Cypher talked to his holographic son, who was making good progress. Unable to help Kitai himself, he directed, "Go left, Kitai. You'll save time. You'll have a straight shot without having to go through any tunnels."

He sighed as Kitai moved to his right.

"Damn it."

Kitai bolted up the slope, fast and fluid. It was an easier climb than his last effort before flunking out of the Rangers. He figured Bo and Rayna and the others would be far behind him by now. He missed them as he scampered with confidence and soon was enveloped in the ionic cloud, white and thick, that was causing the interference. It consumed the upper portion of the mountain and changed everything. Kitai realized he was effectively blind and could not see a predator, native or alien, if it was farther than two meters away from him.

Kitai readjusted a handhold and then looked at his sleeve and saw that the smart fabric had altered color to jet-black and adopted the texture that would protect its wearer from most harm. Danger was nearby; he couldn't see it, but he knew it was coming. He just didn't know from where. He tried to penetrate the dense mist around him visually but saw nothing.

However, he heard scuttling, something nearing him. Instinctively, he withdrew his cutlass and activated it. He moved backward a few meters and found an entrance to a cave, something he had missed the first time he'd passed it.

The cave was all onyx. Kitai had never seen anything so dark yet so shiny. There were stalactites and stalagmites cluttering the cave, and that made maneuvering tricky. The growths appeared to be made entirely of diamonds, something Kitai had never heard of happening back home. He had no time to study the fascinating find, instead running into the depths of the cave. All that mattered right now was that the Ursa was here, hunting him. There had to be a way out, hadn't there? He continued to move, trying to control the mounting panic in his chest, when he spotted a shaft of light dropping from a crevice in the cave's ceiling. All he had to do was follow that and he'd exit the mountain, above the damned clouds, he hoped, and activate the beacon.

Such satisfying thoughts were banished when a terrifying, unearthly scream echoed off the crystalline walls. As the sound vanished, he could hear claws against crystal and stone. Viper had followed him into the cave. He had no choice but to go deeper and hope a second exit presented itself. One hand brushed against a stalagmite, and the sharp-edged diamond protuberances sliced into his palm. He needed speed but was forced to move carefully.

A second scream reminded him that there was no margin for caution. Recognizing there were no other exits evident, Kitai knew it was time to change strategy. He held the cutlass before him, uncertain how many of its different configurations he actually knew how to activate, let alone use. Instead of worrying about it, he found several stalagmites to hide behind, giving him a view of the entrance. His eyes rose to the shaft of light; he hoped he'd still have a chance to use that escape route.

Watching the crevice, he was interested in the mist that had seeped through from the clouds outside. As he studied it, he saw something unnatural move in the mist. Before he could react, the Ursa shifted from camouflage mode to its natural hideous form and hung from the ceiling. The beast let Kitai take in its powerful form before the hide shimmered and blended in with the rocky ceiling, disappearing once more. All Kitai could hear was its claws against the rock, moving away, toying with him, making him sweat with fear, turning Kitai into a tasty morsel.

He crouched low, trying to use the stalagmites as a shield.

Looking around, he saw that a large crystalline structure had fallen across two tremendous boulders, creating a crude bridge. Cautiously, Kitai moved under it slowly, seeking protection. Peeking out, he spotted dust drifting down from directly above his position. Without warning, the Ursa became visible and dropped the three meters separating them. It landed atop the crystal bridge, snarling and smelling awful. Kitai wanted to wretch but gritted his teeth and remained beneath the crystal, which was cracking from the impact and the weight of the beast. His fingers twitched, and the cutlass fell from his grasp.

As he looked once more at his opponent, there was a flash of hope when he saw that two shards of crystal had pierced the Ursa's body, trapping it in place. Unfortunately, Kitai was similarly trapped as he tried to move only to discover that his foot was trapped underneath a shattered section of the crystal bridge. His boot protected his foot from injury, but he was still stuck and needed to free himself in a hurry. It would have been comical to be an observer watching the two life-forms struggle to dislodge themselves from the same predicament. Only it was not funny to Kitai. This was life or death, not just his but his father's, too.

Worse, the Ursa had six limbs and was using several to try to pry itself free while one was pushing down, trying to crush Kitai's foot. The human was fighting back, struggling to lever himself free, but was failing with every attempt. Done with the crystal, the Ursa's free claw was now swiping the air before the teen's face.

Suddenly the claw vanished, going to the aid of the other limbs in freeing the body, allowing Kitai the precious moments he needed to yank his foot away from the crystal chunks and roll free. Grabbing the cutlass, he spun about, ready to slay the impaled beast. Instead, he turned about and his weapon shook with the force of an incoming blow from the Ursa. It was powerful enough to send the human flying three meters backward into an outcropping. The air was expelled forcefully from his lungs as his back hit the rocks.

The impact dazed Kitai, who remained low, trying to absorb the pain throughout his body and regain his strength. As he gathered his energy, he watched with renewed terror as the Ursa pulled itself off the twin shafts of crystal, dark gray blood trailing from the wounds. Now free, it stood for a moment, seemingly checking its own limbs, letting the blood pool atop the crystal floor. Kitai had no choice but to run.

The Ursa was right behind him, roaring in pain and

fury, hurting his ears. Energetically, Kitai leaped off the ground, propelled himself at an angle off the side of the cave, and flipped through the air to avoid fresh stalagmites and stalactites, hoping they would slow the beast. Instead, the charging creature shattered the crystal structures and kept running toward the cadet. And it was gaining.

Kitai spotted a small crevice to his left and low to the ground, and he dived headfirst through the narrow space. Sure enough, he took some bruising as he landed, but his guess had been right: It was too small for the Ursa to follow. Instead, it thrust claws at him and bellowed but didn't make contact. In a rage, the Ursa threw its weight at the space, shattering the crystal walls. As debris fell, Kitai scrambled to his feet and continued deeper into the cave. He acrobatically ran, jumped, and leaped around, over, and under crystal impediments.

Just as he thought he had gained some distance from the Ursa, which was charging through the natural formations, it reached forward and clipped Kitai's leg with its claw, sending him sprawling in pain. Rather than give in to it, he used the momentum to roll quickly and resume running. As he moved deeper, Kitai began to notice the tunnel growing narrower.

The Ursa was gaining on him.

Finally, Kitai spotted an opening into a narrow cave, maybe a meter wide. The Ursa was too big to follow him in there. He slid into the cave and caught his breath, listening to the monster's howls of anger and frustration. After it was done yelling, Kitai peered into the tunnel. The Ursa studied the opening, spying Kitai within, and then backed away.

That was when Kitai realized how truly intelligent the beast was. He hadn't stopped to realize that stringing up the animals was a sign of cunning. It wanted him scared since it fed off his fear and used it to track him. Now it was waiting him out. This was a deadlier foe than he'd ever imagined.

As he considered that, he watched the Ursa through the small entrance. The creature stared back and then placed one claw on the crystals and another on the rock wall. Within seconds, it seemingly vanished before his eyes, taking on properties of both minerals. Daring him to try to escape. Instead, Kitai edged farther back a meter and rested his injured body against the crystal wall. It felt safe, but he knew full well that just before him, somewhere out there, the Ursa waited for him, camouflaged and startlingly silent.

The waiting game had begun.

Kitai squeezed his eyes tight, shutting out the images from nearly five years earlier. Calling to Senshi, wishing she'd hide with him. He opened them slowly and stared out the small cave entrance. He tried to see a movement, something that would show him where the Ursa was hidden in plain sight.

Although he saw nothing, he did hear the steady drip, drip, drip of blood. He couldn't see the gray droplets but knew they were there.

That was when the Ursa came into view, once more hanging upside down, literally crowding the entrance, as close as it could come to the human. First one claw, then another reached inside the cave, trying to reach Kitai but failing. That seemed to frustrate the beast more than anger it. It stretched deeper this time and nearly nicked Kitai. To retaliate, he waved the cutlass before him, forcing the limbs back through the entrance. Once the Ursa backed off a bit, he shimmied himself farther back into the cave.

With its limbs out of reach, the Ursa used another of its formidable weapons and spit several black globules of venom at Kitai. The paralytic agent missed his face by centimeters, striking the back of the crevice. The next attack finally proved successful as one of the black masses hit the lifesuit and his exposed skin. The mere touch of the icky, vile-smelling stuff caused him to scream. He knew this would slow down his reflexes and give the Ursa a decided advantage.

The Ursa managed to wedge itself into the crevice, its sheer bulk wearing away the edges. As it neared Kitai, it spit more black poison in his direction, and the law of averages dictated that a second bit of the gross venom would make contact. He continued to crawl backward. The Ursa matched him centimeter by centimeter. As Viper closed the distance to its prey, the Ursa once more tried to snatch Kitai with its fore-claws but failed to reach him. It spit again, pressing its advantage.

Kitai continued to shimmy back, not daring to take his eyes off the beast. As a result, he missed the fact that he was running out of space. Before he knew it, he was slipping, and gravity took hold of his slender form and yanked. Suddenly, he was falling. Not far, maybe two meters, but enough to surprise him before he struck a rock. Pain radiated from the impact, and he grunted more than once but refused to scream. Instead, he flipped from the rock, spun around, and continued to fall, this time much farther down. He remembered how sailors fell to their doom in *Moby Dick* and feared he was about to join them.

That was when he hit water and confused the novel with his own situation. He nearly swallowed a mouthful as he sank low. He threw out his arms and legs, spreading them to distribute his weight evenly. Without taking the time to hold his breath, he had precious little oxygen in his system and needed to get control of his situation. Fast.

Steady but still underwater, he opened his eyes, impressed that the smart fabric in his lifesuit still provided some illumination. Twin spots of light from his shoulders let him see maybe two meters in any direction. As he hurriedly assessed his position, he saw a shaft of light waver in the water. Light meant escape and, he hoped, freedom. A chance to complete the mission and save his father. But if he made it down here, could the Ursa have followed? And did it know how to swim?

He hadn't sensed the kind of impact a creature of its bulk would have made, but that didn't mean anything.

Feeling the lack of air start to burn, he began to swim toward the light. In looking back, he couldn't recall where he felt the first bite, but suddenly his body was enveloped with tiny sightless fish with big teeth taking nips. He'd heard of such fish but couldn't recall their name. Instead, he felt them ripping his lifesuit, which he didn't think possible.

As quickly as the fish attacked him, they disappeared faster. Kitai began to wonder what had changed but knew in a heartbeat why. The Ursa had made its way to him and was now approaching, its six legs propelling it through the water at a fast enough rate to worry him. One leg and claw slashed at Kitai, narrowly missing his leg.

Turning away from the predator, Kitai pushed off and swam as hard as he knew how. He was swimming for his life in almost total darkness, his shoulder lights flickering thanks to the fish tearing at the integrated bodysuit. He continued toward the streaming light. The Ursa was right behind him and closing.

Kitai, already breathing hard and laboring, pushed himself even harder to pick up speed. There was now desperation mixing in with his practiced strokes. The lights flashed briefly on an unusually beautiful group of stalactites just before him. It was a straight, unimpeded line to the light, but that also played to the Ursa's strengths. As he swam and tried to control his mounting panic, Kitai strained to strategize. He veered off and swam through the stalactites, pushing off each one for extra momentum. Sure enough, he was putting much-needed distance between him and the bulky beast.

What happened next was confusing, largely because Kitai was disoriented. He was rushing so far, so fast underwater that he grew confused. He was uncertain which way was up and knew he needed to find out quickly before he drowned. A few bubbles escaped his lips and traveled down.

How are bubbles going down? That isn't right.

Kitai flipped himself around and followed the bubbles, which rose to the surface. As he broke the surface, he spotted the light and took a much-needed breath. As he reached the light's contact point with the water, Kitai saw that he was at the bottom of a vertical shaft of rock that traveled roughly twenty-five meters above him to where daylight awaited.

Despite his weariness, Kitai left the water, pulling himself up on a jagged piece of rock, which cut into exposed parts of his flesh now that the lifesuit was compromised. He took several deep breaths to center himself and then positioned his feet on either side of the shaft to brace himself. He reached out with his arms, pulled himself up, and then began the slow, steady climb to the surface.

Before he went several meters, though, the Ursa burst from the water and reached for its prey. One claw snagged Kitai's leg, but once more its bulk prevented it from succeeding. It could not fit into the shaft and follow Kitai. In fury the beast tried to pull the human toward its gaping mouth. Kitai looked into the maw with its sharp teeth, moist tongue, and dark innards. He screamed. Two claws had gotten purchase and begun dragging him backward. His legs scissored to break free as his arms pulled his body upward. Both efforts worked, and with a sudden rush forward, he was free. As he clambered up, the Ursa bound out of the water in a final attempt to grab him and bring him down. Fortunately, the effort failed and the Ursa fell back to the underground lake.

Kitai was in pain. The tiny cuts were not deep, but there were enough larger cuts to be felt with every muscle movement. He was tired. He was hungry. There was no one around to help him; there was no rescue on its way. All this roiled within him, and he finally let it all out in a yell of pain and fear.

Without looking down at the Ursa, Kitai climbed. He had little choice, and so he continued to the surface, focusing on the next handhold. The next step. As he rose, the beast's roars diminished until they finally faded away and he could put it out of his mind for now. The meters vanished beneath him and he lost track of time, but the light grew brighter and he felt the beginnings of a breeze. The surface was beckoning.

The timeless void ended as his head rose above the shaft, and he once more saw clouds and sky and black mountain. He pulled himself to the surface and stood, panting. His lifesuit was still damp, and drops of water fell from the obsidian surface, which was glistening in the waning sunlight. To his surprise, it was snowing. The air around him was filling with flakes, but as they adhered to his skin and lifesuit, he noticed they were not crystalline water droplets but something ashy. Then he remembered. This was a volcano, and it was still very much awake. From where he stood, there really were no safe places to climb. He was standing essentially on the edge of a cliff, and it was a long way down.

ii

On the *Hesper*, Cypher Raige was waging war with himself, forcing the fever-induced flashbacks away. He remained frantic as he feared the worst for his son. There had been no communications for some time now, and Kitai's signal appeared to be lost. So did the Ursa's avatar, making him go mad with worry and concern. If the Ursa had killed Kitai and lived, it would continue to hunt and eventually find its way to him. Somehow, he knew, it would locate the sole remaining human on

Earth and kill him. Or he would bleed out, leaving behind a somewhat rancid corpse for the Ursa.

A beeping sound caught his wavering attention, and he saw that Kitai's vital signs were registering. *He's alive!* The screen representing Kitai's lifesuit camera winked back on, and Cypher saw the dark mountain. His son was alive and above the ionic interference. All he had to do was activate the beacon. But what was he waiting for?

Kitai steadied himself, having ascertained his current whereabouts and situation. His breathing was once more under control, but his stomach was demanding attention. He was out of MREs and would have to tough it out. He began to reach for the backpack and the homing beacon when he was distracted by the sounds of an avalanche. Or so it seemed to him. He turned toward the sound and saw the shaft being torn apart. Rocks fell into the entrance, and there was an unmistakable sound of claw against rock. The Ursa was forcing its way up to continue its hunt for Kitai.

The security chief had been right. Once the beast imprinted on Kitai, it would not stop until it or Kitai was dead.

It was beginning to occur to Kitai that it might be him.

But first he had to save his father.

He reached for the beacon, but before he could activate the signal, a claw grabbed his legs and pulled. The teen fell face-first into the hard rock. Both hands flew open with the impact, and the beacon flew one way and the cutlass another.

Kitai tried to scramble to his feet, but the Ursa, still trying to emerge from the shaft, smacked him into another rock and then hefted him into the air, tossing him away like a rag doll. As he hit the ground, he felt blood gush from his nose and pain in his neck. He wanted to get up, run away, but he couldn't. He hurt too much. This was it.

The Ursa, once it reached the surface, was going to claim its prey.

995 AE

Nova Prime City

Senshi was most certainly her father's daughter, preferring things to be just so. She rose every day at the same time whether she was on or off duty. There were the calisthenics to stay in shape, followed by a light breakfast, and then a run before cleaning up and dressing for the day. She invariably tied her long black hair behind her in a fashionable bun, barely pausing to notice her brown skin and bright eyes. Most days, dressing meant putting on her uniform.

She loved the Rangers, their sense of camaraderie and community. Although she could have applied to join at thirteen, she wanted to make sure she could ace the rigorous mental and physical testing, and so she worked hard for another two years. On one of his rare visits home, she made her father, the general, watch her practice portions of the test on a deserted field. She scaled rock walls, traveled by a zip line, and demonstrated hand-to-hand combat skills. She was so proud of how well she was doing that the final component, the mock cutlass battle, was going to be no problem.

Instead, she was black and blue for days. Her father was one with his weapon, athletic and graceful as he put on a one-man demonstration of forms until he used the cutlass to sweep her off her feet, letting her fall ass-first onto the hard ground.

He reached down to help her up and finally gave her a smile of approval, something withheld the last few hours.

"I think you'll do," he told her.

His rare praise gave her the confidence to apply to the Rangers the next morning.

After completing the two-part training period, she was thrilled as she crossed the stage and received her badge while her father watched. He looked taller than ever in his crisp white uniform. Nothing compared with that feeling of elation, of accomplishment. Their eyes met, and she saw all his love and pride revealed as if for the first time. She couldn't help but steal a glance at her mother, Faia, and younger brother, Kitai, as they cheered from the second row.

A week later she moved out of the family's tidy, tiny apartment, preferring to bunk with her fellow Rangers until the time came for a place of her own. She visited the family for meals, and the first time she arrived, she brought her cutlass with her to show Kitai.

After dinner, she put on a demonstration for him, with both parents watching intently. She showed him several of the many configurations of the C-10 model, pirouetting and explaining several of the attack forms she had been taught. He watched with saucer eyes and clapped in delight.

Faia was full of praise, but Cypher pointed out things she was doing wrong, taking her outside to spend the next two hours working with her. She did not take offense at his criticisms or argue but worked intently. This, after all, was how he showed he cared, and she loved him for it.

Now, four years later, she was nineteen and already had been promoted to Ranger, second class. Senshi Raige was on the fast track to commander, determined to do her father proud. More than that, she knew that the moment she took the Ranger oath, she was committing to a way of life that her family had embraced dating all the way back to Earth. While her little brother played, she was immersing herself in the family history, starting with the first Supreme Commander of the Rangers, Skyler Raige II. It wasn't long after they arrived on Nova Prime before the title of Supreme Commander was retired in favor of Prime Commander. More recently, her great-grandmother Khantun was even the Imperator for a brief time, and now her father was the Prime Commander. Although he might be *expecting* her to replace him one day, she *wanted* the job.

Kitai might have tested off the scales in terms of Ranger potential, but he was still young and not interested. Their mother seemed resigned to his entering the Corps at some future point but acted as a counterbalance to Cypher's infrequent comments about what was expected from him. Instead, the boy was currently excited about the Landing Day celebration, being a typical boy.

She reveled in being a Ranger. She enjoyed being out on patrol, getting to know the city's nooks and crannies, watching how businesses found new uses for the remarkable smart fabric. The skies buzzed with mag-lev traffic, and the city was thrumming with life.

It had been fairly quiet, giving her a chance to brush up on her piloting. She had expressed an interest in the Varuna Squadron and was taking extra lessons back at command. Scheduled for her first solo flight in a few weeks, she'd already invited Braden to come watch. He might be a civilian, but he was a cute civilian, and they had been dating for months now. Faia had even started questioning how serious they were getting, but Senshi was living in the moment and was not focused on that kind of a future. Not yet. There was time for that. The Raiges tended to marry and start families later than the average person, and she was fine with that. It brought less pressure.

All of that ran through her mind as she put on a fresh shirt and shorts before heading to the rec center. The spacious training and physical recreation facility was deep within the mountain housing the Rangers, kept cool by the natural rock and lack of windows. There were discrete areas for weight training, for calisthenics, and a general-purpose parquet floor for other activities.

She began a light jog around the perimeter, warming

up before going out later on patrol. Halfway around, she noticed that Kiara Kincaid, another nineteen-year-old Ranger, was lifting weights on her own. As she passed, Senshi called out a friendly, "Hey, K!" and kept moving. On her next circuit, Kincaid dropped her free weight to the cushioned mat and joined her on the track.

Kincaid was curvaceous where Senshi was lean and muscular, a marked contrast that got remarked on more than once when the Rangers from their class went out drinking. Somehow, Kincaid added a dollop of sensuality to her every movement, earning her more than a few admirers among the Rangers and citizens alike. Senshi couldn't help but notice their differences because both families measured the other with minute precision. She grew up constantly being compared with Kincaid's accomplishments and found herself mentally competing with Kiara, whom she genuinely liked, in most everything from bust size to obstacle course times.

"Quiet shift?" Senshi asked her running mate. She was already beginning to sweat.

"Gate duty is boring," Kincaid answered. "Nothing ever happens."

"True that," Senshi said. "It still beats the alternative."

"Does it? Wouldn't you rather have, I don't know, a band of marauders come charging across the desert?"

"You've been watching too many vids. There are no marauders. The occasional brigand, sure, but those are crazy solos, not organized."

"A girl can daydream, can't she?"

"Sure, and better marauders than Ursa."

"What's the matter, doesn't the OG's daughter want to take down an Ursa all on her own?"

Senshi bristled at the jibe, not hearing it for the first time. Yes, she was Cypher Raige's daughter, and yes, he was the Original Ghost, meaning there was undue pressure on her to replicate his remarkable feat. She joined the Rangers because that's what Raiges did, but did she want to do *everything* her dad did?

"I'd rather blast them from the sky," she said.

That earned her a fresh appraisal from the redhead. They continued jogging in silence until, finally, Kincaid asked, "Are you trying out?"

"Already training to qualify," Senshi said.

"Varuna Squad. Huh."

Senshi recognized the tone. It meant Kiara Kincaid was seriously considering the Varuna Squadron for the first time. After all, as the latest generation of Raiges and Kincaids to serve in the Rangers, the centuries' old rivalry between the families was continuing through them. She couldn't recall how it all began back on Earth, but somehow it endured the century-long voyage to Nova Prime and flourished when the tripartite government was formed. A Kincaid developed the F.E.N.I.X. tech to repel the Skrel, then another Kincaid turned that into the cutlasses they still used today. Raiges kept the planet safe and secure. Members of both families were found in the historic records of the Rangers, the Savant's Mirador, and the Primus's Citadel. Both families served Nova Prime with pride, but the tensions rose and fell between the families with regularity. Earlier this century, a Kincaid went down as the worst Prime Commander, supplanted by Senshi's great-grandmother, who was considered the greatest. And now her father was in charge while the best the Kincaids could offer was a Chief Medical Officer.

Yeah, no pressure on the girls.

They continued to jog quietly as other Rangers arrived to do their own workouts. Men and women began their routines while two were setting up a net for what appeared to be a volleyball game.

"Now, Santana, he's got some nice moves," Kincaid said, jerking her chin toward a very muscular man in his thirties. He was doing isometric exercises in just his shorts.

"And you know this how?"

"We've danced," Kincaid replied. "A few times."

"I date closer to my age," Senshi said.

"And closer to your weight class," Kincaid said.

"So I like them lean, big deal."

"I prefer my Rangers to have some power on them," Kincaid said, waving at the bearded Santana.

"Gotta jet," she said. "I go on duty in a bit."

"Hope you see some action," Kincaid said, her tone intimating she didn't necessarily mean official Ranger business.

Senshi swallowed her retort and split from the track, heading for the lockers and a quick shower before going on patrol.

She was on the evening shift for the month of Egypt and was patrolling with Janus McGuiness, a man just a few years older than she was. He was broad-shouldered and had nice sandy hair.

"You watch the Meteors' game last night?" he asked as they rounded a corner not far from where her family lived.

"Their defense is . . ."

"The word you're searching for is *sucks*. The fourth quarter was a travesty," he said.

"The Comets took every advantage," she agreed. "Kochman was on fire. What'd he score, seven or eight in the last minutes?"

"With luck, they can beat the Sapphires next and stay in the playoff hunt," McGuiness said. He grew thoughtful for a moment and then added, "Why don't you and that guy . . ."

"The name you're searching for is Braden," she said, a smile finding its way to her lips.

"Yeah, him. You, him, Mallory, and me," he suggested.

"Sure; if the stars align, it sounds ideal," she said.

Senshi was about to add something more about the

Meteors' poor defense when their navibands simultaneously sounded off.

"Ursa," McGuiness said, his voice dropping into the deadly serious tone that reminded her of the general. "Four spotted in town."

She was studying the feed on her own wrist device and saw that one was nearby. Close to the apartment building where her family lived. That became her priority, and she broke into a trot. McGuiness was on her heels.

"You see something?"

"We have to evacuate the people, and I'm starting at my house," she declared. He merely followed along, which was wise of him. Her family meant everything to her, and she wanted to make sure Faia and Kitai were safe.

The complex, carved deep into the cliffs that made up Nova Prime City, was a honeycomb of oblong apartments. Their home was a few floors above ground, meaning she had to make certain they were on their way to the nearest shelter.

"You ever see one?" he asked from behind.

"Just the vids during training," she answered over her shoulder. No one was certain how many were left after the last incursion four decades earlier. Some definitely had survived, and the fear was that they had been breeding. However, no one knew where they lived, and so it was an ever-present threat.

"They've gotten bolder, coming into the city as they please," he explained.

"Why can't we find their home?"

"If you could camouflage, would you make it easy to find your nest?"

"Point taken," she said just as the alert siren pierced the cool evening air.

Instantly, there were the sounds of panic and movement. Senshi increased her speed as the apartment structure came into view. Other Rangers came from the opposite direction, and McGuiness, the senior officer in the area, gestured for them to fan out, enter the other buildings, and escort people to shelter.

"One is two blocks over!" one of the others, an older man, shouted.

"Faster, then!" McGuiness replied.

McGuiness followed Senshi into the family's building and gestured at her. "I've got the top floor. You get the kid to safety."

She leaped up the stairs three at a time and was quickly on her family's floor. Senshi banged on doors, yelling for them to get to safety, then shouldered her way past those crowding the corridor to get to her own door.

The automatic locks recognized her naviband signal and allowed her into the apartment. "Mom!" she called. No answer, so she must be at the turbine labs, working late again. Kitai at eight was old enough to put himself to bed.

"Kitai!" she yelled, hoping he was not scared despite the siren still blaring.

She strained to listen for his high-pitched voice amid the sounds of people and Rangers yelling. Ignoring the commotion behind her, she moved toward his room.

"Kit?"

"Senshi!" he replied, finally making himself clearly heard.

He wasn't coming out of the room, and so she ran across the distance and found him still in bed, a reading tablet by his side. She burst through the smart fabric that acted as the room's door, cutlass at the ready, and he grinned at her.

"Kit!" she said with frustration. "Why aren't you out in the hallway? Why didn't you come when you were supposed to?"

He didn't reply, and she realized he was scared. Who wouldn't be, with an Ursa alert and no parent in the apartment? Part of the price of being a Raige was hearing many Ursa stories.

"Never mind," she said, deciding that determining the reasons for his paralysis would be of no use. "Kit, we have to go. Right now."

He stared at her, his eyes seeming to focus on her weapon.

"Right now!" she yelled, insistent.

That seemed to do the trick, and as he struggled to climb out of the hammock, his foot got caught and pulled one end of the bed from its fittings. It wrapped around the boy as he fell hard to the floor.

"Oh, for God's sake," Senshi muttered as she started to move toward him so that she could disengage him.

The background noise was overwhelmed by a loud, terrifying screech. She'd heard that sound before, but only on vids. This was live and far closer than she was comfortable with. After all, she was in her own home, trying to get her brother to safety. This was not the time for her first meeting with the six-legged killing machine.

The Ursa's cry made her brother freeze, still tangled in the hammock. Honestly, if she weren't eleven years older and a trained Ranger, she'd probably be paralyzed with fear, too.

Instinct took over, and without realizing it she thumbed the controls on the center of the cutlass; thousands of filaments curled to life, forming twin blades.

"Is that . . . ?" Kitai said in a strangled whisper.

Senshi nodded.

"They surprised us," she explained to Kitai. "They keep invading the city at random times," repeating what McGuiness had said just minutes earlier. She stepped forward quickly and swung the cutlass toward him. As the blade neared her brother, Kitai let out a startled cry, but the cutlass neatly cut away at the hammock, freeing him. He tumbled to the ground with a thud and wriggled free of the bonds.

Senshi spun about, the cutlass in both hands now, and tensed, awaiting a fresh cry so that she could gauge where the beast was. She prayed she could get her brother to safety, but if it was already in the building, the odds of that happening were slim to none. Over her shoulder, she asked in as confident a tone as possible, "You're not afraid, are you?"

"No," Kitai said, but she could tell he was close to freaking out.

There! A second high-pitched howl of animal fury, and Kitai jumped several feet in the air.

"Yes," he admitted.

She nodded in confirmation, refusing to admit that she, too, felt a cold knot form in her stomach. She might have trained for this, but not here, not in her home. Instead of replying, she turned and faced the doorway, tensing her body.

It was coming.

There were unmistakable sounds of the claws snapping against the floor in the hallway. All human sound had drained away. While she had tried to coax Kitai to action, her fellow Rangers had cleared the floor, apparently just in time.

"Kit," she said softly, "get under the bed."

Kitai scrambled under the torn and twisted hammock, useless now for supporting him but still good for hiding under. Having pulled it completely over his head, he then backed up toward the corner.

"Senshi, come on," he called to her.

She didn't spare him a glance or reply but already knew there was nowhere near enough room under the bed to hide. And she remembered what her brother clearly had forgotten. The Ursa worked predominantly with its sense of smell. Hiding under the bed wouldn't work as well as he had hoped.

All that she could focus on was protecting Kitai. She was his sister. She was a Ranger.

There wasn't much time and even fewer options available to her. She finally spied the rounded glass box with plants in it. It was Kitai's attempt at an indoor garden, but now it could be used for something far more useful. Quickly Senshi brought her fist down on a button at the end. The lid obediently slid open as she swept her cutlass around and attached it to her back with its magnetic clasp. Her hands free, she quickly unloaded the plants from the box, dumping them all over the floor, sending dirt flying everywhere.

Tight, but it will do. The soil and plant residue will help mask his scent.

She shoved the box toward Kitai, who hadn't moved a muscle. Lowering herself to his eye level, she urgently said, "Climb in here, okay?"

"But . . . why?" He was not thinking clearly despite all the stories the general had told him.

"So it won't be able to smell you. Hurry up!"

That snapped him into action, and he climbed in while she turned her attention to the sounds outside the apartment.

Where is it?

Satisfied he was secure, she put the case's remote control into his hands. "Hold on to this."

"But what do I use it for?" he asked.

"You use this when I tell you to. Or when a Ranger tells you to. Other than that, don't come out. No matter what.

"That's an order," she added sternly.

She knew that those were words Kitai would respect.

His fingers hovered over the controls when she stole a moment and took his face in her hands. His skin was soft, smooth, unscarred by life. She would die before that changed. And she probably would.

"Did you hear what I said, little brother?"

"Yes, Sen—"

Once more they were interrupted by an Ursa's roar, but this one announced its presence in their home. Maybe it was their conversation or the sudden burst of the soil smell in the house, but none of the reasons mattered. It was here.

Without hesitation, she pushed his hands atop the remote, closed the glass case, and then whipped her cutlass from its resting place, summoning it to life. She hefted the C-30, appreciating its solidity, and triggered the twin blades. Kitai was safe, and so she could focus entirely on the Ursa, which now was prowling her mother's relaxation room. It once had been her bedroom, before she'd chosen to reside permanently in the Ranger barracks, making the transition from daughter to Ranger complete.

The Ursa was quiet and stealthy, but she knew it was there just as it knew she was nearby. Calmly, she assumed the classic horse stance, cutlass pulled back in two hands, ready to swivel and thrust the moment she could see the beast.

Senshi stole one look behind her, making eye contact with the terrified Kitai. Her hands made a downward gesture, keeping him low and safe. She nodded with confidence, assuring him he would be safe. This was what big sisters did.

As carefully as she could, keeping the cutlass behind her, she eased toward her old room. Then, spotting the Ursa's shadow and noting its position, she changed her mind and began spinning her cutlass in a figure eight, letting it whir in the air. As she did, she issued the command to voice activate the naviband.

"This is Raige on the second floor. The Ursa is here. In my house. I have one child with me, but he's secure. I could really use some backup. A Ghost or two if you could spare them."

Her father had been the first Ghost, years before. Since then, there had been a few others who exhibited the same remarkable ability to mask their presence from the Ursa. There had been Daniel Silver, whom she met just once. And Blackburn, but he had gone missing and wasn't someone her father liked to talk about.

McGuiness acknowledged her signal but added that reinforcements were minutes out. She wasn't sure she had minutes, not with that thing in the room next door. That was why Ursa squads were required to have eight members.

"And you're where?"

"Just heading back from the shelter. I should be with you in two minutes," he told her.

She doubted that. She knew where the shelter was, and it was more than two minutes away. There was no choice: To save Kitai, she would have to engage the beast on her own.

This was what she trained for. What she lived for.

The Ursa chose that moment to walk into the room. It moved steadily on its six feet and clearly had a bead on her scent. If it imprinted on her, she was dead. If she could avoid that, she had a fighting chance of surviving. The Ursa must have sensed they were in tight quarters, and it stalked back and forth, blocking her only exit. She spun the cutlass about, making certain the creature knew she would not go down without a fight.

The figure eights were good for show and to loosen her muscles but also allowed her to build up momentum, and when the time was right, she lunged right at it. She hoped to inflict a good wounding blow and slow it down long enough for the reinforcements to turn up. As the weapon neared the Ursa, it backed up several meters. A quick thrust from one of its legs sent furniture crashing about.

Senshi sidestepped, allowing the furniture to tumble past her. At the same time, the Ursa tried to move in on her. Senshi pivoted and jabbed. The creature knocked the point of her weapon aside but failed to knock it out of her hands. Gritting her teeth, Senshi struck back, and that began the give-and-take, the thrusting and the jabbing. The Ursa bunched its powerful hind legs and lunged for her, but Senshi dropped low, bringing up the cutlass in a move that she was certain would impale the creature.

But it didn't.

The Ursa landed clear of the weapon. That caught Senshi by surprise, momentarily making her falter. Her confidence rocked, she tried to bring the cutlass back around so that she could slice into the beast's body.

That hesitation, that slowness of thought cost her.

The Ursa was faster than she imagined, and before she could register its movement, a clawed foot lashed out and struck her. Talons cut into her right shoulder. She felt her skin split and then a rush of blood followed by intense pain radiating from her shoulder up her neck and down her arm. Her cries of pain sounded weak compared with the bellow of the beast.

The impact forced her backward, opening a space between them. She tried to backpedal and increase the distance, but the pain was all-consuming. The beast closed the gap, and she raised the cutlass with her good arm, ready to retaliate. Instead, with a swift wave of a leg, the creature knocked the cutlass from her unsteady grip. She heard it clatter to the ground but dared not take her eyes off the beast, certain it would lunge if she tried to retrieve the weapon.

The Ursa shifted its stance, and she took a chance, moving toward the fallen cutlass, but the beast howled anew and froze her. She was a Raige, and they never froze in battle. But she froze now, and it cost her.

A claw stabbed into her leg, going right through the Ranger uniform and into muscle. It closed and pulled, and she felt tendons and muscles and veins being ripped from her body. Another of the legs thrust into her stomach and repeated the grisly action.

Senshi's sight grew dim, for which she was thankful, not at all wishing to see her insides on display. Her mind clouded with images of Kitai, safely in the case; of Faia, off someplace else, clueless to the fact that her only daughter was bleeding out in this very moment; of Cypher Raige, the Prime Commander, watching her actions with disapproval and pointing out all of the cutlass maneuvers she *should* have used.

All she wanted was to please him, to follow in his footsteps and carry on the proud Raige name. Instead, she was dying, no longer able to feel the pain.

Senshi knew that the creature reached out and knocked her off her feet, which didn't take all that much effort considering that one of her legs was little better than grated cheese. Although she no longer could focus or feel the pain as shock bathed her nervous system, her ears worked just fine as the Ursa let out a fresh roar. She matched it with her own terrified shriek, a duet of life and death.

The beast was atop her now, three legs pinning her down, each cutting fresh wounds into her battered body. It dripped saliva on her, and it was rank. Her vision went from blurry to dim to dark. She was dying. It would have been easy to think that she had failed the Rangers—and perhaps she had—but she found some solace in knowing that her baby brother would live to see another day. She hadn't failed her family. The thought brought her a measure of peace. She hoped they would forgive her for leaving them. She hoped her father would forgive her. In a small voice, as if he were close enough to hear her ask, she softly said, "Dad."

The Ursa crushed her mangled body. Senshi welcomed oblivion.

1000 AE

Earth

i

Kitai lay on his back, a dying snow angel. His crimson blood was mixing with the ash's clear white. He tried to reach for the cutlass on his back but came up with air, forgetting it was nearby. He let his arm fall and looked down at the limb as the gray ash adhered to his wet skin.

He thought, *That's really pretty.*

He closed his eyes and there were Senshi's loving eyes as she leaned close to him.

Then he saw the mother condor, fighting to protect her babies.

Senshi's eyes darted around the room and fixed on a rounded glass box with plants in it.

The bee jousting with the spider in a lightning flash.

Senshi is leaning close, whispering in his ear.

He crawls from the nest, protected by the dead condor.

The bee ceases to struggle, then breaks its bonds.

Kitai is swimming in the shaft of light, his lungs ready to burst.

Senshi takes one final look toward Kitai. She nods confidently and makes a down-handed gesture to indicate that he should stay low.

That everything is going to turn out just fine.

On the raft with Senshi. Her lips brushing his ear, to impart a secret. He hears her say, "Forgive yourself."

* * *

Kitai opened his eyes in the cooling air. The gray ash was lightly coating his body. He studied himself and realized he was being layered head to toe in the ash. Skin, blood, and smart fabric were vanishing beneath this new gray skin.

His reverie was broken by the sound of the Ursa finally breaking through the top of the shaft. Although he couldn't see the camouflaged beast, he could hear it steady all six limbs on the mountainside. It was now free to kill him.

Kitai was not worried. He was breathing steadily, his mind focused on something other than the Ursa.

The Ursa approached him at a deliberate pace, not rushing the kill. As it moved forward, closing the gap, it did not notice that the ash was also coating its invisible form, rendering it visible. Dusted, it could no longer rely on camouflage.

The Ursa continued to move toward its target, gray ash coating every portion of its hideous body. Dark blood seeped from its wounds, acting as a paste to keep the ash from flaking off. Kitai watched as it slowed down, seemingly confused for the first time. It swiveled its neckless head back and forth, clearly trying to regain his scent. And failing.

A small smile crossed Kitai's face for the first time in what felt like days. He pushed himself up to rest on one knee, careful not to make a sound but also no longer worried about the creature. Rising to both feet, he stood, his back to the Ursa, and concentrated on his surroundings.

Kitai's vital signs resumed their even baseline reading, and the warning lights flickered off. Cypher studied them, certain the system had not malfunctioned, and then settled back with a wince, watching the screens around him. Everything remained stable and steady. His son was seemingly in control of the situation. That was when he noticed a tear splash against the back of his hand. Cypher looked down at it; flicked his eyes once more to the screen, which remained unchanged; and let the tears finally come. It was the only thing he could do that didn't physically hurt. That, and watch his son do what so few had done before.

Kitai knew that he was standing high atop a volcanic black mountain. That an Ursa, which had imprinted on him, was standing just meters away. That the means for his salvation were in his hands—the cutlass to deal with the Ursa and the homing beacon to save his father.

Time seemed to slow down as he concentrated on his breathing, mastering his emotions and achieving a state of being he had never felt before.

For once, he was finally in control. He wasn't, before— not with Senshi, and not with the kind mother condor. But that was okay. He was helpless then, but they had risked their lives so that he could keep living his own. That's how much they loved him.

That's how much Kitai loved his father.

Sure in what he had to do, Kitai walked almost casually past the Ursa, which continued to turn in a complete circle, seeking its prey, and bent to collect his cutlass. Now armed, he returned to the Ursa and defiantly stood before it, face to face. The ash continued to fall, flakes settling on his cheeks, almost anointing him on the planet of his forebearers.

Grasping the cutlass with both hands, he tapped in a command, splitting the armament into identical parts. Now hefting twin-bladed weapons, he tightened his grip and ran toward the Ursa.

A gray ghost charged across the rocky terrain, almost invisible to anyone watching.

The other ashen figure finally heard the approaching footfalls and tensed itself for a renewed battle.

It was not to be.

Instead, Kitai moved toward a rocky growth and launched himself high into the air, sailing through the distance and landing on the Ursa's back. Noting where the wounds continued to leak its noxious blood, Kitai plunged the dual cutlasses into those access points and buried them deep.

The Ursa screamed, but in a tone Kitai had not heard before. It was clearly a scream of unimaginable pain. Perhaps this was the first time the beast had felt its own mortality. It shrieked and spun about, writhing and attempting without success to dislodge the tiny human on its back.

As the Ursa bucked, Kitai gripped both pieces of his weapon tightly and rode it out, slamming repeatedly into the beast's bony body. He banged an elbow against a piece of metal that the Skrel had woven into its flesh for additional protection. That made him loosen one hand, and he nearly lost his balance and his position atop the beast. Done with riding and wishing to end it, he tapped a pattern into both handles, and the weapons altered their configurations.

Once more the Ursa bellowed in pain as the twin cutlass halves sliced through sinew, muscle, and bone as they reshaped. Kitai pushed deeper, and the spear end of the left cutlass emerged from underneath the creature. With a tap, the spear tip retracted, leaving a gaping fresh wound, and more of its blood poured forth.

Another tap and now the right cutlass formed a sickle shape that was shoved deeply enough to pierce through the roof of the Ursa's mouth and emerge a wet, gooey thing from the maw. The human continued to slice away at the beast, literally gutting it from the inside.

He didn't think about the cruelty being inflicted. Nothing mattered to him but ending this threat and completing the mission. Kitai was focused solely on his task, on being in control for the first time, and on taking command of the situation. It was how he was trained.

It was who he was.

He was Kitai Raige, the culmination of his ancestors.

Another tap.

Another scream.

Another tap.

Another scream.

But this time the Ursa faltered, no longer steady on its six feet. Sensing its own death, the creature let its instincts take it to the edge of the cliff. It would die by falling, and it would take its prey with it.

Another tap.

No more did the beast yell. Instead, the Ursa slowed its pace toward the edge of the mountain.

One final tap, and this time the creature lowered itself to the ground, its energy spent. Less than a meter from the cliff, it collapsed.

ii

The camera moved so violently, Cypher feared becoming seasick, but he felt so crappy to begin with that he barely noticed.

Things slowed down in time with the Ursa's death throes, and now the camera was showing his son still on the dead Ursa's back, as the beast's legs finally gave way and it dropped to the ground.

His son dismounted from the creature, taking the cutlass pieces, still dripping with gore, out of its dead carcass. With a yell and a strain of spent muscles Kitai stared down at the beast, daring it to move.

Two more taps, and the cutlass pieces reshaped themselves into the sickle swords. Cypher felt a chill run through his body, seeing his son, now a man. A warrior.

A Ranger.

*   *   *

Kitai felt no joy. He also felt no fear. The threat had been dispatched, and he remained in place, studying the beast. He noted that his shredded lifesuit had shifted from black to rust, the smart fabric no longer sensing immediate danger.

Wiping the gore from the blades on the ash-covered hide, he brought the two pieces together and re-formed the cutlass into a single tool. Climbing down from the beast, he walked over to his fallen backpack and retrieved it. Once it was in place, he affixed the cutlass to it and began to walk higher up the mountain.

Still feeling in command of his surroundings, Kitai was bursting with controlled energy and used it to propel himself gracefully up the mountain. The rock and ash soon were joined by snow until his boots sank centimeters into pure white powder. The temperature dropped with each kilometer he walked, and still he climbed undeterred. Thoughts of exhaustion, hunger, and pain did not exist. Only the mission did.

He had to blink twice to clear his mind as he reached the peak. There, atop the world, he saw for a hundred kilometers or more all around. Instead of admiring the world in its natural beauty, he focused on powering up the homing beacon, and within moments it had cycled to life and signaled readiness. With one hand, he raised it high into the cool air, slamming the button that would summon help.

The beacon thrummed with power, and a bright white light raced into the starry night. He knew that the humans were wise when they left Earth. Between here and Nova Prime, the arks dropped buoy satellites. They were dubbed breadcrumbs and acted as tethers between worlds. Now the ancient satellites would act as relays, ensuring that the signal would race across the light-years home.

The signal sent, Kitai was satisfied this phase of the mission was completed. He could return to his father and care for him, keep him alive, until help arrived.

Cypher Raige was not entirely sure what happened after he saw Kitai begin his final ascent to the top of the mountain. His fever was higher, and he no longer had the adrenaline surge to keep him focused. Instead, delirious, he succumbed, satisfied that help was coming.

The next thing he saw was a thin, bright vertical line. Something was cutting into the darkness. He had no idea how much time had passed or why the *Hesper* had grown dark.

He saw figures, two, maybe three, maybe six. All he could make out was the shapes with bright light behind them. He saw something silvery, too, but had no idea what he was looking at. People said that when you died, you sometimes saw a white light and you were to walk toward it. He never imagined heaven having Rangers waiting to greet him. Maybe being Prime Commander had its perks after all.

If I'm dying, I shouldn't still be feeling so much pain, should I? And if I were dead, why do I feel like I'm being gripped and lifted?

He shut his eyes and drifted off.

Next thing he knew, he was being carried. It was a feeling he recognized, and that meant he was not dead. At least not yet. He was now inside the silvery space. Was it the belly of Moby Dick? Were an Ursa's innards silver? No, it was an artificial setting, not organic. That was when his mind told him he was being carried between ships, between the wreck of the *Hesper* and the rescue ship.

Kitai's signal had gotten through.

Kitai, finally feeling rested and refreshed after being rescued, wished he had something other than his tattered lifesuit to wear. He would have liked a Ranger uniform, but that would come with time. There was no way Velan could refuse him now.

He had dreamed of surpassing all the Raiges who'd preceded him, up to and including the general. After his experience on Earth, he might not be quite ready to surpass his father, but he felt that he was much farther along than he'd been a few days earlier. Amazingly, it had been just a week before that he'd been on Nova Prime, feeling like life had kicked him in the teeth. Now he had visited Earth, seen amazing things, and single-handedly killed an Ursa. Kitai still needed time to process all he had experienced and accomplished.

The rescue ship arrived as if by magic, a feat of Lightstream engineering he was curious to learn about, but for now he was just glad they had come and gotten to his father first. He was hours from death, and their emergency medical section allowed the Rangers to stanch the blood loss and repair the damage. Cypher had done much to help his own condition, but now the medics had to worry about infection and repair. It would be some time before they knew the full extent of his injuries and recovery time.

Kitai was just happy to have his dad alive.

Walking through the main corridor of the class-B ship, he watched as Rangers did their duty with precision and little chatter. Then he came across a technician studying a monitor that appeared familiar. Before the man was a silver device that was physically connected to the console. It had to be the recorder that every ship contained, filled with all pertinent data and logs for just such occurrences. On the screen he recognized the image: the unaware Ursa. Kitai slowed down and watched in fascination, barely remembering what he'd endured. The creature really had had no idea where Kitai was, had truly lost the scent.

Sensing he was no longer alone, the technician, an older man, turned and studied Kitai. He looked once at the screen, then looked back at Kitai. The teen saw a shift in the man's expression. He was clearly impressed by Kitai's efforts on Earth. Curiosity was replaced with something else.

Respect.

It was only after he was rescued, after some sleep and hot soup, that Kitai had a chance to reflect on all he had done. He had wanted to follow in his father's footsteps, wanted to be a Ranger. What he never had anticipated was that he would become a Ghost, too. He was the eighth, part of an elite group.

Kitai continued to move through the ship until he reached the small room where his father, the Original Ghost, rested on a cot, attended by two medics. He looked better than he had before they'd left Earth's surface, which pleased Kitai. Still, he was paler than usual, a look of pain on his face that no drug could treat. Under the blankets, Kitai knew his mangled leg was healing but might never recover fully.

They were checking vitals and generally fussing over him, so it took Cypher a few moments before he realized his son was standing in the entrance. When he did, he interrupted them and spoke.

"Stand me up."

The medics looked from one to another and then down to the man on the cot. It pained Kitai to see his father so helpless. So normal.

"General . . ." one of them said.

"I said stand me up!"

Without waiting, Cypher started to sit up, prompting the medics to swing into motion. They helped him rise, and that was when Kitai realized it was both legs that had been so badly damaged. They were encased in braces that helped administer painkillers, stimulate cellular regeneration, and provide support. The medics helped him swing the braced legs to the deck, and then each took an arm and helped Cypher rise to his feet. The effort took a lot out of his father, who winced but gritted his teeth and made it to an upright position.

Father and son studied each other for a long, silent moment.

Cypher raised his hand and crisply saluted his son.

Kitai was stunned and pleased in the same instant.

Kitai returned the salute just as neatly and then broke into a smile as he ran forward and gently embraced his father.

Close to each other for the first time in what felt like forever, Kitai reached his father's ear and whispered, "Dad . . ."

"Yes."

"I wanna work with Mom."

Cypher chuckled a little at the joke. Kitai realized his sense of humor still needed work, but this was a good moment. Neither wanted to let go, but the medics respectfully separated them and lowered his father back to the cot.

As the ship left Earth's orbit, preparing the powerful engines for the trip home, Kitai studied the monitors, taking a last look at the planet. It was raining when they took off, a fresh, cleansing rain that would replenish the pools and lakes that sustained life.

The jungle would endure. The cycle of life would continue.

A different monitor showed the ocean, and to Kitai's surprise, there was something breaking the surface. It was the size of a whale but looked like no whale he had ever seen before.

Kitai stood over his father's sleeping form. Cypher was going to be like that for most of the trip home, healing.

The planet being left behind was also slowly healing, and life would continue to evolve.

Eyes still on the vanishing green and blue planet, Kitai took a chair and sat by his father's side.

Soon the ship had cleared the solar system and engaged the Lightstream engines, propelling them into wormhole space and back to Nova Prime.

One would not blame Kitai if he spent the entire journey home lost in daydreams of the accolades and adoration he, the youngest Ghost, was certain to receive once he set foot on Nova Prime. But his only concern was the man lying quietly before him.

Cypher Raige was many things to so many people— the Original Ghost; the Prime Commander; the reason Skrel were no longer winning the war—but, to Kitai, Cypher had only one name: Dad.

And he was his son.

Cypher Raige was the first to ghost, making him an Ursa-killing machine and Nova Prime's new hope for survival.

Kitai Raige, his son, became the eighth human to exhibit such amazing self-discipline.

In between were six incredible individuals who also found themselves able to mask their presence from the Ursa.

Here now are three of their amazing stories.

The remaining three tales can be found in the book After Earth: A Perfect Beast *by Michael Jan Friedman, Robert Greenberger, and Peter David, available now in print or as an eBook from Del Rey Books.*

AFTER
EARTH

Ghost Stories

REDEMPTION

Robert Greenberger

The sun was warm as usual, but not oppressively so, and Anderson Kincaid wanted to play in the sand. His mother took a rare afternoon off to bring the seven-year-old to the park. Accompanied only by the boy's baby-sitter, she left word that she was not to be disturbed for anything short of a supernova. This was strictly family time, a rarity given her responsibilities for the population's medical needs.

She smiled as Anderson rushed from her grasp to the mounds of sand before him. Given how dusty Nova Prime City could get, it never ceased to amaze her that the boy still asked to go play in the sandpit. She briefly worried that he would inhale the fine particles and choke, but Norah shook her head at the maternal instinct to want to protect her child. It was this sense of protecting life in all its myriad forms that tied her to the people.

Rather than swallow the sand, he stomped around on it with white sandals and then planted his rump and squirmed, indenting the space until he was comfortable. His baby-sitter, a young man named Jason, stepped over and handed him a cloth bag filled with tools to shape the sand. Anderson patted the faded red shovel atop the sand and giggled. He delighted in this, and the sound reminded her of what she herself had been like as an infant, first encountering the sand. Anderson began digging with a purpose that attracted the attention of boys and girls of various ages. Soon five children were busily constructing some sort of fort or castle.

Norah Kincaid was content to sit and watch. Life on

Nova Prime was never easy, but the people were enjoying a nice respite. Their alien enemies, the Skrel, had not been heard from in decades, and their vile creations, the rampaging Ursa, had been largely wiped out. The last attack had been around thirty years ago, and all but a dozen of the Ursa had been killed. Those remaining beasts were elsewhere on the planet, and every night, as part of her prayers, she asked that the United Ranger Corps or age would destroy them and keep her people safe.

Those prayers appeared to have been answered—there were very few such sightings in the last handful of years.

As a result, the people once more were gazing up at the stars, wondering what else was out there. The news was filled with word that the latest anchorage, Avalon, had been successfully opened for business out in the next spiral arm. The planet Tau Ceti beckoned nearby, and Norah's cousin Atlas had been captivated by the notion since he was a boy. Such thoughts were good ones, but the actions they might lead to were a constant source of concern. Humankind had fled Earth nearly a millennium ago and, hundreds of years after that, learned they were not alone in the universe. There were dangers out there, including but not limited to the Skrel. She had understood the warnings against tempting the fates and the hand of the creator, but there remained those who wanted to explore. It was human nature, and rather than fight it, she sought ways to embrace the yearnings while tempering them with grounded reality.

Anderson stood up, grinning at her and waving the shovel. "Come see!" he commanded.

She rose and took three steps toward him to admire the formation of a massive structure. There were towers clustered together and several smaller buildings in a semicircle. Clearly, he was the architect and had convinced the others to build from his ideas.

"All you need now is a moat to protect the village," she said admiringly.

"What's a moat?"

Before she could answer, sirens broke the sounds of play. She knew that sound all too well. She reached out and grabbed Anderson, who was in the process of covering his ears, his eyes clenched in disapproval.

"What is it, Mama?" he shouted.

She didn't answer him as her eyes darted from side to side, seeking some sense of the alarm's source. Jason looked at her, and she nodded in confirmation: an Ursa sighting. He reached into a satchel and removed a communications device. She might have taken the afternoon off, but her oath meant she could never shed its responsibilities. She took the comm unit from him and spoke into it.

"This is Dr. Kincaid. What is happening?" she asked.

The voice on the other end replied, *"At least six Ursa have entered the city. One is by the main market, the other heading toward the park! You said that's where you were going; if you're there now, get out of there. Rangers are in pursuit."*

"I'm coming in," she said, Anderson squirming in her arms. She handed the device back to Jason, who already had collected the toys. "Emergency protocols should already have begun. If not, someone is going to be flogged." People were screaming and rushing about, children wailing almost louder than the siren. There was so much noise that she didn't yet register the commotion at the other end of the park. A squad of eight Rangers had rushed in through the far gate, their shape-shifting weapons—called cutlasses—configured into swords.

Norah swiveled her head around. Where was the Ursa?

The octet of Rangers also seemed confused, forming a loose ring back to back, scanning the park. People continued to flee.

She studied the men and women, noting just how young and nervous they appeared. No doubt they grew up on tales of the genetically engineered monsters that the Skrel sent to the planet with frightening regularity, all in a vain attempt at ridding the world of life for some unknown reason.

They stood their ground, uncertain where to go. If they weren't moving, neither was she. She tightened her grip on Anderson, who studied the Rangers in their brown smart fabric uniforms with fascination. He knew what a Ranger was; after all, her older cousin Lucius was Prime Commander, and Anderson, even as an infant, was drawn to the uniform. It was in the Kincaid blood and had been for many generations.

One Ranger heard something and looked up. Norah followed her gaze and looked at the brown- and yellow-leafed tree.

That was when she heard it: the unearthly, ferocious cry of an abomination. It became visible amid the foliage, bellowing in a horrible tone. Her nightmares had manifested, and she had to flee. In the rush of activity, Anderson squirmed free and rushed across the sandpit, away from her. She cried out to him, but with the siren and the other noises, her words were swallowed and the boy, unaware of the danger, headed right for the Rangers.

The moving target was all the Ursa needed, and it leaped from the tree toward the boy.

Time slowed for Norah as her heart slammed against her chest, each beat drowning out all other sounds.

Anderson finally stopped moving and watched the Ursa in the air. He was paralyzed with fear.

One of the Rangers also leaped into action, trying to draw the Ursa's attention, but the monster had other ideas.

The last thing Norah saw before her world went black was the Ursa's maw opening to devour her son as the Ranger's bladed weapon swung through the air.

The boy woke up hours later. Norah never left his side. She was accompanied by her husband, Marco, a slightly paunchy man with dark, slicked-back hair and a mustache that once had been fashionable but now seemed oddly out of place. Anderson was groggy, blinking repeatedly as he looked around the room before focusing on his parents.

"Where . . . am I?" he croaked.

A nurse, also present, leaned over and gently squeezed water from a yellow bulb into his mouth. He swallowed, sputtered, swallowed again, and seemed to be becoming more alert rapidly.

"Hi, love bug," Norah said, tears streaming down both cheeks.

"You're in the hospital, Andy," his father said. "How do you feel?"

He shrugged. "I dunno . . . sore. What happened?"

Anderson drifted off before he could hear the answer. Over the next few hours he could only hazily recall snippets of conversation. None of it seemed real to him, but it all sounded scary, so he took comfort in sleep.

He heard his father ask, "Can it be reattached?" His mother sobbed. The doctor started talking about prosthetics and how far they had progressed through the years.

Anderson also heard his parents arguing, and that hurt him in ways different from the ache in his shoulder. He heard his mom saying, "I never should have stayed in the park." His father was agreeing but sounded very angry.

As he fully woke up, he wasn't sure what to expect. All he knew was that he ached all over and was very thirsty.

"Mom?"

Norah turned to look at her son, and he saw that her eyes were red. His father was right behind her, his hand on her right shoulder.

Shoulder. He turned to look at where he ached. All he saw was a huge bandage and beyond that . . . nothing.

"Mama! Where's my arm?!"

"The Ursa was about to kill you, but the Ranger stopped it . . ." she continued.

"The creature took your arm," his father said as gently as possible. "It could not be reattached."

Anderson blinked, his left shoulder under thick white bandages shuddering in response. "But I feel it. Mama, you're a doctor; can't you put it back on?" The question sounded so reasonable, and it was, if you were seven. Norah Kincaid, though, knew that there were limits to what medical science could do.

Just then, a middle-aged man of Asian descent entered the room, followed by a different nurse with a rolling cart. Atop it was a readout of Anderson's vital signs that the man consulted before looking at the boy.

"My name is Dr. Zeong, Anderson. How do you feel?"

"What about my arm?" he asked, ignoring the question. "Mama's the best doctor on Nova Prime. Can't you put it back on?"

"The arm was too badly damaged at the base for successful grafting," the doctor explained in a low voice. "I'm sorry, son, but it couldn't be saved."

There was some talk about prosthetics, which he knew meant a fake arm, and that didn't interest him. As he lay back in the bed, he tried to recall what had happened. He remembered the sandpit, then the siren. And he remembered the Ranger who ran toward him.

"Mama," Anderson said, breaking the silence. "What happened to the Ranger who saved me?"

She sighed heavily and kissed his forehead. "She died doing her duty to protect you."

He nodded at that and thought a lot about the Rangers as the adults chattered among themselves about things he couldn't follow or care about.

Year after year, Anderson grew up, training himself to qualify for the Rangers. Every few years, as his body continued to grow and develop, he would visit the hospital, where a new arm had to be attached. There were weeks of clumsiness as he adjusted to each new prosthetic; this usually was accompanied by some depression and frustration as the simplest tasks proved difficult.

Never once did Anderson think his arm was "fake"; that was a little boy's way of thinking. As he matured, he treated the arm as a real limb. Thanks to the smart fabric technology woven into the synthetic skin, it actually tanned in the sunlight, even freckling to match the rest of his body.

As Anderson grew, he studied the history of the Rangers and his family's lengthy connection to them. His family could trace its proud Ranger heritage to at least 306 AE, when Carlos Kincaid became the first Kincaid to be named Prime Commander. He pestered his cousin Lucius for information about what it was like and what was required and never tired of hearing stories of the family's Ranger-related exploits. Despite the tarnished reputation of his grandfather, Nathan Kincaid—considered the worst Prime Commander in history—Anderson wrote several school reports addressing the man's notorious tenure as Prime Commander.

He also learned more about the Kincaid family's lengthy rivalry with the Raige family. It stunned him to hear the genuine hatred in his family members' voices as they recounted how the Raiges had stymied the Kincaids' progress time and again. For every achievement his family had, such as developing the cutlasses, the Raiges seemed to trump it. He didn't know any Raige in school, and they remained an abstract concept to him with the exception of Cypher Raige. The Ranger had been his cousin Atlas's close friend despite the familial animosity, and Anderson had met Cypher a few times. The tall, stern, quiet man was the epitome of what it meant to be a Ranger. But more than that, he was a legend. The year Anderson lost his arm, Cypher Raige managed to do something they called ghosting—becoming invisible to the Ursa. It enabled him to become the first to kill the creature single-handedly. It sounded like the stuff of myth, but Atlas and his mother had assured him it had happened. Cypher himself never wanted to talk about it, disliking being the focus of attention.

Growing up meant overcoming the replacement arm's limitations. He constantly adjusted it to match the strength and dexterity of his right arm so that he could play sports and function without an unfair advantage. Working with weights and other equipment, he honed his muscles and improved his endurance. He learned how to box and shoot, how to ride, and how to fence. The teen was guided by his father to balance the physical with the mental, which meant not neglecting his studies. Though not at the top of his class, he was proud of his accomplishments.

At night, Norah arrived home from her work and tended to her son. Even though his body was exhausted and his mind weary, he would absorb her lectures on the philosophies of Nova Prime and its people. Although the Kincaids had a deep connection to the Rangers, several served as the Savant and as such were in charge of the scientific community of Nova Prime. Currently, their aunt Liliandra led the planet's religious order as the Primus. Their family served the planet in whatever honorable way possible. When those lectures occurred, he reminded her time and again that it was all well and good, but he was determined to qualify for the Rangers. Testing began as early as age thirteen, but he wanted to make sure he nailed the admissions the first time out. She nodded encouragingly and continued her lectures as he fell asleep.

Maybe it was her medical training and her concern for the sanctity of life, which was constantly at risk, but she didn't necessarily encourage him in his pursuit. She did, though, know he had been focused on this path as a form of atonement or honoring the dead, and she couldn't argue with that.

Then came the afternoon the eighteen-year-old appeared at Norah's offices in a sweat-drenched shirt, a towel wrapped around his neck. Maybe it was the glistening sweat, but it appeared to her that Anderson was glowing.

"I'm ready," he told her.

"For a shower, I would think," she replied tartly, sniffing at him in disapproval.

"Fine. But after the shower, I'm going to go sign up," he announced.

She said carefully, "Is this truly what you want?"

"Mom, it's all I've been thinking about since the attack," he said in a tone that indicated this was old territory. His mother pressed the point.

"Yes, and it has been good to stay focused so you can heal and get strong. But now that you are fit, you have so many other options. There are other ways to serve the people."

"I already heard Aunt Liliandra and how wonderful the augury is," the teen said. "I don't care."

"Show some respect for your aunt and the faith," his mother said. "I don't know where I'd be without it. I prayed and prayed you'd survive that awful attack."

"I did, Mom. I did because a Ranger risked her life for mine. Aren't you always telling us to give back? This is me, giving back."

"You could explore medicine or other fields," she said. He had heard it all before and knew she was just trying to get him to at least consider other careers. But after so many years being focused on the Rangers, nothing else felt quite right. "You really have your mind made up?"

He nodded.

"All you see is the noble sacrifice, and all I see is a dead woman, cut down before her life could really develop. You've already lost one arm, and it nearly killed me. I just don't want to lose the rest of you."

"You won't, Mom," he swore.

He walked over and hugged her.

"I want you to be proud of me," he said.

"Always," she replied. They stood in each other's arms for a few silent moments.

"If that is what you wish, then I will not stop you," she told him at last. "Shower first, United Rangers second."

He knew that Phase 1 testing was a grueling mix of physical activity and mental recall. There were two dozen others testing that cycle, and he was determined to top them all. He had barely any body fat and was pure muscle, able to dead lift over 114 kilos—impressive for an eighteen-year-old—and that was without any enhancement to the prosthetic arm. He omitted its existence on the entrance forms and never mentioned it to the others. The synthetic skin was perfectly blended to match his natural skin tone, and he stayed in a T-shirt whenever possible. Being a Kincaid meant he knew the regulations by heart, and among them was the archaic prohibition against Rangers having prosthetic limbs. Nope, he was going to do this evenly matched against the others.

Well, maybe not that evenly matched. Being a Ranger was in his blood. He proudly carried over seven hundred years of Kincaid dedication to service.

He outran the men, outclimbed the women, and sparred them both into submission.

Stepping into the dreaded booth, he was able to recite facts and details way beyond what the artificial intelligence was asking him. He also finished in what he imagined to be record time.

There was nothing stopping him from being approved for Phase 2 testing.

That night, there was a knock on the door of the family's home. Anderson's younger sister, Kayla, ran to answer it while he was reading. All he heard were hushed voices and some sort of commotion that caught his attention.

Clicking off his reader, a barefoot Anderson padded through the fabric curtains into the main room. Standing in the middle of his home was Commander Rafe Velan, the man in charge of training and testing the cadets. The tall, broad man had a close-cropped head of graying hair and a weathered face. Anderson's mind was reeling; he had never heard of such a personal visit being made. What on Nova was happening?

"Commander!" he said, snapping to attention despite wearing a light shirt and baggy trousers. His sister imitated his stance, stifling a giggle.

Velan, a stern look in his eyes, twitched his mouth a moment before saying, "At ease . . . kids."

Anderson exhaled while trying to remain at least somewhat presentable; Kayla fell into a chair.

"Are your parents at home?" Velan asked.

"Dad's out getting something for dinner, and Mom's at her office, as usual," Kayla said.

"I see. May I speak with you alone, Cadet Kincaid?"

"Kay, get lost," Anderson said, looking intently at his sister.

She made a face at him, smiled sweetly at Velan, and skipped out of the room. The commander, meanwhile, looked around the room, clearly uncomfortable. That got Anderson concerned. Something was wrong if the commander himself was in his house. How he wished his mother were there.

"Sir, may I get you a drink?"

"Thank you, no," Velan said before swallowing hard. "I will get right to the point. You *cannot* be a Ranger."

Anderson blinked once, then twice.

Kayla peeked through the bottom of a curtain, trying to eavesdrop, but he glared at her and she vanished back behind the curtain. He hadn't imagined something so blunt and definitive. Now it was his turn to swallow and collect himself, trying to control the roiling emotions he felt.

"Sir, may this candidate inquire as to why?"

"At ease, Anderson," Velan said emphatically. "You're not in the program, and we know each other. In looking over your application for admission, the computer sent up a red flag. And I believe you know why."

Anderson stared at the commander, trying to hold in the warring emotions deep in his chest. His dreams were about to become bitter ashes.

When he didn't reply, Velan continued: "You lied, son. Had I seen the application, I would have remembered your accident and prosthetic arm and pulled it from consideration. You know the rules, I believe."

"Sir, yes, sir," he said weakly.

Velan nodded at that. "You knew about the prohibition, but you applied anyway and tried to sneak by. You were dishonest. Is a Ranger dishonest, Cadet?"

"No, sir!"

"Why lie, then?"

"The prosthetic is a *part* of me," Anderson began. "I have lived with it for over half my life, and it doesn't make me any less fit for being a Ranger."

"Our regulations have a prohibition against Rangers having any prosthetic devices that may malfunction in the field, compromising the Ranger's welfare and the safety of the Rangers around him," Velan said, practically reciting the manual.

"Has it happened to anyone before?"

"Not that I know of," Velan admitted, and if he could not think of an incident, it probably never had happened. Velan was a legend at the academy, a battle-tested man who was a walking, talking rule book. "But the rules were written a long time ago."

"Then with respect, sir, considering the advances of prosthetics, maybe it's time for those rules to be reviewed and revised."

"A good point and one that will be taken under consideration. But meanwhile, the prohibition remains on the books, and it therefore excludes you. Right now, the larger issue is you being deceitful, which I cannot tolerate within the corps. I have to say, Anderson, I am disappointed you would lie. It dishonors yourself and your family name."

"The arm has never once let me down, just like I won't let the Rangers down. You can't discriminate against me—it wasn't my fault, and it's not all I am. Let me prove it."

"You hid the truth from the Rangers, and it sounds like you're hiding it from yourself, too," Velan gently said. That seemed to end the discussion, and Anderson knew he was not going to win the argument.

"Does my mother know?" he asked.

"I felt I owed it to you to tell you first," he said, sounding genuinely sorry. "Would you like me to discuss this with her?"

"No . . . thank you, sir," Anderson said. "I can tell her of my own failing."

"You didn't fail," Velan said. "This has nothing to do with your ratings and everything to do with you hiding a disqualifying factor about yourself. Truthfully, you shouldn't have even been allowed to try out in the first place. The thinking was that if you proved to be simply not up to the demands of the position, this would all be moot. The fact that I had to come out here just to have this discussion at all is your victory, not failure. Your scores were incredibly impressive. Then again, I would expect no less of Atlas's relative."

The future that Anderson had spent more than a decade working toward had suddenly vanished, and now that reality was sinking in. It hurt in a way his shoulder and missing arm never did. The pain was a psychic one, coursing from brain to heart and back again. Now all he wanted to do was scream at Velan, but he suspected that would be an irreparable mistake.

"I think I'd better go, Anderson," Velan said, beginning to turn. "If you want me to speak with your parents, just call my office. I wish it were otherwise, since I know you would be an asset. Good night."

With a voice that was as dead as his career, Anderson Kincaid said, "Good night . . . sir."

It was a few days later, when the pain of the rejection had faded to a dull ache within his heart, that Anderson truly sat down to examine his options. He was powerfully built, and it appeared that only the Rangers had the limitation on prosthetics. Scanning the feeds, he considered various opportunities, but many were for labor and offered no real sense of a career. He most definitely didn't want to be a laborer or an athlete (for fear someone would also be whispering "fraud" at every competition) or provide personal security for the elite.

Then he spotted a position with the Nova Prime Civilian Defense Corps. They were looking for qualified candidates for civilian patrols.

Kincaid did a quick scan of the agency and realized it was sanctioned civil defense. He hadn't previously noticed or concerned himself with any other options, blinded as he was by dreams of the Rangers. Now, though, the NPCDC looked like a perfect fit.

"A Kincaid, eh?" the slightly overweight desk officer said. "Haven't had one of those yet. Why us and not the Rangers?"

Anderson had anticipated the question, although he didn't like discussing it. Just seeing the artificial arm and hand should have been clue enough. But then again, not everyone paid attention to details.

"My left arm is a prosthetic," he said in a flat tone.

"Lemme see," the man said, extending a beefy hand.

Anderson complied, meeting the hand with his own. The man rolled up the sleeve a bit and examined the detail work, which simulated skin, arm hair, and even fingerprints to match the other hand. He whistled.

"That's the new K-class arm," the man said.

Kincaid blinked in mild surprise that the man knew that and flexed the fingers for him, suddenly swelling with pride, since the man clearly wasn't patronizing him.

"Works great, the best one yet," Anderson agreed. "You have any problem with prosthetics?"

"Not in the slightest," the man said. "Bill McGirk. Fill this out, and once you pass the physical, you're in. And you'll look better in the uniform than I will."

McGirk was a man of his word, and within days, Anderson Kincaid was being shown the pulsers used by the NPCDC, which were not regularly carried but cached in case of emergency. Most of the work involved patrolling public spaces, looking for mischief, petty theft, and other troubles the Rangers didn't have to focus on. They were first responders to medical emergencies, and so he needed a week of paramedic training, which he had an aptitude for despite ignoring his mother's lessons through the years.

He enjoyed the long shifts and felt a sense of purpose as he walked the streets of Nova Prime City. McGirk was right about one other thing: He looked damn good in uniform, its sheer fabric diffusing heat and wicking away sweat, keeping him comfortable.

Anderson also liked patrolling with Virginia Marquez, a petite woman near his age. She was pretty and sassy and easy to get along with. They would walk the streets together, and bit by bit he was getting to know the neighborhoods in the sectors, picking up the vibes each area gave off. In many ways, it was like he was a newcomer, experiencing the city for the first time. There were the areas where the technicians worked, the smell of the animal herders and farmers with their own ripe odors, the manufacturers who always had recyclables littering the edges of their buildings.

"What's the strangest call you've had?" Kincaid asked her the fourth week they were patrolling together. It was morning, and as the suns climbed the sky, the heat rose and the city woke up. There was a quiet followed by the growing sounds of the people getting ready to work or play. There was always the smell of freshly baked goods, and he learned early on when to be near the bakeries so that bakers would toss them hot rolls—their way of saying good morning.

Marquez, her long hair knotted in an elaborate style with various wooden pieces holding it in place, thought about it for a while. "It might have been the time I was called for a domestic disturbance. Neighbors called just before dawn, claiming there was a horrible fight going on next door and they heard things breaking. I got there with my partner, Cotto, and we knocked once to be polite before we kicked in the door."

She fell silent, munching on the roll.

"Well?"

"There was no fighting. They were making love. A lot of it, apparently."

Kincaid nodded and grinned at her. "Learn anything?"

"Nothing you need to worry about," she teased, and quickened her pace.

"You miss your arm?"

Marquez settled onto the bench next to him, shoving the beer stein in his direction, letting some of the foamy head spill onto the worn table. They had knocked off work a little early and met others at their favorite bar to toast Anderson's first year in the service.

"I was so young when it happened, I think about it more than actually miss it. At night, sometimes, I think I can still feel it, still flex my real muscles and point with my fingers. I was told the sense of the phantom limb would fade with time, and I guess it has, but I don't stop thinking about it."

"But you should be thinking about the path it set you on," Lars Svensen said. He was a five-year vet with blond hair, blue eyes, and pecs the women swooned over. As a result, he made certain to wear his uniform shirt open beyond what regulations allowed for; not that anyone complained. "You could have been a Ranger."

"Yeah, you could have been a Ranger and flown over all this planet or trained until you were ready to cry," Kelly Alpuente added. "I mean, really, what do they do when not fighting Skrel and Ursa? They train to fight Skrel and Ursa."

"And when was the last time you saw a Skrel ship?" Marquez asked.

"It's been a while," Anderson admitted.

"And when was the last significant Ursa attack?"

"Nine fifty-one AE. The Skrel deposited a hundred on the ground; the Rangers took out eighty-eight of them," he mechanically replied.

"You're on my trivia team," Alpuente said with a smile. "I might have gotten the year right but not the rest."

"It's that Ranger prep," Marquez said. "You really wanted to be one of them, didn't you?"

He merely said yes and drank his beer. He was happy with the corps and had made some valued friends. The last years had been good ones, and he was pleased with the work. They were happy with him. It all should have been good and this should be a joyous celebration, but like his phantom limb, being a Ranger still felt like a phantom career, the reality versus this substitute.

Kincaid threw himself into the conversation, drank one beer too many, and let Alpuente take him home for the night, unaware of the longing look Marquez shot him.

Flames had blackened the side of the honeycombed complex. Non-smart fabric materials were catching fire and adding to the heat and light. People were still being evacuated when Anderson finally showed up to assist. The call for reinforcements had gone out only ten minutes prior, so he thought he had made good time, but he recognized that every minute meant more property lost, more life endangered.

McGirk had arrived to take point, sweating in the heat, soaking his uniform beyond the fabric's ability to keep him cool. He looked haggard as firefighters behind him were spraying foam directly on the flames.

Kincaid and Marquez had been pulled off their regular assignment to lend assistance to the firefighters. They first were handling crowd control, and thankfully, everyone followed orders without trouble. Then McGirk came toward them, pointing at Kincaid.

"Kincaid, the firefighters are shorthanded. You're strong; I need you in there searching for stragglers," McGirk said, shoving his right thumb in the direction of the burning building.

"I'm a little underdressed for that," Kincaid began when a fireman shoved a rubbery yellow suit at him. Without hesitation or additional comment, Marquez helped him step into the one-piece outfit, which quickly fastened around him. He was handed a pair of orange fluorescent gloves that fit over the sleeves and then were molded around his wrists, adhering to the bodysuit. Finally, a cowl was applied, fastened, and finished with goggles and breathing apparatus. The oxygen had a metallic tang to it. He felt a little silly, but it was regulation and he was now insulated for brief periods so that he could enter the structure and see if people were trapped.

Marquez patted the side of his face, which Anderson found oddly affectionate until he realized the woman was merely activating the communicator built into the breathing mask.

"You hear me? Am I coming across clear?"

"Crystal."

McGirk gave him a thumbs-up, adding, "Go find 'em, kid."

Kincaid walked toward the building, seeking a safe entry point, and wound up climbing through the remains of a burned-out window. He half stumbled his way through, regained his footing, and paused to study his surroundings. The fire had pretty much charred the furniture and belongings so that there were dark heaps of what once had been useful materials. He saw no loss of life and walked into the next room. There was enough noise from the flames, the foam, and general shouting of orders that he decided against adding to the noise by calling out. Instead, he methodically worked his way from room to room, apartment to apartment, and floor to floor. It promised to be a long, tedious process.

The first two floors proved empty, just remnants of what once had been people's homes and lives. Little had survived the heat and flame, which hungrily devoured what it could. He had never bothered to ask what had caused it, but whatever had happened had happened fast, long before the firefighters could arrive to stop the spread. The foam left a sticky residue everywhere, tinting the blackened furniture and walls a dull green.

As he climbed the emergency stairs up to the third floor, he heard something above—a wall, most likely— give way, crumbling with loud thuds that actually shook the stairs. He tightened his grip and continued upward, listening for any cries that might indicate an injury. His breathing seemed to grow louder in his ears with every step.

The first four apartments he checked were damaged and empty, but the fifth was where the structure fell apart. The rooms were almost pitch-black, with charcoal masquerading as furniture. The collapsed wall had divided a living room from a bedroom, leaving structural supports that had burned through. He suspected the fire might have started there or nearby, but he'd leave that to the trained investigators to confirm. He gingerly kicked at rubble, seeking evidence of a living being that might be trapped beneath. There was nothing remotely human, and after a few minutes he gave up.

Turning, he readied himself for the next apartment,

his throat beginning to long for a cool drink, when he saw a figure dart by the doorway.

"Hey!" he called out, but there was no response.

He tried to move both quickly and cautiously, not wishing to cause walls or floors to crumble beneath him. The figure had made it to the end of the corridor and had entered the last room on the left. Skipping the ones in between, Kincaid stalked the person, wishing he had a pulser with him just in case.

Peering through the doorway, Kincaid was surprised to see the person was an old man, seemingly unharmed by the conflagration. He was wandering in circles, as if he was searching for something, looking increasingly confused. Kincaid took one step into the room, and the old man finally noticed him.

"Have you seen my reader?" he asked Kincaid.

"Sir, are you all right?" he asked the man, who looked anything but all right.

"Absolutely," the man said distractedly as he opened a drawer. "Thank you for asking."

"You *do* know this building is on fire? It's unsafe, and you should come with me."

The man paused in his search and looked at Kincaid as if for the first time. Studying him from head to toe, the old man gaped. "What are you?"

"Civilian Defense Corps, sir. I'm searching for survivors, and you look like one."

"Survivors of what? Are the Skrel attacking?" He was clearly addled, perhaps even mentally ill.

"Not the Skrel; a fire. I need to get you out of the building."

"I need my reader; I have to finish my book before class," the man complained. Kincaid realized his argument was not getting through to the poor man. He still wondered how he was totally unscathed by the fire, but that was a mystery for another time. The one wall crumbling made him feel as if he were inside a ticking bomb. He stepped forward decisively, grabbed the man's left wrist, and hefted him into the air and across his shoulders in the traditional fireman's carry. He tested the added weight and the floor held, and so he took one step and then another to make certain they could escape. The moment the old man was across his shoulders, he became remarkably placid, like a kitten slumping when its mother carried it by the nape.

"McGirk, I have a survivor. An elderly man, physically unharmed. We're coming down from the fifth floor."

"Acknowledged. Medical corps will be standing by. Stay safe, kid."

"No kidding."

The old man stayed quiet as Kincaid made his way slowly down the steps until finally, several agonizingly long minutes later, he emerged from the building. Two members of the medical team ran to him and eased him from Kincaid's shoulders to a stretcher, where he was quickly checked over.

Kincaid ripped off the mask and breathed in air that smelled of smoke.

"Nice work, kid," McGirk said as he walked over. "What's his story?"

"No idea," Kincaid admitted. "Don't know and frankly don't care. The guy needs some help, and I'm too sore and tired to really think about it."

"You're done. They got the fire under control, and the firefighters can check out the rest of the place. When are you next on?"

Anderson thought a moment and answered, "Second shift."

"Get some sleep and come in late. Marquez can keep the peace until you show up."

"Nice work, Anderson," she said, giving him a hug that lingered a bit longer than normal. He pretended he didn't notice and thanked her.

Collapsing into bed back at his apartment, Kincaid thought that this was why he had signed up: to protect the people, to use his body in productive ways. It was a good way to live.

* * *

The following day, he reported for work and was heartily congratulated and razzed by the others for his heroism. He shrugged it off in the locker room but inwardly felt very proud of upholding the Ranger ideals even if he was still a corpsman.

On the street with Marquez, though, he felt he could really express those feelings. They'd been growing increasingly comfortable with each other, a true bond forming between them. Today he noticed she had done her hair a different way.

"I like it down like that even though it's not regulation," he said.

"Thanks, but there are few hair regulations. You keep thinking we live by the Ranger code, but we don't. We are looser and have far more fun."

"Just what do you do for fun?"

"Long-distance hiking. I really like getting out on the Falkor Desert, seeing what's out there."

"You walk far enough, you'll get to New Earth City," Kincaid said.

"No, I go looking for reptiles. I'm a secret herp."

"Herp?"

"Herpetological, silly. Reptiles, snakes and things."

"Really? That sounds really . . . different."

"Says someone who has clearly never handled a snake," she said. "Look, come over after shifting and I'll let you have a feel."

She was blushing as she said that, but he was certainly interested enough to accept her invitation.

It was a good way to live. Then why didn't it feel like it? Anderson had grown comfortable with his life, and the year 997 AE had been a particularly satisfying one for him so far. He had the corps, he had friends, and his apartment was taking on his personality. Kayla was old enough to no longer be annoying but a loving sister and good friend. His parents continued to ask about a spouse, and his mother—still the city's head physician—asked about grandchildren to occupy her during her impending retirement. But he was not interested. Not yet, anyway. He was twenty, in his physical prime, and creating new generations of Kincaids could wait.

Over the last few weeks he and Marquez let things take their natural course, and a romance was developing. She introduced him to her snake, Merlin, then let him feel the reptile's skin and compare it with her own far hotter flesh.

Since that torrid night, the two were seeing each other both on shift and off duty. Now both were getting teased by the others, but all approved, even Alpuente, who seemed to have first dibs on Kincaid.

It wasn't all Nirvana, though. He felt a great deal of affection for her, but it was clearly secondary to his mission, and that caused problems. The previous night, he had stayed at her place, and after they had made love for the second time in a few hours, she straddled him, her hair tickling his nose.

"Do you always do everything with military precision?"

"Did I do something wrong?"

"No, not at all. To be honest, you're the finest lover I've had. You're definitely a keeper, Andy."

He frowned at her. "There's a 'but' coming, isn't there?"

She shook her head, but her eyes were no longer merry. "You are technically proficient, even creative, but you never feel fully committed to this . . . to us."

He propped himself up on his elbows and stared into her eyes. Was she trying to break things off? She had just said he was a keeper, so what was happening?

"Andy, you have yet to let go of your dream. You've told me about being denied entrance to the Rangers, and I get how soul-crushing that must have been. But you have a good life, a good career. You have *me*. But that isn't enough, is it?"

Anderson Kincaid had no proper response to that question.

Instead, he slid out from under her and hurriedly dressed, returning home to his place and his thoughts.

He was on second shift the following day, walking toward the huge outdoor market. Fresh produce and crops had been brought in hours earlier, and the place was teeming with people haggling, bargaining, and gossiping. In other words, another typical day in another typical week, and Kincaid was okay with that. He and Marquez could walk in comfortable silence and just soak in the local ambience.

As he pondered a choice between green and leafy or juicy and succulent for his dinner, their radios crackled to life.

"All corps, this is a priority alert. Ursa have been sighted in the city. Rangers are in pursuit, but we need to begin clearing the streets. The siren is about to go off, so be prepared for a panic."

Marquez thumbed a button that acknowledged the alert and quickened her pace toward the market. "That place is a zoo under normal conditions; this is not going to be easy," she said. "What was it you said a while back? Only a handful left from the last attack?"

"A few, but we have no clue if they breed or not," he said, matching her pace.

"I'm voting for not," she said, and her next words were cut off by the siren coming to life. It was long and loud and had the desired effect of catching everyone's attention. From the speakers nestled within various structures, a recorded voice announced, *"This is not a drill. All citizens are instructed to remain inside or report to the nearest shelter."*

Marquez understood the populace, and sure enough, people were moving in anything but an orderly manner. Some ran, some scooped up purchases, some continued to bargain. Awnings began collapsing, and goods for sale were being sealed in containers. People screamed in panic or shouted for loved ones. Everyone moved. Movement was good; all the corpsmen had to do was steer them to shelter.

Kincaid thought about the Ranger response. This was what they prepared themselves for and what each one dreamed about: killing an Ursa and claiming a prize, having a story to tell, or being part of a legend. He longed once more to be fighting alongside them but knew that was never going to happen. Instead, he would have to herd the people and keep the streets clear so that the Rangers could do their jobs.

Although it was not part of corps protocol, Kincaid maintained his own weapons training, making certain he could fire a pulser with either hand and be certain his target would fall dead. He was adept with various bladed weapons and had even dabbled in archery to perfect his eye-hand coordination. Aiming had to be precise, as it might mean the difference between life and death. In the case of the Ursa, it meant hitting their meat and not the smart metal that was bonded to their skeletons to give them a layer of protection. They were unearthly, hideous creatures, and in his mind's eye he replayed the one that had nearly killed him almost two decades earlier.

A Ranger had died to save his life, and he owed a debt for her sacrifice and her memory.

Emergency shelters to protect people from sandstorms or lightning—and yes, Ursa attacks—dotted the city, marked with a glowing symbol that promised safety. Anderson windmilled his right arm while his prosthetic left arm directed citizens toward the nearest shelter. Marquez had jogged over to make certain it was open and powered. She then helped funnel the people through the dual doorways.

People continued to make noise, adding to the siren's wail, and Kincaid wished for earplugs but gritted his teeth, ignored the discord, and kept directing them toward a safe haven. The great mass continued to flow from the market toward the shelter.

A roar, the sound of which brought back waking nightmares, pierced the panicky noises. An Ursa was close, and he hoped the Rangers were on its heels. He glanced over his shoulder and saw people fleeing in all directions away from the covered open-air market. The creature had to be in there.

Kincaid rushed to the space between the twin doors and entered a code on the keypad. A panel smoothly slid open, and he withdrew three pulsers. Tucking one in his waist and tossing another to Marquez, he felt better about dealing with the imminent threat.

A Ranger emerged from behind the shelter, out of breath and covered in dust. "Have you seen it?"

"In the market, I think," Kincaid replied.

"Keep the people moving in there; we've got this," he ordered somewhat needlessly. The comment bothered Kincaid, who took it as an insinuation that he wouldn't do his job unless a Ranger directed him to.

The Ranger sprinted toward the Ursa and, no doubt, his fellow Rangers. If Anderson recalled correctly, the rules stated that—when available—a minimum of eight Rangers were required to confront one of those beasts. People got out of the Ranger's way and kept streaming toward the shelter. Marquez continued moving them through the doors while Kincaid surveyed the scene. They didn't need to speak; each understood the other well enough by now that words were unnecessary.

Kincaid watched as the cutlass-wielding Ranger dashed into the market, where sounds of destruction were competing with the siren. He wished there were an off switch for the alarm; by now, everyone had gotten the message.

A body came flying through an opening in the market and crumpled to the ground. It appeared to be missing a leg, and blood pooled around the figure. Marquez gestured for him to keep his position.

"Don't go, Andy!"

"There are civilians still inside."

She crossed over to him, eyes flaring. "It's suicide! This is what the Rangers exist for. And you are not a Ranger. Let it go."

"But they're not here and I am."

"Okay, Andy, so you live and breathe being a Ranger even though you're not in uniform. What does the manual say about fighting the Ursa?"

"Eight Rangers, no less."

"You are an army of one. How do you reconcile that?"

He stared at her, speechless.

"I didn't know you had a death wish."

"How can I face you tomorrow if I don't go do this? How could I live a life with you if I knowingly let that monster kill the innocents?"

"If there were an army of us, I'd have your back, but right now it's just us. We can't go in there and survive."

"Gin, I have to. I have to try or I couldn't live with myself."

Kincaid ran toward the body, but as he drew closer, it was evident the person was dead. He focused his attention on the market itself, an ever-changing cluster of prefabricated stalls and stands where every food and drink imaginable could be found. As he neared, the corpsman could see the creature, which was huge and moved erratically. However the Skrel bioengineered those things, they were far from elegant creations designed for maximum carnage. The six limbs ended in razor-sharp talons, and the maw was stuffed with pointed teeth. He knew they were sightless, using their other senses, mainly that of smell, to locate and lock onto their prey. Right now it was rampaging and destroying in search of human life.

He knew Virginia would do her job, protecting the perimeter while he went after the beast, but he had no idea if she'd still be there when the mission ended. A part of him was planning a future that included her, but with every step forward he was trampling that dream, risking the first tangible happiness he'd had in years.

The deserted stalls appeared to frustrate it, and the

Ursa tore through thin metal and wood and Plasticine as if they were all cotton-weight fabric. Behind it, Kincaid could spot two more Rangers in addition to the one who had charged toward it. That one could not be seen, and he hoped the man was not dead.

He spied the Rangers deploying their cutlasses. Lightweight and versatile, cutlasses could quickly morph into a dozen or more shapes depending on need. Right now, all the Rangers' weapons appeared to be in sickle formation, clearly intended to hobble as many of the creature's legs as possible and bring it down. Of course, first they had to catch the thing.

Then Kincaid saw another Ranger spring from hiding, his cutlass shaped like a needle, and fly toward the beast, ready to pierce its tough hide. The Ursa, though, must have smelled the man and reared up on its hind legs, the forward limbs shredding him in the air. Organs and blood spilled to the ground moments before the dead body followed. The Ursa roared not so much in triumph but because it could.

Quickly, it turned around and charged toward the Rangers, who scattered out of its way. The creature chased the ones who ran to the left.

This was Anderson's chance. He rushed forward and grasped the fallen Ranger's cutlass. Now that he was wielding it, there was little to differentiate the corpsman from the Ranger, and Kincaid recognized he had a debt to repay, first to the woman who had saved his life and then to his family's legacy.

He had to move carefully to avoid alerting the monster but also so that he wouldn't slip on the messy pools of blood, viscera, and squashed fruit. The sickly-sweet smells made him want to gag, but he swallowed it down and kept approaching the beast as it continued its charge toward the Rangers. The other Rangers were out of sight; either they had run away or they were stealthily approaching it.

The siren finally cut off, and Kincaid whispered

thanks to the heavens, just as his mother had taught him.

He focused his hearing and heard the clatter of taloned paws moving the Ursa along, the cracking of worn wood, and the crackle of the cutlass in his hand.

Then he heard a different sound, a low, plaintive resonance. Not human and most certainly not Ursa. It then struck him that livestock was also on display at the market, mostly as a petting zoo for the kids while the parents shopped. Demonstrations were put on to teach the children how the animals contributed to society. These were not happy noises, and he heard shuffling about. The animals were spooked, and that could only mean the Ursa had decided it was lunchtime.

Kincaid crept closer, hands tightening and retightening their grip on the cutlass. He had never hefted one before and had no real clue how to make it alter its configuration. If the scythe shape was particularly sharp, that might be all he needed.

An animal cried out, with others repeating the sound at a lower volume, and he knew the Ursa had slaughtered one, maybe a horse. He hoped to catch the Ursa unaware, preoccupied as it was with eating whatever poor animal had lost its life before its time.

He worked close to the pens, and as he rounded one corner, he came upon the remains of more Rangers. One's torso had been torn apart; another's head was severed from the neck. The man's head had rolled a few feet away, the look of shock on its face frozen in place, a sight Kincaid wanted to forget immediately. Instead, it seemed to find a place in his mind, right next to the image of the charging Ursa at the playground when he was a child.

The Ursa paused in its consumption, suddenly aware of Kincaid's presence. Sightless, it turned toward him but held its ground. Dim light reflected off the smart metal protruding in a haphazard pattern around its body. No way could a single shot from that distance take out the beast. Heck, pulsers were useless at point-blank range. Kincaid had to get closer but was having trouble making his feet move. Perhaps the Ursa would have to come his way; it was a terrifying thought.

He knew that if it imprinted on him and his fear, it would hunt him down until one or the other was dead. Kincaid had other plans for his death—first and foremost being that it would not be for a long time—and so he did the only thing he could: shuffled backward, away from the creature, hoping it would stay to finish its meal. There were still Rangers operating and no doubt more coming. The Rangers' main mission was to protect the world; his primary job was to protect the citizens *here*, right now.

To his surprise, the beast took a bite of intestine and proceeded to ignore him. He couldn't fathom it. The things were supposedly killing machines. The only thing he could surmise was that the Ursa considered him too puny or weak to charge right now. On the one hand, he was relieved. On the other, he felt vaguely insulted.

Making no sudden movements, Kincaid headed toward the periphery of the market. He heard human sounds and stopped to listen: They were coming from underneath a collapsed fabric stand. Judiciously stepping over debris, he approached the mound of colorful fabrics and sundries. Individually, each bolt of cloth was light enough, but one atop the other, they created a weight that clearly had someone pinned beneath.

He kicked over a few bolts and called out, "Who's there?"

"Miranda," a whimpering voice replied.

"Hi, Miranda. I'm Anderson, and I'm here to free you. Are you hurt?"

"My arm," she said, and gasped.

He knew about arm injuries and quickly began shoving the fabric out of the way. As he dug through at least a yard's worth of cotton, wool, linen, and other materials, he encountered wooden and metallic shelving that had gotten tangled up with the bolts and was not loosening easily. He strained at a particularly stubborn bit of metal, and his right arm ached.

Kincaid rarely thought about what made his left arm unique, but he knew that it didn't tire, didn't ache, and was far more durable than his right arm. He tried never to rely on its superior strength—he insisted his doctors calibrate it to male norms—but he also knew it was never a precise process and the prosthetic arm remained somewhat stronger. Now he wanted super strength, the kind he remembered from stories he had heard as a child of strong men such as Samson and Superman. He now wanted to be as mighty as they were for real and save Miranda.

As he applied all the pressure he could muster, the metal began to crumple in his hand, which closed vise-like. He gritted his teeth, feeling the muscles in his neck, chest, and legs begin to strain. Still, he didn't let go, and bit by bit the metal began to give in to the pressure. With a popping sound, it twisted and finally came free, nearly pulling Kincaid off his feet. After regaining his footing, he reached within the opening he had created and continued to yank bits of metal and wood and cloth away. He managed to create an opening and paused to peer within.

Miranda had to be fifteen, if that, and was a redhead with long curls that flowed over her yellow dress, which was now bloody and torn. The arm she complained about was pinned beneath a sewing machine, and she was lying at an angle that prevented her from moving it herself.

"Hi," he said to calm her.

She grunted and gave him a panicked look. "I can't feel it," she said.

That didn't sound good at all. He renewed his efforts and managed to reach the machine from his side of the mess. Using the cutlass as a pry bar, he levered the machine high enough for her to move her entire body, taking the limp arm from underneath. She began moving toward the opening he'd created. He pulled her through and then stood her up. He gingerly reached for her to examine the arm, but she threw herself at him and gave him a one-armed hug.

He called in his find and asked for help so that he could continue his search. Once he closed the signal, he said, "Get out of here. There's an Ursa by the animals, and I don't want it finding you."

"What about you?"

"This is my job. You go get that arm examined," he said.

She wiped away tears with her good hand, hugged him a second time, and turned to make her way outside.

Within the next fifteen minutes, he found more dead bodies, crushed from machinery that had toppled on them, and the corpse of another Ranger. His entire body had long bloody rows carved into it by the Ursa's talons.

With every step, his mind remained fixed on the Ursa's noisy position. He kept his radio on low so that he could hear reports from elsewhere around Nova Prime City. It sounded like many Ursa had come simultaneously and were wreaking havoc everywhere, which might mean Ranger reinforcements would be delayed, especially if they didn't know the Rangers at the market were among the dead.

He turned his back to the Ursa's position and called in to the corps what he had discovered, insisting the information be relayed to the Rangers. They had to know he and Marquez were the only trained form of defense in this crowded part of the city. Of course, it didn't feel crowded now as people huddled in shelters or hid within their homes.

As he turned back toward the Ursa, he saw Miranda standing in place. She was clearly in shock and hadn't gone far. This was a complication he did not need.

"Go!" he said, waving his arms in the direction of the entrance.

"I'm scared," she said, holding her injured arm.

"All the more reason to get out of here," he said.

She hesitated.

With a growl all his own, Anderson grabbed the girl, picked her up, and began moving her out of the Ursa's way. He didn't have time to play games with her and couldn't turn his back on the beast for too long. Sure enough, it took being moved just a few feet to shock her back to reality. Her eyes went wide; she let out a gurgling yelp and began running.

The Ursa roared, and Kincaid heard a thick wet sound as something hit the ground. Feeding time was over, the hunt was on, and they were the targets.

Then he heard the snarl, and it was closer.

Miranda was out of sight and presumably off to safety. That freed him to focus entirely on keeping the Ursa from hunting other humans. He looked left and right and noticed the roof. There were long sheets of pliable metal that helped shade the stalls. Fastened in place, they could provide support.

Powerful legs propelled him upward. He grasped an edge and pulled himself up. He then threw himself belly down on the roof, cutting his cheek in the process, and withdrew his pulser, taking aim. He fired a series of blasts that cracked in the air like fireworks, the bolts of energy filling the air between him and the charging Ursa.

Sure enough, it slowed the beast down as it emitted a noisy sniffing sound while its talons scraped the hard ground. Once it appeared to lock onto Kincaid's scent, the creature sped up again. Anderson sighed at his plight, aimed, and fired again. Not that he could kill the creature with the pistol, or with both pistols if it came to that. He wasn't even sure if the cutlass would be enough, but he needed to keep the Ursa occupied so that the Rangers had a chance to arrive.

His wrist gauntlet contained a small screen that usually flashed a variety of information; he orally commanded it to display a schematic of the market. He needed a plan other than blindly shooting at the Ursa until it leaped up and gored him. Bright red lines appeared on the black screen, and his eyes traced one pathway and then another. Below him, the Ursa snarled and roared, nearing his position and ready to leap up and meet him on the roof.

He saw a course of action and scrambled to the next slot in the roof to his right, leaning down and firing as he moved. The beast roared and followed, gathering enough momentum to leap off the ground and slash at him.

Kincaid kept moving in a diagonal path, leading the creature back toward the animal pens. It climbed neatly over the crushed booths, ignoring everything in its path, intent on reaching the annoying pulser and its owner. He hurried along until he reached the desired slot and then fired again.

The beast sped up, charging with abandon. As Kincaid ran, he fired a pattern of blasts not at the Ursa but at the roof in front of it. Without pausing, it leaped toward the roof, but it had the misfortune to land exactly where Kincaid's pulser had done its work. The weakened floor buckled under the creature's great weight, and suddenly it fell into a mound of rotting food and decomposing animal dung.

The beast expressed its displeasure with its loudest roar yet, and Kincaid covered his ears. Unfortunately, the pit was not deep, and once it collected its wits, the Ursa would climb back up. But at least it was preoccupied for a little while, giving Kincaid time to come up with a new plan.

"Kincaid here. Where are the Rangers?"

"*Moser here,*" came a voice he didn't know. "*They're all over the city. Where are the ones dispatched to the market?*"

"All dead. Where the hell are the reinforcements?"

"*Coming.*"

"Not fast enough. Please pass that along."

"*You okay?*"

"For now."

His fingers stroked the cutlass before pressing and

squeezing random sections; sure enough, the device sprang to life as the strands of programmed metal altered at one end, curving and refashioning itself into a hook shape.

"Get me those reinforcements."

"Roger that."

The Ursa was not idle during the conversation. It regrouped and used its powerful legs to scramble out of the muck and back onto the ground, roaring with every step. Of course, now Kincaid could not only hear the beast but smell it, too; his nose wrinkled in revulsion.

The moment it settled on the ground, the Ursa tensed and leaped up, its short forearms grabbing the thin metal of the roof, its talons ripping into it. With an effort it made its way onto the roof, where Kincaid was already on his feet.

Now they were on the same level playing field, and the advantage had shifted from the corpsman to the foul-smelling creature. He started swinging the cutlass at the Ursa, connecting with legs, joints, clawed hands. But the Ursa continued plodding toward him. Realizing he wasn't harming it at all, Kincaid turned and ran.

The Ursa charged.

Kincaid counted on the beast being too heavy for the wafer-thin metal roof. Sure enough, the roof creaked and groaned, adding to the Ursa's bellowing tone. The beast had gone maybe another six feet before the roof began to buckle. Another few feet and the roof became wobbly. As the Ursa gained on Kincaid, the metal started coming free from its moorings.

What Kincaid did not count on was plunging to the ground with the Ursa.

Both fell with a loud crash, Kincaid's right shoulder absorbing the impact. It took all his willpower not to cry out in pain as he landed atop the ruins of a shoe peddler's stand. He scrambled to regain his footing, taking a moment to come up with a strategy.

The Ursa, despite its ungainly shape, had a good sense

of balance and was upright and snarling, once more locked onto Kincaid's position.

A plan, however sketchy, was still a plan, and Kincaid ran to his right, down a relatively unscathed corridor of the market. His shoulder ached as he pumped his arms; he had to push past it. Within several strides he could hear the great creature coming after him, screaming at the top of its lungs. It wanted him badly.

He darted down side aisles, jumping over boxes and leaping into a forward roll to avoid a pillar barring his path. All along, the creature barreled forward, tearing through one thing after another, unrelenting in its pursuit.

Kincaid was running out of the market. He'd be exposed soon, and then the creature could home in on him and end it.

That was when he remembered the park and quickened his pace. He emerged from the dim shadows of the market and into bright sunlight. Blinking repeatedly as his eyes adjusted, he kept moving forward, crossing the street from the market to the park. Fortunately, it was deserted.

Lining the park were old trees. Kincaid darted toward one and leaped, grabbing one of its thick limbs. His right shoulder complained, but he worked past the pain as he swung himself up and over, landing on the limb. He scrambled to the next highest branch, climbing until he was a good fifteen feet off the ground, ideally too high for the Ursa to reach with a single jump. His shoulder let him know he would be paying for this once the adrenaline rush wore off. He looked forward to being alive to enjoy the pain.

He finally was safe enough to look behind him, and the damned thing was out of sight. It had shifted to camouflage mode, blending in with the serene park surroundings. Kincaid hoped more Rangers would arrive soon, wondering just how intelligent the beast was, doubting anyone could say with certainty.

His entire life seemed to take place in a park. It was

in one similar to this that he had lost an arm, saw the Ranger sacrifice herself, and begun on a specific course. Despite Velan rejecting him for the Rangers, Kincaid now found himself fighting an Ursa one on one. He idly wondered what Velan would make of that considering that he would first note that the regs called for a squad of no fewer than eight. Going solo against the creature might appear to be suicidal, but Kincaid was determined not to begin and end his life in a park. He would survive this—he was not done with life yet.

It was quiet. *Too* quiet. He tried to focus on his surroundings, but Virginia's face kept materializing in his mind. He had to stay alive and apologize. Or own up to losing her.

His nose wrinkled in disgust, interrupting the reverie and warning him a second before a roar confirmed his sense of smell.

The still-invisible Ursa bellowed once more to attract his attention but mostly to strike fear into him. The more pheromones he released, the easier it was for the creature to lock in on his position. It struck the tree with its talons.

His arms wrapped around the tree as it shuddered with every stroke. Kincaid realized, as his flesh pimpled with goose bumps, that it intended to shred the tree until it collapsed and he fell.

He held tight with the artificial arm and began shifting his feet on the branch so that he could make the leap to the next tree over. He had no desire to be the Ursa's victim and started scrambling as far from the creature as possible, taking it deeper into the park and away from the people hidden close to the park's edge.

It didn't take him long to travel six trees away from where he had started, although he could feel how weak his right side was getting. The Ursa, now fully visible in all its ugliness, dutifully followed, stinking and thundering and clawing the entire way. Running out of trees and out of steam, he considered his options. He had the cutlass, not that he really understood what to do with it; he had two pulsers, one almost out of charge; he had an artificial arm that might outlast one or two swipes of those claws. But that was about it. Peering past the monstrosity, he saw that no help was coming his way.

This might actually be the end.

His mind drifted back, and he considered what he had accomplished. Within the last few hours, he had saved some lives and kept an Ursa from harming others. He had served the corps with distinction, saving that man from the fire among other heroic acts. He'd laughed; he thought he might even have loved, even if he had screwed it up earlier that day. If it ended right now, it would be seen as a good life, one that honored his debt and respected the Kincaid family tradition even out of a Ranger uniform. If he was to die here and now, he could accept that.

The first Ursa had chased all the fear from him years before.

Following the Primus's teachings, he prayed to the creator of the heavens and the universe, thanking the being for giving him a good life, one that honored his family name. He prayed that the creator would look after his parents and sister and that humanity would continue to thrive on Nova Prime.

His mind was so busy preparing for his imminent death, it took him a moment to realize it had gotten very quiet and his immediate world had stopped shaking. The Ursa was done with the tree and was skittering in a semicircle, seeking something. At first, Kincaid thought that help *was* coming and the creature had sensed it first.

But no, it was something else.

The creature seemed to have lost his scent, just as earlier it had turned right at him and hadn't reacted. This was his chance to escape to safety. But that would mean the creature would be free to stalk some other living being, and that did not sit well with him.

Instead, he lowered himself branch by branch to the ground. The Ursa never noticed, intent on figuring out what had happened to its prey. Kincaid stalked the Ursa from the rear. He moved dangerously close, holding his breath from the stench.

There was no sweat, no fear.

The beast turned toward him, unaware of how close the human had come.

Kincaid held a pulser in his right hand and was hefting the hook-shaped cutlass in the other. He had been studying the creature and saw several spots that looked more vulnerable than others. He could strike from the rear. Although it would be inelegant and far from fair, this was war, and in war, fairness was a luxury.

Swinging with all his might, he hooked the end of the cutlass into the Ursa's hide and yanked. Through the creature's blood he could see a hint of tissue, and he pulled harder while firing a series of point-blank bursts from the pulser. The cutlass continued to tear into the creature's hind leg joint, searing the purplish muscle and tissue. As the Ursa screamed in a tone that spoke of its pain, Kincaid turned and ran with whatever strength he still possessed. He did not look back, nor did he drop the weapons, clutching them for reassurance. The Ursa tried to run after him but was badly hobbled.

Kincaid kept running the way he had come, back past the trees and out onto the street. Looking left, he saw the street was clear, and then he looked right and spotted a Ranger speeder landing in the middle of the avenue.

Eight Rangers, cutlasses at the ready, were leaping out of the vehicle as it still kicked up dust.

"I wounded one of them in the park," he said between gasps. They nodded in silent acknowledgment and rushed past him. Stretching out his artificial arm, he rested against the side of the speeder, sucking in warm air and trying to calm himself.

He remained where he was for several minutes, his breathing and mind calming down in unison. At last, a female Ranger emerged from the park, spotted him, and flashed a thumbs-up.

"We have it contained," she said, smiling at him. "Lieutenant Divya Chandrark."

"Anderson Kincaid. Did you kill it?"

"They're working on it," she admitted. "What happened?"

Kincaid gave her a report as if she were McGirk and he were delivering a formal after-action statement. She nodded, eyes widening now and then.

"You're saying the thing looked right through you? And then lost track of you later? Ursa don't do that. You do that *to* them. Sounds like you ghosted, just like the OG."

"OG?"

"The Original Ghost. Cypher Raige. Made himself so disconnected from fear that the Ursa couldn't find him. He was the first to take one out single-handedly."

He had, in fact, known that, but he had failed to apply the notion to himself because it had seemed so distant to him. He'd been so busy trying to stay alive that he simply hadn't questioned how he was doing it.

"Well, the OG still has one up on me. I just stuck it and ran."

"Still, you got close enough to do that."

He just nodded in amazement. Apparently the competition between families was still ongoing.

After the debriefing with the Rangers, they went their way and he headed back to headquarters. Along the way, he ran into comrades who already had heard about his accomplishment. He swore gossip traveled by smart fabric.

When he entered the locker room, Virginia stood by his locker, freshly showered and dressed in a clingy pale purple sundress.

"Hi," he said.

"Hi," she replied, her tone neutral. He couldn't read

her expression and had no sense if they were lovers, partners, or even friends anymore.

For a moment he paused and looked deep within. He'd been doing that all day, looking for answers, and this must have been his lucky day because the solutions were magically appearing.

"I've been a jerk," he said.

At that, her eyes twinkled and she replied, "But you're a talented jerk."

"You've made me so happy, but I only realized that when I thought I'd chucked it away to go die fighting the Ursa. I risked you, risked us, to possibly die."

"But you lived. Better than that, you ghosted. That is so freaking amazing."

She hurled herself at him, and he caught her in his arms, letting the enhanced arm help lift her high off the ground. They laughed together as he twirled her about.

After he placed her back on the ground, they smiled at each other. "I need a shower," he said. "Then we can go celebrate."

Slipping out of the dress, she said, "I'll scrub your back."

Days later, there was a knock at his door, and Kincaid, recuperating from his injuries, answered it in his casual shirt, clutching a beer. Marquez, in a silk robe, lounged on the couch.

Cypher Raige, in his snow-white uniform, stood in the doorway, and his eyes rose and fell, taking in the sight. Kincaid nearly dropped the bottle as he snapped to attention.

Raige stood patiently in the doorway until finally the younger man realized what was going on and stepped back, gesturing for the Prime Commander to enter. He stole a glance over his shoulder to see Marquez frozen in place, unable to dash out of sight.

"Prime Commander Raige, may I introduce you to Virginia Marquez," he said as formally as possible.

She clutched her robe tightly closed as she rose with as much grace as was possible and stepped forward, shaking the man's hand. "A pleasure," was all she could muster. Raige merely nodded in her direction. She then demurely took up a position on a chair, still within earshot of the men. Raige seemed fine with that although Kincaid was certainly feeling awkward, as if he were violating some rule he had forgotten.

"I hear you ghosted," Raige said, his eyes now taking in the apartment, which Anderson was pleased to have kept neat. Not white glove neat, but good enough.

"So I'm told."

"Nice work. Anderson . . . May I call you that?"

"Of course, sir."

"Anderson, ghosting is a rare ability. We've counted only a few who have managed it. Three during the recent Ursa attack, yourself included. That's pretty elite company to be in."

"Yes, sir," Kincaid said, suddenly feeling years younger and burning once more with a desire to wear the uniform.

"We owe you a debt. Your actions kept people safe and allowed the Rangers to perform their duty."

"That pretty much sums it up."

"Nova Prime City owes you a debt of thanks. We'd like you to join the Rangers."

At last, he thought.

And then a moment later, he realized it was a fine offer but a late one. It was all he had wanted—all he had needed—for so long. But now he had what he needed: a home, a career, and someone to share his life with.

Kincaid shut his mouth and took a deep breath.

Raige remained ramrod straight, his face unreadable.

"Your cousin Atlas asked me to preserve and protect this society when he left Nova Prime," Cypher Raige said thoughtfully. "Of course, those rules were probably written before the Ursa even showed up here. Maybe even predating the Skrel. Things were very different back then."

"Yes, sir, they were."

"The rule, all the rules, I think, need a fresh review. Ones like this need to be looked at with our current society and its requirements." Raige paused, letting the comments sink in.

"Thank you, Prime Commander," Anderson said slowly, fighting to find the right words and to meet the man's piercing gaze. "But I respectfully decline the invitation. The rules remain the rules, and they forced me to give up a little boy's dreams and find a man's dream instead. I found it, forged a path for myself, and I am content."

Raige let that sink in and then looked directly at Marquez, who immediately blushed but was grinning with pride. He nodded once.

"You're standing on your own two feet, and your accomplishments certainly allow you to make your own choices for the future. It's a shame the Rangers will lose a ghost, but it's the Defense Corps' gain. Maybe one day the Rangers can steal you back."

"Thank you, sir," Kincaid said.

He paused, looked past Kincaid's shoulder at Marquez, and nodded her way in farewell. "Good luck, Anderson."

"Thank you, sir."

"A word of advice," Cypher said. "The next time you answer the door, see who it is first so you're both properly attired for the visit."

As Raige stepped out into the night, Kincaid looked down to see he was still standing at attention wearing just a shirt and boxer shorts.

Marquez looked at him and smiled.

"White would've looked good on you."

AFTER
EARTH

Ghost Stories

SAVIOUR

Michael Jan Friedman

Jon doesn't know where he is. All he knows is that he's awake and that there's a face looming over him. A familiar woman's face.

How long has it been there? He can't say. Maybe a long time, maybe not.

A name breaks the surface of his mind. "Doctor Gold," he says, his voice sounding strange—thin and coarse—in his ears.

Her expression changes, her mouth turning up at the corners and her cheeks bunching under pale green eyes. "Yes," says Doctor Gold in a voice like music, "it's me, all right. Do you remember *your* name?"

"Blackburn. Jon Blackburn."

"Excellent. How do you feel, Jon?"

It isn't easy for him to comprehend the question, though it should be. It's not a difficult question. It's what people ask one another every day.

"How do I feel?" he echoes.

"Are you uncomfortable?"

"My brain's wrapped in cotton. Everything seems . . . I don't know. *Vague.*"

Doctor Gold tucks something behind an ear. "Good. That's how you're supposed to feel."

Supposed to . . . ? Why? Jon hasn't always felt this way, has he? "What's happened?" he asks.

"You're in the North Side Medicenter," says the doctor. "You had a procedure. Do you remember anything about it?"

He doesn't.

"What kind of procedure? Was I injured?"

"No." Doctor Gold points to the holographic screen on Jon's left, a black one with bright gold lines undulating across it. "We did some work on your amygdalae. You remember what those are?"

Jon thinks for a moment. "Parts of the brain."

"That's right. And why would we work on those parts?"

Again Jon concentrates. But he can't come up with anything. Just a flash of something big and pale moving across his field of vision.

The doctor's expression changes again. Her mouth returns to its original shape, and her eyebrows come together in a knot of flesh above the bridge of her nose.

"It's all right, Jon. We'll talk about it later. For now, just get some rest."

Jon starts to protest, but Doctor Gold holds up a hand, her fingers long and slender.

"No talking," she insists. "*Rest.*"

Then she does something at the side of Jon's bed, and suddenly Jon's very sleepy. He watches the doctor's face shiver like a reflection in a wind-struck pool. Then he feels himself dropping into a deep, echoing darkness.

The next time Jon wakes up, he knows where he is and has a better idea of why he's there. Doctor Gold isn't present at the moment. But there's a nurse in the room, a big dark-haired man, walking over to take a look at him.

"It's all right," Jon says. "I'm fine."

"Terrific," says the nurse, though he looks concerned. "I'll get your doctor."

"Go ahead," Jon says.

The nurse goes as far as the entrance to the room, stands half inside and half out, and calls to someone down the hall. A moment later, he comes back inside.

"It'll be just a minute," he says.

"All right," says Jon.

Funny. He doesn't feel the vagueness anymore, but he still feels different. Lighter somehow, as if a burden had been lifted from him.

Suddenly the nurse is back in the room. "Sorry. Turns out it'll be more than a minute. Do you mind waiting?"

Jon finds that he doesn't mind at all.

He leans back into the pillow and wonders how long it will be. Not that he cares. He just wonders.

Despite what the nurse has said, it doesn't take long for Doctor Gold to show up. She has long blond hair. She tucks some of it behind her ear as she sits down on the edge of his bed.

"Feeling better?" she asks.

This time he knows how to answer. "The cotton's gone."

"That's good. Do you remember anything more about your procedure?"

"I remember that you operated on my amygdalae."

"Not me, actually. That was Doctor Nizamani. But yes . . . your amygdalae . . ."

"The amygdalae control fear." He recalls having heard someone say so.

"That's true."

"You wanted me to be unafraid." He recalls that, too.

"*You* wanted it as well, Jon. That's why you volunteered for the procedure."

"I . . . volunteered?"

Doctor Gold tilts her head to one side. "Do you remember the Ursa, Jon?"

He sees the flash of something big and pale again. *As pale as a fish's belly.* "Yes. They kill people. They're predators."

"They are. And we've been dealing with them for hundreds of years on and off. We get rid of them, and then a new wave appears, each one more difficult to exterminate than the last. Does this sound familiar?"

"Yes."

"Excellent. You also recall that the Ursa in *this* wave are better hunters than the ones we've dealt with in the past. That's because they have an ability they never had before. They sense our *fear*.

"Lately we've discovered that there are people who can elude the Ursa—people who don't experience fear under certain circumstances. We call them Ghosts. Unfortunately, there are only a handful of them, and they can't be everywhere—which is why there were hundreds of lethal Ursa attacks in the last year alone."

Was that a lot? Jon didn't know.

"Then we asked ourselves, 'Why not explore the possibility of *creating* Ghosts?' In other words, taking away the ability to experience fear. We experimented with a number of ways to do this, but none of them completely eradicated the fear response. That left us with just one approach: the one we pursued in your case."

"A procedure."

"Yes."

"On my amygdalae."

"It was Doctor Nizamani's idea. He knew that the amygdalae process sensory information and react by instilling in the brain what we know as fear. And he'll tell you that they do so for good reason. Without fear, our ancestors would never have been spurred to flee from saber-tooth tigers and other predators.

"So what we were talking about was going against nature. That's something we don't do around here when we can help it. But the Ursa are taking a terrible toll, Jon. We have to try any approach that has a reasonable chance of success. And we thought if we took away your fear—"

"I could be a Ghost."

"Yes. And if it worked in your case, it might work in others."

Jon thinks about that. "*Did* it work?"

"What do *you* think?"

He examines his mental state. "I don't *feel* any fear. However, I don't think there's anything in this room I'd be scared of. Is there?"

"Nothing," the doctor agrees.

"Then am I undetectable to the Ursa?"

She shrugs. "There's really only one way to find out. But first you've got to recuperate from your surgery." She starts to leave—to go on to her next patient, Jon imagines.

"Will you continue to visit?" he asks.

Doctor Gold stops long enough to say, "As long as you need me."

Soon Jon receives a visit from another doctor: the one who performed his surgery. Doctor Nizamani is a small man with a big head and a dark beard flecked with gray. One small spot on the left side of his chin. Doctor Nizamani's mouth, like Doctor Gold's, pulls up at the corners. And like Doctor Gold, he asks Jon what he remembers. When Jon responds, Doctor Nizamani makes notes on a personal access tablet.

"Are you experiencing headaches? Other discomfort?"

"No," Jon says.

"Good." Doctor Nizamani studies the computer data on the hologram beside Jon's bed, calling up one screen after the other. Finally, he says, "I want you to walk up and down the hall, get some exercise. Your nurse, Marcus, will accompany you. How's that sound?"

"Sound?" Jon says. He's not sure what the doctor is asking. "You mean . . . ?"

Doctor Nizamani pats Jon on the shoulder. "Never mind. Just walk."

Then the doctor leaves. The nurse with the dark hair approaches Jon.

"Ready to take a walk?" he asks.

Jon says he's ready. With the nurse's help, he gets out of bed. His legs are weak, and they shake a little.

But he walks.

Jon and Marcus negotiate the length of the hall four times. Then Marcus helps Jon back into his bed.

"Nice job," Marcus says, extending his hand.

Jon looks at it, wondering what Marcus expects of him. After a while, Marcus takes his hand back. "That's okay," he says.

Jon has no idea what Marcus is talking about.

The next morning, Jon and Marcus walk again. Afterward, the nurse tells Jon he can take his meal in the cafeteria instead of in bed.

The cafeteria contains eight rectangular metal tables. It's empty except for a couple of other patients sitting at the table nearest the window.

One of them is a tall fair-haired man who is missing an arm. The other is a woman with dark skin and a long black braid. The right side of her face, including one of her eyes, is covered with a bandage.

They're eating food from blue ceramic trays. Jon sees perhaps fifty such trays stacked by a wall alongside a buffet counter offering perhaps twenty choices of casserole, sandwich, salad, and soup.

Marcus says he'll be right back. "Enjoy yourself."

Jon considers the nurse's choice of words. *Enjoy?* He scans the buffet. Nothing appeals to him. But he knows he has to eat.

"Hey," says the fair-haired man, his voice echoing a little as he addresses Jon across the room, "I felt the same way the first time. At least it's hot."

Felt? "I don't—"

"It's all right," says the woman with the dark braid. "After you're here a while, you get a little crazy. Grab some food and sit down."

She pats the bench beside her. Jon doesn't know why.

Following her instructions, he gets a tray and places some food on it, then goes to a table and sits down.

But before he can lift a forkful of casserole to his mouth, the fair-haired man says, "If you want your privacy, we're fine with that. But we'd prefer it if you'd join us."

"Come on," the woman says. "We won't bite."

Jon doesn't understand the reason for the comment. He hadn't *expected* her to bite.

"Or," said the man, "we can join *you*."

Jon doesn't object. A moment later, the man and the woman bring their trays over and sit down.

"Arvo," the man says. "Arvo Lankinen. Good to meet you."

"Yada Srasati," says the woman. She looks at Jon for a moment. "How do you feel?"

"The cotton's gone," Jon replies.

"The cotton?" Her skin bunches up over the bridge of her nose the same way Doctor Gold's did.

"You mean your head is clear?" Arvo asks.

Jon turns to him. "Yes." He sees his companions exchange glances and doesn't know why.

"It's all right," Yada says. "You've been through a lot. It's going to take time before you're back on your game."

"I suppose so," Jon says.

As they continue to converse, he learns that Arvo and Yada are Rangers. Their injuries are the result of Ursa encounters.

"Listen," Arvo says. "I want to tell you how much I appreciate what you're doing. You're making a sacrifice, I know."

"But if it works," Yada adds, "we may be able to get rid of the Ursa once and for all. And if that happens, there'll be less misery in the world." She touches her bandage in the vicinity of her eye. "A whole *lot* less."

Misery, Jon thinks. He doesn't know what to say to that, either.

Over the next couple of days, Doctor Nizamani is the only physician who comes to visit. Jon wonders where Doctor Gold is. One morning, after Doctor Nizamani checks Jon's data screens, he says, "I'm clearing you for light exercise. You know where the gym is, right?"

"Yes," Jon says.

"You can use any of the machines with the green signs. The yellows and the reds, you'll work your way up to. Got it?"

"Yes," Jon says. "Can I go *now*?"

"Absolutely."

The gym is down the hall, on the right. Jon knows because he has passed it on his walks.

When he enters the place, he sees Yada there. She's running on a treadmill, her braid flopping up and down.

Jon's been eating with her and Arvo whenever he sees them in the cafeteria. To an outsider, it may look as if they were friends. To Jon, they were just three people sharing the same table until their meal had been consumed. Sometimes there are one or two other patients there as well.

Sometimes there's no one and Jon eats alone.

There's a female attendant who directs him to an apparatus with a green sign even before he asks, and so he gathers that she already has received instructions from Doctor Nizamani.

When Yada realizes that Jon is in the room, she stops exercising, picks up a towel, and walks over to him. "Jon," she says, dabbing at the exposed portion of her face, "I missed you this morning at breakfast. Arvo's been discharged, you know."

"I wasn't aware of that," he says.

"Don't worry; he'll be back to visit. I made him promise that."

Jon doesn't understand why he would be inclined to worry, or why Yada would ask such a thing of Arvo, or why Arvo would agree to it. But then, he's finding there are lots of things he doesn't understand.

As he and Yada speak, a couple of other patients enter the gym. One, a fellow with a shaven head and thickly muscled arms, is ensconced in a mag-lev chair. Another, who moves stiffly, is bandaged around his middle.

They're new to the medicenter, they say, but they know about Jon's procedure. Like Yada, Arvo, and the other injured Rangers on the ward, they thank Jon for his sacrifice. They express the hope that his courage will help them wipe out the Ursa.

"Bet you can't wait to get out there," the man in the mag-lev chair says.

Jon doesn't know why he would be unable to wait. Anyway, he has no choice in the matter. "My doctors won't allow me to leave the medicenter until I'm ready."

The man in the mag-lev chair looks at him for a moment. Then his mouth turns up at the corners, and he says, "Damned doctors!"

The others open their mouths and make a sound Jon doesn't recognize. Or rather, he recognizes it but can't put a name to it. It sounds like *ha-ha-ha-ha*.

Yada seems to notice his lack of comprehension. She makes eye contact with the others. Soon they stop making the sound.

"Jon's probably got a routine he needs to start," she says. "Let's let him get to it."

"Sure," says the man in the mag-lev chair. "Can't hunt Ursa till you're back in shape, right?"

Jon assumes that the man is right.

Jon's starting to doze off on his bed, fatigued from his workout in the gym, when Doctor Gold enters his room.

"Hey there," she says.

Jon sits up. "I didn't know if you were coming back."

"You can't get rid of me that easily." She checks the data on the hologram beside his bed. "Did you see Doctor Nizamani today?"

"This morning. He cleared me to work out."

"Excellent." She continues to check his data. "That means you're making progress."

"I have a question."

Doctor Gold turns to him. "What's that, Jon?"

He tells her about Yada's request for information the other day in the cafeteria: *"How do you feel?"*

"I didn't know how to answer her," he says. "I still don't. Then, just a little while ago, in the gym, someone said something and everyone made a sound. I didn't know what to make of that, either."

Doctor Gold tilts her head to the side. "What was it that person said?"

Jon did his best to replicate the remark: "Damn doctors!"

She looks at him for a moment. "Was the sound anything like this?" She re-creates it almost perfectly.

"Yes."

Her mouth pulls up at the corners. "It's laughter, Jon. The people in the gym were *laughing*."

"Laughing." He points to her mouth. "And what's that?"

"What's *what*?"

"What you're doing with your mouth." He uses his thumb and forefinger to push her mouth up at the corners. "*This*. I see it all the time."

Doctor Gold's brows come together over her nose. She puts her hand over his and removes his fingers from her face. Slowly.

"I was afraid this might happen," she says. "We took every precaution, ran as many tests as we could on primates as well as on people. But in the final analysis, we've never done this kind of surgery on a human being."

"You thought *what* might happen?" Jon asks.

"It's not just fear that originates in the amygdalae, Jon. Other emotions are connected to those parts of the brain as well."

He tries to follow her logic. "Are you saying I'm no longer in touch with my emotions?"

"I'm saying it's possible. And even if you *have* lost touch, it may only be a temporary situation. Despite the way it looks to Doctor Nizamani, your brain may not have healed completely."

"What if it has?"

Doctor Gold doesn't answer right away. "Then—and I know this sounds disappointing—the situation may be permanent."

Jon considers the possibility. He doesn't feel disappointment.

He doesn't feel anything at all.

That evening, Doctor Nizamani, too, makes the observation that Jon has been distanced from his emotions.

"This is a challenge," he says, "not only because you're incapable of feeling but because you're incapable of perceiving emotions in others. If you're going to work with other Rangers, you'll have to have some idea of what they're feeling."

"How can I do that?" Jon asks.

"Emotions are most often conveyed through facial expressions. I'll arrange for an automated tutorial on the subject. It'll be part of your daily regimen."

Jon agrees to participate in the tutorial. He wonders what he will learn.

It's an unusually warm morning in the desert. Jon has been given permission by Doctor Nizamani to sit outside in the medicenter's courtyard, a place with ocher-colored ceramic pots full of colorful desert flowers. He's watching the second sun top the horizon when he receives a visitor.

It's neither one of his doctors nor one of his nurses nor even one of the injured Rangers on his ward. This visitor has a round face and curly red hair. She wears a dark blue robe clasped at the throat. She asks: "Do you know who I am, Jon?"

"Yes," he says. "You're the Primus." He has seen her many times before on his computer screen but never in person. "Your breath smells like cinnamon," he observes.

"How . . . kind of you to say so," says the Primus. "Would you mind if I spoke with you for a little while?"

"No, I wouldn't mind."

Her mouth turns up at the corners, but he knows what that means now. The Primus is *smiling*.

In the brief time Jon has spent with Doctor Nizamani's tutorial, he has learned to recognize a half dozen facial expressions. The smile is one of them.

"Now," the Primus continues, "you're probably thinking I've come to talk to you about your decision to undergo brain surgery. Heaven knows I made my position on that subject known to the Prime Commander when it was first contemplated. In fact, I spoke to him about it every day—both him *and* the Savant."

Jon doesn't know what to say to that.

"As you can imagine," says the Primus, her expression hardening, "I was against it."

Jon doesn't imagine *anything* these days. He only observes and reacts.

"But what's done is done," the Primus says. "The only thing we have to talk about now is what effect the surgery has had on you."

"I have discussed the effects with my doctors," Jon says.

"I have no doubt of it. But their concern, and the Prime Commander's, is how useful you can be as a weapon. My concern is your humanity."

"I'm still human," he says. "It's just that I've been altered."

"You *have* been altered; on that we may agree. But . . ." She shakes her head. "You see, Jon, we're all born with souls—you, me, and everyone else. But your surgery, for which you volunteered, seems to have cut you off from the part of you that *feels*."

"So I've been told."

"It was exactly what I feared." She leans forward. "Feeling is what makes us who we are, Jon. Do you believe that?"

"I haven't thought about it."

"Well, it's true. Without compassion, without love, we're no different from the animals. Or, for that matter, from the machines with which we surround ourselves."

Jon isn't an animal *or* a machine. He wonders why the Primus would imply otherwise.

"This isn't the first time we've ventured into new territory, child. Technology constantly conspires to strip us of the qualities that make us human beings. This challenge is only the latest in a long history of such challenges."

"But I *am* a human being," Jon insists.

"Not in the way that matters most," the Primus says. "So why am I here? What's the point if you're no longer one of God's chosen creatures? The point, Jon, is that you can still be redeemed. You can still pray to heaven—and I mean *pray*—to be remade in the image God intended for you. And if you want to do that, I can help."

Jon isn't inclined to be remade in such an image, not even enough to inquire about the effort involved. "That won't be necessary."

The Primus sits back in her chair. A tear grows gradually in the inside corner of her left eye and tumbles down her cheek.

"Very well," she says, her voice trembling slightly, "you may say that now. But there may come a time when you understand what you've done, a time when you fear for your soul. And when—"

"I'm beyond fear," Jon says.

The Primus looks at him for what seems like a long time, her eyes wet and shiny. Then, without another word, she gets up and leaves him sitting there.

As alone as he was when she appeared.

Jon graduates to the machines with the yellow signs in the gym. Yada says she's proud of him. She also says she'll be leaving the hospital soon.

"I can't go out in the field anymore," she tells him, "but I can still make a contribution. I'll be working with the Prime Commander's office to educate the public about Ursa attacks."

She smiles with the half of her face he can see. "I expect to hear good things about you."

Jon looks at her until she looks away. To do otherwise, he has been told, is rude. Then he begins exercising on the yellow machines.

They turn out to be more demanding than the machines he's been using. When he finishes, he's more fatigued. However, he knows exercise is necessary if he's to get out of the medicenter and do what's expected of him.

That night, Jon has a dream.

There are two people in it. They look familiar, but try as he might, he can't seem to identify them.

When he wakes, he can still see them. One is a male, perhaps fifty years old, with a long face, dark eyebrows, and a thick shock of silver-gray hair. The other is a female. She, too, is about fifty years old, but her hair is light brown with only a few streaks of gray.

When Doctor Gold comes to see him, he describes the dream to her. She doesn't comment right away. She instead brings up a picture on her data tablet and asks, "Are these the people?"

They are. "Who are they?"

"They're your parents, Jon. Adabelle and Gregory Blackburn."

He looks more closely. He has seen himself in a mirror. He looks for evidence of heredity in the picture—and finds it.

"You have your mother's eyes," says Doctor Gold as if she can read his mind.

"I seem to," he agrees.

"And your father's chin." She points to it. "You see the cleft?"

"Yes." *My parents*. He looks to the doctor. "Is it possible for me to see them?"

As on other occasions, her eyebrows, which are very fair, come together in a bunch of skin. He knows now that this is an expression of consternation.

"I'm afraid it's not, Jon. They're dead. They were killed in an Ursa attack six months ago."

He turns back to the data tablet. "Dead," he echoes.

"Yes. In fact, it was their deaths that spurred you to volunteer for the surgery. You said it was the only way you could make their deaths count for something."

Jon continues to study the image on the tablet. He doesn't feel any anger now. But something—curiosity, perhaps—draws him to the people in the picture.

"I'm sorry," Doctor Gold says.

Jon recognizes the expression as one of sympathy. "Your condolences are acknowledged," he tells her.

Days pass, an alternation of light and shadow punctuated by visits from Doctor Nizamani, Doctor Gold, and occasionally other doctors as well.

Yada leaves, as she said she would. The damaged Rangers in the medicenter smile when they see him but seldom speak to him. He can hear them whisper things: "It's Blackburn." "Better cut out the jokes." "Don't want to hurt his feelings."

In the gym, Jon's promoted to the red machines. He finds them a challenge, just as he found the green machines and the yellow machines a challenge at first. But he's getting stronger. He can see that. He believes his doctors see it, too.

Pretty soon he'll be fit for duty.

Jon has another dream.

He's standing in the desert, watching *Explorer I* lift

off from an airfield outside Nova City, its destination a world in another star system. Jon is eight, nine, perhaps ten years old. His father's hand rests on his shoulder.

"I wish my grandfather was alive to see this," says Gregory Blackburn. "If not for him, none of this would have happened."

Explorer I glints in the light of the first sun as it rises into the flawless blue of the sky. Higher and higher it climbs. Then it's gone.

Jon's father's parents, Grandpa Masters and Grandma Sheila, are making whooping noises. Jon's parents are embracing.

They are smiling, all of them. He knows now what that means. *They're happy.*

When Jon wakes up, he finds himself looking at the ceiling of his room in the medicenter instead of the sky. The airfield, his parents, his grandparents . . . they're gone.

But it wasn't just a dream, he realizes. It really happened. He had forgotten, but now he remembers.

It happened.

He wonders about his father's grandfather. Did I ever meet him? *Did I know anything about him before my procedure?*

He gets dressed and goes to the medicenter's library, where he sits at a workstation near the transparent wall along the corridor and looks up his family's genealogy.

Jon finds that his paternal great-grandfather, Elliot Blackburn, was born in 883 AE. As an adult, he became the spokesman for a group of engineers that made presentations to the Tripartite Council advocating the official exploration of neighboring star systems. After all, they said, the Ursa had been the cause of misery for hundreds of years. It made sense to settle a planet that would provide an alternative for those sick of the bloodshed.

Elliot Blackburn died without making much headway on behalf of his cause. However, his oldest son, Masters, picked up where his father left off. When Savant

Ella Dorsey broached the idea of a space colonization program in 951, it was at the urging of Masters Blackburn.

Dorsey's idea was opposed by both the Primus on religious grounds and the Prime Commander for reasons never publicly stated. However, Jon's grandfather continued to speak in support of colonization to professional organizations and civic groups.

Finally, in 960, Brom Raige—who had become Prime Commander only a year earlier—tilted the Tripartite Council in favor of a space program.

Tähtiin Industries, which had been working privately with the Savant, possessed plans for an interstellar vessel. With the Council's support, Tähtiin began developing what it called *Explorer I*.

Jon's father, Gregory, had *Explorer I* in mind when he entered the terraforming program at Nova City University's Thermopoulos School of Engineering. His dream, he said in his valedictory address, was to prepare a home for humankind free of the fear that had plagued Nova Prime for hundreds of years.

Jon's mother shared this dream, though she took a different route to it. Inspired by her mother, a Ranger flier in the Varuna Squadron, Adabelle Bonnaire became one of the youngest pilots in the history of the Corps. Her goal, according to her Ranger file, was to helm an interstellar vessel to the first new human colony in almost a thousand years.

Jon's parents met at a conference sponsored by Tähtiin Industries in 968. Gregory Blackburn was twenty-five at the time, a year older than his wife to be. They married a year later.

They didn't realize their dreams, Jon notes. His mother didn't helm *Explorer I*. His father's terraforming program wasn't needed. Yet on that airfield, they were happy that humankind was following the course in which they believed.

Jon has never aimed for the stars. His goal as a Ranger

has been to destroy the threat represented by the Ursa on Nova Prime.

However, he has something in common with his forebears: He began by wanting humankind to be safe from fear.

Later that morning, Jon sees Doctor Gold. She smiles at him and asks, "How are you feeling?"

He isn't sure how to answer that. He reminds her of his deficit in the area of emotion.

The doctor reddens. "Sorry. I guess I wasn't thinking."

"It's all right," he says, having learned that a blush represents embarrassment. "This is a new experience for you as much as it is for me."

She smiles again. "Thanks for understanding. And allow me to rephrase the question: Have you noticed any changes in your mental state?"

He assesses himself along those lines. "I've been thinking a lot, more than I ever did before. About my family, for instance." He tells her about his dream of the airfield and what he did afterward. "I wonder if I'm trying to replace feeling with thinking."

"That's interesting," she says.

He looks at her. "Is it?"

"Well, yes, of course it is." Then she adds: "Everything about you is interesting." And she turns away from him to check the data on his holographic screen.

Something changes in her expression, but Jon can't decipher the change. His tutorial covers only so much.

"Is something wrong?" he asks, venturing a guess.

Doctor Gold shakes her head—a negative response, he's learned—and says, "Everything's fine." But she continues to study the data.

Then she runs out of screens. But instead of turning back to Jon, she turns away from him.

This behavior, too, was covered in the tutorial. "You're uncomfortable," he observes.

"No," Doctor Gold says. "Just tired. I haven't slept a lot lately."

He's seen his records. He had difficulty sleeping, too, after his parents were killed. "An inability to fall asleep may be the result of unresolved emotional issues."

She looks up at him. "Where did you hear that?"

"It's noted in my file."

Doctor Gold laughs softly. "Right. You're a smart guy, Jon."

His records support her observation. He placed first in his cadet class in all measures of intelligence.

"Very smart," Doctor Gold says. She places her hand on his and leaves it there.

In the tutorial, such behavior is described as an indication of emotional involvement. Jon asks Doctor Gold if he is reading her gesture correctly.

She takes her hand away. "You're getting better at interpreting behavior, Jon, but in this instance you're reading into it a little too much."

"Then you're not emotionally involved?"

"I'm part of the medical team assigned to your case," she says. "Let's leave it at that."

He agrees to do so. After all, she's his doctor.

As Jon was taught, he doesn't look away from Doctor Gold. He intends to wait until she does it first.

But she doesn't look away for a long time.

Jon is sitting at his usual workstation in the medicenter library, looking up more information on his family, when he feels a hand on his shoulder.

Looking back, he sees a tall, broad-shouldered man looming behind him. "Mind if I interrupt?" he asks.

"No, sir," Jon says, rising from his chair.

His visitor is Prime Commander Raige. He and Jon

met more than once before Jon's procedure. That, too, is noted in Jon's file.

Raige says, "Good to see you again, Ranger." He salutes.

Jon knows why.

"Let's sit down," Raige says. "No need to stand on ceremony." He pulls a chair over from the next workstation, then points to Jon's chair.

"It's a courageous thing you're doing for us, Blackburn. Extremely courageous. We wouldn't have selected you if we thought you were going into this precipitously. But you heard all the risks, and you volunteered anyway.

"As you know, I am one of this procedure's biggest supporters. It's not just a matter of getting one more Ghost out there in the field, as valuable as that will be. If this works, there will be a lot more like you. An army of Ghosts. These Ursa are tougher than any we've faced before. Deadlier. We have to try anything and everything to keep more people from dying."

Just then, Jon catches a glimpse over Raige's shoulder of someone out in the hallway, on the other side of the transparent wall. It's Doctor Gold, he realizes. *And she's crying.*

Jon is familiar with the behavior. After all, it's the first one he studied. *But why is Doctor Gold engaging in it? Most of the time crying reflects sadness. Is Doctor Gold sad? For what reason?*

If she comes inside, he thinks, *I'll ask her.* But she remains in the hallway. Jon continues to watch her and to wonder.

"Is something wrong?" Raige asks. He looks back over his shoulder, perhaps trying to see what Jon sees. "What's out there?"

"Doctor Gold," Jon says.

Raige's eyebrows come together in a knot of flesh, reflecting a measure of consternation. "Gold?" he says.

"Yes. She's one of my doctors."

Raige shakes his head. "I haven't heard of a Doctor Gold. Maybe she's new."

"She's out there." Jon points to the hallway, where she's still crying.

Raige looks over his shoulder, then back at Jon. "Hang on a second," he says. He takes out his personal comm device and punches in a sequence. "I need you," he says into the device. "Now."

A minute later, Doctor Nizamani enters the library.

"Why is Doctor Gold crying?" Jon asks him.

Doctor Nizamani looks at him for a moment, then turns to Raige. "Gold?"

"I was hoping *you* would know," Raige says.

Nizamani looks at Jon again. "Why is Doctor Gold crying?" Jon asks a second time.

Doctor Nizamani shakes his head. "There *is* no Doctor Gold."

Hallucinating? Jon thinks.

"Don't worry. It's not entirely unexpected," Doctor Nizamani says.

"I'm not worried," Jon says.

Raige pats him on the shoulder. "He means *me*, Ranger. But I'm not worried, either. And neither is Doctor Nizamani . . . right, Doctor?"

Doctor Nizamani's mouth pulls up at the corners. A smile, Jon thinks. But one that was tighter than normal.

"That's right," Doctor Nizamani says. "There's no cause for *any* of us to be worried." He sits down on the edge of Jon's bed. "It's perfectly natural. You've been cut off from your emotions. You're finding other means of support."

Jon doesn't understand.

"Doctor Gold," says Raige, "isn't real."

"More than likely," Doctor Nizamani says, "you've cobbled her together from other women you've known in your life."

"Not real?" Jon asks.

He looks for Doctor Gold out in the hallway. If he can persuade her to come in, it'll be obvious that she's as real as Jon is.

But he can't find her. *She's gone.*

"He's fine," Doctor Nizamani tells Raige. "It's nothing to be concerned about."

"Our expectations are the same?" the Prime Commander asks.

"Exactly the same," Doctor Nizamani assures him.

"Expectations?" Jon asks.

"That you'll be able to ghost," Raige explains.

But ghosting isn't on Jon's mind at this moment. He can't take his eyes off the empty hallway.

Jon is confused by the question of Doctor Gold's existence.

On the one hand, no one seems to know a doctor named Gold. Doctor Nizamani in particular is adamant that she's an artifact of Jon's imagination.

On the other hand, Jon has spoken to her. He has shared his thoughts with her. On those occasions, she seemed as real as Doctor Nizamani or anyone else.

In the end, the result is the same: Doctor Gold doesn't come to see Jon anymore. A week goes by, and there's no sign of her.

It's just as well. Jon will be sent out into the field in a couple of days. He has to spend all his time preparing for that moment.

He studies video records of Ursa encounters. He trains with his cutlass, a new one, apparently, rather than the one he used previously. And, sitting around a table with the team that's been assigned to him, he runs through one strategic scenario after another.

Thanks to his limited familiarity with human expressions, Jon has some understanding of how his squad mates look at him. They see him as distinct from the rest of them. A valuable asset, to be sure, but *different*.

Doctor Nizamani says their opinion of Jon will change once they're out in the field with him. At that point they'll establish a bond. Jon takes Doctor Nizamani's word for it.

Finally, he and his squad receive a mission. Jon is curious to find out if he'll meet Prime Commander Raige's expectations. Of course, no one will know until Jon encounters an Ursa.

Blackburn's orders take him and his squad to a school building on the South Side of Nova City. The day before, one of the creatures got into the school and killed two of the students there.

Raige and his command staff have noticed that Ursa sometimes revisit the scene of a recent kill. It's their hope that Blackburn and his squad will encounter the creature as it returns in search of more victims.

As squad leader, Jon leads the way through the front doors of the school and down the main hallway. Despite everyone's efforts to be quiet, they make scraping sounds with their boots that echo from wall to wall.

The others seem to be bothered by the sounds. Jon knows that the scraping may give their presence away, but he's not bothered by it.

A classroom comes up on Jon's left. He indicates with a hand gesture that he's going to take a look inside. The others assume positions in the hallway in case an Ursa comes charging out.

Jon opens the door, but there's no Ursa beyond it. The room is quiet, empty. However, it's clear that an Ursa was there at one time.

There's blood on the floor. A good deal of it, in dark, dry blotches where it dripped and collected and in streaks where the children's bodies were dragged by the Ursa across the room.

A couple of chairs have been overturned. There's blood on them as well.

Saturria, a squarish, muscular man, curses between clenched teeth: "Bastards." Jakande, lean and quick, draws a deep, ragged breath. Though Tseng does neither of these things, a single tear traces a path down her cheek. No sooner has it fallen than she wipes it away.

They're reacting to the evidence of the children's deaths, Jon notes. *Even though they're trained to confront such a sight, even though they have probably seen death before.*

Jon himself has no such reaction.

Perhaps because he's not distracted, he hears something. *A ripping noise.* He recognizes it as one of the sounds an Ursa makes in its throat.

With a hand signal, Jon gets the attention of the other Rangers. Then he points to the direction from which the sound came.

They take their places around the room. Noiselessly, their cutlasses assume the shapes the Rangers want from them: pikes, blades, hooks.

They wait, their backs against the walls, their eyes fixed on the doorway.

All but Jon. He takes up a position by the entrance that doesn't block the doorway but makes it impossible for the Ursa to miss him. If, of course, it's capable of detecting him at all.

As the Ursa gets closer, the sound it makes changes, becoming louder, deeper. More terrifying, as well, if the looks on the faces of Jon's teammates are any indication.

Then the creature comes around a corner out in the hallway, and Jon gets his first look at its pale, powerful form. He can see its huge black maw, which is ringed by double rows of sharp silver teeth. He can see the talons that are hard enough to score metal, hear them make soft clicking sounds on the floor.

Despite the Ursa's apparent lack of sensory organs, it has a range of senses. Humanity's scientists have examined Ursa carcasses and identified organs that facilitate hearing, smell, and touch. It's only a sight organ they haven't found, long ago leading them to the conclusion that the creatures can't see and that their creators, the Skrel, may not be able to do so, either.

The Ursa, however, more than makes up for the deficit with its ability to perceive fear. This sense is its most acute by far. That's why Ghosts are so valuable to the colony, valuable enough for Doctor Nizamani to invade a man's brain and permanently impair its functions.

The data, drummed into Jon in briefing after briefing, sift through his mind. There's another piece: the Ursa's ability to utilize camouflage with the help of color-changing cells in its skin. But this specimen, like a few others the Rangers have encountered, makes no attempt to conceal itself.

It simply advances.

Jon can hear the breathing of his Rangers, quick and shallow behind him. They're not like him. They're disciplined, but they're afraid.

But what they do and how they feel are all but irrelevant. This mission isn't about them. It's about *him*.

As Jon stands there and watches, the Ursa proceeds the length of the hallway—slowly, fluidly, despite its angular alien anatomy. It doesn't pause to look into other classrooms. It heads right for the one occupied by the Rangers.

Jon steps out into the hallway, placing himself in the beast's path.

With its increasing proximity, Jon can see the smart metal woven into its hide. It's what makes the Ursa so difficult to kill even when a Ranger gets in a good stroke with a cutlass. A death blow can be made only in the creature's unshielded spots above and below—nowhere else.

Suddenly the Ursa roars, its voice like rocks cracking in half. Jon can feel the sound in his bones. It moves closer, still closer, until it's almost close enough to touch.

A sour metallic stench issues from its gullet, like that of human blood but more powerful. It's the smell of its venom, an oily black substance capable of eating through flesh, bone, and even metal.

Nonetheless, Jon stands his ground.

If the Ursa detects his presence, it'll make short work of him. It'll tear him apart as it tore the children apart.

Such an outcome would be a source of disappointment to Jon's medical team as well as to the Prime Commander. It would refute the idea that fear can't be surgically eliminated after all.

Yet that's an outcome Jon may have to face.

Suddenly, the Ursa gathers itself and leaps. Jon brings up his cutlass, knowing what little help it will be at such close range.

But it's not Jon the Ursa is attacking. It sails past him through the door of the classroom, its target one of the Rangers behind him.

He looks back in time to see the creature pounce on Saturria or, rather, on the spot Saturria occupied until a fraction of a second ago. Saturria himself rolls across the floor, his reflexes saving him.

But they won't save him a second time. Jon can see that as the Ursa rounds on the Ranger. It's imprinted on him, Jon thinks. *It'll stay after him until it kills him.*

Jon's job as squad leader is to keep that from happening.

Tseng configures the blade of her cutlass into a pike and tries to spear the Ursa, but her point glances off the smart metal in its hide. Still, she draws the creature's attention.

It's all the distraction Jon needs. Pelting across the room, he leaps onto the Ursa's back and drives his cutlass deep into the creature's soft spot.

It's a small target, an easy target to miss, but he hits it dead on. The Ursa bellows and tries to flip him off its back, but Jon hangs on. He taps his fingers in the required sequence and transforms his cutlass into a blade.

Then he turns it inside the creature, tearing its insides apart.

In a spasm of pain, the Ursa finally does wrench Jon loose, sending him crashing into a wall with stunning force. But the damage to the creature has been done. It won't survive much longer.

Knowing that an Ursa can kill even in its death throes, Jon directs his squad to leave the room one by one. Then he joins them outside in the hallway.

Through the transparent pane in the classroom door, he sees the Ursa writhe in agony, smashing walls and cabinets and windows. It's only after several minutes have gone by that it collapses and lies still.

Jon hears a cheer go up among his squad mates. He understands why. They're alive and the Ursa is dead.

The mission couldn't have gone any better.

Jakande and Tseng and Saturria pat one another on the back. The others do the same thing. But no one pats Jon.

"I'm pleased," Raige says.

Jon looks at the Prime Commander across the man's desk. "Because I was able to ghost when the time came."

"That's right. We've been working for centuries trying to figure out how to beat these things, and we've finally got the answer. It's one thing to find a Ghost once in a while, usually by accident, and another to be able to *make* one any time we want. That tips the odds."

Jon knows something about odds. They are reducible to numbers, to ratios, which are a lot easier for him to grasp than hopes and dreams.

"It does," he agrees.

"And you did that," says Raige, "because you had the courage to take a chance no one had taken before."

Jon is familiar with the facts. What's more, he has a sense of what the Prime Commander is trying to do: instill a feeling of pride in him.

However, he doesn't feel any pride.

"We've got other volunteers who've been waiting in the wings," Raige says, "hoping to get the same chance you did. But we didn't want to contact them until we made sure the procedure had the desired effect. Now that we know it does . . ."

"You'll operate on them as well," Jon says.

Raige nods.

Jon wonders if the Prime Commander will ask him to speak with the volunteers. He doesn't think so. After seeing his lack of emotion, they may not wish to have the operation after all.

But he doesn't say what he's thinking.

The other Rangers in Jon's squad spend a lot of time together. He notices that. They talk, they engage in laughter, they spar in the barracks.

Jon isn't inclined to take part in such behavior. He remains separate from the others. He does the things he has been trained to do—work out his body and inspect his cutlass—and very little else.

When he eats, he eats alone. And he doesn't linger in the mess hall. He remains there only long enough to take nourishment and then leaves.

Once he saw a woman with blond hair walking ahead of him in the hallway and jogged to catch up with her. She turned around and looked at him with eyes that weren't green. Eyes that weren't Doctor Gold's.

Doctor Nizamani asks Jon how he's getting along with his squad mates. Jon tells him the truth.

Doctor Nizamani says, "The squad has been together for more than a year. You're the newcomer. Give it time."

But as time goes on, Jon doesn't interact any more with his fellow Rangers. If anything, he interacts with them even less. So little, in fact, that he doesn't think it would be troubling to him if they had died in the Ursa attack.

Maybe he would have grieved for them before his operation. But not now.

Questions come to mind with increasing frequency, questions Jon finds difficult to answer. One is why he should kill Ursa.

They present a threat to humanity, true. But he's no longer human as far as he can tell, so why act on humanity's behalf? What makes the Ursa any less worthy of survival than the colonists they hunt?

Jon has no answer.

Days after Jon's first mission, he and his squad are dispatched to a power station on the North Side of the city where an Ursa has attacked the workers.

From all indications, the Ursa is still inside. So are the workers, who got off a single truncated distress call, though it's not clear if they're still alive.

The power station is a massive orange-colored mound designed to blend in with the red earth of the desert. Even before Jon disembarks from the Ranger transport that has brought him to the scene, he sees the ragged hole in the exterior wall where the Ursa crashed through it.

He starts for it even as his squad hops off the transport behind him. There's really no reason for him to wait for them. At this point, they're just a burden to him.

Jon picks his way through the rubble created by the Ursa's entry. Inside the power station it's cool and quiet except for a low hum. If there's an Ursa present, it's not making a ruckus.

That suggests two possibilities. One is that the creature already has caught its prey. The other is that it's detected the approach of Jon's squad and camouflaged itself in order to stalk it.

Jon taps his cutlass and watches its metal fibers form the pike configuration. His favorite. The one he consistently finds most useful.

He recalls the layout of the station, which he studied on the way over. The facility has two main access corridors that run perpendicular to each other, crossing in the middle, where the power chamber is situated.

There are doors along the corridors. *The workers may be hiding behind them*, he thinks. *Or their remains may be lying somewhere*. He doesn't see any evidence of bloodshed in the corridor. *But that doesn't mean anything. It's a big place.*

He approaches the power chamber, senses alert, cutlass at the ready. The chamber, which is made of a blue-gray ceramic material, houses an apparatus that uses magnetic fields to generate energy-rich plasma, which then is pumped into a complex web of underground conduits.

The chamber has a small window on each corridor. Jon isn't focused on it, and so it's a surprise when he notices movement through the window.

One of the workers, he thinks. *A male.* He's still too far away to tell if the worker's injured.

At the same time, the worker seems to see Jon. He beckons to someone inside the chamber, someone Jon can't see. A moment later, two other workers crowd the window.

A scenario begins to unfold in Jon's mind as he advances. *The workers took shelter in the chamber. It kept them safe. But they can't leave for fear of the creature.*

Jon holds his hands out, the empty one palm up. He's learned that this gesture poses a question. In this case, the question is: Where's the Ursa?

The workers return the gesture, signifying that they don't know. Yet they have line-of-sight access to all parts of the station. So the creature has camouflaged itself. This is valuable information.

They're now on even footing, Jon and the Ursa. Neither can be seen by the other.

Unfortunately, the creature won't reveal itself until it's about to pounce. With the workers constrained to remain in the power chamber, they won't become prey. That leaves only one other possibility.

Jon turns to his squad mates, who are coming up behind him. He points to the one nearest to him, Tseng, and says: "You and I will scout ahead. The rest of you remain here."

Jon doesn't know if Tseng understands what he has in mind. Either way, she doesn't hesitate. She moves down the hallway with him, her cutlass a pike like his.

The Ursa could be anywhere. They watch carefully for a sign of it. However, they reach the power chamber without getting such a sign.

The chamber is encircled by a strip of open floor about fifteen feet wide. It's enough space to hold an Ursa who could be monitoring its prey, smelling their fear through the air vents in the chamber.

Waiting for them to emerge.

It no longer has to do so, Jon reflects. *If it's here, or anywhere in this vicinity, I've given it another option.*

He's barely completed the thought when a huge form seems to materialize out of thin air. It's a blur of pale hide and smart metal blue, and it strikes Tseng before either she or Jon can make a move.

Tseng goes flying backward and skids across the floor. She finally stops thirty feet away.

She's already dead, her chest caved in by the impact, by the time the Ursa lumbers after her. But she's served her purpose. She's brought the beast out of hiding.

Jon's squad mates go after it. They weave a web of silver with their cutlasses. But there's not much room for them to operate in the corridor, not nearly enough for them to surround the Ursa as they've been trained to do.

Jon watches as the creature swipes at Saturria and

tears his arm off. The others come forward to cover him while Jakande applies a tourniquet.

Jon looks at the cutlass in his hand. He might be able to kill the Ursa with it. But he feels no desire to do so.

His fellow Rangers are in mortal danger, but that fact doesn't faze him in the least. He isn't human anymore. The Primus was right about that—he sees that now. He has as much in common with Tseng or Saturria or Jakande as he does with his cutlass. In other words, *nothing*.

Then he realizes that someone's standing behind him. Turning, he sees that it's Doctor Gold. She's wearing the same white lab coat that she wore at the medical center, a lock of her hair tucked behind her ear, her eyes the same pale green.

The other doctors insisted that she wasn't real, that she was a figment of his imagination. But she *looks* real, as real as any of the Rangers who followed him there.

"Doctor Gold," he says. "What are you—?"

"Jon," she replies, her voice tight and urgent yet just as musical as he remembers, "you've got to help these people. You've got to kill the Ursa."

"Why?" he asks.

Her brow puckers. "Because I'm *asking* you to."

It isn't much of a reason. But because it's Doctor Gold who's asking, Jon accepts it.

The Ursa is completely unaware of him. He capitalizes on that fact, taking a run at it and eyeing the one vulnerable spot on the creature's back.

He misses it on purpose.

But he comes close enough to make the creature shriek with pain and rage—to hobble it, slow it down, and force it to address the invisible threat behind it rather than the visible prey before it.

It jerks him off its back, sending him crashing into the wall. Something snaps in his side, but he manages to scramble to his feet.

"Get out!" he yells despite the pressure in his side. "And take the workers with you!" He turns and gestures for the workers in the power chamber to leave it and run.

They do as he asks, falling over one another to get out of the chamber and down the corridor. But the Rangers hesitate. They have their duty, after all.

Again he yells: "Get out!"

With obvious reluctance, they follow his order. The Ursa turns to go after them, but Jon won't let it. He stoops to pick up Tseng's cutlass and, without breaking stride, leaps onto the creature's back. Then he drives the point of the cutlass into the center of the Ursa's soft spot.

The creature whirls, no doubt intending to confront its attacker. But Jon is still on its back. He transforms his cutlass into a blade, cutting up the Ursa inside. Then he turns it back into a pike and into a blade again.

With each transformation the cutlass does more damage, weakening the beast a little more. Finally, Jon pulls his weapon out of the Ursa and drives it home again, even deeper than before.

It's a mortal blow.

Making a gurgling sound in its throat, the creature whirls, rears, and tears at the air with its forepaws. Jon slips off it and presses his back against the wall, then slides away so that the Ursa doesn't kill him with its death throes.

In what seems like an attempt to dislodge the cutlasses, the monster slams itself against a wall. But it only succeeds in driving the weapons in deeper.

The Ursa goes wild. It spins, crashes into one wall and then the other, screams in its agony.

Jon doesn't know what a complete human being, someone still in touch with his emotions, would see in the Ursa at this point. A menace that has to be finished before it can kill again? A beast that needs to be put out of its misery?

A moment later, the question becomes moot. The Ursa takes one more long, lurching stride. Then it falls over on its side, shudders, and dies.

A gout of venom spills from its mouth and pools in a slowly widening circle, viciously eating the floor beneath it, hissing and raising twists of black, oily smoke. Then even the smoke and the hissing stop.

It's over.

Jon has never been so close to a dead Ursa. As it lies there, inert, he comes to a realization: He has something in common with the creature. The Ursa is a biological machine, engineered to carry out one purpose and one purpose only: to kill. And so is he.

So is he.

Jon looks around for Doctor Gold. She's gone. Somehow he's not surprised.

He takes stock of himself. A couple of his ribs are broken, and half his face is bloody from a cut over his eye. Otherwise he's unscathed.

But his victory means nothing to him. Victory, defeat . . . they are simply events in a featureless series of events, strung together one after the other, all of them meaningless.

Then Jon hears something and realizes he's not alone. At first he thinks the workers have come back for some reason. However, the sounds are too loud, too heavy. There are other Ursa in the station.

More than one, he thinks.

Even if they can't detect him, it'll be difficult for him to finish them all off. Not that he cares what they do to the Rangers or the workers or other Novans. But *Doctor Gold* seemed to care.

Which is why, holding his side, Jon makes his way to the power chamber.

On the way, he passes Tseng. Her eyes stare up at him. They don't look any different than they did a few moments earlier. But there's a trickle of bright red blood from the corner of her mouth that tells Jon she's dead.

He continues to the chamber. Its door is open, the workers having left it that way. Jon moves to its control console and slides his fingertips along its black command strips one by one, increasing the pressure of the station's magnetic fields on its plasma supply.

Just then, the Ursa shed their camouflage. Jon was right. There are three of them.

They don't know he's there. They also don't know what he is planning.

A blinking red danger light comes on, causing every surface around Jon to strobe with its lurid reflection. He continues to increase the pressure. A voice, echoing throughout the enclosure, warns him that conditions in the facility are reaching a critical level—one that will result in its destruction.

Jon isn't daunted in the least. In fact, destruction is precisely the outcome he has in mind.

In the golden light of morning, the air mercifully cool on his skin, Cypher Raige walks through the debris field that was, until the events of the day before, the site of the North Side Power Relay Facility.

Raige has spoken at length with the survivors of Blackburn's squad. They have all said the same thing, that both Blackburn and the Ursa were destroyed in the explosion.

The magnitude of the blast seems to support their observation. There are chunks of ceramic composite—pieces of the relay facility—hundreds of meters from the building's footprint. Nothing exposed to such a massive release of energy can have survived.

Raige frowns. *And yet . . .*

The Savant's forensic team has discovered bits of flesh containing Ursa DNA. Plenty of them, in fact. It's no less than what Raige expected.

But as many scientists as the Savant has put on the job, not one has been able to turn up a sign of *human* DNA.

It's puzzling, to say the least. And Raige doesn't like

puzzles. Especially when they have such a profound effect on his colony's prospects for survival.

He considered approving four surgical procedures along the lines of Blackburn's. However, given the mysterious circumstances of Blackburn's demise, he will have to put those procedures on hold.

A shame, he thinks, but he has no choice. Until he knows more about Blackburn's death, he can't allow another Ranger to undergo amygdala surgery.

It's a bitter development, as bitter as the smell of ashes in Raige's nostrils. He'd had high hopes for Nizamani's program.

Such high hopes.

The second sun is beginning to melt into the western horizon, its race run, and every rock and grain of sand in the desert is touched with fire. The San Francisco Mountains in the north seethe as if made of lava. A much smaller, more distant chain in the south writhes in what seems like agony.

From Jon's vantage point on a high bluff, he sees for miles in every direction. What he doesn't see—doesn't *wish* to see—is any part of Nova City.

That is why he has made the trek out here. To be alone in the desert, far from his fellow human beings. Far from their striving and their purposes and their emotions.

If he had stopped before reaching this point, someone might have found him and tried to persuade him to go back. But not now. He is beyond their reach, beyond their help. He is exactly where he meant to be.

It has taken him days to reach this bluff. On the first day, he became thirsty and then hungry. On the second, his hunger and thirst got worse. On the third, it was difficult for him to go on.

But he went on anyway.

A normal man would have balked at the idea of walking into the desert without food or water. A normal man would have done whatever he needed to do to survive.

Jon has no needs. No needs at all.

He only has preferences. He prefers to escape the way others look at him. He is tired of explaining his lack of motivation to them. Not that he blames them. He was their hope, after all. But he's become something else, something more like the Ursa he was supposed to destroy. They have to accept the fact that their hope was misplaced.

So he has come to this place to be alone, to let nature— *his* nature—run its course. To let the desert claim him in its own good time.

Does he wish he had never become a Ghost? Never undergone the operation that gave him the ability to go undetected by the Ursa at the cost of his humanity?

Certainly, his life would have been different. He knows that, thinks about it. But he doesn't feel any regret regarding his decision.

He doesn't feel *anything*.

And in the fiery stillness of the desert, under a perfect blue dome of sky, he waits. For what?

For something that might not appear. After all, he can't control his life, not even the last bit left to him. Even as he searches for it in the great, dark expanse, he knows he may be denied it.

The sky turns black. The stars come out. He falls over on his side, too weak to sit up. But somehow, he finds the strength to right himself.

Then he sees something off in the distance.

A tiny figure, limned in starlight. A feminine one in a white lab coat. It's an odd garment to wear in the desert.

As the figure gets closer, he recognizes the blond hair. It tosses in the breeze, obscuring the figure's face. But only for a moment.

Then he sees it clearly and knows it's *her*.

Again he falls over on his side, and the ground is cool

under his cheek. But this time he can't push himself up no matter how hard he tries.

"It's all right," she says, her voice as soft as the wind. She sits down beside him. "Don't get up on my account."

"I didn't know if you would come," he says.

"Yes, you did. I told you I wouldn't abandon you."

He realizes that she's right. He knew. He knew all along.

She looks up at the stars. A tiny piece of their light is reflected in her eyes. "It's beautiful here."

"Is it?" he asks.

"I guess you'll have to take my word for it."

She puts her hand over his. It's warm with life, much warmer than his hand. There was a time when he would have loved that touch, or so he believes.

"How long can you stay?" he asks.

"As long as you need me," she says.

Jon waits for her to look away, as his training has taught him.

She never does.

AFTER
EARTH

Ghost Stories

ATONEMENT

Michael Jan Friedman

Cade Bellamy had it all planned out.

His men—Andropov's, really—were posted throughout his warehouse as well as outside it, their pulsers set on an only *slightly* less than lethal level of force. His supply of stolen electronic components—also Andropov's—had been extricated from ample stacks of legitimate goods and piled in the center of the floor for inspection. And his client, a manufacturer of vintage ground vehicles who loved the idea of paying less for parts, was due to arrive in a matter of minutes.

All set.

This was the first deal Cade had set up entirely on his own. But if all went well, it wouldn't be the last. After all, Cade had his sights set on a black market operation of his own someday—one that would be even bigger than Andropov's.

That was how the world worked, wasn't it? *You take care of yourself.* He had learned that the day his mother died. *You take care of yourself.*

"All over but the accounting, eh?" said a voice behind him.

Cade looked back over his shoulder at the man to whom he owed most of the credits he had ever made. Andropov's features were thick, blunt, as if someone had started to make his face out of putty and lost interest before he got around to finishing it. Andropov's eyes, which were light colored, seemed alive only because the rest of his face looked so dead.

But he had been good to his protégé. *Damned good.*

And his protégé, in exchange, had made him a pile of credits.

"The accounting is my favorite part," Cade said.

"How well I know that," Andropov said. "No doubt you've decided how you'll spend your cut?"

"I think I'll get me a new skipjack," Cade said. He stroked his day's worth of beard as he pictured it. "The latest model. Bright red. Hell, make that a fleet of skipjacks, one for each day of the week."

"After this," Andropov said, looking around the warehouse, "you'll have *earned* a fleet of skipjacks." He consulted his wrist chronometer. "You're sure your client will be on time?"

"I'd bet my life on it," Cade said.

Then he heard the shout from outside: "Rangers!"

It shouldn't have come as a surprise to him. After all, he had gone a long time without the Rangers catching him. Five *years*.

People who made their living on the black market generally figured they would last a year, maybe a year and a half, before the authorities caught up with them. Two years was almost unheard of—and Cade had lasted *five*.

So even though he had known the odds were stacked against him, he had begun to feel like he would *never* get caught, like his luck would never run out.

And now it had.

Cade would have reached for his hip pulser if it had just been a rival busting in on him. But the Rangers? There was no point. Not when they had those cutlasses in their hands. As good as he was with a pulser, he was no match for those things. They'd slice and dice him before he got a decent shot off.

So he followed plan B: He ran.

Not out of the warehouse, because Cade was sure the Rangers had blocked all the street exits. They were known for that. Instead, he resorted to a way out they didn't know about: the trapdoor under a container in the corner that looked as heavy as all the others but was in fact completely and utterly empty.

Andropov, who was closer to it, was already moving the container aside. *Even better,* Cade thought.

Using the other containers for cover, Cade took two quick steps and dived full out across the room. He heard more shouting: the Rangers reacting to his attempt to escape. But none of them had a clear look at him or he would already have been pinned by someone's cutlass.

He hit the floor, rolled, and dived again. Still nothing. *I'm going to make it,* he thought.

Another voice inside him, unbidden, said: *Of course you are. You're Cade Bellamy.*

As he landed on the floor again, skidding forward on his belly, he saw that Andropov had already lifted the trapdoor and was slipping into the tunnel beneath it. But before Cade could join his mentor, Andropov closed the door.

Cade cursed—but not because he was disappointed in Andropov. Had their positions been reversed, Cade would have done the same thing, no question about it.

Scrambling over to the door, he tried to yank it open. But it wouldn't budge. *Andropov's locked it from below—so the Rangers can't follow him.* Again, it was no less than what Cade would have expected.

He looked around for another option. He wasn't going to let the Rangers catch him. *No way.* Another escape route would present itself somehow. He just had to be ready for it.

What he *wasn't* ready for was for the wall beside him to *implode*.

The impact sent pieces of wall flying at him. Most of the pieces missed, but one caught him square in the temple.

Everything went red for a moment. A *long* moment. Then Cade's vision started to clear, and he saw what had happened to the wall.

An Ursa had crashed into the warehouse like a transport cruising at full speed. The genetically engineered creatures were created by the Skrel, a hostile alien species. After a failed attempt to eradicate mankind centuries earlier, the Skrel introduced the human hunter-killers to Nova Prime in order to cleanse the planet of all human life.

He caught a glimpse of the thing's black hole of a mouth, its alien weave of pale flesh and gray smart metal, its cruel curved talons. Then it was on top of one of the Rangers, pinning him to the ground, spewing globules of black venom on him. The Ranger screamed as the venom ate through his uniform and into his chest. A second later he stopped screaming, twitched a couple of times, and lay still, his insides hissing away.

Cade felt his gorge rise, battled it back down, and reached for his pulser. But it was gone. He looked around, couldn't find it in the swirl of dust and debris. Obviously, it had fallen off his belt when the Ursa had burst into the building.

Sometimes a single kill was all the creature required. It would dig in and forget about its other potential victims. But not this time. The Ursa's head swiveled around, its maw opening and closing, its jagged teeth clashing as if it craved something more. It had no eyes; Cade knew that in lieu of sight Ursa were able to detect pheromones secreted by fear and lock onto their victims.

And from all appearances, it seemed to settle on Cade.

The thing was only a couple of meters away from him—a pitifully short leap away. Too short for him to scramble for cover and have any hope of making it.

All he could do was steel himself, fully expecting the Ursa to grab him and dissolve his guts as it had dissolved the Ranger's.

But for some reason, it didn't. It lumbered past him as if he weren't even there.

It's not going after me, he thought wildly, scarcely

able to believe his luck. *It's not going after me. Why isn't it going after me?*

It sprang at another Ranger instead. Her squad mates slashed at it with their cutlasses, keeping the thing at bay. But the Rangers' defense wouldn't last forever. Eventually, the creature would break through and dismember its prey.

As it always did.

And then what? Cade wondered.

How long would it be before the monster finished the Rangers and remembered the morsel it had left behind? It might not even wait that long.

Escape, he thought. *There's got to be a way out.* And he had to find it now, while the Rangers were still distracting the creature.

But he was trapped in a corner of the warehouse, the Ursa blocking his way out. He couldn't get to the front door, couldn't get through the hole it had made in the wall, couldn't even find the trapdoor under the wretched landscape of debris.

That was why he had to do something to the Ursa before it did something to him. But what?

Then he realized that the answer to his question had been a few strides away from him all along. He had just been too focused on the Ursa to know it. Just this side of the monster, lying on the floor next to the lifeless hand of the Ranger who had dropped it, lay a cutlass.

It was long, thin, gleaming in the harsh glare of the overhead lights. And it could kill an Ursa—Cade had seen it happen once, when he was little. He had seen a squad of Rangers fighting one of the creatures; one Ranger leaped onto the Ursa's back and drove her cutlass into the thing's soft spot. He had convinced himself that *that* is what real power was: forcing your opponent—be it life, some monster, or a client thirsty for stolen goods—into submission. *Believe you cannot be touched, and you* won't.

Of course, he'd never used such a weapon in his life.

But he knew the Rangers used finger pressure to change the thing's shape. How hard could it be?

I just have to reach it before the Ursa sees me. He licked his lips, which suddenly felt very dry. *Just . . . get to it.*

Cade hadn't lived his life making safe choices. He was a gambler. And to that point, he had always won. *I'll win this time, too,* he assured himself. *Watch me.*

And he went for the cutlass.

Funny thing . . . even after Ursa imprinted on their intended victims, they were known to turn on would-be attackers. And in this case, Cade was a would-be attacker. But the thing didn't seem to notice him.

Not when he grabbed the cutlass, not when he rolled, and not even when he popped to his feet within striking distance of the creature. As it turned out, he'd been wrong about the weapon's controls; now that he saw them, he had no idea what to do with them. He let the cutlass remain in its spear form as he targeted the Ursa's soft spot and stabbed at it from behind.

But what Cade hit wasn't soft. It was hard enough to deflect his attack.

Bellowing with rage, the thing spun to strike back at him. *Uh oh,* he thought. Its maw dripped blood and gore as it opened to take a chunk out of him.

Except it didn't. The Ursa just stood there, looking confused somehow.

Cade took a couple of steps back, but the Rangers behind the Ursa didn't. They went after it from behind. And they, fortunately, seemed to know where it was vulnerable.

They didn't all hit their target, but at least one of them did. A cutlass sticking out of its back, the monster reared and screamed.

Cade didn't think; he just reacted, hauling back and throwing his cutlass with all his might. It skewered the Ursa through its throat or, rather, what looked like its throat. He wasn't a scientist; he couldn't say.

The thing staggered around, crashing into containers and ripping them open so that their contents went flying everywhere. Cade knew that if it hit him with one of its flailing limbs, he would be dead—no question. But he pressed his back as far into the wall as he could and stayed out of harm's way.

Finally, the Ursa collapsed onto the warehouse floor, the silver shaft of Cade's cutlass still protruding from its throat and the other end protruding from its back. But even then it wasn't dead. It still thrashed a little every few seconds for what seemed like a long time. Finally, it seemed to lie still.

You've got to go, Cade told himself, even though he wanted to stay and revel in his victory.

There would be more Rangers descending on the place. He had to get out before they got there.

But even as he urged himself to run, he was wondering what had kept the Ursa from killing him, what had kept it—it seemed at the time—from even knowing he was there.

Stop wondering and go! he thought, his instinct of self-preservation overriding his curiosity.

He went.

But he hadn't taken two steps before he found a Ranger barring his way.

She pointed the business end of her cutlass at him and said, "*Freeze.* You're not going anywhere."

Cade had never been in a jail cell before. He couldn't say he especially liked the accommodations.

But then, he had always prized his freedom; that was one reason he'd avoided the constraints of a traditional job, traditional hours, even traditional people. But his cell, a small gray windowless space with a bed built into the wall, a ceramic sink, and a ceramic bowl, was about as constraining as it could get.

Of course, he wouldn't be consigned to the place for any length of time until he'd had the benefit of a trial. Even black marketers got that. Not that it would matter in the long run.

After all, they caught me with stolen components. That shipment alone would be worth a few years. And they probably had evidence of other transactions he had made, or they wouldn't have gone after him in the first place.

I'm screwed, he thought, plunking himself down on his bed just as the door to his cell whispered aside, revealing a tall, broad-shouldered figure standing in the corridor outside. The guy, whose face was half in shadow, was wearing a Ranger uniform.

But he wasn't armed, and so he wasn't Cade's escort to the courtroom. *Then who . . . ?*

The guy entered the cell, and the prisoner got a better look at him. A good enough look to get him wondering what the hell was going on.

It wasn't every day Commander Rafe Velan of the United Ranger Corps paid a visit to a lowly black marketer.

"Bellamy," Velan said, his voice deep and resonant. It echoed in the cell.

"That's right," Cade replied cautiously.

He had seen Velan on news broadcasts since he was a kid, it seemed. He felt like he knew the guy. But there was a world of difference between them.

Cade's mind raced. Velan wasn't there to shoot the breeze. *He wants names, I bet. And he thinks I'll be freer with them if it's a commander doing the asking.*

Except it wasn't going to work. Cade was a lot of things, but a snitch wasn't one of them.

"Listen," he said, "thanks for the visit and all, but—"

"I'll make this short," Velan said, interrupting him without apology. "I've got a proposition for you. You can rot here in prison for the next eight years, which is the sentence you'll likely receive, or you can do your colony a favor."

Cade smiled. "A favor . . . ?"

"Yes. You can help us eliminate the Ursa."

It took Cade a moment to figure out why Velan would want his services in that regard. But before this went any further, he figured he ought to set the record straight. After all, Velan would find out on his own soon enough. "I haven't exactly earned a reputation for honesty, but I should tell you that what I did in the warehouse—"

"Is exhibit a rare talent. Our psych people think you've lived on the edge for so long, fending for yourself, you just don't react to danger the way other people do. Fear has been replaced with survival instinct. Whatever the reason, it's a talent we *need* if we're ever going to get rid of the Ursa."

"What I meant to say," Cade pressed, "is I don't know how I did it. Or, for that matter, how to do it again."

Velan shrugged. "We believe your lack of fear enabled you to remain invisible to the Ursa—to *ghost*. It's possible it was a one-time thing, and equally possible that the next time you confront an Ursa, it will tear you apart. But it's also possible that you'll do exactly what you did before, with or without the knowledge of how it happened."

"You really think so?"

"Would I be standing here if I didn't?"

Cade considered the proposition. "So it's a crapshoot."

"Ultimately, the question is whether you've got the stomach for a little gamble."

Cade chuckled to himself. *A gamble?* "Now you're talking my language."

Cade had barely sat down on his bunk in the cadet barracks before he found a woman looming over him, a rawboned woman with dark skin and thick copper-colored hair. He gathered from her rust-brown uniform and the insignia on her shoulder that she was a squad leader. *His* squad leader if the way she was glowering at him was any indication.

He got to his feet. That was how they did it in the Rangers, wasn't it? They stood whenever a superior officer was in the room.

"You're Bellamy," she said in a voice like iron. It wasn't a question.

Nonetheless, he said, "Yes, ma'am."

"I'm Tolentino. You're mine now."

Cade couldn't help smiling a little.

"Something funny?" she asked.

He shrugged. "Was just thinking that this gig might not be too bad, after all—"

"Get dressed," she said, obviously not amused. "We're training at the ravine in twelve minutes. Past the command center, on the left. If you're late, you'll be cleaning boots the rest of the day. And just so you know, those boots can get pretty rank." She seemed to enjoy telling him that. "By the way, the ravine's a good ten minutes away. I'd get started if I were you."

Then she left him sitting there.

Screw her, he thought, watching her go. He glanced at the neatly folded uniform on the bunk beside him. *She thinks I'm going to jump just because she's got more muscles than I do?*

Really?

Of course, there *was* the little matter of jail time.

As it turned out, it didn't take long to pull on a uniform and a pair of boots. Not long at all.

Cade stood on the dusty red dirt flat, shaded his eyes from the glare of Nova Prime's twin suns, and considered the shiny metal structure bridging the ravine up ahead of him. It was like a child's set of monkey bars except that the bars, which were held in place by magnetic forces, could reconfigure at any moment.

As he had learned moments earlier, they could rotate, pivot, elevate, or descend. They could cluster together or spread apart. And there was no way for Cade to know in advance which position they would take.

The ravine was ten meters wide and six meters deep, which meant a drop would be painful if not quite deadly. To get through the monkey bars and reach the flat beyond it, Cade would have to adapt. He wasn't worried. He'd been adapting all his life.

"Ready?" Tolentino asked.

She held up a slim black personal access device. With it, she could stop the bars from moving if safety demanded. But from what Cade had heard about the exercise, safety *never* demanded.

"Ready," said Cade, his voice all but lost among six other responses. His fellow cadets were lined up on either side of him, crouching to get a better jump.

After all, the first three to get over the ravine would watch the other four try a second time in the rising desert heat. And the last two in that second group would spend the afternoon cleaning everyone else's ordnance. So there was an incentive to do well.

Not that Cade needed one. He liked challenges, always had. And this was an opportunity to show the cadets he was as good as they were even though they had been training far longer than he had.

"Go!" Tolentino barked.

The seven cadets took off as one, pelting across the few dozen meters that separated them from the ravine. It took Cade only a couple of seconds to find out he was the fastest of them.

But then, he'd spent his life running from the law.

As he approached the ravine, he lifted his knees and expanded his stride. If he didn't leave the ground until he absolutely had to, he would minimize the amount of time he spent among the monkey bars.

Three, two, one, he thought. *Now jump!*

By waiting as long as he had, Cade was able to bypass

the first rank of bars. But as he reached between them for a bar in the second rank, it rotated from horizontal to vertical. He managed to grab it anyway, but it slipped through his fingers.

No! he thought as he began to plummet into the ravine.

Fortunately, there was another layer of bars below the first one. Throwing a hand out, Cade hooked one with the tips of his outstretched fingers. And somehow he held on, wrenching his shoulder as he swung back and forth like a pendulum.

His fellow cadets, who had been more conservative in their approach to the ravine, blotted out the suns as they swung from bar to bar overhead. Bitterly, Cade acknowledged that he had outsmarted himself.

Twisting about, he latched on to a bar that put him back on the right path. Then he began handing himself across the ravine, his arms straining hard with the effort.

But as the wall of the ravine loomed ahead, he confronted the fact that he still had to climb back to the top layer. His first impulse was to try to swing himself up and hook a bar with his foot, but he was no trapeze artist. Then another tactic occurred to him.

He waited until he reached the wall. Then he kicked hard, hit the inclined surface, and sprang back as hard as he could. The angle of the wall and the force he exerted propelled him high enough to grab a bar in the upper layer.

From there he swung back and forth and finally, pushing himself to his limits, wrestled himself over the lip of the ravine.

As he got his feet beneath him, he saw that a few of the cadets had already begun sprinting for the finish line. Ignoring the fire in his arms and legs, Cade took off after them.

Two of them beat him. He edged the third one by half a stride.

Didn't win . . . but I didn't lose, *either,* he quipped to himself.

As the rest of the pack caught up, Cade drank in a deep breath, pointed to the two who had finished ahead of him, and said, "Nice run."

They glanced his way but didn't say anything in return. Cade wondered why.

"You trying to make me look bad?" someone asked from behind him.

Cade turned and saw the cadet he had edged out.

She had dirty blond hair and almond-shaped eyes, in fact, the nicest eyes he'd seen in a long time. And a thin white thread of scar that ran from the corner of her mouth to her jawline.

"Ericcson," she said, using the back of her hand to wipe the sweat from her forehead. "Nava Ericcson."

"Cade—"

"Yeah, I know. The Ghost in training."

He smiled. "I guess my rep's preceded me."

From the other side of the ravine, Tolentino called out the names of the first three finishers, Cade among them. "Everyone else will be crossing over again in five," she said.

Nava turned to Cade. "So can you do it?"

"What? Ghost?" He shrugged. "I did it once."

"That's once more than anyone else I know."

The two cadets who had finished ahead of them walked by. They didn't say anything. They just looked at Cade.

"What's with *them*?" he asked.

"They resent you," Nava said.

"Resent *me*? For what?"

They were the ones who had grown up with mothers and fathers, for God's sake. They were the ones who'd had it easy in life.

"They've wanted to be Rangers since they were old enough to crawl. They dedicated themselves to that idea. They studied. They trained. And they dealt with the anxiety of knowing that despite all their studies and their training, they still might not make it.

"But you didn't have to worry about any of that. Velan just waved his magic wand and fast-tracked you through Ranger training. At least, that's how it looks to them."

"Is that how it looks to *you*?"

"I don't want to join the Rangers so I can strut around in a uniform the color of month-old pumpkin pie. I want to join so I can fight Ursa. Maybe even, in my craziest dreams, end the threat of them altogether. If you can help us do that, I don't *care* how you wound up here."

If, he thought. That was the question, wasn't it?

In the heat of the afternoon weeks later, Cade's squad had to respond to a simulated Ursa attack.

The idea was Prime Commander Cypher Raige's, according to Nava. He had set up a couple of city streets out in the desert, or at least what *looked* like city streets. The buildings were real but empty and unpopulated.

And as a squad patrolled them, a mechanical construct would be released from an unannounced point of entry.

The construct was designed to resemble an Ursa, move like an Ursa, react to counterattacks like an Ursa. Except, of course, it spewed black dye instead of venom, left red marks instead of wounds where it struck with its talons, and didn't eat its prey on those occasions when it won the encounter.

Tolentino led the squad down the street as she had done in the past. But now Cade was part of it. He had graduated from his accelerated training program, one of eight Rangers moving slowly and deliberately, four on one side of the street and four on the other, cutlasses in hand.

He eyed the windows on either side of him, the doors, the intersection up ahead. Others were keeping an eye on the street behind him. That was the way it worked. They were a team.

Cade had never depended on others to do his work for him, but he cooperated. He wasn't in the black market anymore, after all. He was a Ranger, as hard as that was to believe.

As luck would have it, he was the one who saw the thing first. It was on the rooftop across the street, hardly visible from his angle on the ground. But he had spotted his share of Rangers over the years, and they weren't nearly as big as a mock Ursa.

Exactly as Cade had been instructed, he touched the navi-band on his arm to alert the others. But as he did so, the simulated creature leaped. A moment later, it landed in the middle of the street.

Dutifully, Cade awaited Tolentino's orders. "Surround it," she barked. "Don't let it get away."

Standard procedure. Cade took up his position. His squad mates took up theirs. The beast focused on one of them—a stocky guy named Smithee—and went after him.

Cade was on the opposite side of the circle. Seeing his chance, he broke into a run. When he reached the construct, he leaped up onto its back and drove his cutlass into its soft spot.

He saw the spot light up in red even before he fell to the ground. *Construct killed,* he thought. *Mission accomplished.*

As he got to his feet and dusted himself off, he was pretty pleased with himself. Nava smiled at him and shook her head, no doubt more than a little impressed.

But truthfully, it had been easy.

Easier, in fact, than climbing up the construct's back to retrieve his cutlass. The first time he did it, he slipped and fell back and landed on his butt.

Everybody laughed. That was all right. *Let them. They know who put away the Ursa.*

He tried again. This time he recovered his cutlass. *Then* he fell on his butt.

Tolentino hadn't said anything to Cade about his "kill" as the squad awaited transportation back to the Ranger barracks. But as the ocher-colored transport appeared over the desert, the squad leader tapped Cade on the shoulder and said, "Join me."

Cade walked with her, grinning, pleased with the fact that he'd distinguished himself on day 1. No doubt, Tolentino wanted to compliment him on the work he'd put in.

And who was he to argue with her? *I've been busting my butt. I deserve some recognition.*

When they were a few dozen meters apart from the rest of the squad, Tolentino stopped and turned to him. "At ease," she said.

Cade stood at ease.

"You know why I singled you out?" she asked. "Why we're talking here, apart from the others?"

He didn't want to seem immodest. "No, ma'am."

"It's because I'm disappointed in your performance."

Disappointed . . . ? It took a moment for the word to sink in. "What are you talking about?" he asked. "I've done everything you wanted from me—done it better than anyone in the squad."

Tolentino's gaze was hard, unyielding. "Not the way I look at it. I gave you an order to surround the Ursa. You diverged from that order."

"I saw an opportunity," he argued. "I took advantage of it."

"And put the rest of your team in danger. No one got killed this time, but next time it won't be an exercise. It'll be real."

"I thought the whole point of my being a Ghost—"

"You ghosted," said Tolentino. "I know. *Once.* But

neither one of us is a hundred percent sure you can do it again. Right?"

He clenched his teeth, refusing to give Tolentino the satisfaction of a reply.

Her eyes narrowed. "I asked you a question, Ranger."

Crap. "Right."

"And until we know for sure that you can do the things the rest of us can't, let's focus on teaching you to do the things we *can*—like staying alive, and making sure the others in your squad do the same."

Cade resented the remark. Was it his job to worry about his squad mates or to kill the construct?

"And by the way," Tolentino added, "when you made a fool of yourself climbing up to get your cutlass back? Your squad mates weren't laughing with you. They were laughing *at* you."

That stung. No doubt, she had meant it to. Cade wanted to hurt her back but he couldn't—not if he wanted to stay out of jail.

"Got it?" Tolentino asked.

He nodded coldly. "Got it."

"Got it, *what*?"

"Got it, *ma'am*."

"You'd better," she said. "Because I'm not clearing you for field duty until you do."

If Cade's first day was bad, his second was worse.

Tolentino put him through one grueling drill after another, matching him up against his squad mates singly and in pairs. His speed and agility were second to nobody's, so he didn't have a problem keeping up physically. But when it came to things like strategy and teamwork, it was clear he had a lot to learn.

Even to him.

In one exercise, Tolentino drew a circle in the dirt with her cutlass. Then her Rangers had to stand inside it and, using their own cutlasses as quarterstaffs, knock their opponents out of the circle. They were given padding for their heads, ankles, and hands, but not enough to keep a solid whack from drawing blood.

In round 1, Cade beat a fair-haired woman named Bentzen, sweeping her legs out from under her. In round 2, he drove the end of his cutlass into the chest of a guy named Zabaldo.

That put him in the final round. He would face Kayembe, a monster of a man with a weightlifter's chest and thighs the size of Cade's torso. Kayembe had reached the final by besting Tolentino in the second round, so he wasn't just big—he was crafty.

Kayembe smiled when Cade stepped into the circle against him. "Looks like you and me, Ghost Man."

"Figure that out all by yourself?" Cade asked.

His opponent's smile faded. "I was going to go easy on you. Now . . ." His voice trailed off suggestively.

"Don't do me any favors."

"Commander *Velan* did you the favor," Kayembe said. "It's up to me to show him how wrong he was."

"Assuming you *can*," said Cade.

If he hadn't backed down in the back alleys of Nova City, he wasn't going to do so for the likes of Kayembe. Not even if he *was* one of the biggest human beings he had ever seen.

Tolentino held her hand up between them. "Ready?"

Cade and his adversary said "Ready" at the same time.

"Go," Tolentino said, dropping her hand.

Kayembe began by striking at Cade's feet. *Not a bad approach*, Cade had to concede. Even if he kept himself from falling, he would be off balance when he came down.

Unless, of course, Cade had paid attention when Kayembe had tried the same opening gambit on Nava, on whom it had worked. Anticipating it, Cade jumped high enough to avoid the stroke but not as high as Kayembe might have expected.

Then he planted the end of his cutlass in the ground and, using the weapon like a vaulting pole, kicked Kayembe in the face.

The big man staggered, but not far enough to step out of the circle—which was why Cade bent, thrust his cutlass between Kayembe's legs, and pushed. Already off balance, Cade's adversary couldn't stay upright. He toppled like a tree, raising a cloud of dust where he landed.

But he didn't stay down for long. In a heartbeat, he was back up, reaching for Cade's throat. It took Nava and two other members of the squad to hold Kayembe back, and it looked like even that wouldn't be enough until Tolentino intervened.

"Atten-shun!" she snapped.

The squad straightened, though Kayembe still glared at Cade as if he wanted to kill him.

Tolentino eyed Cade, then Kayembe, then Cade again. "Kayembe," she said, "do I need to remind you of the punishment for Rangers who go after their squad mates?"

Kayembe's mouth twisted. "No, ma'am."

"Good." Her gaze hardened. "Not that I entirely blame you. I distinctly said no one was to strike an opponent other than with a cutlass. Did you hear me say that, Zabaldo?"

"Yes, ma'am," came the reply.

"How about you, Ericcson?"

"Yes, ma'am," said Nava.

"And yet Bellamy seems to have missed that instruction. Pity. It's costing him the championship of our little tournament—and a couple of hours of his free time this afternoon, which he'll spend doing everyone's laundry."

Cade was going to protest. After all, the Ursa didn't play by the rules. *Why should I?*

But in the end, he thought better of it. He wasn't going to change Tolentino's mind, so what was the point?

* * *

Later on, Cade had the mess hall all to himself. But then, no one else had spent a couple of hours doing his squad's laundry.

He was just lifting the first bite to his mouth when he heard someone come in. Casting a glance over his shoulder, he saw that it was Nava.

"Mind if I join you?" she asked.

"Hope you like the smell of laundry detergent," he said, glad for the company though he wouldn't have admitted it.

Nava sat down across the table from him. "Very inventive, what you did this morning."

Cade shrugged. "Tolentino didn't seem to think so."

"She *did* say no body-to-body contact."

"That's not the way it works in the real world." He gestured expansively, including the entire mess hall. "Only in *this* one."

"But *this* is where you're training. And if we maim each other here, there won't be anybody left to protect the colony."

"I come from a different place, that's all. You said it yourself. I didn't aspire to be a Ranger all my life."

Nava nodded. "I heard you were involved with the black market."

"I had to be involved with something. I had to *survive*."

"What about your family? They thought that was all right?"

"I didn't have a family. My mother died when I was five. My father . . . I never had the pleasure."

Nava's expression softened. "How did you live?"

"After Mom's death, I started running errands. Guys would pay me to take messages back and forth for them. They figured the Rangers wouldn't arrest a kid. As I got older, they gave me more to do. Things just evolved from there."

"Must have been rough."

"I didn't look at it that way. I mean, I had nothing to compare it to. I figured everybody had to look out for themselves, not just me."

"No one gave you a hand? *Ever?*" Nava sounded incredulous.

"People offered me help now and then, sure, but they always had an angle. They were really trying to help themselves. And if I trusted them, if I did the things they suggested . . . let's just say I wouldn't have lasted very long."

"You're a Ranger now. You can put that behind you."

Cade shook his head. "It's not that easy. I'm not used to trusting people, doing what they say just because they've got an officer's insignia on their shoulder."

"So following orders isn't your strong suit."

He chuckled. "Like you didn't come to that conclusion on your own."

"People change, Cade."

"Not everybody."

She put her hand on top of his, but only for a moment. "We need you too much—need your talent too much—for me to let you talk that way. You're a gift. And we'll do whatever we can to hang on to it."

He looked Nava in the eye. As much as he wanted to trust her, he couldn't help wondering if she had an angle, too. "Nobody's ever called me a gift before."

Nava smiled. "There's a first time for everything."

On Cade's fifth day of training, he ran afoul of his pal Kayembe again. It wasn't as if he *intended* to tick the guy off. It just happened.

Their squad was up in the San Francisco mountain range on maneuvers. After all, Ursa liked to hole up in remote places sometimes, especially the mountainous kind. And when they did, it was up to the Rangers to flush them out.

Cade and Kayembe were paired off, searching a high canyon, moving from strong sunlight to shadow and back again. They were supposed to rendezvous with the rest of their squad at a specified point.

Unless they found something. But they wouldn't. It was just a maneuver. A hike, really. Just so they would know their places in case they *did* have to hunt down an Ursa someday.

Kayembe didn't talk. Not to Cade at least. If the big man had been paired with someone else, it would have been different. But he had nothing to say to Cade.

After twenty kliks or so, Cade noticed something shiny in the wall of the canyon. Squinting at it, he saw that it was a plaque. *Out here? In the mountains?*

He moved closer to get a better look at it, stood there, and shaded his eyes. "In commemoration of Conner Raige's victory over the Ursa known as Gash," it said.

"Who's Conner Raige?" he asked Kayembe.

The big man glanced at him, narrow-eyed. "Prime Commander. Long time ago. Let's move."

But Cade wasn't ready yet. He looked around at the red-clay mountains, trying to imagine somebody— some *Raige*—slashing away at an Ursa in the narrow confines of the canyon.

"I said let's *move*," Kayembe insisted.

Cade ignored his partner. After all, this was Ranger stuff. Ranger *history*. Maybe if he knew more about it, more about Conner Raige, he could figure out what he himself was missing.

"Must have been a big deal," he thought out loud, "if the guy got himself a plaque for killing a—"

Suddenly, Cade noticed a point of bright red light on the chest of Kayembe's uniform. At the same time, the big man cursed and pointed to Cade. Following the gesture, Cade realized there was a point of red light on his chest as well.

"What the hell . . . ?" he said.

Kayembe spit out a curse, his eyes full of anger. "We've been tagged, you idiot."

"Tagged?" Cade asked.

He had no idea what his partner was talking about. But Kayembe's expression told him it wasn't good.

It was Tolentino who had tagged them, it turned out—with a laser beam from a vantage point higher up the mountain. Rangers weren't supposed to stop and read plaques, apparently.

"You lose focus, you die," Tolentino told Cade and Kayembe afterward, when the squad had reassembled. "How does it feel being dead, gentlemen?"

The penalty? A two-hour run in the desert the next morning. Full packs, no stopping, not even for a drink. Cade wasn't happy about it. Kayembe was even less so.

When they got back to the barracks, the others were waiting for them, smiles on their faces and taunts on their tongues. They seemed to think it was funny. Despite all the pain he had been in that morning, Cade might have found some humor in the situation as well.

But Kayembe felt otherwise. Pointing a long, thick finger at Cade, he growled, "I don't *care* if you can ghost. I'd rather have somebody else—*anybody* else—watching my back than a screw-up like you."

Cade could feel the others' eyes on him. They didn't say anything, but they didn't have to. They felt the same way Kayembe did.

A screw-up.

It hurt—more than Cade wanted to admit, even to himself. After all, he wanted to show them he could be a Ranger, too. But he wasn't going to say anything in his defense.

Why should he? They had all had it in for him from the beginning. Even Tolentino.

I'm a screw-up? he thought, glaring back at Kayembe. *Well, screw* you.

But he didn't say it out loud—not when he had so much to lose. He just kept his mouth shut and walked out.

It was raining when Cade got to the place on D'Agostino Road.

He stood across the street from it, his hands shoved into the pockets of his jacket, his collar turned up against the weather. He could see an orange light through the dirty windows, feel the beat of music in his bones if he concentrated hard enough.

The place was called Regina's. No one knew why. If it had been owned by a woman named Regina at one time, she had faded from memory long ago.

Cade remembered the first time he'd been inside. He had been twelve. He had walked in with guys he worked for, guys who were regulars in the place. Nobody questioned his being there, not even when he ordered a drink he clearly couldn't handle or when they had to throw him on a cot in the back because he'd passed out.

He thought he heard a peal of laughter across the street, muted by walls and distance. It didn't take much for people to laugh in Regina's, he recalled. Pretty much anything got them going.

Of course, it could have changed since he'd been there last. But he doubted it. It had been only a few weeks—the night before the Rangers arrested him, in fact.

Cade knew everybody in Regina's, knew every face. He'd had good times with them. He wanted to have those times again.

But he hadn't made the trip just to join the party. He had received a request on his personal comm unit from an unidentified friend. Except he knew from the choice of words who the friend was. The only thing he didn't know was why that friend had asked Cade to meet him at Regina's.

But he would find out soon enough.

Regina's was exactly how Cade remembered it—loud and crowded, redolent with alcohol and sweat, and something sweet he had never been able to identify. He found Andropov sitting at a table in the back, flanked by a couple of his men. New ones, of course, to replace the ones Andropov had lost in the raid on the warehouse.

"I'm pleased you could make it, my friend," Andropov said. He got up and extended his hand, which was large and meaty.

Cade clasped it. "I wish I could say it was easy. The Rangers are everywhere." And though Velan hadn't given Cade any formal restrictions, he might not have taken kindly to the idea of Cade visiting one of his old haunts.

He sat down opposite his mentor. Andropov looked the same. But then he had gotten away that day in the warehouse. He hadn't been running in the desert with a full pack on his back.

"Drink?" asked Andropov.

Cade shook his head. "No thanks." The last thing he wanted to do was return to his barracks with liquor on his breath.

Andropov grunted. "You're not holding it against me, I hope, that I escaped the Rangers without you?"

Cade shook his head. "Not at all. It was every man for himself."

"I'm glad you understand."

"You said you had something to discuss with me."

Andropov nodded. "So I do. Something that I discovered. Because, as you know, I have contacts in the courts."

Cade knew, all right. When he was a boy, he had delivered things to people. One of them had been a court clerk.

"It's good news," Andropov continued. He put his elbows on the table and learned forward. "A week from now, the charges against you will all have been dropped."

Dropped? Cade thought.

"You look surprised," said Andropov. "Me, too. I figured you would have to prove yourself as a Ranger first. But your superiors appear to be a trusting lot. They began petitioning the court to clear your record the day you joined them."

Dropped, Cade repeated inwardly.

"So you don't have to stay with them," Andropov told him. "You can leave a week from now, free and clear. Which brings me to my proposal . . ."

Andropov described a shipment for which he needed a customer. But Cade wasn't listening to the details. All he could think about was that he could leave the Rangers in a week, and how sweet that would be.

"What do you think?" Andropov asked.

"I'm in," Cade told him. After all, he would need some credits when he got out.

"Excellent," Andropov said. "You were lucky for me, my friend. I think you can be lucky that way again."

Maybe the man was right. *Maybe my luck is coming back.*

Cade got back to his barracks an hour and a half after he had left, flushed with the prospect of getting his old life back. *Who needs the Rangers?* he asked himself.

They had been on his case since the minute he showed up. Tolentino especially. He'd seen it at the ravine that first day. He'd seen it after he disabled the construct. He'd seen it after he beat Kayembe in the tournament, and again in the San Franciscos when he saw the plaque.

They hadn't given him an inch. And he had taken whatever abuse they wanted to throw at him because he didn't want to go to prison. But soon he wouldn't have to worry about that.

Cade imagined himself walking up to Tolentino and shoving his uniform in her face. Maybe even decking

Kayembe before he left. *Yeah.* He would do all that and more.

He was thinking about that, thinking hard, when he heard yelling from inside the barracks. One of the voices was Nava's.

A real Ranger would probably have entered the barracks without a second thought. But Cade wasn't a real Ranger. He was a street kid at heart, a criminal, so he didn't walk in. He went to a place where the fabric walls of the barracks came together and peeked inside.

Just in time to see Nava kick Kayembe's cutlass, which had been propped against his bunk, halfway across the barracks.

Kayembe glared at her. "Are you nuts?"

"Cut him a break," Nava snapped. She turned to Zabaldo. "You, too."

"I haven't said a *thing* to him," Zabaldo protested.

"That's the problem. It's like he doesn't exist."

"What's it to you?" Bentzen asked.

"He's a *Ranger*," Nava said.

Kayembe sneered bitterly. "Not a *real* Ranger."

They're talking about me, Cade realized.

"Says who?" Nava demanded. "*You?*"

"He didn't earn it," Kayembe said. "You *know* that."

"Since when do they ask *you* to decide who's earned what?"

Kayembe poked himself in the chest with his thumb. "I went through the selection process. I busted my *hump.*" He looked around. "We all did."

"That's great," Nava said. "And why did you do it?"

Kayembe looked confused. "To become a Ranger."

"To fight Ursa," Bentzen said, who seemed to have a better grasp of where Nava was going with this.

"To fight Ursa? Well," Nava said, "that's a coincidence, because that's why Bellamy's here, too. He wants to fight Ursa as much as we do. He wants to make a difference. Who are we to tell him he can't?

"Especially if he can ghost. You know what that would mean to us? How many Ursa we'll be able to take

off the board with a guy like that? Or do you *like* losing your friends and having not a damned thing to
show for it?"

That seemed to shut them up.

"If they're right about Cade," Nava continued, "the
Ursa can't see him. But *we* can. So stop pretending he's
not here, because he's one of us. One of *us*."

No one objected. Not because they had gained respect for Cade, because as far as he could tell, they
didn't have any to begin with. It was because of how
they felt about Nava.

And how Nava felt about *him*.

Cade was touched. Hell, no one had ever stood up for
him that way before.

But what if his ghosting turned out to be a fluke—*a
one-time thing*, as Velan had put it? What if he wasn't
the difference maker Nava hoped he was?

How hard would she fight for him *then*?

That night, Cade's squad was assigned crowd-control
duty at the East Side Arena, a huge, ivory-colored amphi-
theater open to the stars.

The occasion was a concert for kids who had lost
loved ones to the Ursa. Cade had never heard of the
performers, but they were loud and quirky and perfectly suited to their youthful audience if the applause
they got was any indication.

Cade and Nava had been stationed on the curved
walkway just behind the nosebleed seats. In the Arena's
early days, a couple of mischievous spectators had gone
over the rail and tried to climb down the facade, only
to fall to their deaths. Since then, it had become the
Rangers' job to watch the walkway.

Nava smiled. "If I'd known they used Rangers here,"
she said, "I'd have tried out even earlier."

"We're not just here to enjoy the music," Cade reminded her.

Tolentino had made him paranoid. He was sure that if he lost focus for even a second, she would find out about it.

Nava shrugged. "Who's enjoying the music?"

"Then what?" Cade asked.

Nava looked around. "The way the place lights up the night. The way the air smells, like some kind of perfume. It's nice."

He slid her a look. "Really?"

"Uh huh. And it's even nicer being up here rather than down there."

"If you say so," he said.

Suddenly, he realized that her eyes had locked with his. What's more, he found it hard to turn away.

Cade had thought Nava was nice-looking from the moment he met her. But now that he saw her with the stars in her eyes, she looked absolutely beautiful. And her scar only made her more so, somehow.

Before he knew it, she was leaning closer to him, bringing her mouth up to meet his.

"Don't," he said suddenly, surprising himself. *Am I crazy? A pretty girl is trying to kiss me and I'm turning her down?*

Still, he couldn't do it. Nava thought he was going to be a Ranger for the long haul, and he wasn't. In no time at all he would be free of the Corps, doing what he did best—working the black market.

She was the one person in his life who had stood up for him. He wasn't going to let her get hurt.

"Why not?" Nava asked. "No one's looking."

"Because we're *Rangers*," he said, lying through his teeth.

"And Rangers can't have love affairs?" She made a face. "Is that a rule or something? Because if it is, I've never heard of it."

"I don't know if it's a rule, but it's still a lousy idea." His mind raced. "What if we wind up fighting an Ursa side by side? How are you going to survive if you're worrying about me? How am *I* going to survive if I'm worrying about *you*?"

"I'd be worrying about you anyway. You're a member of my squad."

"I mean me in *particular*. There are a million things to think about out there. You don't want to add one more."

Nava shrugged. "Then I'll ask for a transfer to another squad."

"Squads work together sometimes. They get mixed and matched. We can't take that chance."

"You don't think this is stupid?" she asked. "I've never met anyone like you."

Cade could see only part of her face, but she looked like she was in pain. "This is hard enough," he said. "Don't make it harder."

Nava eyed him a moment longer. Then she said, "All right," with only a faint note of bitterness in her voice and moved farther down the walkway. "If that's the way you want it."

It wasn't. But he wasn't going to put Nava in a position to hurt herself. Anyone else, but not her.

As the days passed, Cade became more and more certain that he had done the right thing back on the walkway.

Nava didn't speak to him much, but that was all right. She was better off this way.

It occurred to him that they could get together after he left the Rangers, but he didn't think she would want that. She was a Ranger. He was going back to the black market. Not exactly a match made in heaven, was it?

Meanwhile, something funny happened. The less Cade gave a crap about impressing Tolentino and the others, the better he seemed to do his job, at least in everyone else's minds. And the more he did that job, the more easily he was accepted.

Even by Kayembe. At least a little bit.

Go figure, Cade thought.

Then, the day before Cade's charges were supposed to be dropped, he and his teammates got the news from Tolentino: They would be engaging in an Ursa hunt, Cade's first. To his surprise, he was excited about it. But then he would have a chance to ghost again.

Or fall flat on his face.

But at least he would *know.*

They were dispatched by mag-lev transport to Old Town, the original settlement from which Nova City had grown. Old Town, as Cade remembered it, was a place full of narrow streets and alleys, any of which might afford an Ursa a place to hide.

When he got there, he saw that the streets were even narrower than he had recalled. It wasn't a plus from a strategic point of view. Rangers had always done better when they had a chance to surround the beasts.

Still, Tolentino put half of them on one side of the street and half on the other. They stopped at each intersection, knowing that any Ursa they encountered probably would be camouflaged but might betray its presence with a set of tracks in the soft red dirt underfoot. When they didn't see anything, they moved on.

Suddenly the monster appeared—out of nowhere, it seemed—a sinewy six-legged mass of pale flesh and blue-gray smart metal with a huge black maw and razor-sharp talons.

Tolentino called out an order that sent Kayembe and Bentzen at the thing from different sides. Cade could see that the Ursa was confused—so much so that it didn't know which of them to imprint on first.

Then it made a choice—and it was Kayembe. It took a swipe at him with one of its paws and nearly got him, but he managed to scramble backward in time. Seeing that the creature had picked its prey, the other Rangers knew they had to distract it or see Kayembe sliced to ribbons.

Zabaldo was the first to take a serious hack at the Ursa. Nava followed suit. Cade caught himself watching her every move and forced his eyes to avert. *Focus,* he reprimanded himself.

With each Ranger attack, the monster whirled and roared, but it didn't go after its tormentor. Having imprinted on Kayembe, it wouldn't go after anyone else until it had ripped the big man apart.

Cade knew he was leaving. He didn't have to risk his life to save Kayembe's. But if he hung back, he might never know if he could ghost again as he had done in the warehouse.

Was it worth sacrificing himself to find out? *Hell no.* But he wouldn't have to. All he had to do was keep his cutlass at the ready. If it looked to him like the Ursa was going to attack him, he could defend himself.

Was there a risk? Sure. But Cade was a gambler. He *liked* the idea of a little risk. All he had to do was get between Kayembe and the creature, where it would perceive him as an obstacle if it perceived him at all—and remove him as only an Ursa could.

Here goes, he thought, allowing the others to continue the fight as he sprinted past Kayembe and took a position behind him. That was where Tolentino had told him to go in an encounter. "Behind whoever the Ursa imprints on," she had said.

This Ursa was noticeably bigger than the creature Cade had encountered back in the warehouse. *Bigger and faster.*

He remembered the way that other Ursa had gone by him as if he weren't there. At the time, he hadn't even realized what was going on. But this time he knew *exactly.*

But what if what had happened in the warehouse was a fluke? What if it was only that first Ursa he could hide from and no others?

Then Kayembe won't be the only casualty today.

As the big man retreated past Cade, the Ursa followed. And Cade stood there, counting on the luck that had always seen him through, no matter how tough the situation.

The creature opened its maw and shrieked. Cade could see its teeth, a jagged circle of death. He could smell its breath, rank with the shreds of its last human meal.

He waited until he was sure it would try to rake him with its claws or spew its venom at him. And then he waited some more. But the Ursa didn't go after him.

At the last possible moment, he threw himself out of harm's way, and the thing went past him.

I'm invisible to it! he thought. *I'm goddamned invisible!*

But Kayembe was still at risk. Nava and Bentzen closed with the Ursa to try to slow it down and give Kayembe a chance. But there was only one guy who could save the big man, and that was Cade.

The Ghost.

He didn't owe Kayembe a thing. But he owed *himself* something. He owed himself the look on his teammates' faces when they saw what he could do, and maybe regretted the way they had treated him.

He still wasn't an expert with his cutlass, but he was good enough. The Ursa had two soft spots. One was underneath, a big target but difficult to reach. The other was on its back.

With that in mind, Cade configured his cutlass into a spear, got a running start, and leaped onto the beast's back. Then, before it could shake him off, he drove the point of his weapon into the Ursa's soft spot.

Or at least what he *thought* was its soft spot.

It was hard to aim with the thing moving so quickly beneath him, and hard to know whether he had hit the right spot. But his luck held. The spear didn't hit a piece of smart metal.

It dug in a good half meter, as far as he could have hoped.

Then the Ursa shook him off.

But it didn't matter. By the time Cade stopped rolling, he could see that the creature had begun to stagger, his cutlass sticking up out of its back like a toothpick in a big ugly hors d'oeuvre.

Fall, he thought.

It fell. And shuddered. And then stopped moving altogether.

Cade grinned as he got to his feet. And he continued to grin as he climbed up onto the Ursa and pulled his cutlass out of it. It came loose with a soft, slithering sound.

He wiped the cutlass clean on the Ursa's dark, gloopy hide. Then he climbed down and returned the weapon to its cylindrical, undifferentiated shape.

Luck is on my side again, he thought. He could do anything he wanted. He could bait an Ursa, for God's sake, and get away unscathed.

Cade stood over the monster and pounded himself on the chest with his fist. *Who's the man now?*

And the irony was that he hadn't broken a single rule. He had done *exactly* what Tolentino had asked him to do.

But even as he congratulated himself on his victory, he saw that his fellow Rangers were gathering farther down the street. *Why?* he wondered. *The Ursa is over here.*

Then he saw that someone was lying on the ground, and he ran over to join them. *Not Kayembe,* he thought. The thing never caught up to Kayembe; Cade had seen to that.

Then who . . . ?

He didn't see her until he had joined the knot of Rangers, didn't see that it was *Nava* stretched out on the ground. She was lying face up, eyes closed, one arm twisted behind her back. Caught by the dying Ursa's flailing claws.

No . . .

Cade's knees got weak. His cutlass fell from his fingers. He pushed his way past the others and dropped to his knees beside her.

"Nava?" he moaned.

There was blood on her face. *Lots* of blood. He grabbed her shoulder and shook her. "Nava!"

Somebody pulled him back, but he slipped free and fell to Nava's side again. Bentzen ran a mag-scan the length of her body.

"She's alive!" Cade growled. "She's *got* to be!"

Then he saw Bentzen shoot Tolentino a glance and shake her head. Cade's throat closed with grief. Tears squeezed out of his eyes.

"No!" he screamed, his voice cracking. "No!"

But he couldn't deny it enough to make Nava breathe, to make her live again, to make her open her eyes. Nobody could.

Cade didn't sleep that night. He kept thinking about Nava lying there in the street in Old Town, her face covered with blood. Her eyes—those beautiful eyes—closed forever.

Because of *him*.

He had finally begun to drowse off when he felt someone shaking him. It was Tolentino.

"Commander Velan wants to speak with you," she said.

Velan? Cade got out of his bunk and pulled on his uniform, all the while wondering what the commander wanted with him.

First sun was just creeping over the horizon when Cade entered Velan's office. Velan's adjutant waved him in.

"Bellamy," Velan, said as Cade entered. "Close the door."

Cade did as he was told. Then he stood at attention.

"You're probably wondering why I called you here," Velan said. "The answer's a simple one. I wanted to know when you're planning to leave."

Cade swallowed. "Sir?"

"We're not idiots, Bellamy. There's a leak every now and then, which is what allowed your friend Andropov to find out when the charges against you would be dropped. But we've got informants as well, which is why we were able to arrest Andropov last night—and, incidentally, find out what he had told you.

"Mind you, it wasn't a secret that we'd be dropping the charges. I would have told you that myself if you'd asked me." Velan sat back in his chair. "You're a free man, Bellamy. There's no prison sentence hanging over your head. You can go."

Then he turned away to examine the graphics on a holographic display at his side, as if Cade no longer existed. Because in the commander's world, he didn't.

I've got what I wanted, Cade thought. So why was he still standing there? Why wasn't he halfway out the door?

"I want to stay, sir," he said, the words sounding like they were coming out of someone else's mouth.

"Stay?" Velan echoed, something like annoyance in his voice. He cast a sideways glance at Cade. "What makes you think that's still an option?"

"Why . . . wouldn't it be, sir?"

"Leaving aside the question of what you planned to do and whom you planned to do it with, I have to look at how you performed as a Ranger. According to your company leader, you're not particularly suited to what we expect in the Corps. Self-reliance may be a positive trait when you're running illegal goods on the black market, but we prefer our Rangers to work together, as a team."

"But . . . you said you needed *Ghosts.* . . ."

"We do, in the worst way. But only if they can work within the Ranger framework—which you, apparently, can't do. I'm not placing the blame for this on you, Bellamy. If anything, it was my mistake trying to fit a square peg into a round hole."

And he returned his attention to the hologram.

Cade had been dismissed. But he wasn't leaving. After a while, Velan noticed that. "Is there something else?"

"There is, sir. I'd like to remain a Ranger."

The commander shook his head. "I'm afraid the decision's already been made."

"I've got unfinished business with the Ursa, sir." Cade felt a surge of resentment. "You don't want me to be a Ranger? Fine. I'll go out and hunt them on my own."

"That's against the law."

"The law never stopped me before, sir."

A muscle rippled in Velan's jaw. "Why so adamant about staying, Bellamy? You couldn't stand being a Ranger, according to Andropov."

"I've changed my mind, sir. Nava Ericcson . . . She died while I was thinking about *me*. About what I could do."

"Don't flatter yourself, Bellamy. Ericcson's death wasn't your fault."

"But I could have prevented it. She stood up for me, sir. Trusted me." Cade's throat began to ache. "You don't find trust everywhere. You don't find people who care about you. That's a gift—like my knack for surviving, like my being able to ghost. *A gift*. And when someone gives you one of those, you don't give it back. Not if you've got half a brain, you don't."

"And you think you've got half a brain?" Velan asked him.

Cade straightened. "I do now, sir."

Velan looked at him for a long time. Then he sighed. "It's against my better judgment, but I'll let you try it again—with a different squad. Understand, it'll be a whole new start."

Cade nodded. "Thank you, sir. You won't regret it."

"But this is *it*, Bellamy. If you can't hack it *this* time, you're done. You understand?"

"I do, sir."

Velan eyed him a moment longer. Then he said, "Dismissed."

Cade left the office. Then he crossed the compound in the direction of the barracks, determined not to screw up a second time.

* * *

Cade's new squad didn't contain a single veteran except for his company leader, a lean, bearded man named Gwynn. No one else had more than a couple of months of Ranger service under his or her belt.

They were reminders of how helpless he had felt as he watched Nava die. How completely and utterly helpless. For all his ghosting ability, he hadn't been able to do a thing to save her. He had been so concerned with leaving the Rangers, he ended up losing the one person he cared about.

And yet there he was again, facing the possibility of a terrible loss. People were depending on him, putting their lives in his hands. And as far as he could tell, not one of them had faced a live Ursa before.

Cade trained with them as he had trained with Nava's squad. No—even harder. But he didn't learn their names.

After all, there was a Nava among them. He didn't know which of them it would be, but the odds were good that one of them would die under the claws of an Ursa. And what would it be like for him to see that—to see another human being get torn apart because he couldn't kill the monster soon enough?

Cade remembered something his mother had told him just before she passed away. Insanity, she had said, quoting someone from way back, maybe even somebody from Earth, was doing the same thing over and over again and expecting different results.

So maybe he was insane. But he was going to do everything in his power to keep what happened to Nava from happening again. His mother's death hadn't affected anyone but him, but Nava's death would be different. It would *mean* something.

Cade didn't demand perfection just from himself. He demanded it of his teammates as well. He hounded them without respite, without consideration for the way they felt about him. He kept after them even when Gwynn didn't seem inclined to do so.

Clearly, they didn't like it. A few of them barked back at him. One guy in particular, a big red-haired guy almost the size of Kayembe, looked ready to go after him after Cade chewed him out on the far side of the ravine.

"Who the hell do you think you are?" the guy demanded.

When Cade didn't answer, the guy took a swing at him. Cade ducked and planted his fist in the guy's belly. And when the guy doubled over, Cade cut him down with a blow to the side of the head.

Gwynn could have disciplined him, but he didn't say a thing. He just called out the names of the Rangers who would be negotiating the ravine course a second time, as if nothing had happened.

Then came the squad's first training exercise with the mechanical Ursa, out on the streets built in the desert. Everyone followed Gwynn's orders, but it wasn't Gwynn they kept glancing at to see if they were doing everything right. It was Cade.

And he was fine with that.

He *wanted* them to know he was watching. He *wanted* them to know they couldn't get away with anything less than their best.

It was after he had plunged his cutlass into the construct's back, as he was drawing it out again, that he caught a glimpse of a shadow passing over the squad. The kind of shadow an Ursa would make if it were leaping from roof to roof, even if it were otherwise camouflaged.

He wanted to yell, but instead he touched his naviband and said, "Ursa!" Then he leaped off the back of the mechanical construct.

A moment later, the creature appeared in the middle of the street.

"Surround it," Gwynn barked, exactly as he was supposed to.

They fanned out, four Rangers to each side of the street. But Cade's assignment was different from anyone else's. As a Ghost, he was supposed to find a soft spot and go for the kill.

He was looking for an opening, confident that he wouldn't be seen by the beast until it was too late, when the Ursa suddenly went after Gwynn. He had gotten too close, Cade realized. But then, corralling one of the beasts wasn't an exact science. It was easy to make a mistake.

Gwynn managed to activate his cutlass's blade configuration in time to deal the Ursa a slash to the face, but that didn't stop the creature. It smashed into the squad leader with bone-rattling force, sending him flying backward into the base of an ersatz building.

Cade had the opening he had been looking for. While the Ursa was busy with Gwynn, he would be able to land on it and plunge his cutlass into the soft spot on its back.

But Gwynn would be mauled first.

He knew that with the same certainty with which he knew his own name. And he couldn't let it happen. He had seen Nava spill her blood on the ground, and he couldn't bear the thought of that happening to another of his teammates.

So Cade leaped onto the thing's back and used his cutlass to vault over it.

He twisted in midair and came down between the Ursa and Gwynn. The monster didn't see him, of course. He could have gotten out of the way at the last moment and remained utterly unscathed.

But that wasn't his plan.

Going hook with his cutlass, he buried its business end in the Ursa's mouth. Then he yanked it to the side for all he was worth.

The move pulled the Ursa off its course, keeping it from sinking its teeth into Gwynn. However, it also forced Cade to take the brunt of its charge. He twisted

his body at the last moment to try to avoid the impact—
but he couldn't.

The next thing he knew, he was lying on the ground
not far from Gwynn, the metallic taste of blood thick
in his mouth. He had taken a beating. But he was still
alive, still able to think, still able to find his cutlass in
the dirt.

As he regained his senses, he saw that his teammates
were in disarray. Their strategy had gone haywire, and
their leader was sprawled on the ground, unconscious
and maybe worse.

"We can still do this," Cade said into his navi-band
even as he went spear with his cutlass. "Hit it from behind. Turn it around."

The others went into action. All they had needed was
a little push.

As they attacked the Ursa, it did exactly what Cade
had hoped: It turned on them, giving him the opening
he needed. Dragging himself to his feet, he ignored the
injuries he had suffered in his collision with the monster, took two painful steps to gather some speed, and
leaped onto its back.

Still stunned, he wasn't moving as quickly as he had
before. But he managed to hang on when the Ursa tried
to dislodge him, lift his weapon above his head, and
drive it deep into the thing's back.

Then the Ursa *did* dislodge him. He hit the ground,
rolled, and looked up to see what had happened.

What he saw was the beginning of the beast's death
throes. The spear had done its work. They *all* had.

But Cade didn't stay there to watch the Ursa die. He
picked himself up and staggered over to where Gwynn
still lay on the ground.

Be alive, he thought. *Be alive . . .*

The squad leader's face was bruised and bloody. Pitifully so. And he wasn't moving. *Is he even breathing?*

"Gwynn . . . ?" he said.

No response.

A second time: "Gwynn?"

He was about to start mouth to mouth when he saw Gwynn's eyelids flutter open. Cade heaved a sigh of relief. *He's alive*, he thought. *Alive*.

Still, the guy was going to need a doctor. Cade could hear his teammates behind him, making the arrangements.

Gwynn groaned at him through swollen lips, but Cade couldn't make out what the squad leader was trying to say. He leaned down and put his ear next to Gwynn's mouth.

What he heard was, in words like the rusting of weeds, "What took you so long?"

Cade laughed.

"What'd he say?" one of the others asked.

Cade laughed again. "None of your damned business."

He felt a hand on his shoulder. Then another. Then someone else grabbed hold of him, and yet another hugged him from behind.

Before he knew it, he was part of one big embrace. Not just a bunch of Rangers sharing a victory but something more than that. He had survived. But—more important—so had *they*.

Together.

Cade was hot and dusty and more than a little stiff-muscled as he exited the transport that had brought him and his squad back from the San Franciscos to the Ranger compound. He was looking forward to a shower and some shut-eye.

What he encountered instead was Velan's adjutant, standing there by the transport. "The commander wants to see you," the guy said.

Cade had a notion why that might be. "All right," he said, "let's go."

He cast a look back over at his teammates. They looked concerned. Maybe they were right to be so.

After all, Cade had risked his life to save Gwynn back at the desert training facility a few days earlier. And a Ghost, as Gwynn himself had pointed out more than once, was too valuable to risk that way.

Unfortunately, he'd had no choice. He couldn't have let Gwynn die the way Nava had died. Faced with the same choice again, he would have done the same thing.

Surely Velan'll see that.

When they got to the commander's office, Velan's adjutant said, "Go ahead in."

Cade opened the door, but Velan wasn't in evidence. "Sir?" he said, wondering if the commander might be under the desk looking for something he'd dropped.

"It's all right," said the adjutant. "He'll be right back."

Cade took up a position in front of Velan's desk. How much trouble could he possibly be in? He had killed the Ursa, for God's sake. He had saved Gwynn's life. He hadn't followed orders precisely, but—

Finally, Velan came in. "Ranger."

Cade turned to his superior. "Commander."

Velan walked past him and sat down behind his desk. He didn't look happy. But as far as Cade could tell, the guy *never* looked happy. "At ease, Ranger."

Cade assumed the more relaxed position.

"There's something I should have shared with you a long time ago," Velan said, "when I first offered you a place with the Rangers. If I had, we might have avoided some difficulties."

Cade just stood there and listened.

"Ghosts are critical to our efforts to eliminate the Ursa, no question. But so is *every* Ranger. Everyone has a contribution to make. Some people are capable of learning that lesson. Others are not."

Cade didn't quite get where the commander was

going with this. *Is he talking about what happened at the training facility?*

Velan looked at him a moment longer. Then he said, "I made a mistake. You weren't meant to be part of a Ranger squad."

What? Cade thought.

The words didn't seem real. They couldn't be. After everything he had been through? After everything he had accomplished?

No, he thought. Just that: *No*.

"Permission to speak freely, sir?" he snapped.

"Granted," Velan said.

Cade pointed to the commander. "That's the biggest load of horseshit I've ever heard. And if that's your final word, you're not half the Ranger I thought you were."

Velan's eyes narrowed. "You're a judge of Rangers now?"

"Damned right I am."

"And that's the way you speak to a superior?"

"You gave me permission, remember?"

The commander frowned. "So I did."

"And as long as I've got that permission, I'm going to tell you what—"

Velan held up a hand. "Hold on, Bellamy."

"Or what?"

"Or you're going to miss the rest of what I was going to say." He cleared his throat. "As I noted, you weren't meant to be *part* of a Ranger squad. You were meant to *lead* one."

Cade straightened up. *Lead . . . ?*

"Well?" asked Velan. "No comment? No *thank you, sir*?"

Cade grinned. "Um . . . thank you, sir."

The commander nodded. "It's my pleasure, Ranger. And I mean that as sincerely as I've ever meant anything in my life." He held out his hand and opened it to reveal an insignia, the kind squad leaders wore. "This is yours."

Cade took it. "I didn't expect this. I . . ."

Velan made a face. "Is this going to be a *long* speech, Bellamy? Because I've still got things to do today."

Cade shook his head. "No, sir. Not long at all. Again, thank you, sir." As he left Velan's office, he could think of only one thing:

How proud Nava would have been of him. How very, very proud.